LOOSE KANIN

BOOK 2 OF GLASS KANIN

KIA LEEP

PULSAR PUBLISHING

BOOK I SUMMARY

After dying on set of his debut *Supernatural* TV show ripoff, Kanin ends up Between, a space between dimensions. There he meets Noli, an elf, who's also gotten stuck between worlds. As a magic spell pulls them back into reality, a predator in the dark attacks Kanin, stabbing him through his soul.

The horror of Between quickly fades as Kanin and Noli fall back into reality—but not into their original bodies. Kanin ends up in a homunculus core shaped like a small glass flask, while Noli falls into the body of a toy clockwork octopus. The two have accidentally been caught in a wizard's spell intended to power a magical automaton designed to do his yard work.

Kanin learns how to maneuver the world as a tiny glass flask, leveling up and taking a Wizard class to help him perform spells and gain mastery over his fragile body. Before he can figure out how to communicate with his summoner, however, the predator from Between strikes, killing Kanin's only hope of returning home.

Noli and Kanin are forced to flee, searching for help before the spell keeping them stuck to their temporary bodies runs out and they're thrown back Between, where they'll face permanent death—if the predator doesn't consume them first. After many days on the road, and a failed attempt to get help, they make it to the nearest village, where they attempt once more to flag down assistance. Noli transcribes a "cheat sheet" for Kanin to use to communicate, while she writes a letter explaining their situation to send to her wife. But just as they're ready to break down the language barrier, the predator returns, and this time Kanin understands a horrible truth: it's summoned by his own unwitting actions.

After the predator possesses Kanin, killing two travelers and crippling Noli in the process, Kanin flees the village, as much to find help elsewhere as to protect everyone from himself. With Noli unable to walk, Kanin is her only hope of finding help before their spells expire.

While on the road, Kanin survives the elements and battles undead creatures—and also befriends a devilish rogue named Zyneth. Zyneth takes Kanin to the nearest city, where he hopes to find the help he's looking for. However, the friends of the two slain travelers also catch up with Kanin, intent on avenging the deaths of their comrades. Destroying his only means of communication, leaving him injured and alone, his spell timer approaches the end. Just as Kanin has given up, however, Noli finds him with the help of people they'd met along the way.

With renewed hope, they once more begin to search for a wizard who can free them. Simultaneously, Kanin discovers he's capable of extending the timer on their spells himself—but it would require tapping into the predator's void powers to do so. With time running out, Kanin performs the spell to extend their lives just one more day, although the cost means the next spell he casts will summon the murderous predator from Between once more.

Finally, Noli's wife catches up to them, and helps usher everyone back toward her home—and Noli's comatose body. Kanin reluctantly agrees to perform the spell that can bind Noli's soul to her body, but doing so summons the predator. Zyneth gears up to fight off the predator as Kanin sews Noli's soul back into her body, but not before the vengeful travelers find them. After a three-way battle, Kanin finally resolves the fight by confronting the predator head-on and sealing it within his inventory.

With the predator gone—at least, for now—and Noli's soul returned to her body, Kanin sets his sights on achieving the same.

CHAPTER ONE

OR MAYBE BOB ROSS

Call me Michelangelo.

I'm a right Frida Kahlo. A fucking Leonardo da Vinci—and let's just throw the rest of the Ninja Turtles in while we're at it, because no one in the history of art has seen anything like this. Not on Earth, anyway.

I finish Sculpting a piece of glass, breaking the rod into three sections in the air before me. Like puppets on invisible strings, the glass levitates at my beck and call. I line them up with the rest of the construct: Good. They're all the right size.

Chain, I think, activating the spell.

[Activated,] Echo replies, the mental voice accompanying a visual overlay of the mana I lose from casting the spell.

The three pieces of glass snap together like magic, which, I suppose, it is. I Chain the string of glass to the main body as well. When my magic is active, it glows with an eerie black light. As I complete the spell, however, the color fades away, and now the glass pieces remain attached to each other despite having no apparent connective tissue. I take a step back to admire my work.

Spread across the kitchen table like a body at a morgue, the construct is incomplete, but starting to look human. It's got arms, legs, hands, and now, thanks to my latest addition, some toes. All made of glass, of course. If I could work with other materials, I would.

The head remains a bit of an enigma. Currently a large chunk of glass is just sitting next to me on the table, waiting to be Sculpted, but I haven't decided on a shape yet. Since my soul is in my vial, I figure that should go in the chest. But what should the head look like? Once I Sculpted it into a stagnant face, like an ice statue, but Rezira was very adamant about not keeping any creepy decapitated doll heads in her house. And to be fair, it did fall pretty squarely in Uncanny Valley. More to the point, though, looking out of a wobbly bumpy surface like that was pretty disorienting. Maybe something simple, like an orb, would be best for now. I don't need a mouth, ears, or eyes, anyway, so basic is probably better.

I cast Sculpt, deciding to play with the shape of the head once more. Maybe this time I'll figure something out.

[Activated,] Echo says. Then, [EXP threshold reached. Level up!]

[Name: Kanin]

[Species: N/A]

[Class: Wizard]

[Level: 9]

[HP: 10/10]

[Temp HP: 325]

[Mana: 56/56]

[Void: 100%]

[Role: Homunculus]

About damn time! I've only been Attuning, Sculpting, and Chaining glass 24/7 for the last month. I'll take that tiny boost in mana reserves, too, thank you very much. Still no increases to base HP, looks like. Underwhelming. But I guess I shouldn't be surprised. Without the body to give me a boost in temporary hit points, I'm still just a little glass vial that can die via misplaced boot.

But not forever, hopefully. If I'm going to learn a way to get my real body back, step one is to become more mobile. And for that, this glass shell will have to do.

It's kind of ironic, really. When I first got shunted into this world, I was doing everything in my power to stop from getting stuffed into a glass homunculus body. Now, I'm spending every waking hour of the day trying to make one. Funny how that happens.

The cottage door swings open and Noli steps inside. "Oh!" the elf signs with a delighted flourish. "He's got feet now! That's adorable."

I set down the piece of glass I was working with. *Adorable* is not really what I'm going for. "And *manly*," I sign back. By now my signing glass is more than just floating clusters of toothpick-sized shards; I've got fully articulated hands at my disposal. It doesn't have great grip for picking stuff up, but it's a far cry from what I was working with just four weeks ago.

Rezira snorts. She pauses chopping up the vegetables for dinner in order to face us and sign, though she simultaneously speaks aloud for my benefit. "It's glass. Unless you're going for anatomical accuracy, it's not going to be manly."

"I could do that," I threaten. Don't mock me, it'll only make me more determined.

Rezira grimaces. "Oh please, no. It's bad enough we've sacrificed our kitchen table to this freaky glass marionette. That's the last thing I need to look at while I'm cooking."

"Your fault," I sign, glancing around the cramped living space. "Should have made the room bigger."

"Oh, excuse me," Rezira says. "I didn't plan on housing a snarky pint-sized freeloader when I built this place for my wife."

"That's enough, you two," Noli signs, smiling gently at our banter. She sets a dead rabbit she was carrying on the counter, gives Rezira a quick kiss, and then goes to hang up her bow and quiver. "Need help with dinner?"

"No, no." Rezira waves her off. "I've got this." She turns back to her chopping board as Noli wanders over to me, standing above the kitchen-table-turned-assembly-line.

"You're almost done," she observes. Noli picks up the hand of the glass body, rolling its wrist and articulating its fingers. In a weird disembodied way, I can feel everything she's doing—every bit of that body is glass I first Attuned, after all. It's how I'll control it once it's finished. I suppose I could even have it march around by itself, but that sort of defeats the purpose.

"Do you know what you'll do once it's done?" she asks.

Isn't that the million-dollar question. "I need to learn more," I sign. "About the void. The predator. Between." Not to mention magic in general, and this entire world. I don't even know what I don't know.

Noli nods. "That makes sense. The predator... is it still...?"

"No sign of it coming back," I sign. It's been a month now. Hopefully that means it's permanent. But I should be prepared in case it's not.

However, that's not my top priority. "Also, I want to get my body back. Like you."

A flicker of something flits over Noli's face. A grimace? Noli doesn't grimace. "I definitely understand wanting to be in a normal body again," Noli signs. "But... er... Well, it's been a few months, hasn't it?

And when we first met, you told me the reason you ended up Between was because you'd died."

Ah. Right. She's not wrong, but she's also lacking a crucial piece of information: my body didn't die in *this* world. I had to pass Between to get here, and that place seems to exist outside of space and time—maybe it's not a stretch to hope for a Narnia type situation. Maybe I can get back to Earth right when I left it. If I can just reach my body within a few seconds or minutes of the accident, if I can use magic to heal it up... maybe I still have a way to reclaim some sense of normalcy.

Maybe there's a way to go back to being *me* again.

Which brings me to a conversation I've been wanting to have for a while, but lacked the vocabulary to really dig into. I still don't have all the words I want, but I suppose now is as good a time as any.

"I didn't die on Lusio," I sign. I'd only learned the name of this planet a few days ago.

Noli tips her head. "You didn't die?"

"No," I tell her. "I did die. But not here. Not in this world."

Noli stares at me for a moment. "I'm sorry?"

"I'm not from Lusio," I sign. "I'm not from this world."

Noli blinks. Then she turns around and tugs on Rezira's elbow. "Dear?" she signs as Rezira turns to look. "I think you better be part of this conversation."

"A human?" Rezira repeats after I've explained everything I can. "I always pegged you for a halfling."

I don't know if I should be offended or flattered. "You believe me?"

The women exchange a look.

"Different planes of existence are well known," Rezira says. "But they're pretty much just arcana sources. They're not worlds—they're not full of people, and you certainly can't live there. There's stories of the Old People world-walking, bringing technologies and cultures and languages back from other places—but those are just stories. Any truth to them crumbled away with the Ruins thousands of years ago."

"But of course we believe you," Noli adds. "I don't know why you would make such a thing up. And it explains quite a few things, like why you can't write in the common script."

"Or why you don't recognize any cities or countries," Rezira says.

"Not to mention, how you were able to understand my signs when I was just a little toy," Noli agrees with a chuckle. "Rezira could barely even understand me like that. But you said that's because you have a... what was it... an echo in your head, translating these things for you?"

"Yes," I sign. "She tells me information about the world. Magic. Levels. Experience. You don't hear her, too?"

Rezira shakes her head. "I've never heard of anything like that."

Well that confirms what I've suspected from the start. If it was that easy, I would have been able to write in English and their Echos would have translated it for them. But the question is, *why* am I the only one with an Echo? Why can I see stats and numbers like all of this is some kind of video game when no one else seems to be aware of them? It has to be linked to the fact that I'm not from this world. But I'm stumped on the why.

"But if your world really doesn't have magic," Noli asks, "how are you so good at it?"

Rezira nods along. "That's why I thought you must have been a halfling. They've got a natural inclination for the arcane. But really? Human?" She laughs. "They're like the least magical people out there."

Maybe that's why no one on Earth can do magic. Or... maybe they could? I mean, I'd always chalked that kind of stuff up to superstition, but given what I know now...

"Echo," I sign again. "She helped me learn."

Rezira grunts. "Handy."

Noli shakes her head. "What does all this have to do with your body? You don't think... I mean... you're not planning on leaving?"

My insides twist unpleasantly. "My body isn't here. I want to get it back."

Noli and Rezira exchange another look. I hate it when they do that. It's like they can convey a whole conversation in just a glance, and I'm the one left wondering what they've just said behind my back.

"Like I said, traveling to other worlds is practically unheard of," Rezira says. "It's myth. Stories. Where would you even start?"

"I came through the Between," I sign. "I must be able to go back that way."

"Maybe," Noli signs, hesitant. "If it is possible, I've never heard of anyone achieving such a thing."

But Trenevalt did. He pulled Noli and I from Between. And I have access to the Between as well—even if that tiny pocket of null space is currently occupied by a murderous shadow monster that wants to control my mind and eat every soul within reach.

Details.

"What about this?" I ask. I mentally reach for a jar tucked away behind the bookshelf, placed out of the way—and out of sight—intentionally. Most times I can forget it's there. But anytime I'm within range, just like with my glass, I can feel it, like an extension of my body.

I call my Attuned void from the jar, and the ink-like shadows swirl up onto the table and settle around me. Even just holding their form in my mind like this makes me feel slimy. They might no longer belong to the predator—they might have been crucial in saving Noli's life—but accessing them still summons too many bad memories.

Unfortunately, it's also the only lead I've got.

"Void is related to Between," I sign. "And also powering my homunculus spell." I tap my glass, inside which my hollow form also seems to be full of the stuff. Ever since I trapped the predator in my inventory, the ink level in my vial hasn't decreased. "If I learn where it comes from, how to use it, maybe I can find a way back."

Noli frowns, her brows pinched in concern. "I don't like this. You just said you know practically nothing about magic. And now you want to play with something none of us understand? Try to reinvent space-rending magic lost millennia ago? Assuming it ever existed at all." She shakes her head. "Why not leave well enough alone? You're nearly done with your body." She gestures to the lifeless glass shell. "You could just live here in peace. Move on. Make this second chance at life whatever you wish."

Move on? Easy to say for someone who got their body back. Who can sleep and eat and smile. Who doesn't have to worry about the smallest accident shattering them to pieces. Who doesn't have to relive the memories of killing people and consuming their souls.

Anger boils up inside me. I jab a hand at the glass shell on the table. "This isn't my body! It's not me. Just temporary. A tool."

Even Rezira looks concerned now. "You know that's not what she meant. But if you really died, then your real body is probably long gone by now. Noli's right—you've got a second chance, which is more than most. This body might not be ideal, but—"

"Ideal?" I interrupt, clumsily and angrily repeating her sign. That's the understatement of a century. "You have no idea what it's like."

Noli smiles, small and sad. "Maybe not Rezira, but I do. I might be the only one who does."

My glass falters. Of course she does. But some selfish part of myself only feels a sting of jealousy at her words. She knows what it's like—but for her, it ended a month ago.

"Then you understand why I can't stay like this," I sign.

Noli presses her mouth in an unhappy line. Instead of responding, she holds a hand out to me. My frustration deflates as I touch my glass to her finger. She doesn't have to say anything. Whatever I decide, she's here to help. She always is.

A knock comes at the front door, and a line of runes above the entrance light up in response. Noli and Rezira glance its way as the door opens, and a friendly form steps inside.

"I think I've found it," Zyneth says, taking in the three of us as he flashes a smile. "The perfect shape for the head. I got the idea in…" He trails off, belatedly registering the room's tense mood. He glances from Noli, to me, to the void I have hovering nearby. "I feel as though I'm interrupting something," he remarks, awkwardly shutting the door behind him. "Pray tell. What did I miss?"

Chapter Two

ANKLES

Rezira refills Zyneth's cup of tea as he sits back in his chair, eyebrows raised, blinking repeatedly after I finish my story. Finally, he takes a sip of the tea, then sets the mug down.

"Well all that certainly explains your financial illiteracy," he says.

Not exactly the response to 'I'm a dead alien from another planet' I was expecting. And what does he mean, illiterate? "I know how to use money."

As usual, Rezira translates for Zyneth any time Noli or I sign.

"But no concept of value," Zyneth replies. "I noticed when we were in Harrowood. And the last few times I've brought back glass for your project. You never commented on the cost."

Should I have? I'm suddenly playing back all the interactions we've had around money in a new light. "Was it expensive?"

Rezira gives me a flat look. "He paid for all the materials to fix Attiru's shop."

"Yes, he's quite rich," Noli adds with a laugh.

Zyneth grimaces. "I'd assumed you didn't say anything because you were just being polite."

Rezira barks out a laugh. "Well I wasn't terribly interested in scaring off our mysterious, yet affluent, benefactor."

"Oh." I awkwardly shuffle my glass. I don't have two pennies to my name—or whatever goes for pennies in this world. I haven't really been paying attention. I'd offer to pay him back, but the prospect of finding a job here seems about as unlikely as it is unattractive. "Sorry. I didn't mean to... use your kindness."

"Take advantage," Noli supplies, slowing the signs down for me. I'm getting pretty fluent with the basics, but Noli still slips me some more complex words and concepts a few times a day.

"I don't particularly see the point of having money if it can't be used to help others," Zyneth says. "But that's enough about me. I must say, I thought I was done being surprised by you. You're really set on trying to find a way home to retrieve your body?"

"I am."

Noli glances away when I say this, and Rezira just frowns.

Zyneth, however, scratches thoughtfully at his chin. "Binding your soul back to your body would be tricky enough as it is without the fact that it's on another world. I suppose the best place to start looking into the issue would be at the Athenaeum of Miasmere."

Noli looks at him in surprise. "Really?"

"You're not serious about helping him?" Rezira adds. "I expected you to see the folly in this idea."

"Kanin is his own person," Zyneth says. "He's fully capable of making decisions for himself. I'm merely offering insight on the best path forward."

Rezira shakes her head. "It's reckless."

"If suggesting a trip to the library is reckless," Zyneth says, "then I shudder to think what alternatives you would suggest."

His support fills me with gratitude. Noli and Rezira had me starting to question myself, but it's nice to know Zyneth has my back.

"Where is it?" I ask. "The library."

"A few days' travel, by way of telepads," Zyneth says. "The Athenaeum boasts Valenia's largest scholastic collection, so it should be no surprise it's in the capital." He pauses for a moment. "Which is Miasmere," he adds. "Sorry, I forget you aren't familiar with geography here. Retroactively, so much of our interactions make more sense now."

That's not bad. I could draw up a circle, refresh my spell, and be ready to go by this afternoon. "When can we leave? Will you come with?"

"Hold up, now," Rezira says.

"Zyneth is likely too busy for such a venture," Noli adds, looking at him. "You always have so many jobs to return to."

Zyneth's mouth pulls tight for a moment, but then he waves it off. "I can take time away. It shouldn't be a problem." He turns to me. "However, you may be getting ahead of yourself. If you want to peruse a library with any efficiency, you'll need a form more suited to the job."

We all look down at my creation. Practically complete, save the head. He's right, though. If I want to carry around books and flip through pages—not to mention draw less attention and avoid getting crushed by any misplaced tomes—this body is the answer.

"It's almost done," I sign. And it's about time I tested it out.

"Are you waiting on anything?" Zyneth asks. "You could control it now if you wanted to, right?"

"Yes." I just wanted to finish all of it, first. It would be harder to get used to walking around on two legs again, only to change the design and throw myself off balance once more.

Or maybe that's just what I've been telling myself.

"You have an idea for the head?" I ask. He'd been saying something about that when he first came in.

"Oh yes! I'd nearly forgotten." Zyneth grabs his pack, then roots around for something inside it. "It's not glass, but the shape got me thinking. A current issue of yours is seeing out all angles at once, correct?"

"Yes." I've gotten used to it somewhat, but too much motion on different sides gets dizzying.

"Well what about having different parts of your vision you could turn on and off," Zyneth suggests. He pulls a carved wooden decoration out of his bag. It's shaped like a pyramid.

"You want his head to be a paperweight?" Rezira asks, skeptical.

I'm also not really getting it. "I can't turn parts of my vision in a piece of glass on or off. The whole piece sees, or doesn't." Add in the vision from my core vial—which I can't ever turn off—and it all can get a bit overwhelming. The last time I dealt with too many sources of sight at once, it just about broke my mind.

Zyneth shakes his head. "If you created the shape from four separate pieces of glass that you then Chain together, you could activate your sight in just one side at a time. Or two if you like." He flips the pyramid upside down, tapping each of the four triangle-shaped sides. "Maybe just start with one in the front. Or two, if you wanted to treat each side like an eye. Might give you better depth perception—honestly, I don't really understand how your vision works."

That makes two of us.

"And then you could cover up your core," he continues. "Hide it beneath a cloth or something—that might help stop you from seeing things from multiple angles at once."

It's an interesting idea. And there's no reason not to give it a shot, I suppose. "Alright. Let's try."

I summon the hunk of glass that's slated to be the head and activate a Sculpt.

If I keep it as a single piece, then I'll be seeing out of all sides at once, just like I currently do with my core. To try what Zyneth is suggesting, I'll need to break it into separate pieces. I set to work on that, segmenting the glass into five different chunks. Then, I start to replicate the shape of Zyneth's inverted pyramid. One square piece, four triangles. I hold them together to make sure they all line up properly, then activate a Chain. The pieces snap together, snugly secured in the form of a prism, yet still five distinct planes of glass.

That's the easy part.

Echo, I want to activate vision on the front piece of glass, I say.

[Affirmative,] Echo says. [Mana cost: 0. Activated.]

Like flipping on a TV, a second vision source appears abruptly in my mind. I'm looking at myself: a three-inch glass vial full of black ink. Four glass legs strapped to the sphere, with a pair of small glass hands hovering nearby. But I can also see the pane of glass that I'm looking through: I'm looking at myself, looking at myself, looking at myself...

Ugh. I can already feel a headache coming on. I turn the pane of glass away, and my whole vision swivels with its movement. I tip to the side, dizzy, and nearly fall over before I catch myself. It's too much. I can't parse all the different things I'm seeing at once.

Turn it off, I tell Echo, wishing I had eyes I could squeeze shut.

[Deactivating vision in Attuned glass.]

Abruptly, the second source of sight vanishes.

Whew. That was awful.

"Are you alright?" Noli signs, leaning forward. "You almost fell!"

"I'm okay now," I reply. "Just too much at once. Not used to seeing twice." Sensory overload.

Noli nods with a grimace. "I think I understand. I could hear when I was in that body." She gestures toward the clockwork octopus toy still sitting on a bookshelf.

"What?" Rezira looks at her. "You could?"

I hadn't realized either. She'd never said anything about that. How much had Noli been grinning and bearing everything for my benefit?

Noli chews at a lip. "It was uncomfortable. Confusing, at first. I started to get used to it a bit toward the end, but... I couldn't really make sense of it. I didn't like it."

Rezira squeezes her shoulder. "Sorry."

Noli smiles back at her, putting a hand over her wife's.

"Is it not an option, then?" Zyneth asks me. He looks disappointed. "Blast. I thought I was onto something."

"It might work," I sign, considering the head. The sight through that piece of glass had actually been pretty clear, when it wasn't incredibly disorienting. At least it wasn't all warped like my current vision, as if everything I see is through a fish-eye lens. "If I cover up my core, like you suggested."

"Don't push yourself," Noli signs. "You've already spent the whole day working on building your body—your *construct*—up."

"I'm okay," I sign. Besides, I've already waited long enough, and with the library waiting for me, I'm ready to be on the move. "I want to try."

"Is there any way we can help?" Noli asks.

I set the head back down on the table, then hoist myself up onto the body's chest. "Yes. Do you have a cloth?"

"I'll get something," Rezira grumbles, standing up to go rummage around in the kitchen.

While Rezira works on that, I consider the chest area. I could create a cavity here for my core to fit into, like some kind of crystalline heart.

But there's a part of me that feels claustrophobic about embedding myself in this glass form. What if I fall and get skewered by my own broken shards? What if I run out of mana and can't Sculpt my way out?

"I'll need a way to hold my core," I sign. "A way to keep it safe."

"Hmm," Noli considers, tapping her lips. "Wait! I know." She gets up and digs around a chest near her bed. A moment later, she returns with a necklace.

She grins sheepishly, removing the piece of jewelry that hangs from the middle. "You *are* shaped like a pendant with that little hook on your back. What if you wore it like a necklace? Er. Wore yourself?"

"The body has no neck," Zyneth points out, eying the chain. "How would he wear it?"

Excuse me, I haven't even agreed to this idea yet.

"Good point," Noli signs. She holds the necklace up to my glass construct, turning it this way and that. Then, she taps a spot on each shoulder. "Could you put little hooks here? I could use that to tie them to either side."

Still not wild about this idea. But Noli seems so excited, so... I guess I could give it a shot. I activate a Sculpt and start creating the hooks Noli suggested.

"Next will be to attach it to you, I suppose," Noli signs. "Do you mind, Kanin?"

I wave her over, still focusing on my Sculpt.

"Alright then. Hold still." Noli delicately latches the clasp around my hook, which suffice to say is an extremely weird sensation. "There! All done. Now we just need to fix it to the body, once you're ready."

I finish the Sculpt as Rezira returns with a small drawstring bag. "Would this work?"

As uncomfortable as I am with the idea of getting stuffed into a bag, that's pretty much exactly what I was looking for. "Yes, thank you. Noli, can you help again?"

"Of course." She holds out her hand, and I step into her palm. Noli holds the cloth sack with her other hand, looking between us with a grimace. Hah. Nothing like stuffing your friend into a cloth sack.

Noli smiles apologetically, then gently slips me into the bag and cinches the top shut.

My world goes dark.

Panic wells up for a moment, all too reminded of Between and the predator. But I can still feel the rough texture of the fabric around me. And more than that, I can feel my glass. I force my nerves to calm.

I'd heard that shutting one sense off can make the other ones more attuned to your surroundings, and now I'm experiencing that in a very disembodied sort of way. I can feel my glass construct on the table almost as if I'm seeing it. And while I can no longer hear Noli speak—well, *see*, I guess—it's still odd to hear the quiet shuffles of the others in the room. Rezira and Zyneth are remaining quiet—I guess everyone's holding their breath to see what happens next.

My world swivels, and then abruptly stops moving as I come to rest on a surface. From the outside, I can also feel something soft resting on my construct's chest.

For a moment, I think of the homunculus shell in Trenevalt's cabin. That was what—two months ago? It feels like worlds away. That small, fragile homunculus shell I had found so terrifying. The horrific idea of being bound to it. And here I am, replicating the same thing. But this one is bigger—more human looking. And I'm doing it on my own terms.

"Okay," Zyneth says, after a moment. "The necklace is secure."

I reactivate my vision in one of the panes of the head piece, and the world lights up once more.

It's way less disorienting this time. At least now I'm not seeing double. Although actually, weirdly enough, only having vision that can see in one direction at a time feels a little restrictive now. Maybe I've gotten more used to that omni-vision than I thought. But this way helps me feel a little more human.

"Kanin?" Zyneth ventures. They probably don't know if I can see yet. "You alright?"

"Yes," I sign with my signing glass. But wait—now I have actual hands I can do that with, don't I?

I lift one arm. It feels like trying to control a wet noodle. The fingers flop uselessly until I focus on them, forming a fist. The glass tinkles quietly as the fingers close around each other. I try again, bobbing it to sign, "Yes."

Noli lets out a relieved breath. "Good! Can you sit up? Do you need help?"

One thing at a time, jeeze.

Which is about how I need to take it.

I move a hand to either side and press them against the table, leveraging myself upright. And I'm greeted with the bizarre image of a glass torso sitting up in front of me. Oops. I left the head on the table. Since I haven't Chained it to the torso yet, it's still just sitting there, watching the rest of me get situated. I summon it next, levitating the inverted pyramid to float above the neck. I can worry about Chaining it later, if I need to. Although with the current flexibility in how I can swivel and point it, maybe a Chain isn't necessary after all. I'll just have to remember to not leave it anywhere.

I take a moment to gather myself as I look around, and find Noli, Zyneth, and Rezira staring back at me with expressions that range from awe to horror.

Rezira is the first to break the ice. "Well this is the weirdest fucking thing I've ever seen."

Zyneth's eyes are dancing with amusement. "This makes getting stabbed by the void monster entirely worth it."

"How do you feel?" Noli asks. "Be careful! Go slow."

No shit. I already feel like I'm about to capsize. It's the strangest sensation. I have to concentrate on each piece of glass to get it to do what I need it to do. That's nothing new, but doing that for hundreds of connected pieces at once is a bit much. I'm also levitating them, in a way, just like my signing glass, but their weight—and the weight of all the pieces they're Chained to—is keeping the body completely grounded. Maybe, if I was able to consciously hold every piece in my mind at once, I could make it float. For now, though, it's baby steps.

"Strange," I sign, fumbling through the movements. I try to focus harder. Elbows, wrists, fingers. "I feel heavy."

Rezira snorts. "You managed to get even worse at signing."

Noli covers her mouth, behind which is an obvious smile. "No, he's doing great! It's just a little stiff. And make sure to close your hand all the way there, otherwise that's, ah, a slightly different meaning..."

"Yeah, this way means *shit*," Rezira says. Then she helpfully repeats the sign so I can see the difference. What a bro.

Noli slaps at her hands, dissolving the signs, and Rezira laughs.

I bring my own hands back down to the table, curling my fingers around the lip and squeezing tightly. Slowly, I pull myself around to dangle my legs toward the floor. Toes, feet, legs, hips, knees... Whoops! I catch myself just as an arm starts to go out. And arms. Don't forget to focus on arms.

"Careful!" Noli signs. "Don't go too fast."

I've been stuck at a crawl for two months now. *Fast* is a dream.

I scoot forward a little more, trying to hold as many pieces of glass in my mind as I can. Still sitting, I press one foot against the floor. Then the other.

"Might want to give it a minute," Zyneth says. "Feel everything out. There's no rush."

Now I know what Neo must have felt like after escaping the Matrix. Nothing is moving quite how I expect it to—every limb threatens to keep giving out. But if I want any of this to change, if I want a shot at recovering my real body, then this is the first step on that road.

I push myself to my feet.

I'm taller than Noli. Just as tall as Zyneth. A few inches shorter than Rezira. But I'm meeting their gazes at eye level, and it feels absolutely amazing. It might not be *my* body, but I finally have a *proper* body. A humanoid body. I have two legs, two arms, a head—

The world tips. Noli's eyes go wide. Zyneth reaches out a hand. Rezira says, "Oh, shit—"

Ankles, I realize as my legs collapse. I forgot about the ankles.

And then I fall to the floor in a shattering heap of glass.

[253 points of Fall Damage sustained,] Echo says.

[Fall Damage Resistance Level Up!]

Chapter Three

Not Exactly Licit

It takes three days to fix everything. Luckily the cloth sack prevented any of the shards from spearing through my vial, but it's a terrible mess to clean up. I'm still finding bits of broken glass swept between cracks in the floorboards when they pass within my range.

It took me about a month to build the body the first time, but that was mostly due to all the time spent collecting and then Attuning enough glass to make up the body. Now that it's all Attuned already, I'm only limited by how fast I can re-Sculpt everything given a pool of only 56 mana. Zyneth gives me a couple recharges, which helps. But reassembling each limb is still a meticulous process.

"Okay," I finally sign, after checking the body over for the upteenth time. "Ready to try again."

"Maybe we should help this time," Noli suggests. "All that glass seems rather heavy, but Rezira could hold you upright."

Rezira and I look at each other.

"If she wants…"

"I guess if he needs it…"

"Or perhaps I could take an arm," Zyneth suggests. "And maybe Noli if you wanted to help with his other side. You could lean on us until you feel comfortable letting go."

A much better idea. And two less limbs to have to think about. "Alright. Let's try that way."

Once more, I have Noli obscure my vial with the pouch so I can turn on the head's sense of sight. It's slightly less disorienting this time, now that I know what to expect, and I once more allow myself to be strung up like the necklace I apparently am.

Okay. Round two.

I cautiously sit up as before, swinging my legs over the side of the table. Zyneth and Noli stand to either side, and I awkwardly put an arm around each of their shoulders. They pull upward and I try to take some of the weight off of them, levitating the glass in each arm, but my attention quickly switches to my legs as I begin to put weight on my feet. This time, don't neglect the joints.

"Easy," Zyneth murmurs, as I stand from the table.

Whew, he's awfully close, isn't he? I mean, it's not like I didn't ride around on his shoulder for several days like a little glass parrot, but being in this more human body, holding onto him with more human limbs, it feels more intimate. An embarrassed warmth rises within me, which I pray isn't *actually* a warmth anyone else can feel.

As I pause there, just trying to stand in one place, Noli grunts.

I shake myself out of the intrusive thoughts. "Sorry," I say with my signing glass, given my hands are a bit preoccupied.

Even trying to levitate as much of my glass as possible to offload the weight, I'm pressing down on Zyneth and Noli, and glass is damn heavy. Still leaning on them (as little as I can manage), I take my first shaky step. The foot drags heavily across the floor. I set it down. Shift my weight. Now for the other one.

With Zyneth and Noli's help, I make a slow lap around the room. So much for hitting the ground running. I must look like some kind of hospital patient trying to build up their muscles again.

After about ten minutes of shuffling around the cottage, I can feel Noli starting to tremble. Someone who's *actually* building up her muscles again after her body had been in a magical coma for a month.

"That's enough," I sign, gesturing back to the table. "I'm ready for a break."

Well, Noli is, but I'd rather not call attention to it. The two help set me back down on the table, then step back with wide grins. They look happier about this than I do.

"Great job!" Noli wipes some sweat from her brow. "No falls this time."

Thanks to them. I'd stumbled once or twice, but they'd always caught me. "Still a lot to practice," I sign.

Rezira shakes her head. "Stop using those dinky pieces of glass to talk. You need to practice with your body's hands, or you'll always sound like some kind of country bumpkin."

"Don't you guys live in the country?" I ask.

Rezira replies with a rude gesture.

Zyneth chuckles. "I think it was good progress, at any rate. Keep it up and we might be able to head to Miasmere in another few weeks."

"Weeks?" I can't wait that long. "I have to get faster."

"Not too fast," Noli signs. "Another fall will only set you back again. Just try to take it slow."

Ugh, I hate being treated like I'm, well, like I'm made of glass. Okay, maybe their concern is valid. I just wish it wasn't so damn frustrating.

"The joints are difficult," I muse. "They don't move right." If I could crack that problem, walking might be easier.

"No tendons or muscles to restrict the movement," Rezira says. "A little hard to simulate elastic ranges of motion when all you've got to work with is glass."

She's right. "Maybe I could add something?" Attach strips of leather along joints or something.

"There's no harm in trying," Zyneth says. "I'll keep an eye out for viable materials on my next trip into town. Which actually may be soon."

"Again?" I ask, disappointed. He's left twice since I've been at Noli and Rezira's place, each time gone for over a week.

"Sorry." He grimaces. "Another job came up. This one might take longer than the last—a few weeks, perhaps. But when I get back, we could experiment with the pseudo-tendon material, as Rezira suggested."

Once again, no explanation of where he's going, or what the job entails. I'd consider it sketchy as fuck if I haven't been getting to know the guy. He doesn't seem like a bad person. So why all the cloak and dagger?

"When do you leave?" I ask.

"Perhaps tomorrow, or the next day," he says. "I've already spent five days here. Time to check back in."

"Where?" I ask.

Zyneth cocks an eyebrow. "You've a lot of questions, all of a sudden."

"I'm curious what you do," I sign. "How you make so much money."

Noli laughs nervously. "Kanin, that's rude. His employment is none of our business if he doesn't want to share."

Rezira tips her head. "No, go on. I'm rather curious myself."

Zyneth glances between us, clearly uncomfortable with the sudden confrontation. I almost feel a little bad at putting him on the spot—but my nosiness wins out.

"The less you all are involved, the better," Zyneth finally relents. "It's not exactly licit work."

Noli's eyes widened. "You mean it's something illegal?"

"A little late to try to keep from involving us, don't you think?" Rezira adds. "You already spend all your time between jobs at our house."

"I'm sorry," Zyneth says. "You're right. I should never have done that. If you'd like for me to leave now—"

"No!" Noli cries. "Absolutely not. No one is getting kicked out. Right, Rezira?"

The orc blows air out her nose. "I mean, I don't know. Maybe we should hear a few more details about this *illicit job* before making any decisions. No offense, Zyneth."

"That is completely fair," he replies, shoulders uncharacteristically hunched. Compared to the typical nonchalant and confident Zyneth I'm used to seeing, this version looks like a scolded schoolboy.

Whoops. I opened a bit of a can of worms here, didn't I?

Zyneth is still hesitating, but Noli waves a dismissive hand before he can answer.

"Whatever you need to say," she signs, "you can chew on it until tomorrow. You're staying the night regardless. Perhaps if it *is* something worth addressing, we can discuss how this might affect future visits then. But you're here now, and that isn't changing."

Zyneth nods, fidgeting with the cuff of a sleeve, but he doesn't appear mollified. "I appreciate the hospitality. I've some thinking to do on the matter myself. Rezira raises fair points about my presence here involving the rest of you. It might be best if I limit future visits, in frequency and duration."

"But the trip to Miasmere," I object. "My research at the library." And currently my only lead on discovering how I might get my body back.

"As I said, I will return," Zyneth says. "And you need time to get used to operating that new body, anyway."

But that'll be weeks! Biding my time is the last thing I need. I'm sick to death of moving slow.

Zyneth shakes his head before I can object. "As Noli said, we can continue this discussion tomorrow—when we've all had time to think through our priorities."

I, for one, don't need to think too hard about mine.

"Well," Rezira finally sighs as an uncomfortable silence threatens to settle over the room. "I suppose I should get things ready for dinner."

"Have we got any of that rabbit left?" Noli asks, seemingly eager to disperse the cloud that's still hanging in the air. She heads over to the wall, where her bow and arrows are mounted. "I've been meaning to go out hunting again."

Rezira waves her on. "I'll never say no to fresh meat. We're also low on mugroot while you're at it."

"Great." Noli slings her quiver and bow over opposite shoulders. "Be back in a few hours. And *please*, Kanin, go easy on this body, won't you?"

"No promises," I joke.

She smiles, briefly, with worry in her eyes, then heads out.

"Actually," I sign, after she's gone, "I need help outside, too. I want to renew my spell."

Rezira's eyes brighten. "Does this mean I get my dining room table back?" They'd been sitting out front eating their meals on a pair of hand-made rocking chairs ever since I'd commandeered the table for building my glass body. "Gods' grace, I can't wait to use my table again."

"Maybe," I sign. "I was feeling generous, but with all this attitude…"

"Careful," Rezira says. "Keep tempting fate and I'll just shove you off the table."

"That'll be another three days to rebuild. Doesn't sound productive."

Rezira snorts, holding out an arm. "You want help, or what?"

With her and Zyneth's shoulders to lean on, we make our way outside. I call the Attuned void to follow after—a crucial element to working my spell circles. We slowly head around to the back of the cottage, and I marvel at the sensation of soil and grass underfoot. It's so different experiencing the world through this body as opposed to a teacup-sized orb of glass. I'd nearly forgotten what walking feels like. The simple pleasure of soft ground under your feet.

"Here?" Rezira asks. There's a clearing where the grass has been dug away to reveal a patch of dusty earth. I can still see the impressions of the last circle I'd drawn a few days ago, though the features are weathered from yesterday's afternoon rain. Why Rezira had to ask for clarification is obvious, however.

The circle is barely three feet across, sized for a vessel the size of a pint, not a person. I'll need to redraw it if I don't want to deal with the hassle of unclasping my core from the necklace and then putting it back on again.

"Here is fine," I sign, and they lower me to my knees in front of the circle.

"Anything else?" Rezira asks.

I just focus on staying upright. "No. I've got this. Thank you."

"Let me know when you want to come back in," Rezira says, then waves as she heads off.

"Anything I could help with?" Zyneth asks, lingering nearby.

"No," I sign. Without Rezira to translate for him, I try to keep my words simple. Zyneth's picked up some sign language as well, but without Noli to sit down and practice with him every day, like she does with me, his vocab is a lot more basic. Then again, I'm only two months into learning the language myself—though I'm pretty damn proud of how far I've come in that time, if I'm being honest.

"Thanks for your help," I sign, sending my extra glass to scrub out the circle. I'll need it at least twice the size. *Echo, bring up a diagram of the Core Bond spell circle,* I tell her.

[Affirmative.]

I've recreated it enough times now that I'm starting to memorize the pattern, but I'm still too nervous to try the spell without a reference. I don't want to risk missing anything—I don't want to risk messing a spell up, like Trenevalt did.

Zyneth sits down next to me, legs tucked up toward his chest and arms draped over his knees. "Mind if I watch? I've some time to kill."

It's strange. Part of me feels a little hurt by him—that he's still keeping things from me. That he's leaving again so soon. But, paradoxically, I'm glad he's here, and his presence at my side fills me with comfort.

"Of course." I finish flattening out the dirt, then begin to sketch out the outermost circle. "Could you lend your magic?"

Zyneth squints at the signs. "You want to know if I could boost your spell?"

"Yeah." If he doesn't mind. Given my low mana reserves, I can only go about one day before a refresh. Not a problem, as my passive mana generation is up to 1 point every five minutes now, so I can save up enough mana for a daily spell renewal in a few hours. But it's definitely anxiety inducing to just be one missed-spell away from an untimely death. Not to mention, the mana cost keeps me from working on my glass body. With Zyneth to help, his entire mana pool boosts the spell's duration to about ten times what I can manage.

"I can lend some," he says. "Not all, unfortunately. It would be wise for me to not drain myself today when I plan on leaving tomorrow. Never know when you might need a spell or two."

"That's fair." I work on the second major circle next, prescribed just inside the first.

"Sorry," Zyneth says. "Didn't catch that one."

"Thank you," I sign instead.

Zyneth is quiet as I continue adding components to the circle. The ten-pointed star. The correct cross hatches and semicircles.

"Is it terribly different?" he asks. "The world you come from."

I finish my first pass at the circle, and consult the diagram Echo's manifested in my vision. "Yes." Where to even start?

"Were you a wizard there?"

I sign laughter. "No. No magic."

"You couldn't do magic?"

"There isn't any."

Zyneth rocks back, eyebrows raised. "No magic in the whole world? I... I can't even imagine. How strange."

"Not as strange as here," I counter.

But Zyneth shakes his head; he doesn't know those signs. "Do you miss it?" he asks.

I hesitate. I mean... of course I miss home. That should go without saying. There's my career, and everyone I've ever known, and... well, my body, obviously. Yet I still pause before signing, "Yes."

Somewhat bothered by the question, and still not entirely sure why, I turn my focus back on the circle. Double and triple checks aren't turning up any mistakes. I send my Attuned void to overlay the circle, the shadows pouring into the diagram like ink.

"Help up?" I ask, gesturing to the circle.

Zyneth stands, taking my hands, then braces himself with a grunt as I pull myself to my feet. I sway, and he catches me. I stand there for a moment, leaning on him.

"Ready?" he asks after a moment.

No time to think about him. I focus on the feet. The ankles. The legs and knees. Gradually, I push off of Zyneth, holding myself upright but not letting go. Okay. I think I got this. "Yes."

He steps forward, gingerly picking his way across the circle, as nimble as a dancer. I'm just doing my best to not screw up the lines. At the center, he hesitates.

"Should I step out?"

"Yes." Probably. I mean, who the hell knows what would happen if an already living person was in the middle of this spell—I'm certainly not willing to find out.

"Alright. I'm going to let go."

Ankles, don't forget the ankles. Slowly, Zyneth releases my hand, and I'm left standing on my own. The ground seems so far away from up here.

Zyneth backs out of the circle, but remains just outside the outer ring. He holds up both hands, a yellow glow forming in each palm. "Ready when you are."

Activate Core Bond Renewal, I tell Echo. And my circle jumps to life.

In contrast to Zyneth's yellow, my magic illuminates the circle, managing to glow in some surreal hue of black that nearly hurts to look at. A familiar warmth floods through in my soul. I bring up a display of the spell's mana as I feel my own pool depleting:

[Core Bond: 78 mana]

Zyneth's magic joins the spell as well.

[Core Bond: 89 mana]

I let it continue until Zyneth lowers his hands, cutting off his magic supply; it's only a few seconds after that the rest of my mana is depleted as well.

[Mana: 0/56. Core Bond: 543]

[Mana depleted. Spell complete.]

The light fades, and I'm still standing. That's over a minute without anyone supporting me.

"Well done," Zyneth says, stepping back into the circle to offer an arm. "You're already far more steady on your feet."

Which might be an accomplishment if I only intended to be walking three weeks from now. But that's not good enough—not if I want to leave with Zyneth tomorrow.

Ambitious? Maybe. But I have a plan.

I call the void up to my hand as we pick our way back out of the circle. I picture the ink layering over my fingers, and the shadows oblige, forming an onyx glove over my glass. The image is all too familiar, and summons memories I spent the last month and a half trying to box away. I suppress a shudder, but close my hand into a fist, feeling out the sensation. I don't love it, but just like this glass body, it's a means to an end.

Time to get to work.

Chapter Four

SHADOW AND GLASS

I insist on staying outside that night. Sitting around and watching them all eat delicious food—which probably smells and tastes fantastic—when I can't do any of that just rubs salt in the wound. I'd rather be out here with my own thoughts. Not to mention, magic.

Rezira was on the right track when she suggested adding something elastic to my glass limbs to simulate tendons. I'm not convinced leather is the answer, though. I won't be able to sense them until they're pulled all the way taut, and that sounds like a recipe for accidental limb breakage. No, I need to have more precise control than that.

I'll start with the hands first. Thanks to practicing signs, I've gotten best at simulating finger movements anyway.

Splaying my hand before me, I summon a mental picture of what I want. False tendons bracing the back of each joint. Restricting the motion to just what a normal, human hand could do.

The void reacts immediately, splitting into dozens of tiny pieces to secure itself to each digit. It only uses a portion of the whole Attuned void volume, which is great considering I'm going to need a shit-ton more for all my other joints. But even then, I don't think it will be enough.

Once the void is settled, I flex my fingers. The void is helping to guide my motions, just as I intended. Of course it is—it can only do what I intend. But even after using it a dozen different times to renew my Core Bond spell, a part of me still regards it with deep suspicion, as if it will develop a mind of its own at any moment.

For now, however, it's working. I compare it to the hand that I didn't add void to: even its basic movements look more artificial. Puppeted. I must be doing something right.

Holding it up against the starry sky, the shadows sink into the joints, vanishing beneath the moonlight. Shadow and glass. Maybe it would be pretty if it weren't so alien—if it didn't fill me with such a deep instinct of wrongness.

Lowering my hand, I recall the void and have it rejoin the baseball-sized blob of ink-like magic floating beside me. Now for the real test.

I start with my ankles and knees: those are the most crucial points, I think. Shadows peel away from the main volume, wicking toward each joint as I picture the forms they should take. Hips next. Back. Feet, probably, something along the bottom...

I suddenly wish I had an anatomy book to help, but I'll have to make do as is. My limited supply of void runs out before I can add any to my arms or hands, but I don't need those to walk.

I stretch a leg out, flexing it. The movement feels stiff, a little too restrictive, so I pause to rearrange the void until it feels... well, *normal* isn't the right word, but at least a little more familiar.

After a few more minutes of tweaking, it's as good as I can get it from the ground. Time to try it out.

Bracing an arm against the side of the cottage, I slowly pull my legs beneath me. I push myself up to one knee, then pause. Tense. Don't hesitate now, this is the easy part—

In one move I push myself to my feet. And I feel... stable, actually. I'm hardly leaning against the cabin. Gingerly, with a *tink* of glass on wood, I take my hand away. No one holding me. No table to sit back against. Just me, standing on two legs, all on my own.

Like I had before I'd been sucked into this world.

Okay, well, not *just* like I'd been. I'm a little less fleshy now I guess. Significantly less attractive. But just this much feels amazing.

Choosing to heed Noli's advice about not taking things too fast (sometimes she might be onto something) I start by bending my knees. The movement feels pretty good, so I pick up one foot, then the other. My balance is actually fantastic. *Too* fantastic. I wasn't this good with just the glass. It has to be the void, trying to fulfill my intent. Not just the order to act as tendons, but each subconscious order as well, like "stay balanced, keep me on my feet." A sort of auto-stabilizer. Begrudgingly, I have to admit that's pretty useful. I still don't completely trust it. But I guess even *if* a hint of the predator lives on in the void, it would still have some incentive to keep me alive. After all, without me, it loses its only means to enter the physical realm.

What a comforting thought.

Shaking off memories of the predator, I return my focus to walking. And even before I take the first step, this time I know: I've got this.

The grass brushes across the arch of my foot as I take a step. The ground is cool and soft against the humid, warm night—the kind of rejuvenating cold that makes you want to rebel against the summer heat. The kind of crispness that makes you want to run. I take another step.

Giddiness tickles through me. It's almost effortless. I'm not just walking, I'm strolling. I push myself a little faster. There's no fear. No uncertainty. I can do this. I can walk! I break into a jog, then a run. Wind is blowing through my glass. I want to laugh. It's incredible. I feel so free! Finally, *finally*—

My foot catches on a branch. Panic lurches through me as I crash forward, and I only have a moment to throw my arms out in front of me, desperate to protect my core. The void leaps to my hands, cushioning the fall—

Then I hit, my right knee striking first, closely followed by both hands. I feel and hear something crack as I skid forward. Several some-things.

[41 points of Fall Damage sustained.]

Pain spikes up my right leg and arm. I fall onto my side, and wince with the sting of another crack.

[7 points of Fall Damage sustained.]

My right leg is on the ground two feet away. A chip of glass is next to my hip. A crack has spiraled up my left arm, but it's still intact.

Shit.

"Well that's significantly less damage than before," Zyneth says. "I thought I was about to go fetch a broom."

I whip my head in his direction. He's reclining casually against the back of the cottage, watching.

"How long?" I ask, then quickly stop signing as I can feel the cracks spreading through my broken arm like dozens of tiny hot needles. I activate a Sculpt and begin to repair it.

"Just in time for the show," he says. "You improved remarkably fast. I suppose that's related to you not shattering into a thousand pieces?"

I glance at the void, sitting idly nearby. I hadn't even consciously told it to break my fall. And it hadn't, entirely, but I guess a pint of malleable shadows can only do so much.

I finish repairing my arm, then levitate my leg over and line it up with the stump beneath my hip. It's strange to look at. Such a seemingly dire injury should hurt more than this. And don't get me wrong, it does hurt, but the pain is no different from the cracks I'd had in my arm, or the small chip of glass missing at my hip. Like the size of the injury is irrelevant.

"You going to help?" I ask him as I start Sculpting my leg back in place.

"Seems like you've got it handled." But he pushes off the cottage to stroll my way. I'm done with my leg and working on the hip when Zyneth stops nearby, crouching down beside me. He watches in silence as I finish fixing myself up. I Check my health just to make sure I didn't miss anything.

[HP: 8/10]

[Bonus HP: 312/312]

Good. The last couple bits of HP should heal up naturally in the next few minutes, and it looks like I didn't miss any chipped pieces, either. I glance at Zyneth and find him staring back.

He sighs. "Kanin. What are you doing?"

"Fixing my body."

"No," he says. "That's not what I mean."

I call the void over and begin painstakingly reforming the tendons I'd lost when it cushioned my fall. "Learning how to walk?"

"That's not what I mean either," Zyneth says.

I start with the feet, working up. "I'm not sure what—"

"*This*," Zyneth says, gesturing to the void. "What are you doing? You wouldn't even let the stuff touch you a week ago. Now you're incorporating it into your body?"

"Temporary body," I stress with a tinge of defensiveness. "It's just to help strengthen the joints." Just a means to an end.

He shakes his head. "Sorry, I didn't get most of that."

"It helps me walk," I sign, slowing down the movements. This must be what Noli felt like trying to teach me signs when we first met. Okay, she probably still does.

"But why?" he asks. "You don't need to push yourself like this—compromise your values just to get a little faster."

I stiffen. I'm not compromising shit. I'm trying to get over my fears, not let them hold me back. There's nothing wrong with that.

"I need to move faster," I sign instead. "You're leaving tomorrow. I'm coming with."

Zyneth blinks. "Tomorrow? You won't be ready by then."

I finish layering all the void back among my joints. Placing a hand on my knee, I push myself to my feet. "I am."

Zyneth frowns with worry, standing as well. "Maybe you *can* expedite learning to walk. I watched you run across this clearing before falling on your face."

"Hey—"

He holds up a hand. "You're a quick learner and you're creative, I'll give you that. You keep coming up with solutions to things I never would have even considered. But once you come up with a plan, you rush into it. You don't plan two steps ahead of where you set your feet down. Physically, maybe you're ready to walk out of here tomorrow. But mentally, I worry you're not ready for the road ahead."

Pardon me while I roll my nonexistent eyes. "Before, you said I'm free to make my own choices. Even if they are bad." Which this isn't, obviously.

"You are," he says, though with clear reluctance in his tone. "But this is different."

"How?" I demand.

Zyneth glances away. "Well. For one, I hadn't planned on you accompanying me just yet. I have... business which I had intended to resolve alone."

"Oh." So that's what this was about. He's not worried about me *being able* to accompany him—he just doesn't want me there at all. "Is it dangerous?"

He tips his head. "Not physically."

"Then why can't I come?"

Zyneth taps at his lip in thought, still avoiding looking at me. Then again, I guess there's really no eye contact for him to make. Staring at a floating glass pyramid probably isn't the same.

"Come," Zyneth finally says, holding out a hand. "Walk with me. I'll tell you what I can, and then you can decide if you want to follow."

I don't take his hand, but I do follow.

We step through the moonlit glade, Zyneth's gaze turned contemplatively to the stars—God, he's so dramatic—while I carefully watch my feet.

"The short of it is that I have become involved with a dangerous network of people who do not have others' best interests at heart," Zyneth says, absently fiddling with the sheath of one of his knives. "They largely deal with selling artifacts retrieved from the Ruins on the black-market. It's an extremely lucrative business. The more items that are sold, however, the more the revenue stream threatens to dry up. To keep the supply flowing, they needed someone of a particular set of skills to risk venturing into such dangerous lands to retrieve these objects. In my naivete, seeking adventure, I originally entered their ranks of my own volition." With a grimace, he looks back at me. "I have since had regrets, and have done my best to disentangle myself from their endeavors."

"How did you get out?" I ask.

Zyneth laughs, but there's no mirth in his tone. "I didn't."

He rolls up a sleeve of his shirt, and I'm just now realizing I've never seen him in short sleeves or a vest—and that's because of what's etched over his skin.

There's three spiraling marks tattooed into his arm, each a different style of a gold snake appearing to eat its own tail. The first tattoo is whole, while the second tattoo only has an outline of a snake, as if the drawing has yet to be filled in. The third tattoo is partially complete, the head and half of the body filled with the gold coloring: it's also glowing with a subtle light.

"Spent too many years digging myself into this trench," Zyneth says. "Turns out it's twice as hard to climb back out."

I reach out to touch one, then hesitate. "What are they?"

"Debt," Zyneth says. "Not of the monetary variety. They won't eat themselves away until I've paid back the original balance two fold. The enchantments start burning when they have new jobs for me, and they don't go out until I accept one. Sometimes it's days between jobs—sometimes months—sometimes, I'll have two lit up at once. Those are the best scenarios. When more than one granter has use of me, sometimes they can be pitted against each other. I cleared two more debts that way."

Why do I feel like *cleared* isn't just a benign metaphor for cash exchange? And how exactly is he paying off these debts?

A particular set of skills, he'd said. An image of Zyneth fighting off the nightbanes flashes through my mind, throwing daggers into skulls and electrocuting his assailants.

A chill goes through me. "Zyneth... have you hurt anyone?"

Zyneth's gaze trails up from my hands to my face, looking straight at me for the first time since this conversation began. His expression is blank. "Yes."

My soul sinks. "Have you killed...?"

With that same dead expression, he says, "Do you really want to know the answer?"

For a moment my mind stutters to a halt—and that's all the break in concentration it takes for me to miss a step. My knee buckles even as I realize my mistake. I try to stop my fall, mentally reclaiming my grip on the glass, but I'm already overbalanced, tipping forward—

Zyneth pivots and catches me across my chest, his shoulder jamming into my shoulder while he grabs the one opposite. I stumble another foot forward as Zyneth braces, and we come to a halt.

"Good," I sign, waving him off. "I'm good."

Carefully, he lets go. I roll the shoulder he'd slammed into, but it doesn't appear broken. That was smart. If he'd just grabbed an arm it probably would have snapped off.

But I guess he knows his way around the weak points in bodies, doesn't he?

"You shouldn't come," Zyneth says. "I suspect your opinion of me would change."

That's probably true. I'm still trying to wrap my head around the fact that he's killed someone—maybe multiple someones.

Then again, so have I.

I shove the burgeoning nausea aside.

"Were you protecting yourself?" I ask.

Zyneth rolls his sleeve back down, hiding the tattoos away. "In most cases. If you ask, I will tell you the details."

I'm not sure I want the details. "Why?"

The facade finally cracks. Zyneth looks away, pain scrunching his features. "Because I'm trying not to be that person anymore. The whole reason I'm now paying back debts instead of garnering more is to get out of that world. I want to be better—honest. To tip the scales back by helping people instead of hurting."

I tilt my head. "Like me?" Am I just a weight on his scale of morality? Is that why he's stuck around this long? Why he even decided to help in the first place?

"No," Zyneth says quickly. "That's not what I meant."

It sure seems like it. Zyneth must realize this too, because he sighs. "It might have started that way. But at some point I realized it doesn't really count if I treat it as a transaction. A wrong and a right don't cancel each other out. I need to mean it. To want to help for the sake of helping. Noli—she's a good person. I see how she interacts with everyone, and it makes me want to be better. Which is why I said I'm trying—I'm not there yet. But I'm trying."

His words sting. Noli's actions have given me similar thoughts. I know I probably will never be as selfless as she is, but she gives me a North Star, at least. And just being around her makes me *want* to be better. How can I fault Zyneth for feeling the same?

"I'm coming with you," I sign. His background is… surprising, but it still doesn't change what I need to do.

His eyebrows pinch, skeptical. "Even given what you've learned? I can attempt to keep my work separate, but there is still a good chance that if you travel with me, you will get caught in the web as well. It will be dangerous."

Can't be more dangerous than towing a murder void around with you everywhere. "Doesn't matter," I sign. "I still need to learn a way to get my body back." Then I add, "If you want to help people, you can start with me."

Zyneth's mouth quirks with the hint of a smile. "A bit self-serving, don't you think?"

I never claimed I wasn't selfish. "Sounds familiar."

That gets a quiet laugh out of him. "Alright. I'll agree to this. Tomorrow we'll leave for Miasmere."

Warmth fills my chest, relief and hope trickling out from behind the anxiety that he'd say no. Finally. Finally I'm making progress.

"But first," Zyneth says, amusement returning to his eyes as his gaze dances over my body. "We need to find you some pants."

Chapter Five

NOT EXACTLY PANTS

It turns out a glass body is not particularly designed for people clothes. Noli lends me a pair of her slacks first, but since my body is held together with a series of Chain spells instead of muscles and ball-and-socket joints, there isn't really a waist to cinch the belt around. Zyneth also offers me a shirt, but it hangs loose about my thin glass limbs, making me look like some kind of emaciated crane—and that's when it's not trying to slide right off my body. Turns out lack of friction—or a neck—doesn't help.

Eventually, Rezira gives a grumbling sigh at all our attempts. "You all aren't going about this right. We need to be working with the body he has, not the body he should have." Gee, thanks for the reminder. "Here, let me try." She produces a moth-eaten cloak from the back of their wardrobe and gives it a good shake—sending all lung-owning parties in the room into a coughing fit. Heh. Suckers.

Rezira pats off the dust. "It's a little old." A little?! "But it should do for now."

She drapes the cloak around me, hooking the ends around the knobs of glass I'd formed on my shoulders for the necklace chain to fix to. She uses a pin and a bit of twine to tie the cloth in place.

"Alright. See if that stays," she says.

I carefully lift my arms. The cloth pulls a little at my shoulders, but at least it's not sliding off. I feel a little more clothed now, even though it's really only covering my arms and back. I mean, I'm not *really* naked, considering there's nothing to cover up. But damn, it's sure good to feel like an actual member of society again.

I pivot in a circle, flapping the cloak dramatically around me just to see how it holds—and, okay, maybe because I like the flair. "What do you think?"

Noli claps her hands. "It's perfect!"

"It's not exactly pants," Zyneth says. "But it's a good idea."

Rezira steps back, hands on her hips. She gives me a stiff nod. "It suits you."

Noli beams. "Look at you! Look at how far you've come."

"Not far enough," I sign, and her smile falters. The look stings me with regret.

"Sorry," she signs before I have a chance to say the same. "You're right. But I'm proud of you anyway."

Rezira breaths a heavy sigh out her nose. "So you're really heading out then?"

"We should be on the road in the next hour," Zyneth says, glancing at the window. Mid-morning light fills the cottage with an orange warmth. "I'd prefer to make it to Bluevine by late afternoon, so we may find somewhere to stay in Miasmere before nightfall."

"Makes sense," Rezira says. "You need any supplies? Here. Let me pack you something."

"Oh, that won't be necessary," Zyneth objects.

Rezira engulfs his hand and a good portion of his arm in an iron grasp and pulls him away. "I insist."

Noli chuckles as Zyneth is forcefully steered toward the supplies Rezira has meticulously laid out and is now beginning to explain, packing them away one by one. Noli turns back to me. Her smile doesn't reach her eyes.

"Is it selfish of me?" Noli signs. "I'm sad to see you go."

My soul aches with her words. "I'll come back." I don't know how long it will take, but I'm certain I'll see her again.

"You better," she signs teasingly. Then she looks down at her hands, fidgeting. "But... if you do find a way home, I'll understand if you take it. I want to apologize for the other day. You were right. It's not my place to ask you to stay. What you're experiencing, how you're living right now, I can tell how hard it is on you. You deserve your real body. The one that makes you happy. And I'm sure you are eager to get home." She laughs sadly at that. "You know, the whole time we were journeying together, I kept thinking of Rezira, and how worried she must be, and how I couldn't wait to get home to see her. But I never stopped to think about how you were probably feeling the same. I'm sure there's loved ones you're eager to reunite with as well."

"I..."

There's not.

It's like a slap to the face. What do I have? An estranged dad, a handful of ex-boyfriends, some work buddies, but...

No one. There's no one waiting for me.

The realization sits hollow in my soul.

"It's okay," Noli signs with a comforting smile. "I understand. And I hope you find a way back to them soon." She takes my hands and gives them a gentle squeeze. She lets go just as quick. "Here. Even if you are coming back, I wanted to give you something to remember me by." Noli turns away, fetching something from between the bookshelf and the bed. She returns with a leather satchel. There's a simple design burned into the surface: a small vial of ink.

I sign laughter. "Please tell me that's not me."

Noli grins. "I wasn't finished yet. I didn't expect you to head out so soon. But I knew you'd be needing this eventually, so…"

She flips the top open, revealing my two spell books nestled inside. "You'll have to carry these yourself, now." She also points out where Trenevalt's beaded bracelet—half the beads lit—hangs from one of the clasps like a charm. There's a thin sleeve on the back as well, where she's stored a slate and some chalk. "For speaking with Zyneth. He's getting better, but his signs aren't as good as yours, yet. I know you're still learning to write, but I thought it might come in handy."

"Thank you." I'm truly touched. Even if she didn't want me to go, she's been planning for it all along. I hold out my hands, and she passes me the bag.

I stagger forward, dropping it to the floor.

"Oh! Are you alright?" Noli asks.

I try to hoist the bag up, but I can't even lift it. My arms aren't strong enough.

One trend I've figured out through trial and error (mostly error) is that I can levitate my Attuned glass at will: However, at most, they can only carry something equal to half their own weight before it becomes too heavy and they're no longer able to float.

The cloak isn't an issue, given the whole body's worth of glass supporting it. But it looks like the satchel exceeds my arms' limit.

I could laugh. Two books. Two books! This is pathetic.

Crouching down to floor level, I loop the strap over a shoulder and stand back up. This time, the force of my body, instead of just my arms, is enough to lift it. Problem solved.

The stupidest problem solved.

"I've got it," I tell Noli, who's still fretting over me. "I just have... ah... differences with this body I still need to learn."

"Nuance?" she suggests.

I copy the sign. "Nuances to learn." Lots and lots of 'em.

"I know you'll figure it out," she signs. Noli's gaze traces over my body and sticks on my legs. "Those shadows..."

"Yes." I'm surprised she can even make it out. In the daylight, the void nestled into each joint is almost indistinguishable from shadows if you didn't know any better. Of course, Noli does, and she has sharp eyes to boot. I hadn't explicitly told her and Rezira how I mastered walking overnight, but it was only a matter of time until she noticed. "The null magic."

Noli's lips press together. "That's what's helping you walk?"

"Yes." I wearily brace myself for the scolding.

"I'm glad," Noli signs, looking back up at me with a smile. "I'm glad to see you embracing it instead of shunning it. It's not evil, you understand? It's just another type of magic."

"You said that before." Back when I had to use it to save her. And maybe... maybe now I'm in more of a mindset to hear it. I'm not sure I'm completely trusting yet, but it does just seem to be inert magic. Granted, magic the predator had been wielding. But now it answers to me, and if I'm stuck with this black goo, I might as well make use of it.

"And you're right," I sign. "You usually are."

She chuckles. "All this old age makes me wise."

Wait. How old *is* she? She doesn't look a day over twenty, but I guess she is an elf. They live forever, right? I'd just never really given it any thought before.

Echo? I ask.

[Age: 46]

What the shit.

Noli steps back, looking me up and down, then gives an appreciative nod. "Good luck on your adventures, Kanin the wizard."

That rings even stranger than Noli's age. How has this become my life?

"Thank you," I sign to Noli as Zyneth heads back over with his pack newly stocked with all of Rezira's supplies. "For... for everything."

Noli rubs at her eyes. "If you have a chance, come back here before you go?"

I nod—wow. It feels great to be able to nod again. "Of course." After all, there's no hurry. My first priority is to figure out a way to retrieve my body. Going home is a separate, more confusing issue. Maybe they'll be one and the same, or maybe I'll find a way to be able to magic my body here.

The thought gives me pause. Is that what I want? To live as a human here instead of back on Earth? To leave everyone I've ever known, every place I've ever seen, my *career*, behind? I don't know if I have an answer to that.

But I don't need to, yet. I'll have plenty of time to sort through these thoughts after I find a solution to the body dilemma.

Plenty of time.

"Well," Zyneth says, pulling me out of my uncertainty. "Is there anything else you need to grab before we leave?"

"No," I sign, resting a hand against the satchel Noli made for me. Besides the beads and books, I don't really own anything. Just the glass and void that makes up my body—and since I don't need to eat or sleep, there's no food or bedrolls to pack. "I think I'm ready."

"What are those?" Rezira abruptly cuts in, pointing at me.

I glance to my side. "What?"

"Those!" She reaches out and tugs on my signing glass, which I'd been using to talk in place of the hands actually attached to my body. Unlike the pieces that are connected to my arms, each section of each finger long and round, Chained together to mimic human hands, my signing glass is dozens and dozens of smaller fragments, all clustered together to make a hand shape. More like sand and pebbles than skin and bones.

I wiggle my signing glass. "Back-up hands."

Rezira snorts. "You need to practice signing with the ones on your body. Two disembodied hands floating next to you is just weird."

"It wasn't weird when I was small," I object.

"Yes it was," Rezira says.

I look helplessly at Noli and Zyneth.

"It was a little abnormal," Noli signs. "But, everything about our experience was abnormal!"

"I found it quite bizarre when I first encountered it," Zyneth says, as blunt as ever. "And I must agree with Rezira, it is definitely an unusual sight even now. Your form will already draw quite a bit of attention in the city."

Slightly offended, I tuck my signing glass away in the folds of my cloak. Out of sight, but there's no way I'm getting rid of them—not after everything we've been through. "There. Happy?"

"Ecstatic," Rezira deadpans.

"Just be careful out there," Noli signs. "Listen to Zyneth. He's more familiar with our world than you."

What am I, a child?

"And you take care of him," Noli adds, this time to Zyneth. "I'd tell you to make sure he doesn't break, but he does that a lot, so just make sure he can still be put back together again."

"I will do my best to prevent dire breakages," Zyneth says with a chuckle.

"Oh!" Noli throws her arms around me, pulling me into a hug. She still feels so frail, even weeks after her recovery. But the hug is gentle and warm, and fills me with unexpected emotions I can't quite identify. If I had human anatomy, I think I'd be getting choked up. How long has it been since anyone's hugged me? It was at least before I left Earth. Long, long before.

She pulls back. "I'm bad at goodbyes. Stay safe out there. Don't doubt yourself. You're stronger than you think."

I decide not to point out how this seems to be in direct conflict with her previous fretting. "We'll be fine. You take care, too."

Rezira wraps an arm around Noli as they follow us to the door. The sun is filtering through the trees, bright and cheerful as we step away from the cabin, the women hanging back in the doorframe. For once I regret not having my omni-vision, wishing I could watch them even as I focus carefully on maneuvering the path before me. When we reach the end of the glade I stop to look back. Noli waves, and I return the gesture. My soul feels tight, despite it hanging loosely over my chest. A wave of uncertainty washes over me. For a moment I want nothing more than to turn back, back to these friends and this simple, comforting life. Back toward stability and familiarity.

"Kanin?" Zyneth asks. I look back to find him waiting for me.

The doubt passes. I flex my hand into a fist, the glass clinking against each other. No. When I come back here, it'll be in my own body.

I step after Zyneth, striking out into the woods, as we leave the cabin behind.

Chapter Six

On Sleeping Arrangements

It feels great to be walking through a town while being, you know, person-sized. And also just walking on two legs in general. Regaining a sliver of my humanity is nice. It's not totally the same, though. My bare feet clink against the road, which had been mildly annoying while walking through the forest and dirt roads that led to Bluevine, but now that I'm on cobblestone, I feel like I'm walking on eggshells.

Well. Glass.

Trying not to think about how one wrong step might cause me to break off a foot, fall, and shatter into a thousand pieces, I focus instead on the small city we're walking through. I hadn't been paying much attention when we first passed through town, somewhat preoccupied with my and Noli's mortality, but now I have an opportunity to soak up the sights.

The first thing I notice is a lack of humans. Plenty of dwarves, elves, and orcs around, and a scattering of other species I've seen from time to time as well, such as the cat-like felis and grey-skinned damphyr. No scaly dracid, however, or cambions, like Zyneth. Even so, he doesn't draw many looks. In fact, people are glancing toward me more often than my companion.

"Are homunculi rare?" I ask Zyneth. He frowns at my signs. I heave a mental sigh and get out the slate and chalk. Noli was still working with me on their alphabet, but that's only half the battle. Since everything gets translated to English in my brain, I'm not just learning to write their alphabet, but I have to learn every word in their language from scratch, too. It's been slow going. Signs have come to me way faster—maybe it's an acting thing. I don't know. Long story short, I try to avoid writing when I can.

I awkwardly scribble out the word for "homunculi" and manage to get the rest of my point across.

"Ah," he says once I've finished. "No, they're not particularly rare—although they're most often leased to the wealthy or owned by businesses, so it's not surprising there wouldn't be many in a town as small as this."

The words *owned* and *leased* stir a discomfort in my soul. Rationally, I know other homunculi are just artificial automatons: this world's version of robots. They're not people—they're not like me. But it's hard to shake that disquiet.

"Of course," Zyneth adds, "that's unlikely why they're looking at you. A homunculus made of glass is nearly unheard of. For obvious practical reasons."

Yeah, you wouldn't want your delivery monkey to have its arms break off trying to pick up a heavy package.

"Just stay close to me and no one will bother you," Zyneth says. "They probably assume..." He trails off, probably thinking better of completing that thought.

But I can read between the lines: everyone probably assumes I'm his servant. Great.

We make it to the town's square, where the telepad to other cities is located. For a moment I have a visceral reaction to seeing that stone pedestal; the last time I'd used one I'd been running for my life. Simultaneously, I'd been frightened of being caught Between and forced to confront the predator. I try to push the feeling away. There's nothing to be afraid of. The predator is still trapped in my inventory, after all. Nothing is waiting for me Between. Even so, my soul aches at the memory, and I touch my core.

Zyneth checks the schedule with a teller.

"There won't be another Miasmere alignment until tomorrow morning," the dwarf tells him. "But you can secure a pass now if you like."

"Please," Zyneth says.

The dwarf sets down a flat, golf-ball sized stone with a strange rune carved into it. "Five silvers." He looks at me.

"Ah." Zyneth pulls out a pouch and produces a string of ten coins from within it. He sets the whole string down. "We'll be needing two, actually."

The dwarf's gaze sweeps around Zyneth, as if expecting someone else to be there, and it takes until that moment for it to finally hit me—the teller had been expecting me to pay. And he'd probably been expecting me to hold onto that token, too. Because I'm the manservant.

Zyneth should have skimped him and just paid for one.

Still, the dwarf doesn't object as he swipes the coins off the table and puts a second token down in their place.

"A pleasure," Zyneth says, taking one and passing the other to me.

"Is this a ticket?" I ask as we head away. Last time we'd used the telepad, I hadn't really been paying attention to the specifics of how it worked.

Again, however, Zyneth shakes his head at my signs. This is quickly getting old. Instead I wiggle the stone token we got and sign, "What is?"

"It allows passage between linked telepads," Zyneth says. "Though I assume you already surmised that."

"Why two?" I sign.

That much at least he understands. "The telepad requires one token for every living being that passes through. Nonliving matter can be transported easily enough, which is why he'd originally given me one. Typically, homunculi and other spelled servants can accompany their caster without issue. There's a possibility you could pass through without requiring a token as well, but given you have a soul, I believed it was best not to risk it. We purchased extra tokens for you and Noli last time as well."

Not risking it sounds great to me. And the idea that *something* on this planet recognizes me as a living person—even if that something is only a teleportation spell—is kind of comforting. Kind of.

"I suppose we might as well find an inn," Zyneth says. "Shame. We could have stayed with Noli and Rezira another night, if we'd known the next alignment with Miasmere wasn't until tomorrow. Well, I suppose there's nothing for it. Come, we should be able to find a reputable place near here, the ones closest to a telepad square are often the most expensive yet most comfortable..."

But I'd stopped in my tracks. A person is standing at the side of the road, watching me. At least, I assume they're watching me. They're a head shorter, and appear to be made of stone, with lines of red like cracks in volcanic rock threaded over their skin. A large black marble sits where their eyes should be, and a hole through their chest burns with the flickering light of a fire.

I don't need to ask for a Check to know this is a homunculus.

It turns and begins to walk away.

"Wait!" I close the gap and grab their wrist, and they stop. I'm not even sure why I do it. If I had a heart right now it'd be beating out of my chest. My soul feels tight. Anxiety is crawling through me like static. What am I doing? It's not rational. But I have to know—

[Spell: Homunculus]

[Type: Stone and Fire]

[Level: 10]

[Attack: 20]

[HP: 100/100]

[Mana: 0/0]

No name. No Class or Species or Role. A fear I hadn't realized I'd had uncoils inside of me.

"What are you doing?" a woman snaps. I look down to notice her: a halfling standing by the homunculus's side. "Let go of it!"

I release the homunculus, snapping my hand away as if burned. The creature continues to stand there passively as if nothing had happened at all. "I'm sorry," I sign. What was I thinking? "I'm sorry."

The halfling stares at me like I've grown a second head—or maybe just like my head is made of glass. "Stay back."

"I didn't mean..." I stop when I notice her watching my hands. Not to read, but with an expression somewhere between confusion and fear.

"My apologies," Zyneth says, slipping in front of me. "I did not mean to disrupt your shopping."

I finally notice the basket of books in the homunculus's hand—the one I hadn't grabbed. It all clicks: the halfling was out shopping, and her homunculus was doing the heavy lifting.

"Watch your construct," the halfling snaps. "It tried to attack us!"

"A simple misunderstanding, I assure you," Zyneth says.

"Its hands are twitching—do you see that?" she says, continuing to glare at me. "It's malfunctioning. You shouldn't take it out in public when it's like this! Irresponsible." She narrowed her eyes. "What type is that anyway? How garish."

Zyneth bows his head in apology. "Again, I sincerely apologize. We will leave you be. Come," he says to me, nudging me back. "Let's be off."

I let Zyneth guide me away, too overwhelmed to think of a response. I'm not sure if I'm offended or relieved or—or damn it all, I'm just confused with myself. I know other homunculus are just spells. I know I'm the exception. So why did seeing one shock me like that? Why did I feel so... bothered? I don't even know what that was.

Zyneth doesn't say anything as he hurries me away. I can't tell if he's blushing beneath the blood-red tone of his skin, but I can tell he's a little flustered. Embarrassed, maybe? Is he embarrassed by me?

My offense boils away. Of course he is. I just made a complete scene. The halfling isn't to blame for treating me like a servant—no more than that teller had been. They didn't have any reason to think I was anything other than a mindless construct brought to life with Zyneth's magic. Stupid. That was stupid of me.

"I'm sorry," I sign again. "I don't know why I did that."

He waves off my apology. "No, no, don't. I imagine this all must be... somewhat overwhelming. I'm sorry I didn't prepare you better for what to expect."

I thought of what the halfling said. "Does no one recognize signs? Is it that uncommon?"

"Somewhat," Zyneth admits. "It's most common in Valenia South. The primary inhabitants there speak exclusively through Sign Language. Though even if most people don't speak it themselves, they should be able to recognize it for what it is."

"She thought I was broken."

Zyneth frowns. "Yes, well. I can't entirely blame her. Seeing a person sign is quite different from seeing a homunculus sign. Homunculi cannot communicate. They have no soul or mind of their own. Tell me, if a direwolf were to start barking at you, would your first thought be that it was speaking a language?"

They have direwolves here?

Some half-forgotten instinct makes me raise my hand to my head—to rub my temple or bury my face in my hands, I'm not sure. The moment the glass in my hands *tinks* against my head, I realize what I'm doing and stop. I'm tired of not being seen as human. Even just being recognized as alive would be a step up. "I wish I could just talk to them." I look down at the slate I'm still carrying. "Or write better."

Zyneth gives me a sympathetic look. "I can't imagine the frustration. But you know, there may be a..." He pauses.

"What?" I ask. "What?"

"I don't want to get your hopes up," Zyneth says. "I don't mean to offend, but sometimes I suspect you've angered a god or two. This solution could go either way, and you have cosmically bad luck."

Tell me about it. "What is it?" I ask anyway.

"There's translators," Zyneth says. "They work with most spoken and signed languages. I'm not precisely sure how the magic functions, but I believe it operates on intent. I'm not certain it would work with your native language, considering it doesn't exist here, but it might be worth a shot."

I suddenly recall Noli mentioning a translator when we'd just left Trenevalt's cabin. That was nearly two months ago, but it feels like two years. "That would be amazing!"

"Of course," Zyneth adds, "your first language would only be one of two potential barriers that might prevent it from functioning for you."

"What do you mean?" I ask. The translator not recognizing English sounds like a big enough blocker on its own, but I still have to try.

Zyneth makes a gesture that encompasses all of me. "It is the same issue with regards to the teleportation token. We purchased a token for you because it was best to be safe. You do have a soul, after all. However, when we worked together to defeat the predator, the interaction between our magic was somewhat different, if you recall."

He's right. Rezira had tried using her school of magic—healing magic—on me, and it hadn't done a thing. Meanwhile, Zyneth's artificer magic had worked to top off my mana tanks. And that was because healing magic is intended to be cast on living things, while artificer magic is used on inanimate objects.

Which means that, at least according to their magic system, I fall into the latter category.

"The translator only works on living things?" I ask.

"There's never been an opportunity to use it on anything else," Zyneth replies. "Which is why I am uncertain if this would work or not. I don't know that it has ever been tried."

Well, I'm just a walking "First!" factory, aren't I? But I don't see the harm in giving it a shot. "Where can we find one?"

"Miasmere," Zyneth says. "I know of at least one shop we could stop by. We could take a look around here as well, but they're rather expensive, so I doubt anyone in a remote town such as this would be selling any."

The mention of price makes me uncomfortable. I really appreciate Zyneth paying for everything, and he already confessed to being well off, so it probably isn't a financial strain for him, but it still makes me uncomfortable. I don't like feeling indebted, even if I know he wouldn't see it that way.

"How much?" I ask.

"A few hundred..." He must have figured out why I'm asking, because he stops himself. "Please don't concern yourself with the cost. Besides, we won't be paying for anything if it doesn't work, anyway."

And by *we* he means him, because I won't be paying for anything regardless.

Damn. *Should* I get a job in this world? I mean, I still intend to go home, but how long is that going to take?

And Zyneth isn't the only one I owe. Attiru's map shop was destroyed because of me. I should help them. And then there's Tetara and Saru, the two survivors of the predator's attack, though I know money won't bring back their dead friends.

I suppress a shudder at the memory, and touch a hand to my core once more.

Zyneth grabs us an inn near the central square, and I'm greeted with a weird sense of deja vu as we're directed to our room. He'd bought us a room last time, too—although now there's not the looming sense of doom hanging over my shoulders as we're shown inside.

Zyneth stops dead in the doorframe.

"What?" I ask, trying to peek around.

"Ah, er, I am still getting used to them identifying you as a homunculus as well," Zyneth says, his shoulders hunching up with... embarrassment? "I had just assumed... Well, it was my fault, really, for not specifying."

"What?" Impatient, I push past him into the room and look around.

I don't get it. It's a normal room. Like the one I'd stayed at in Harrowood, there's a desk, a trunk, a window, and a bed.

One bed.

Oh.

Zyneth clears his throat uncomfortably. "I'll go back and ask for a different room. One with two beds this time."

Right—of course the innkeep wouldn't book a bed for the automaton. I would be irritated if I wasn't starting to get used to this treatment. But hey, I guess if it saved Zyneth a few coins, I'm not complaining.

"No," I sign. "It's okay. One will work."

Zyneth's eyebrows shoot up. "Ah, well, I mean... I'm not sure if—the bed is rather small—it seems that would be... impractical." He glances away, flustered.

I stare at him in confusion. What? Why's he acting so embarrassed? And is that a *blush* I see? What did I say? It's just a bed. We don't need two, if...

It hits me like a ton of bricks.

Oh fuck! "No, no, I meant, I don't need a bed!" I hurriedly add, haphazardly scribbling on the slate to try to get the point across. "I don't sleep. I'll just, I can wait outside, or—"

"Oh," Zyneth says, his shoulders sagging in relief. "Yes, of course, that makes more sense." He passes a hand over his face, then looks at me, regaining his composure. "Right. Well, I think I will go... find dinner. Then jump out a window, perhaps."

I am seriously considering doing the same.

"Well, please make yourself comfortable," Zyneth says, hastily backing out of the room. "I will be down in the pub. Feel free to..." Even he seems to realize he's rambling. "...do things. I'll return within the hour." He closes the door, his footsteps beating a hasty retreat down the hall.

I stand there for a moment, waiting for the mortification to finally kill me. When that doesn't happen, I slump against the door, gaze returning to the stupid lone bed.

"Fuck," I sign at the empty room.

CHAPTER SEVEN

SUPER MYSTERIOUS OPERATION

I spend the night sitting on the chair, pushed over against the door and as far away from Zyneth's bed as I can manage. Watching Zyneth sleep would be creepy (ignoring the fact I did that while in ink-bottle form the first night we met, but ink-bottle Kanin was wary and gets a pass), so I spend the time practicing writing and playing with the small handful of spells I have at my disposal.

Now that I don't have the Void stat to worry about—still sitting at 100%, as usual—I can experiment with my spells at will. For instance, I've found that if I feed just a tiny bit of mana into the Lightbeam spell, it merely creates a small beam of light, as the name implies, instead of a deadly laser. Which is probably how the spell is intended to be used in the first place. I use some of my signing glass to create the Lightbeam, which I point into a corner by the door so as not to wake Zyneth, then use some more glass to see if I can block and dim the light. Maybe reflect it back on itself. I create a sort of mini disco-ball shape after a minute of fiddling around, and after another minute of playing with this, trying to make it smaller, dimmer, and more controlled, I'm greeted with a familiar voice.

[New Spell obtained,] Echo says. [Glow, Level 1: Create a small ball of illumination. Mana cost: Adjustable. 1 mana per minute at the dimmest setting.]

Nice, with 56 mana at my disposal, I can keep this spell going for almost an hour. The light glowing from my cluster of glass is softer, dim, and more uniform than the previous scattering of light. It's not focused in one direction, like Lightbeam, but this one is a lot more mana-efficient.

I don't unlock any other spells or skills the rest of the night. I'm not exactly sure how the whole process works, but it seems like there's three ways I can learn them. The first is innate knowledge that I have to dig out of Echo. The Attune, Sculpt, and Chain spells all came from me asking the right questions and prompting Echo in the right ways to get her to reveal what spells I could already do by default. The second is through my Arcane Intuition skill. This lets me automatically learn new spells that I read from a spell book, if I study and read them long enough, but just because I *know* a spell doesn't mean I have the supplies, mana, or other prerequisites to use it. (In fact, I've already read both my spell books cover to cover a few times now, and "learned" every spell I could, though many can't even be activated by my type of magic, and the rest are all concerned with forging homunculus cores, which I have exactly 0 interest in.) And finally, it seems, just playing around with my magic, practicing a new application repeatedly enough, can unlock the occasional ability, like this new Glow spell.

Too bad the last option is complete trial and error, and more often than not all I turn up is error.

Like writing, for instance. I spend a good two hours trying to scratch out the alphabet and some simple words Noli has taught me, but despite having a supposed Foreign Language skill (up to level 4 now, I might add,) I'm absolutely lousy with written words. That translator thing better work.

I spend the last couple hours before dawn examining my void joints and fixing up my glass. Bits of the glass on my feet have chipped away from stubbed toes and kicked pebbles. Forget clothes, I could really use some shoes. I don't have any more glass to pull from my inventory—let alone an inventory I can access anymore—so I make do by Sculpting some glass away from different parts of my body to patch up the sections on my feet. While I'm at it, I also redistribute some of the glass from my torso, which I don't really use anyway, to my legs, which are supporting most of my weight and taking the majority of the load. I feel a little bottom heavy as a result, but it helps with balance and, you know, not ending up with more broken legs. I'll have to grab some more glass from somewhere tomorrow.

Zyneth finally wakes up with the dawn, and I pay careful attention to the wall as he gets dressed and ready for the day. We check out of the room and I accompany him to the pub, where I get to twiddle my thumbs as he eats breakfast. I would typically try to hide my jealousy when it comes to meal time, although, given Zyneth's grimace as he picks through a sludgy bowl of the inn's gruel, for once I'm perfectly happy not to partake.

"Got your token?" he asks when we finally make our way back to the telepad.

I hold up the small carved stone.

"Good. You understand how this works?"

"Yes." Step on the pad when it's our turn. It's not exactly rocket science.

"Right." He steals a worried glance at me. I guess the lack of eyes makes it hard to tell that I'm still looking at him.

"What?" I ask. "Is something wrong?"

He hesitates. "I'm concerned for your wellbeing."

"Why?" I ask. "This isn't new." I've used a telepad with him before. I'd been worried about the predator then, when it was still Between, but now that it's trapped in my inventory, I should have even less to worry about.

"Your mental wellbeing," Zyneth amends. "I've no doubt you'll make it through without mishap, however I understand how these sorts of events can... resurface dark memories."

Literally dark, in this case. But he's worrying over nothing. "I'm fine," I assure him. "I'm excited." Looking forward to it, even. It finally feels like I'm making steps in the right direction. Like I'm making progress. "Will we go to the library first?"

"In Miasmere? No," Zyneth says. "Actually, that's something I wanted to talk to you about. Originally, I'd hoped we would arrive yesterday, and I would have had time this morning to show you to the library before I needed to attend to my errands." There's a strange weight in that last word, and he fleetingly rubs a hand over his arm, where the tattoo is likely still burning beneath his sleeve. "However, with the compressed schedule, I'll need to go there directly. I would prefer if you didn't come with, but the alternative is to leave you unattended in Miasmere, which I find equally disagreeable."

"I'm not a child," I sign. "I can be left alone without—" okay, maybe *falling apart* wouldn't be the best word choice there. "—without getting into any trouble."

Zyneth squints at my signs, seeming to miss some of them, but able to gather enough to appear unimpressed regardless. "If you got lost, where would you go?"

"I'd ask for help," I say, switching back to simpler signs for Zyneth's benefit.

"And if they don't know signs?" he asks.

Oh yeah. Welp. "No time to get that translator first?"

"No." Zyneth sighs. "But you're right. This should be your choice. If you'd rather brave Miasmere on your own, I'd advise you to stick close to the telepad and wait for me there once we cross over. I can come retrieve you after my business is complete."

I hesitate. At least I'm being given the choice. But I hate to admit he's right: this isn't visiting a city in a different state, this is a whole different *planet* I'm dealing with. I can't communicate with most of them, and now that I'm not a glass bottle that can hide in alleyways, I'm going to be far more conspicuous.

I shake my head. "No. You're right. I'll come with you." I'm deathly curious about these suspicious jobs he's doing, anyway.

"Good," Zyneth says with a breath of relief. But his forehead is still pinched with worry. "However, you're not to say—or sign—a word if you accompany me. Don't react to anything anyone says. Don't touch anything. As far as they know, you really *are* a homunculus construct and nothing more. Understand?"

I see we're back to treating me like a child. "I can behave."

He looks at me skeptically.

"What? I can!" I insist. "You won't even know I'm there."

"Alright," he says, though he still doesn't appear convinced. "Just... please be careful. And I realize the hypocrisy in saying this to a glass homunculus with a knack for causing scenes, but please try not to draw any attention to yourself."

"I don't do it on purpose," I sign.

"I know." We step out into the square where merchants and travelers have gathered to wait for their time slot at the telepad. "That's what worries me."

We appear in Miasmere and the roar of the city hits me all at once. White marbled stone rises in spires all around us, shouts and the clatter of city life ricocheting from every direction. The marketplace is colorful and crowded, though a dominant motif of blue and gold highlights the white backdrop like a bright sky day.

There are more people here—different kinds, I mean. Zyneth's cambion species seemed to be fairly rare in the towns I'd previously visited, with only him and Attiru as examples of his species I'd seen until now. But the familiar red forms fill the crowds of Miasmere, along with several new species I've never seen before. Echo identifies one terrifying group of people, with a human upper-half growing out of a horse-sized spider's body, as arachnoids. On the less creepy side of the spectrum are nereids, gilled people who shimmer with an opalescent impression of scales, and dryads, whose skin appear wooden and whose hair cascades with vines and flowers.

There are other less-common species I recognize from Harrowood and Bluevine, but I guess even with telepads some groups of people tend to be more regional. I wonder how long this world has used these telepads for casual travel and trade.

Zyneth steps off the telepad without looking back, and I follow him. I'm not thrilled with playing the part of Manservant, but my curiosity outweighs my indignance. Even with the conversation about his past he and I'd had a few nights prior, I can tell there's still plenty he's not disclosing. Is it nosy of me to go fishing for more clues? I mean, yeah, absolutely. But that's hardly enough to dissuade me.

I gawk at the city as we weave through its streets; it's obviously several times bigger than Harrowood. Not just from the density of the crowds and diverse species, but the height of the buildings around us, and how I can catch glimpses of more of the city's towers even in the distance. Not medieval type towers I'd expect to see on a castle, but great, spiraling, artistic spires: a testament to prosperity and wealth more than conquest.

But as we weave through the streets, our surroundings begin to shift. Something I can't quite put my finger on. The shops and crowds don't seem too different. It's not that the streets have become grimy or dark. But there's a tension in the air that I hadn't noticed back in the telepad square. Now the glances that come my way aren't filled with curiosity, but suspicion.

I resist the urge to ask Zyneth about it. He asked me not to draw attention to myself, and signing to Zyneth while I'm supposed to just be a dumb robot would probably achieve that. I can keep my hands still for an hour. How hard could it be?

Finally we stop outside a ramshackle shopfront not far from the docks. I can't see the ocean, but I can hear the distant roar of waves and shrill cries of seabirds, and I'd like to think the sticky streets are from saltwater rather than less desirable fluids. For the first time since entering Miasmere, Zyneth turns and looks at me. There's a hint of anxiety in his eyes, which surprises me. He opens his mouth to say something, then perhaps thinks better of it, instead signing a hasty and barely intelligible, "Ready?"

I'm starting to understand Rezira's frustration with my early attempts at signing. "Yes."

Without another word, he knocks three times—with a stutter in the middle; some kind of code?—then lets himself in.

Our super mysterious operation takes us into the front room of what appears to be a bait and tackle shop. Fishing gear is crammed into the front window and along mismatched shelves. There's harpoons, buckets of bait, lines, lures, and plenty of strange devices I've never seen before. Even the objects I can identify are altered in peculiar ways, with runes or spell circles carved into the surface of many.

The back counter is empty, so I wander over to a wall to get a closer look at the array of items. Wasn't exactly expecting my first venture into the shady underground of magical society to take me to a fishing hut. A framed picture, yellowing and askew, is jammed between two shelves in one of the few empty slots of the wall. The picture features a small group of people, mostly nereids, standing in front of an exotic metal ship that looks like it swam right out of the movie *Atlantis*. There's a hand-scribbled note on the bottom, which Echo is miraculously capable of translating to "2nd Emrox Expedition."

"What's this?" I sign to Zyneth, seeing as we're still alone, and he's agitatedly fiddling with the sleeve of his shirt. Being here clearly bothers him, so a distraction could do him good.

Zyneth glances at the picture. "One of Gillow's early missions, I suspect. Probably when they were going on jobs instead of assigning them."

A figure emerges from the back room as he's speaking. "Ah, the glory days."

They're a nereid, skin covered in a shimmer of purple-grey scales, blue fins fanning at their neck. Their lips peel back to reveal a pointed-tooth smile, and their eyelids blink sideways as they take the both of us in.

I do the same with a quick Check.

[Name: Gillow]
[Species: Nereid]
[Class: Aquatic Mechanic]
[Level: 39]
[HP: 115/115]
[Mana: 840/840]

"Why, if it isn't the aristocrat!" they say, sneering at Zyneth. "Taken to talking to yourself now, hm? I see all the pressure's finally gotten to you. Dig the new servant. Is that a present from Mother?"

Their words are laced with venom. There's a mocking emphasis placed on *aristocrat,* and I detect something derisive in *Mother* as well. Zyneth glowers, but does not acknowledge either of the taunts.

"You have a new job for me?" he asks, stepping away from the wall. I try to casually follow after him, but Gillow's eyes still briefly flick over me when I move.

"What, no small talk?" they say, leaning on the counter as they casually drum their webbed fingers against the wood. Each claw sticks slightly in the surface before it's pulled away. Gillow's a whole head shorter than Zyneth, but somehow that only makes them seem more dangerous, like a snake coiled and ready to strike. "I could regale you about those voyages to Emrox. I still have the sub, you know. They were quite lucrative jobs, but people stopped signing up when only one in ten ships ever made it back."

Zyneth rolls up his shirt sleeve until the lowest tattoo is showing. It's still faintly glowing. "If you have nothing to offer, then we can consider your summons fulfilled, and I'll be taking my leave."

Gillow sighs. "Always were a stick in the mud. Alright." They flick a finger toward Zyneth, and the tattoo leaps from his arm. Now hovering in the air between them, the snake unravels into its individual lines, then reforms into a new shape: a scroll.

"Three jobs," Gillow says, words appearing on the glowing, transparent scroll as they speak, as if written by an invisible quill. "First, a retrieval assignment. A relic in Mount Carmine. Might be to your elemental disposition, eh?"

Zyneth frowns as he taps on the spell, scrolling through the words written there too quickly for me to read over his shoulder.

"No?" Gillow says, though Zyneth hasn't given any indication he's uninterested that I can tell. "The second one is intel. One of my personnel went missing three weeks ago. They were working on a job at the Athenaeum. Find where they've ended up and who put them there."

Not bring them back alive, I notice. I suppress a shiver at the implication, doing my best to remain immobile and impassive.

"Last, an escort mission," Gillow says. "You'd be serving as a guard for a client who is traveling to Wengon. I know relic retrieval is your typical M.O., but frankly I put out the job call now because we need more guards for this last one. The client—"

"I'll take the second one," Zyneth interrupts. "Intel. I need to stay in town for a while. That job will suffice."

Gillow raises an eyebrow. "Intel it is." The spell snaps back in on itself, spiraling into the shape of a snake once more and settling back on Zyneth's arm. The snake's mouth snaps open and closed as it circles around itself, replacing a sliver of gold with black ink instead: perhaps the amount of his debt which will be eaten away once the job is complete. He still has half the snake to go.

"As for the details," Gillow starts, but Zyneth stops them again.

"Perhaps we should discuss that somewhere more private," he says.

Gillow laughs. "Private? It's only the two of us." They look at me, and unease creeps through my glass. I remain perfectly still. "Unless you're worried your pretty little minion over here is listening in. It's not really from your mum, is it?"

It's a struggle not to squirm under their sharp gaze. Their eyes seem to burrow into me. Do they know? When Zyneth told me to play dumb, I wasn't entirely sure why he wanted to keep my circumstances a secret from these people. But right now, I feel like I'm staring down a shark, and I think I'm starting to catch a hint of why Zyneth was so nervous with the idea of me tagging along.

"No," he says shortly. "I am merely concerned with remaining covert."

Gillow snorts. "Ain't no way to remain covert with a homunculus like that following you around." But they return their gaze to Zyneth. I relax—just a fraction. "Are you ready or not?"

Zyneth clearly doesn't want to be having this conversation in front of me, but it's also clear he can't push it any further without casting more attention—and suspicion—onto me. His voice is tight. "Let's get on with it."

Gillow laces their fingers together. "Excellent. The missing individual is Ossina, one of my runners. She's a nereid, blue-toned, scar on her left jaw. Disappeared while investigating rumors of a Glade relic thought to be kept beneath the Athenaeum. Either Yedzaquib has her, or a rival organization. She had a run-in with the Eels a few days before she vanished. Neither of these parties can learn anything about this job or my existence, or the deal is null and your debt incurs interest. I'm looking for answers within a week."

"A week is hardly time to perform thorough reconnaissance," Zyneth objects.

"It's plenty of time," Gillow says. "You're looking for a missing thug, not the Queen of Carmine. Besides." They give Zyneth a wink.

"If you can't complete it, I've plenty of other jobs in the queue. And you'll be chipping away at this debt for some time."

Zyneth looks like he's just eaten a gym sock. "Is there anything else?"

"No," Gillow says, all smiles. "If you don't need me to write it down, that's all I've got. You two have a good day, now."

Shoulders tense, steps purposeful, Zyneth turns on his heels and heads back out the front door. I follow after, playing the dutiful servant, as a chill runs down my spine. I can't help it—as I reach the door, I cast one glance back at Gillow.

They're watching me. They smile and wave when they catch me looking, and I quickly step outside and close the door behind me.

You two have a good day, they'd said. Not just addressing Zyneth, but the both of us.

CHAPTER EIGHT

CARELESS WITH SWORDS

"Translator first," Zyneth decides before I can ask him what the hell all that was about. Rival gangs? Gillow's creepy obsession with Zyneth's mom? I know he's tied up in some shady shit, but this is just weird.

"Ideally we can find you something suitable before we visit the library," he continues. "Being able to speak for yourself instead of using me as your proxy would make interactions significantly easier."

"Is it dangerous?" I ask. "Revealing I can speak. Gillow—they—were suspicious." I stumble over spelling Gillow's name before realizing Zyneth wouldn't understand the signs anyway, and settle for hoping he just gets the picture.

"Dangerous for you to talk?" he repeats, gleaning most of my intent. "Perhaps. Truly I don't know how most of the world would react. Those that don't know much about homunculi might just assume you're some newer, more complex spell. Those who are more familiar with the magic might understand the implications. I expect many would be fascinated—even delighted. I don't believe most would wish you ill will. Outside of organizations like the one Gillow belongs to."

And you, I think, but deem it best to not voice that part aloud.

"Although," Zyneth adds, "if you're worried, we don't need to look for a translator."

"No!" I hastily sign. "I do want a..." I stop when I realize Zyneth is chuckling. "You ass."

"I don't believe Noli would approve of that language."

I show him another sign she wouldn't like.

"Come," he says, laughing. "The marketplace is not far."

Not far ends up being another hour's walk away, though in that time I'm relieved to see the streets go back to... normal. I don't know if that's the right word. But despite nothing really looking any different, the sense of unease I'd felt around Gillow's shop dissolves back into the carefree, bustling atmosphere I've come to expect.

"Boots," I sign to Zyneth as he begins to peruse the stalls. He gives my sign a perplexed look, and I point to my feet. "I could also use some shoes."

"Ah," he says, noticing my bare feet. "Yes, I see. My, you'll look quite strange in just boots and a tattered cloak, won't you?"

Yeah, thanks for rubbing it in. "You could buy me a nicer cloak, too." I'm too annoyed to feel bad about asking Zyneth to spend even more money on me.

"Perhaps the essentials first," he says. "But if you see anything that could accommodate your, ah, unique anatomy, feel free to point it out."

The bazaar is a fascinating scene. It feels like a farmer's market, an art festival, and a *Cryptid Hunter* convention all got slammed together in half the space. Merchants of every shape, size, and species shout their prices over the crowds, while shoppers swarm the street and duck under colorful swaths of fabric to hunt down the best deals and escape the morning sun. It is getting hot, I distantly realize, noticing a sheen of sweat on the brows of some passersby. I still feel the heat—a little, like the faint warmth of a fire several feet away—but clearly not as much as everyone else here.

I keep close to Zyneth as he carves a path through the crowd, my alarm mounting with every occasional elbow which jostles against me. "Careful!" I sign once, before remembering that no one is likely to understand. No one is intentionally running into me, but they also don't seem to be particularly bothered to avoid bumps and jostles. My anxiety ratchets higher and higher the longer we remain in the press of people, and instead of paying attention to the clothes of nearby stalls, I become hyper fixated on sticking close to Zyneth and trying not to think about getting knocked to the ground and shattered into a million pieces.

"Here we are," Zyneth finally says, stepping to the side of the road and out of the thick of the crowd. I sag with relief as I escape the throng without losing any limbs, and look up at the shop as Zyneth steps inside. It's plainly labeled *Red's Enchantment Stock* and features a simple drawing of an interlocked amulet and ring.

I follow him in to find myself inside what looks like a steam-punk gift shop. Clockwork contraptions line the walls, and display-cases crammed full of rings, bracelets, necklaces, and circlets are pressed up against the front windows and back counter. Even on top of the display cases there's more trinkets, while bins of metal junk and tubs of loose stones are shoved into every available crevice. I amend my initial impression: the room looks like a steam-punk gift shop owned by a hoarder. Although that might just be redundant.

Red, as Echo identifies, is a wooden-skinned daisy-haired dryad, and level 31 Enchantments Artificer, too busy snapping several extra layers of lenses over his glasses as he hunches over a watch-face to notice us entering. I have Echo Check some of the display cases and bins of junk as Zyneth approaches Red with a greeting.

[Ring for enhanced endurance. Amulet of healing: 2/10 uses remaining. Bracelet for poisoning immunity. Ring for fire resistance. Necklace for underwater breathing. Necklace for quicker reflexes. Primed garnet. Primed moonstone. Primed quartz. Simple brass ring. Simple brass chain. Simple brass anklet...]

Seems like all the items in the display cases are the enchanted goods, while the buckets of stones and scrap metal are the unenchanted supplies used to make the expensive stuff. Interesting.

"Red?" Zyneth says, calling to the shopkeep a second time. "My friend, you have company."

The dryad looks up at us through bug-eye lenses. "Zyneth? Oh!" He beams. "Good! Good, yes, please, come inside."

We are already inside.

"Need new weapons?" Red asks, his magnified eyes blinking rapidly through his glasses. "Lose a sword, did you? You're always losing swords. How someone can be so careless with swords, I don't understand. Must be a barrel of enchanted swords out there with your name on it."

The man is twitchy, still hunched over the device he'd been working on, and I'm suddenly struck with the image of a nervous squirrel huddled over a nut.

"No, not more swords," Zyneth says, beckoning me over. "I have a bit of a special request."

"All your requests are special," Red says. "Never a straightforward ask. That's why you're my favorite. Special requests are fun. And also pay better. What's this, what's this?"

He squints at me as I approach the counter. "Uh, hi," I sign, glancing back at Zyneth. I'm not sure if he's expecting me to explain everything.

Red's gaze darts from my hands, to my head, to my chest.

"A homunculus?" he asks. "Glass? I've not seen this before. You want me to harvest its core? I don't know, I don't know—homunculi are not my specialty."

Alarmed, I instinctively place a hand over my chest. Like *fuck* is he going to harvest me!

"No!" Zyneth jumps in first. "That's not why we're here. And he's not actually a homunculus—at least, not exactly."

"He?" Red repeats, watching my hand. Or rather, he's watching me guarding my core. His eyes go wide. "It understands us?"

"*He*," Zyneth again stresses, "is called Kanin, and yes, he does understand. There's a human soul trapped in the core. Which is why we need your help. He can hear us, but has no way to speak aloud. We are looking for a translator compatible with his... unique circumstances."

Red leans forward, wide eyed, fingers twitching excitedly. "That cannot be. No, Zyneth, no, you mustn't understand. A homunculus spell cannot trap a soul no more than a sieve can catch water. There must be some other explanation. Necrotic magic may trap a soul, for instance." He reaches out for my chest and I take a hasty step back.

"You can politely tell this guy to fuck off," I sign to Zyneth.

"Please, both of you," Zyneth says. "Be respectful."

"I said it *politely*," I sign, still keeping out of Red's reach.

"Red, he is a person, as I've previously stated," Zyneth says. "I doubt you would appreciate someone grabbing you uninvited."

Red snaps his hand back. "No, no, I wouldn't like that."

The more I'm around this guy, the more nervous he's making me. Not in a scheming Gillow kind of way, but it's hard for me to pin the guy down. I don't know what he's going to do at any given moment.

Or maybe I just don't take kindly to people trying to pluck my soul out of my chest.

Zyneth looks at me next. "Would you allow me to tell him about your magic? It might help with finding a translator that works. We should be as open and honest as we can."

Red is not exactly an individual I'm excited to spill my guts to. The contents of his shop and his twitchy fingers tells me he's just as likely to dissect my body and sell it to the highest bidder as he is to help us. "Can we trust him?"

"Completely," Zyneth says. "I wouldn't have taken you here otherwise. There are perhaps a dozen shops in the city that specialize in enchanted accessories, but this is the only one I frequent."

Red smiles at that. "That is because many enchantments you ask for are not legal."

Zyneth gave Red an exasperated look. "We're getting off track."

"No," I sign, interest piqued. "Let him talk."

Zyneth sighs. "Please, both of you."

I wave him off. "Alright, alright. Tell him whatever you want."

"Thank you," Zyneth says, though by his tone, he seems a bit exasperated. "Red, whatever translation tools you have at your disposal, bring them out for us to try. Kanin's affinities are glass—obviously—and void. His primary language will not be in any enchantment index you have at your disposal."

"Void?" Red asks, eyebrows shooting up. "As an attunement? Not possible. Too unstable." He excitedly leans over the counter toward me. "Show me!"

I hope Zyneth can feel the glare I'm unable to send his way. Reluctantly, I hold out a hand and call the void from the joints around my torso and arms to form a tiny pool of black over my palm. I leave all the void in place that's being used to support my legs—I'm pretty sure I'd fall over if I took them away now.

Red's eyes go wide. "It is, it is! So concentrated. Never seen undiluted void before. Never so pure. Hmmm, yes, it might be possible for this type of null arcana to trap a soul—the glue of reality, isn't it? Fascinating. Fascinating." He dives beneath his counter and begins snatching up odds and ends.

So glad I can be this guy's source of entertainment for the day.

Another thought occurs to me, though. "How much does this guy know about Between?" I ask Zyneth. Lowering my hand, the void zips back to my joints.

He shakes his head. "I don't know. More than me, at least."

"Would he know anything about how to retrieve my body?"

"What?" Red says, popping back up with an armful of jewelry and strange metal contraptions. "What?"

"Kanin was asking if you'd know anything about the nature of his spell," Zyneth says. "His soul came from another dimension, where his body still remains, and he wants to know if it's possible to access it again."

Red thoughtlessly drops the armful of loot on the counter, and Zyneth winces. "A different dimension? I don't know. Summoning spells require null arcanum—but the summoned object must already be targeted in some way: previously marked by null arcanum, usually. But null arcana is a summoner's specialty. Not me. Ask the wizard who cast the original spell, hm?"

"He's dead," I sign.

Zyneth grimaces.

"It wasn't my fault," I add. Then pause. "I mean. Not directly."

Red picks up a bracelet and shoves it toward me. "This first."

"Um." I carefully pluck it from his fingers, looking between Red and Zyneth helplessly. "What—"

"Never mind." Red snatches it back. He hands me a ring. "Try this."

"How?" I ask. I decide to give it a quick Check before sticking an enchanted ring on my finger all willy-nilly. I'm not stupid.

[Ring of Translation: allows the wearer to speak Common.]

Doesn't hurt to be careful. I put the ring on. Nothing happens. "I'm not sure these are going to work without a mouth," I tell Zyneth.

Red makes a rapid grabby motion with his hand, and I pull the ring off and give it back to him.

"Kanin's right," Zyneth says to Red. "We don't just need translation, but something that can produce the sound."

"Tricky, tricky," Red mutters, digging through the pile. "But, hm, yes. Okay. One moment."

He sifts through a bucket of jewels, grabbing them by the handfuls like a bunch of marbles, mumbling to himself as he tosses the gems back one by one. Eventually he settles on a black stone, then moves back to his tangle of knick-knacks he'd dumped on the counter. He pulls a necklace from the pile—shaking it off for a moment to dislodge an earring, which flings across the room—and strings the stone onto the chain, going abruptly still. I don't think I've seen this guy sit still for more than two seconds the entire time I've been in here. A red light glows from his fingers.

A few seconds later, he blinks, then hands the necklace to me. "This next."

I Check it.

[Amulet of Speech: Fashioned from a Necklace of Projection and Stone of Translation, this amulet is designed to interpret and project the non-vocal speech of species such as merpeople, sprites, and other-worldly souls inadvertently bound to a homunculus core.]

Is it just me or is Echo getting cheekier?

"Does it matter how I wear it?" I ask. I try looping the chain a few times around my wrist.

"I do not have a neck so I cannot wear it the traditional way."

I jerk back, looking at the amulet. Those words had come from the amulet. They were my thoughts. And I heard them—*out loud*.

Zyneth's face splits into a grin. "Was that you?"

"Oh gods. It is really working," I think, and the amulet says.

Well, they aren't *exactly* my thoughts. I don't worship multiple deities, and the translator seems to have an aversion to contractions. Not to mention there's a strangely auto-tuned quality to the words. The voice sounds like the bastard child of C3-PO and Daft Punk.

But dammit. I can *talk*.

"This is amazing," I say, a giddy joy flooding through me. I can't believe it. Finally. After all these months. I'm really speaking! "Thank you," I say to Red. "Thank you so *Expletive* much."

Zyneth raises an eyebrow. I look down at the amulet.

Red snickers. "The translator, ah, may take some liberties with its interpretations."

It takes a moment for Red's words to sink in.

Fuck, I think, and the amulet says, "*Expletive*."

CHAPTER NINE

VAGUE INSTRUCTIONS

"I am starting to understand why Noli dislikes translators," I say. It's still so strange. So alien. They're my words, but it's not my voice.

"Somehow, I don't think it's the lack of swearing she objects to," Zyneth says with a chuckle.

"That is part of it," I grumble. I vaguely recall something she'd said about the translators before: how they don't capture the nuance of her words. "I hate being censored."

Zyneth gives my shoulder a reassuring pat as we weave through the streets. "You heard what Red said. This is only temporary. He should be able to create a more complex charm for you by the end of the week."

There's that, at least. And I know I shouldn't be complaining when Zyneth footed the bill—*again*. I'm going to owe him a small fortune by the end of this.

After Red's place, Zyneth grabs a pair of boots for me next. They're floppy old things, but I need the give in the leather to keep it from inhibiting motion in my ankles and tripping me up. Look at me: slowly but surely putting on clothes like a real person.

By the time we're done with the translator, boots, and gathering various food and supplies Zyneth deems necessary, it's late afternoon. Zyneth finds us an inn and secures a room so he can drop off all his newly purchased items. I'm practically vibrating with impatience when we return to the streets.

"Where is the library?" I ask. It's about time I got some answers. "How much longer until we can go?"

"Actually," Zyneth says, gesturing ahead of us as we walk, "that's why I picked the inn I did. It's right up ahead."

"Where?" I ask. "Is it around that building?" The street disappears behind the curve of an enormous domed structure which I pegged to be some sort of religious temple. The white marbled surface is carved with figures and murals that are several stories high, and even as I watch, I swear the stone creatures are slowly moving across the surface. It gives me a sort of Taj Mahal vibe—if the Taj Mahal was as big as the Colosseum and covered in statues of fantasy creatures.

"No." Zyneth smiles. "It *is* that building. Welcome to the Athenaeum of Miasmere."

I gawk as we pass into its shadow. Features I mistook for decorations and arches are actually windows, stories and stories above us. It's the largest single structure I've seen since coming to this world—hell, it might be bigger than anything I've seen back on Earth.

A distant din of noise begins to surge as we approach. "What is that sound?" I ask as Zyneth steers us to the front entrance. The entrance archway is two stories tall and half as wide, a constant stream of people pouring in and out.

But Zyneth doesn't have to answer: as we step through the library's doors, the roar of people echoes through the stone chambers. There must be a thousand people in here. Floors filled with bookshelves spiral up the walls of the dome, wider across the base and narrower toward the ceiling, allowing a wide shaft of light from the very top of the library to fall all the way to the ground floor. Even so, hundreds of soft lights are strung across the space on white strings, like dewdrops on a spiderweb. In fact, the spider motif continues elsewhere, with dozens of white, cat-sized spiders running along the lines, towing clusters of books behind them to place back on their shelves. People are chatting, laughing, excitedly discussing the contents of tomes and scrolls with their companions—not a single shushing librarian in sight.

"This is not like Earth libraries," I say.

Zyneth laughs as we strike out across the floor.

Already we're in a labyrinth of waist-high shelves that span almost the whole room. And calling it a *room* feels like a disservice when the entire Statue of Liberty could take a nap in here. The ground level is like some strange mix between an art museum and a bazaar; decorative fountains and statues litter the ground floor, interspersed between the shelves, while people seem to be holding loud business meetings in the stacks.

"Where do we even start?" I wonder aloud. To my right is a row of scrolls on a shelf labeled "Agriculture."

"What you'll be looking for is on higher floors," Zyneth said, nodding toward the distant ceiling. "The first floor is public information. Anyone may enter and exit the library and read what they wish at the ground level. Of course, Yedzaquib's helpers are spelled to prevent any of the texts from being taken from the premise." He gestures to one of the spiders as it scurries across a nearby shelf. Up close, it appears to be made of stone, just like the marbled library itself, with a spell circle carved in its back and faint lines of magic tracing across its body.

"However," Zyneth continues, "the library is organized by scarcity of information. While common knowledge can be found down here, the higher you ascend, the rarer the information you will find. At the top is the most valuable knowledge the library contains. And of course, the higher you ascend, the more steep the entry fee."

Fee? This really isn't like Earth libraries at all. "I do not have any money," I say.

"Not to worry," Zyneth says. "The curator does not deal in coin."

Somehow, that makes me more worried.

After ten minutes of wading through the crowd, we finally make it over to a ramp along the wall. There's several different ramps spread throughout the library, and they're all about as wide as a house, gradually inching their way up around the side of the dome in enormous spirals. More shelves of books, scrolls, and stone tablets run up the ramps. Unlike the front door, this entry point is blocked.

A golden spiderweb is knit across the whole passage, at least a dozen feet high and twice as wide. The space between the strands glow with a film of light, and when I cautiously reach out to touch it, the light gives slightly, as if solid.

One of the library's artificial spiders quickly skitters from the wall, across the top of the web, and then down to eye level. I take a hasty step back.

Purple runes light up on the back of the spider, which then swirl into the shape of words. "Admission fees required beyond this point."

I glance questioningly to Zyneth. "How does this work?"

"Let me show you." He steps up to the web and the spider construct crawls out of his way. Zyneth pauses for a moment, as if thinking, then steps forward. The web ripples like the surface of a lake, but otherwise doesn't seem to resist his passage. He stops on the other side and turns back. The runes on the spider swirl into a new form:

Duration: 2 Days

Floor Access: 20

"The payment is knowledge," Zyneth explains. "The more rare, the more valuable, and the more valuable, the higher floors you will have access to."

What the fuck? "It is going to take my memories?"

"No, no," Zyneth says. "It only makes a copy. You've nothing to worry about."

"Oh, yes," I say. "Do not worry about the mind-reading spider magic, Kanin. It is such a common, normal thing."

Zyneth snorts. "It really is fairly normal. I submitted information about the Black Spire. A layout of some of the streets. You may decide how much information you wish to submit; sometimes withholding knowledge can be to your benefit if you know you do not need access to top floors and you plan on returning for a future visit. But in this case, you may want to submit something more rare; information about summoning magic exists on all floors, but the information you're after is likely to be of the less common variety."

"Hold on," I say, still not nearly convinced this thing is as mundane as he claims. "Give me a moment to Check it over myself."

[Memory Net, created by the curator Yedzaquib,] Echo says. [This field is imbued with a variant of the Mind Read spell.]

I wait for more elaboration, but Echo appears to have finished. *What, that's it?*

[Affirmative,] Echo says. [This unit's spell identification capacity is limited. Spells such as Inspect can provide more insight into the intentions and capabilities of arcana.]

I grumble at that, but I guess I can't rely on Echo for everything. I'll keep that Inspect spell in mind for future research. *So it really just reads my mind, it doesn't take any memories from me or anything?*

[Affirmative,] Echo says.

Well, that's something, I guess.

What happens to the copy of my memory? I ask.

[The knowledge stored within Yedzaquib's Athenaeum is gathered from the visiting patrons,] Echo says. [New information deemed worthy enough to be added to the library's catalogue is copied from the donated memories and later added to the stacks.]

Guess I shouldn't go thinking about anything I wouldn't want to be public information, then.

Echo and Zyneth's explanations are slightly mollifying, but this all still seems pretty fucking weird to me. Then again, I guess I'm a soul stuck in an ink bottle piloting around a glass Ironman suit, so who am I to judge?

"Okay," I say, hesitantly stepping forward. But what information should I give it? Something about Earth? I bet that's pretty rare. Unless everyday life stuff is ranked as "common knowledge" even if it is from a different world. What about Echo? That seems to be unique to me, so far as I can tell. And that's something that's this-world specific. Alright, I guess it's worth a shot.

I hold a cautious hand before me, nervously stepping through the web as I think about Echo, her level systems, and ways she catalogs people into certain classes. The light washes over me as I pass through the barrier unhindered, and I don't feel anything in particular as I pass through.

[Warning,] Echo suddenly pipes up. [You have been subjected to a variant of the Mind Read spell.]

Then, half a second later, she adds, [Spell timed out.]

Creepy. But at least now I know Echo will notify me if anything like that happens again.

I turn back to look as the spider's runes resolve into writing.

Duration: 4 Days
Floor Access: 33

"Gods' grace, Kanin," Zyneth says. "Thirty-three?!"

"What? Is that bad?" I ask. "How high is that?"

Zyneth shakes his head. "All of them. That's all the floors."

"Oh," I say. "Well that is good, right?"

"I've never witnessed anyone gain access above thirty," Zyneth says. "What in the world did you do?"

"I do not know! I just did what you said!" I cry. "Your instructions were vague!"

"They were highly specific." Zyneth rubs his head. "What memory did you offer?"

"Echo," I say. "I thought about her and the stat system I can see."

Zyneth blinks. "And you didn't think mentioning an entirely unknown type of magic would be considered rare?"

I strangle the air in front of me before I try to compose myself. "Well I am not exactly an expert on what magic is or is not normal, am I?"

That finally seems to land with him. "Right," he says. "Sorry, I keep forgetting you're from... Well, what's done is done." Zyneth smooths out the front of his shirt. "Let's get on with it, shall we?"

"Is it a problem?" I ask Zyneth as we climb the ramp. "I thought I wanted to get to the higher floors."

"You do," Zyneth says. "But if I'm restricted to level twenty, then I can't accompany you beyond that."

Ah, so that's the crux of the issue. "I think I can handle reading some books on my own."

Zyneth frowns. "It will probably be fine. And I do need to begin investigating the task Gillow has given me, anyway. However... Well, the upper floors can be risky. In order to make it to the top floors you must have knowledge on subjects most of the rest of the world does not. That can attract very powerful individuals."

"Are they dangerous?" I ask, alarmed. Man, this really *isn't* anything like Earth libraries.

"Perhaps," Zyneth says. "Although... I might be feeling overly cautious. The interaction with Gillow this morning still has me on edge."

I'd nearly forgotten about them. To be honest, Red left me more uneasy than the nereid had. At least they hadn't been itching to grab my soul and dissect my body.

"I promise not to pick too many fights," I say, though the translator's voice doesn't quite pick up the level of sarcasm I was going for.

Zyneth nods, though his frown tells me he's still worried. "Just try to keep a low profile while you're up there. Don't draw any undue attention to yourself."

What. "Zyneth." He glances my way as I gesture to, well, all of myself. "*Try not to draw attention?*"

That gets a laugh out of him. "I suppose a glass homunculus isn't the most inconspicuous of forms, is it?"

"You think?"

Zyneth lets out a breath. "You'll be fine. The curator keeps a tight hand on the library, so there shouldn't be any trouble. I just don't like not being there to assist you, should you need it."

His concern would be touching if it didn't imply he still sees me as a helpless little test tube.

Okay granted, just getting bumped into is likely to knock me over and cause me to shatter into a million pieces. But if the upper floors are as deserted as he says, it's the one I'm currently on that I need to worry about.

It takes nearly an hour to weave up the massive incline, which has got to be some kind of fire code violation. Zyneth explains how to use the library and search for subjects as we climb. Similar to how the entry spell worked, it involves thinking about the subject you want to find, touching a web on the end of a bookshelf, and then a string lights up—or doesn't—to guide you to the most relevant books on that shelf. Which sounds like it requires a lot of trial and error, but the shelves are at least generally sorted by subject. I guess this system doesn't much care about who the author is.

"So should I focus on summoning magic?" I ask Zyneth. "Or traveling between dimensions? Or both?"

He shrugs. "I truly am not an expert in any of this. The Between is where this all first started. Perhaps that's the best place to look."

That sounds reasonable enough to me—and maybe it can shed some light on the nature of the predator while I'm at it. Not that the predator is my top priority anymore, now that it's contained, but I'm not going to turn my nose up at any new information I might happen to come across.

As with all previous levels, a number on the railing and a gold line of silk across the floor marks the end of the twentieth level. Zyneth stops, a golden web barrier similar to the first floor blocking his path.

"We can start our research on this floor," Zyneth offers. "There will be plenty of information on Between and different arcana sources on twenty and below."

He's just being nervous again. "Somehow, I doubt reality-hopping magic is going to be in the 'common knowledge' sections of the library."

His lips twitch into a brief smile. "Alright, I can take a hint. Good luck up there. Don't go too far—it will take time just to walk back down. I'll be waiting on floor twenty until you return."

"Thank you," I say, and then pause uncertainly. It's been so long since I've had a body that I'm not sure how to close out this conversation. A hug? A handshake? In the end I awkwardly wave, then turn and step over the line to floor twenty-one.

A rush of excitement fills me as I leave Zyneth behind. Maybe I should feel bad about that. Like Noli, Zyneth has helped me with everything I've needed, without question or compensation, since I got here. Even if they'd never accept it, I owe them both a lot.

But this is something I can do. Researching a way to get my body back finally gives me a modicum of autonomy over my circumstances.

And I'm way overdue to take things back into my own hands.

CHAPTER TEN

HOT AND COLD

Taking Zyneth's advice—and keeping in mind the earlier warning about dangerous folk maybe hanging around the top floors—I only head up another couple levels before I start poking around the stacks.

Already there are significantly less people around. The crowds had begun to thin once we'd made it past floor ten, and they'd gone down to a trickle by floor twenty. Up at my current vantage point, I only notice a dozen other people around, all already sitting at tables, buried in their books. Interestingly, however, there are more homunculi up here than there were in the general sections, the automatons often standing at attention next to their studious summoner, or pulling more scrolls and tablets from the shelves to bring back to their mage. I suppose it makes sense that the people frequenting the higher floors are more likely to be wizards or have the money to lease a homunculus, though seeing them around still creeps me out in a way I can't quite articulate. On the plus side, it means my presence isn't unusual. You know, apart from the glass thing.

At Zyneth's suggestion, I wander over to the nearest shelf and rest my hand against the carving of a web that's embedded in the wood, thinking about the Between, the void, and null arcana. A light illuminates the design, shining just beneath the grain, but it quickly dims and fades out. I step to the next shelf, repeating the process, and the light glows, slightly brighter this time before fading once more.

Well this is some Hot and Cold crap. Even so, I make my way around the shelves, trailing my hand over the surface of each one I pass. The light gets brighter the further I head up stacks, until finally it doesn't fade out at all. Instead, one of the zigzagging lines of web lights up, disappearing around the side of the shelf and out of sight. I poke my head around the corner and see the spider silk following a haphazard pattern which ends at a section of books midway down the stack. I follow the thread to the books it's indicating as the glow slowly fades from the shelf.

The section it's led me to is about planar dimensions. I instinctively touch my satchel, where I have a similar book stored. *Planar Theories*, it's called, with the subtitle *As Relevant to Arcana Sources and the Great Ruins.* You know, your typical light reading. Then again, I'm probably about to dive into some pretty dense stuff with these books, too.

Unsure where to start, I grab one off the shelf—where it immediately slips from my grasp and falls to the floor, narrowly avoiding shattering my foot. God damn it. I need to do something about this lack of upper body strength. And maybe upgrade to steel-toed boots.

Peeling some of the void away from my legs and back—and standing as rigidly as possible to avoid falling over—I grab the book with the shadows and order it back up off the floor. The void obliges—fairly easily, in fact. I guess I shouldn't be surprised the void is stronger than my glass: the predator had been insanely powerful, and this is a piece of that monster. At least it's working for me, now.

As handy as the void is at picking up books, I won't be able to walk anywhere while the void is holding them, which means I'll need to find a different way to ferry items around. Since my satchel is already stuffed full of my own two magic tomes, I set the library book on the shelf and summon my signing glass from beneath my cloak. Quickly working some Chains into the collection of glass, I create a very flimsy glass net which affixes to the side of my satchel. Adding the library book to my bag's side-cart, I send the void back to my legs and back, then make for the nearest table. This is going to become tedious.

I go through the books in a sort of a trial-and-error approach—mostly error—skimming the titles and chapters for something that looks relevant. All told, I dig through perhaps a dozen books over the course of the rapidly-expiring afternoon, gathering a smattering of relevant passages.

Magic, one book reads, after I realize I'm in a bit over my head and have to go back to the basics, *is a fundamental force of existence, as natural as gravity, electricity, or elementary chemicals. While some may assert the field is inherently spiritual, and that there even could exist dimensions which lack its presence entirely, this text prefers to take a more scientific approach. (How could such a magicless world even exist? Would magic, if brought into this world, crumble to nothing, much as an object brought into a reality without chemical forces might dissolve into incoherence? Such speculation, of course, is pure fancy.)*

Magic is observable in everyday life, though more importantly the mechanics through which it is able to be manipulated are well known and repeatable, and even quantifiable. Mana, the volume of magic an individual has access to at any given time, is variable depending on species, practice, and natural talent, however it is measurable in all cases.

And, like chemicals, magic comes in many forms–qualitatively, we call these different fields arcana.

If mana is the cup which limits how much magic you may stow, then arcana are the different liquids which may fill that cup. Each liquid has a different practical use: You would not use alcohol to put out a fire anymore than you would use water to disinfect a wound. Furthermore, each of these arcana arises from a magical source: the well that is used to fill your cup. Which well you have access to is limited by which arcana you have an affinity for.

A summary of common arcana fields and their corresponding sources are listed below. This list is not comprehensive, and indeed there are numerous, if not infinite, planes from which mana can be pulled from, however what follows are the most oft used arcana sources in present society:

The Gyre: Storm arcana, focusing in water, air, and electricity magics

The Pith: Earth arcana, focusing in fire, stone, and metal magics

The Lull: Life arcana, focusing in nature, healing, and necrotic magics

The Abyss: Ocular arcana, focusing in illusion, light, and shadow magics

The Between: Null arcana, focusing in void, mind, and summoning magics

There it is. And that fits what I understand so far about the Between and the nature of the void. All these places–the Abyss, the Gyre, the Between–are actual dimensions that can be traveled to. All sources of different types of magic. And somehow, Noli and I had ended up in the Between.

I guess that makes sense, given the types of magic it enables. But the question is: how can I use that to recover my body from Earth?

I wield null arcana, so if I'm going to learn any new spells, I probably need to start there. And even though my affinity is void (well, and glass, which apparently falls way down into the Earth arcana tree, but that's not particularly useful in this instance), summoning also falls in the same general category, which sounds promising for retrieving my body.

In fact, that the predator came from Between also might hold some key to how I can access it. If I could learn more about the nature of the predator, maybe it'll give me some insight on how I can travel through the Between, too.

Heading over to the nearest shelf, I think about the predator as I touch the web. The markings don't light up. That's odd—usually they're at least dim if the knowledge is stored on a shelf further away. Maybe I'm being too specific. Instead, I think more generally about creatures trapped in the Between and how that might happen. Still, though, nothing.

Seeing as I have time to burn, I head up the flights of stairs, trying shelves one at a time. The library grows quiet the higher I climb, and fewer and fewer individuals are around each new floor I ascend. Over floor twenty-eight, I start to draw looks. There's only one or two people in each of these sections, so any newcomers seem to draw attention—not that my appearance helps. But still, there's nothing on the predator. Nothing even tangentially related. The shelves don't show the slightest flicker of light. Something about this makes me uneasy.

Breaching thirty, the webs are still completely unresponsive to anything related to the predator. Something definitely feels strange about this to me now. Seeing as I've already come this far, I decide to head all the way to the top. As I circle around the dome, each of the higher levels have become shorter and shorter, and when I finally make it to the top of the library, Floor Thirty-Three is little more than a spacious room with a handful of dusty shelves.

No one else is here. The space feels tense and oppressive. Hastily, I do a lap around the room, trailing my hand over every shelf I pass. But not a single thread lights up. There isn't one scrap of information on the predator in this entire library. And if this is supposed to be the world's greatest wealth of knowledge, does that mean no one *anywhere* has information on it?

Unsettled, I quickly head back down. I try to shake away the disquiet the top floors left me with. It would have been nice to learn more about that creature, but I suppose it's not my main objective anyway. I should stay focused on learning a way to retrieve my body. That's why I'm here, after all. Quickly leaving the stifling atmosphere of the upper levels behind, I head back to the low twenties and spend the rest of the day reading books on null arcana and the Between.

I reluctantly leave the library that evening, at Zyneth's insistence, when he's ready for dinner. Seems he's not wild about leaving me here alone overnight, no matter how much more efficient that might be.

By the end of Day One, I've absorbed a handful of new spells, including that Inspect spell Echo mentioned.

[Inspect: Used as a skill, it may glean information about a spell's power, arcana type, and purpose. Additional information may be obtained by activating as a spell.]

[Refraction: A combination of glass and void arcana, this spell incorporates the tertiary abilities of shadow and light to create a low-grade illusory spell which can be used for basic camouflage.]

[Void Whip: A volume of Attuned void may be infused with mana in order to lend power and solidity to the limb.]

Inspect might come in useful at some point: learning more about spells might even help me here in the library. Refraction seemed interesting on the surface, but after I tried to activate it, I found I don't have nearly enough mana for it to cloak my whole body. At most, I was able to make my hand shimmer and disappear, though the light warped through my hand strangely, making it apparent that something was still there. As the spell says, it's only basic camouflage at best.

The Void Whip is curious. Seems like a better offensive attack than trying to stab things with my fragile glass fragments, prone to shattering, although doing so would mean repurposing the void that's currently keeping me upright and walking. I'm also not really planning on getting into any more trouble. Ideally, it's a spell I'll never need.

Hah! That's laughable. Not like trouble doesn't always seem to find me.

"Anything at all?" Zyneth asks me that night over a bowl of steaming noodles and broth. "Leads, at least?"

The crowd here is nearly as bustling as it was on the first floor of the Athenaeum. We're only a block or two away from the library, but the excitement seems to have bled from one scene to the other. Everyone here is always moving, always talking. It's a far cry from Noli and Rezira's quiet hometown of Bluevine. In some ways, Miasmere reminds me of Los Angeles, but the people here are too strange for it to feel familiar.

"I am not sure," I admit. "The lack of information on the predator was odd. And studying the Between does not seem to be the right answer. I understand more about basic magic now, but nothing that would help me recover my body." *Or find a way home.* For some reason, I don't say that part aloud. "I have mostly been researching void magic and the Between. I think going forward I should focus on other fields of null magic, like summoning."

"That sounds like a good plan," Zyneth says, stirring a spoon through the broth thoughtfully. "This was only the first day, after all. I might have six days to fulfill Gillow's job, but you've all the time in the world to browse the Athenaeum's stacks. There's a wealth of knowledge here: You should take your time and learn as much as you're able."

An inebriated customer at the next table over is talking loudly and gesturing wildly to his tablemate, consistently knocking into an array of bottles that almost certainly will be sent cascading to the street at any moment. I wonder if I could swipe a couple to Attune later tonight while Zyneth sleeps.

"I know, you are right," I say, drumming my fingers on the table. Instead of satisfying deep tones, the glass on wood provides a musical tinkling. I stop. "I am just impatient. I want to be moving forward faster."

"You are already mastering magic at a remarkable rate," Zyneth says. "You could probably learn dozens of more spells here while you're at it."

That sounds overwhelming. But it also might break up the monotony. And I suppose anything that might help me get closer to recovering my body—and prevent me from dying in the meantime—is worth my while.

The drunk man finally overestimates his dexterity. One of the bottles falls over from a slap of his hand, then goes rolling to the edge of the table. Zyneth reaches for it. I cast Void Whip.

The void from my legs and spine jumps into a limb of shadows, snapping out to grab the bottle as it tips off the table. I catch it an inch above Zyneth's outstretched hand.

He looks up at me, raising an impressed eyebrow. "See? Progress already."

I set the bottle down on our table then disperse the magic.

[Spell ended. Mana cost: 5,] Echo says.

The shadows had felt almost solid. More *real* than they ever had before. "It will certainly help with carrying books," I say.

Zyneth snorts.

"What?" I demand, a little offended. That wasn't supposed to be a joke.

"I just never pictured you as the bookish type," Zyneth says. "Yet, here we are."

Hm. I suppose, neither did I. I hadn't been much of a reader back on Earth—not apart from reading my scripts. But I guess I hadn't had an important reason to read before now. My very existence hadn't depended on it. And you know, reimagining myself as a bookish type doesn't even feel that strange to me now. Funny how things change. "Here we are," I agree.

As we leave to retire to our inn for the night, I swipe another two bottles from the drunk man's table. Can never have too much glass.

CHAPTER ELEVEN

MAGICAL COMPASS

After a night spent Attuning the glass and using it to patch up various chips and reinforce my book side-satchel, we head back to the Athenaeum in the morning. The easiest way I could solve my predicament is if I could summon my body to me—if such a thing is even possible. As Zyneth heads off to other floors in investigation of Gillow's job, I decide to spend the day focusing on summoning magic instead.

The spiderwebs lead me to a lot of books about forging telepads, which, I suppose, is kind of a summoning magic, but not what I'm looking for. There's even more on summoning monsters, undead, and other types of malicious beasts—which is even further from what I want, though potentially the mechanism through which these creatures can be summoned might be relevant to what I want to do. Trying to ignore the mounting headache from poring over tiny scripts and extremely dense magical theory, I find a handful of passages that might be tangential to what I need.

The art of summoning creatures or objects, one book reads, *is a wide branch of magic that is oft misunderstood. Elemental summoning—conjuring a flame or wind—is the simplest and most common form, and has been greatly explored in other texts in more detail, and so will not be delved into within these pages. Rather, the ability to summon some physical being or construct in its entirety is a much more complex and nuanced topic.*

Contrary to popular belief, a mage cannot simply conjure a demon on a whim. Any living beings that a mage wishes to summon must be marked with a target spell prior to any summoning. Similarly, items may be branded with a spell that allows them to be summoned at will. Without these creatures or items being infused with the necessary summoning magic in advance, conjuring the target is impossible.

Well that doesn't bode well for the "summon my body from Earth" plan. I skim ahead as it takes a tangent on telepads, comparing the mechanism for summoning items to the mechanism used for transporting people between telepads. Apparently, both use null arcanum and several of the same spell circle elements. At least null arcana is one point I have in my favor; apparently most of these spells can only be operated by people with a type of null magic affinity. Small victories.

Finally a subsection on monster summons addresses the issue I'm facing.

So how does a mage initially encounter a creature they wish to summon, you might be asking? Assuming you're not able to pre-arrange a meeting or run into the specimen by happenstance, there are various ways a creature may be tracked down. The most reliable method, of course, is via a Location spell.

Unhelpfully, the book does not go into more depth on what a Location spell is or how it can be used. I guess the author just assumes anyone dabbling in summoning magic would already have a grasp on something so obviously basic. After flipping through the rest of the book and not getting anywhere, I decide to branch out.

I place the summoning book on a return shelf—which is quickly spirited away by a spider construct—and then return to the shelves to look for any information on Location spells.

Over the course of the day, I have to get up several times to swap out books, since I can't carry them all at once, (unless I want to burn through my mana using dozens of Void Whips,) and on more than one occasion I draw the eye of a curious guest perusing the stacks. A catgirl keeps staring at me whenever I step past one of the glowing orbs of light that keeps the room lit, inadvertently scattering a rainbow across her desk. Once or twice, I swear she paws at the reflection. A bald human man glares at me when I nearly bump into him, rounding the shelves. Hastily apologizing, I head back to my seat. Keep a low profile, Zyneth said.

Location spells allow the caster to create a magical compass to the desired target object, one book reads. *They can provide precise locations or a general direction, depending on the design of the spell and the strength of the input focus. An input focus is what allows the target to be identified in the first place, and must be related to the target in some intimate way. For instance, a piece of sentimental clothing owned by the target will result in a stronger and more precise spell than a cup they've drunk from or a stone they've thrown, and hair or fingernail clippings would have an even stronger bond than these. If the target is an inanimate object, such as a dagger, the tool that was used to create it, or the sheath it often resided in, could also be used as focus.*

I read on about the different spell circles that can be used to cast such a Location spell, but I'm worrying this path may be a non-starter as well. If I need some sentimental belonging that's associated with my body, I'm not going to find it in this world. It's a frustrating circle: to summon my body I need to find it, but to find my body I first have to be able to summon something related to it.

[New Spell Learned!] Echo announces as I'm rereading the pages, hoping to find some alternative that could work for my situation. [Spell: Location. A spell which can guide the caster to the targeted source of a relevant focus. Requirement: Spell circle, variable mana, designated focus.]

Well that's nice and all, but it doesn't help me so long as I don't have anything on this planet I can use as a focus.

Or do I?

Echo, I ask, *can a soul be used as the focus for the Location spell?*

[Affirmative,] Echo says. [Although circumstances in which a soul would be separated from its body are exceptionally rare, the inherent nature between soul and body would provide an extremely powerful bond for the focus to trace.]

Hope flutters through me. Is this it? Is this the answer I've been hoping for? Could it be that easy?

What's the mana cost to activate this spell? I ask.

[Mana cost to activate: 20. Additionally, the spell consumes 1 mana per minute that the spell is maintained.]

So not something that could be left on indefinitely, but hopefully I wouldn't need to. I pull out my slate and chalk, glancing back through the pages at the circle designs and adjustments that the spell requires.

Show me the spell circle, I tell Echo. *Targeting my soul as the focus.*

The image appears in my mind the next moment, and I begin to sketch it out on my slate.

I spend maybe an hour perfecting every detail I can manage. Despite my excitement, I try not to rush it. I can afford to take my time, after all, and the last thing I want is a botched spell similar to what ended up pulling me here in the first place. If this works, then the spell should provide me with some sort of "path" I can follow to my body. I don't know how that will play out given my body is on another world, but it can't hurt to try. If nothing else, maybe it will lead me to the next piece of the puzzle I'm looking for.

Eventually, finally, the circle is ready. *Alright, Echo,* I say, leaning back. *Let's ready that Location spell. With my soul as the focus.*

[Affirmative,] Echo says. [Mana cost: 20. Activate?]

I remove my core from the chain around my neck, and slip it from its bag, setting it gently at the center of the circle. With a flutter of anticipation, I activate the spell.

The circle lights up with my magic. Black light swirls around my vial, wisping through the glass. Tendrils of magic curl around my core as I try not to squirm, deeply unnerved by being surrounded by this unfamiliar spell. I wonder if this is how Noli felt when I was trying to put her soul back in her body. The filaments of magic twine together into one strand, and maybe it's my imagination, but I think I can feel something tugging on my soul. Then, the magic stops.

The line vanishes into thin air a few inches from my body. I've seen something like this before: when I use Bond Trace, the predator's thread similarly vanishes as it moves away from my core, because the predator isn't on this plane of existence, but Between.

Is that where this spell is pointing me? I ask Echo. *Is the "path" leading back Between?*

[Affirmative,] Echo says. [As the target object is on a different plane of reality, the shortest path joining the focus with the target object would require traversing Between.]

"Oh, is that all," I mumble. I shut the spell off, uninterested in draining the rest of my mana. Not that I haven't been Between before—but I'm not entirely sure how to get back (without dying) and even then, I'm not sure I want to. Without something tethering you to reality, like, say, a senile wizard's magic-collection spell, or an ink bottle your soul has been bound to, traversing the Between risks ending up in the afterlife. And as far as I understand it, there's no coming back from that.

If I could find a way Between, I ask Echo, *would this spell pull me through it? Back to my body?*

[Negative,] Echo says, and my hope falters. [The Location spell merely provides a direction to follow, not a path to traverse. However, if a spell could be enacted to bridge the current plane of existence with a desired plane, the Location spell may be used to provide the target destination.]

Huh. *So you're saying if I could find some sort of interdimensional-telepad, I could use this Location spell to make sure the other end pops out where my body is?*

[Affirmative,] Echo says.

Which means I wouldn't just be retrieving my body, I'd also have a way back to Earth.

I sit back, trying to take all this information in. Does that mean I could go home? Do I even want to go home? The idea fills me with a strange mix of hope and reluctance. I mean, of course I want to go home. I spent my whole life trying to pursue my dream of becoming an actor—I can't quit now. Earth is where I'm somebody. Where everyone I've ever known lives.

Except Attiru, Rezira, Noli, and Zyneth.

My soul churns, and I shake my head as if that could dispel my unease. I'm getting ahead of myself. This still isn't a real way to get my body back. I don't even know if there is a spell that can do what Echo's describing. Besides, this is just the second day of research. Maybe there's other answers out there.

I push my chair back and stand up—and something thumps to my right, causing me to jump. A man—the bald man I'd nearly run into before—picks up one of the texts he's dropped. The cat girl hushes him, and he glares at the both of us before hurrying away. Careful to not disturb the irritable felis, I quietly re-stow my vial, return the book I was reading, and move on to other shelves.

I can't quite shake the idea Echo had suggested, though. The idea of an interdimensional telepad keeps itching at me. Rezira had said something about this when I first told her I was from another world: there were myths about the Old People being able to world-walk. Something to do with the Ruins, she'd said.

Planar Theories mentioned the various arcana sources and their link to the Ruins. Apparently, various abandoned ancient cities scattered over the world's surface are linked to each of these dimensions, their raw magic spilling out into the surrounding lands. Emrox, the one now sunk far beneath the sea, is the Ruin tied to null magic and the Between. And although it seems I'm far from the only one who has developed an affinity for null magic—Trenevalt and telepad operators being a few others—it's apparently so volatile to manipulate in its raw form that everyone resorts to using the null arcana-infused salt from the sea around Emrox instead.

It seems to me if there's going to be any sort of forgotten world-bridging magic—some scaled-up version of a telepad—it's most likely to be there.

The next time I touch the web on the end of a bookshelf, I focus on the Ruins, Between, and Emrox.

Although it is unknown why the Ruins were abandoned and left to fall into the disarray we find them in today, one tome reads, *one thing remains clear: Each society was built around a specific arcanum source, and that connection is maintained, at least to some degree, to this day.*

The evidence lies in the environment surrounding each Ruin. The bones of dead wildlife are spawned into new beings around the Black Spire. The surrounding woods continue to turn to stone around the Petrified Groves at an estimated rate of one inch per year. The moats of Mount Carmine forever overflow with lava. And if an adventurer is determined enough, it has even been demonstrated that skilled magicians who have ventured into these locations—and survived—were able to harness the arcana there without being limited by their individual mana reserves. Incredible, seemingly impossible acts of magic have been performed at these locations. Whatever spell the wielder may wish to enact, it has the potential to be magnified a thousand-fold.

I excitedly read on, hoping they have some insight into what this would mean for Emrox, but it seems no one has gotten that far. Its inhospitable location—at the bottom of the ocean—coupled with the deep-sea beasts that have become infused with the null magic apparently make it too dangerous for even aquatic species of people to approach. Harvesting the faintly magical salt deposits at the edge of the sea is as close as anyone dares venture.

The rest of the books on this floor don't offer any further insight, so I decide to move up a floor or two. The rarest texts should be at the top, after all, and what I'm looking for has maybe never been attempted before.

At floor twenty-nine, I find another lead.

As before, I take the book back to a desk and begin to leaf through it. There are far less people up here. The bald guy has also wandered up. Every once in a while, a lone patron wanders down.

This book is on Emrox.

The first thing I notice is the map. Or rather, pages and pages of maps. Half the book seems dedicated to sketches of the drowned city, some more clearly defined than others. If I seriously *am* considering trying to visit the city, this is exactly what I'd need. I wish I could take this book with me.

Echo, can you take snapshots or something? I ask.

[Negative,] Echo says, and maybe it's my imagination but I think she sounds mildly offended. [This interface is not designed for such purposes.]

You copied down spell circles and ingredient lists for me before, I note. *Can you copy any of this? Maybe recreate the general map?*

[Negative,] Echo says. [Once a spell has been learned, this unit is able to recall elements of the spell for future use. However, recalling the notional layout of an unknown city does not fall under that domain.]

Damn. No Google Maps for me. It was worth a shot, anyway. I keep flipping through the pages, trying to absorb as much as possible.

A handful of locations are labeled. The Main Gates. The Broken Pillars. There's also a central feature the city appears to be built around, some sort of stadium with an enormous spell circle carved into the center. The circle itself is at least as big as a house.

What about that? I ask Echo. *That's a spell circle. Can you copy it?*

[Negative, as you do not know the spell.]

If I practiced drawing it enough times it might get added to my spell list, and then maybe she'd be able to tell me more about what it could do. I pull out my slate and chalk, use my cloak to wipe off the Location spell, and then attempt to replicate what I can see of the circle. In the picture, parts of the spell are covered up or missing entirely, so I leave those parts blank. My drawing isn't perfect, but since it's not imbued with any magic and I have no idea what other requirements its activation might need, I'm not worried about accidentally setting it off.

After I finish flipping through the book—I find more notes indicating Emrox and null arcana are speculated to be some long-forgotten link to other dimensions—I return it to the shelf. Then I pick up the slate, focus on the spell circle I'd drawn there, and begin searching the stacks once more. Nothing on this level, besides the book I'd just returned, has any information on the circle. I keep heading up.

The library is getting quiet. What was once a roar of people has diminished into a distant murmur. I wonder if magic is muting it, or if it's a trick of the acoustics.

I finally hit another match on floor thirty-two. The light on the end of the shelf zips around the corner, and I follow it to a shelf near the floor. This one isn't covered in books, but scrolls. Given the lack of people and the unlikelihood of me getting in anyone's way, I simply sit on the ground and unfurl the scroll right there.

The paper is old and crinkly. There's writing on the pages, and more spell circle drawings, but the alphabet is in a language I don't recognize.

[Activate translation?] Echo asks.

Whatever would I do without her? *Activate.*

The words snap into focus.

Lost Spells, the scroll reads. There's no marked author. *Circle remnants of The Fallen.*

I'm sure that's fine.

I steadily unfurl the far end as I begin to re-roll the section I've already read. Some spell circles—or at least, partial circles, as many have blank spots in their pattern—contain a paragraph of speculation about what they might have done. Many more, however, are merely labeled things like "Partial circle found in The Green. Year: 732."

It doesn't take long until I find the one for Emrox, and luckily, this one comes with text.

Partial circle found in Emrox. Year: 945. Reinforcement of double outer circle suggests spell containment was necessary. Inner ten-point star comparable to design used in modern telepads, indicating a high likelihood the spell was used for dimensional magic. Author's speculation: If anywhere in this city still maintains a connection to the Between, it is likely tied to this circle. However, the patterns are much more intricate than to simply provide an access point to null arcana. It is the author's belief that the tunnel Between is merely one component of this spell; a stepping stone to power a much more complex magic. Based on what can be made of the circle, and the common mythologies which surround the city—be them truth or fiction—the purpose of this circle may have been to link different physical locations, very likely reaching through the Between itself to link to other worlds—and given the Between's nature, possibly other times.

I feel a rush of excitement. This is it. The spell hat could take me home, maybe even *before* I died. Sure, it's incomplete, yes, it might be a stretch, but it's somewhere to start. And if I can find some way to fill in the blanks, maybe I can activate it without dealing with Emrox. Taking my slate back out, I begin adding to the circle I'd previously drawn, trying to be as precise and detailed as possible. There are still gaps in the drawing, but given the circle's symmetry, I'm hoping I can infer some of what's missing.

[Your magic has been Identified,] Echo abruptly says.

I freeze, a chill running through my soul. *What? What do you mean?*

[A spell has been cast on you to gather information about your nature and magic.]

What the fuck. I look to my left and right—then nearly jump out of my glass as I find a figure standing at the end of the shelf. It's the bald man I'd nearly run into before. He's staring right at me.

Danger.

I don't know how I know that, but every instinct in me is telling me to run. This isn't right. Why hadn't I heard him? Why is he covertly scanning my magic?

Are we alone?

Shit shit shit. Zyneth told me not to go far, but I'm ten floors above him now. What the hell was I thinking?

All I can do now is try to leave out the other side of the shelf. If he doesn't know I'm onto him, maybe I can give him the slip. Okay, Kanin. Play it cool.

"Oh, hello," I say, tucking my slate and chalk back into my bag. "I did not see you there. Sorry if—"

The man's fingers twitch, and a red light flashes from his hand.

[Status Effect: Immobilized,] Echo says. [Your movements have been restrained.]

My body locks up. Every piece of glass frozen in place. At the edge of my vision I can see my hand still holding the lid of my satchel, in the process of letting it go, but at this moment I can't even get a finger to twitch. Panic wells up inside of me like a strangled scream.

The man strolls casually forward. His casualness terrifies me. Like I'm nothing.

"Now," he says. "Let's see what prize we have here."

Chapter Twelve

Masterful Design

Oh fuck oh fuck oh fuck. What was I thinking? Zyneth *warned* me. He told me not to go too high or wander off on my own. And I blew him off like he was babying me.

Okay, calm down. I can figure this out. First I need to know what I'm dealing with.

[Name: Raz]

[Species: Human]

[Class: Flame Artificer]

[Level: 46]

[HP: 100/100]

[Mana: 1051/1055]

Fuuuuuuck.

Raz, the highest level I've seen in this world, strolls toward me with his hands clasped behind his back.

"This must be some mistake," I say, desperately trying to buy time. Will his spell time out? Or does he need to lose focus? "I have done nothing against you."

"Fascinating," Raz says, stopping before me. "I've heard homunculus equipped with basic speech modules before, but never with this much nuance. You *appear* to be a homunculus, at any rate. But I witnessed you perform a spell earlier. Such a thing should not be possible, unless something more is going on here. Perhaps you act as an intermediary for your mage's arcana? Fascinating indeed. Tell me, creature, where's your creator?"

"Dead," I answer, too panicked to figure out what response would be the most in my favor. "And he was not my creator. Now if you would please let me go."

"You're capable of lying? Delightful," he says. "But a homunculus cannot merely stroll up here on their own. They should be bound to the same level as their master. So try again. Where is your creator?"

"It is just me," I say. "I am not lying."

He *tsks* in disappointment, then crouches down next to me. "Such craftsmanship." Raz runs a finger along my hand, and revulsion explodes through me at the touch. "I've never seen anything quite like it. Glass is a peculiar choice." He takes hold of my finger, and in one deft move, snaps it off.

"Ahhh!" Pain jolts up my arm.

[5 points of Sundering Damage sustained.]

"Hmm." He examines the finger. "Not very stable, I see. It could be crafted for better durability. Tell me, did you actually feel that, or is the reaction merely an imitation of life—a complex function of your spell?"

"*Expletive* you," I say. I feel hot and tingly all over, every inch of glass straining to move, to run, to defend myself. The pain in my hand dims to a dull thrum beneath the staticky panic.

"Expletive?" Raz repeats with a chuckle. "Are you trying to swear at me? You may be the most complex simulation of life I've ever seen in a homunculus. Are you sure you don't want to tell me where you came from?"

"I am not a homunculus," I say, fear spiking as his gaze travels slowly over my body, as if deciding which part of me he wants to destroy next. "I have a soul. Please, let me go. I can explain everything, just do not hurt me."

Instead of answering, he grabs my head next—the inverted glass pyramid, and pulls it from where it was frozen above my neck.

"Hey!" My vision spins wildly around, half obscured by his hand. I would have lost my balance if I wasn't frozen in place.

"Strange," he mutters to himself, pulling out a knife. There's runes carved into the flat of the blade, which illuminate as he brings the point up to my head. I can feel heat against my glass as if I'm pressed up against a furnace.

"Wait!" I try, panic welling up inside me. "Do not do this, please, I am a person, a real person, there's a soul in my—AHHHHHHH!"

[7 points of Searing Damage sustained.]

He might as well be cutting into flesh. Searing heat slices through me as his knife cuts off a corner of my vision. A glob of glass drops to the ground, molten. My mind swims in a pain-filled haze. I've broken my glass a hundred times by now, and while it always hurt like a nicked finger or bruised knee, this *burns*. It hurts, it hurts so much more than it should. I want to pass out. To shut my mind down and stop feeling what I'm feeling. But that's the worst curse of this body—I don't ever get a break from existing.

"Hush now," Raz says, as if admonishing a noisy child. "I'd much prefer to get some answers out of you, but I *will* apprehend that translator if you get too loud. You do seem to feel pain, at least—or are producing a very good simulation of it. I *must* find your artisan. Masterful design, really."

"Stop," I croak. "Please." All I can do is beg. Pathetic.

I relax a fraction when he sheaths the molten knife and tucks it away once more. However, his next move jolts my sluggish mind alert.

"Now, what was this you were saying about a soul?" Raz asks. He brushes the corner of my cloak away, revealing my core, hanging on its chain. Only a thin layer of cloth separates me from his grasp. Raz reaches for it.

No, no, no, no, no. The idea of his hand closing over me sends waves of claustrophobia through my body. I have to move. I have to do something!

Immobilized, I blurt to Echo, desperately stumbling over the thought. *It's just restraining me physically, right? I can still do magic?*

[Affirmative,] Echo says.

I don't waste another moment. Activating a Sculpt, I reshape the glass in my head piece, wrapping it around the man's hand like his fingers have sunk into a pile of wet clay. My vision warps insensibly, wrapping in over itself, and I quickly shut the sense off, plunging my world into darkness. But my trips to the Between have left me used to this blindness. I don't need to see to feel.

Raz cries out, shaking his hand, but I only clamp down harder, forming the surface into spikes as I stab into his hand. Now, it's his turn to scream.

[15 points of Piercing Damage dealt. Immobilize effect neutralized,] Echo says.

I sag to the floor, barely stopping myself from toppling over. My head piece still attached to Raz's hand, I scramble away from the insane mage. Pulling out my signing glass while I do, I quickly use a Sculpt to mash it together into a sphere and turn my sight back on in the floating ball—just in time to see Raz smash his hand against the floor, shattering all the glass around it.

[12 points of Piercing Damage dealt.]

[35 points of Bludgeoning Damage sustained.]

"Ahh!" Phantom pain stabs through me as the prism shatters into a hundred pieces, and I can *feel* every essence of myself in that glass fracture apart. But it's not as bad as the molten knife, and I can't let it get to me—I don't have time to nurse wounds. I scramble to my feet as Raz rounds on me, blood dripping from his clutched hand, a snarl on his face. He raises a finger on his good hand, light forming at its tip.

"Lightbeam!" I cry. The fractured pieces of my head snap into configuration, and I pump every ounce of mana I have into the spell.

A searing white light crashes into the mage. He screams, in pain or rage I'm not sure, and I sure as fuck am not sticking around to find out. I keep the Lightbeam on him as I sprint to the end of the shelf, only shutting the spell off as I round the corner and recall the glass to me.

[35 points of Light Damage dealt.]

I race down the spiraling library as fast as I dare. Maybe now that I've gotten away, he won't follow.

"You bastard!" he calls, and I hear a crashing sound, then the rapid thud of pursuing footsteps. Well, so much for that.

It's all I can do to push my legs faster. If I trip now, I'll break off a lot more than just a limb.

[Spell Level Up!] Echo happily declares.

Now is not the time, Echo! I cry.

[Lightbeam: Level 2. The spell now takes 20% less mana to cast, or can be used with 20% increased light damage.]

Oh goody, I am so thrilled to have this information forced through my brain right at this moment when I couldn't possibly have anything more important to be focusing on!

A fireball crashes into the shelf right next to my head. I reel away, stumbling into the railing. My forearm cracks as it strikes the banister.

[5 points of Bludgeoning Damage sustained. Bludgeoning damage resistance Level Up!]

What the hell is wrong with this guy?

[Bludgeoning Damage Resistance: Level 3. Damage taken from bludgeoning related sources reduced by 30%.]

Echo, I swear to fuck.

"How dare you," Raz snarls, storming after me. There's swirling fire in his hands and a red heat shimmering from one of his eyes. A thin stream of smoke wafts up from his other eye, scorched black where my Lightbeam struck him. He paces toward me, steps measured and inevitable, as a venomous sneer stains his face.

If he's trying to look terrifying, he's goddamn succeeding.

There's still another ten floors to descend before I can make it to Zyneth—ten long, grueling circuits down the spiral. It would take at least five minutes, and that's if I were running, and that's if I weren't dodging a deranged mage.

With his 1051 mana against my 56, I can't out-magic him. And with his human body against my glass, I can't outrun him. Backed against the railing, there's only one way to get down quickly that I can think of.

It's probably a terrible idea.

See, technically, I *should* be able to float. I can levitate my signing glass just fine. And as long as the stuff I'm lifting isn't heavier than the glass itself, I can also carry stuff around—like this cloak and Noli's bookbag. The biggest issue I've run into is trying to focus on each individual piece, trying to hold them all in my mind at once. If I don't actively make each one float, then they just become dead weight. Thus, all the walking.

Even trying to get them to float as a tiny walking glass vial, with much fewer pieces to worry about, had been too hard for me. Of course, I didn't have heaps of opportunities to practice, given the crunch time of my spell expiring, but this last month I'd played around with it as I was building up my new body. I could often get whole limbs to levitate on their own: both arms. A leg and a torso. My head and hands. Hypothetically, it's just about remaining focused. Hypothetically, if I concentrate on only levitating all the biggest, heaviest pieces, they should be able to carry the weight of all the smaller ones.

Hypothetically, this isn't suicide.

Raz paces forward, bringing his hands together as a ball of fire grows into existence between his palms. I clutch the railing, my soul fluttering with the horror and stupidity of what I'm about to do. Raz looses the fireball, and I jump.

Chapter Thirteen

SOME DUEL OF FATES SHIT

I ragdoll through the air for one horrifying moment. Paradoxically, I have a perfectly steady view of my body falling to its inevitable doom as the orb I'm using to see through floats peacefully nearby. It's absurd. I want to laugh—or maybe that's the panic. The ground floor is rushing up to me alarmingly fast, and I don't have time to think about it.

I seize my glass. All of it. As much as I can hold in my mind, as complex as I can imagine it. Float, damn you, float, float, float!

And the void reacts, too. It scatters then reforms, infinitesimally small pieces snapping into every Chained joint, stopping my haphazard flails as each limb locks abruptly into place. And for one moment, I can see it all: the whole, instead of individual pieces. Like it's just one continuous form. I latch onto this, mentally grabbing my body and throwing it to the side. I clip the banister as I fling myself back onto a floor and go rolling across the ground.

I feel my limbs break.

[10 points of Fall Damage sustained. 3 points of Bludgeoning Damage sustained. 7 points of Bludgeoning Damage sustained. 23 points of Sundering Damage sustained.]

My health plummets as my foot breaks off—fingers shatter—my forearm cracks. I roll to a stop, stunned and aching, as the floor erupts into chaos around me. People are yelling and scattering, running every which way as pages flutter through the air. I dimly wonder how pissed the librarian is going to be.

No time to rest. I roll myself over, carefully cataloging the location of each injury as I Check myself.

[HP: 8/10]

[Temp HP: 227/315]

[Mana: 11/56]

At least my core was mostly spared. No time to celebrate, though. I'm nearly out of mana—I need to find Zyneth, fast.

What floor am I even on? I look wildly around as I grab my broken foot and hastily Sculpt it back in place. It's crooked, but that's the least of my worries. Looking out across the spiral, I can't see the top ceiling or the ground floor: I must be somewhere in the middle, but am I above or below Zyneth? I guess it doesn't matter. I need to get down and out of here ASAP.

I pick myself up, briefly trying to levitate as I had just a minute before—although perhaps *levitate* is a strong word for "threw myself at a wall." But that moment of mental clarity is past, and the void has returned to bracing the joints in my legs and back. An enigma for another time. I begin limping after the library patrons, who in turn flee from me, screaming. That's fair.

I've barely made it half a loop when I hear a familiar voice. "Kanin!"

Relief floods through me as Zyneth sprints down the slope toward me. So I'm under floor twenty then. Good: less floors between me and a hasty escape.

Concern is plastered over his face. "What in the world is going on?" he asks, taking in all of my injuries. His enchanted blades are in his hands faster than I could see him draw them. "How did you get down here? And where the blazes is your head?"

"Help me get out of here first," I say. "Give me a hand."

Zyneth doesn't even miss a beat. He slings my arm over his shoulder as he lifts the side my crooked foot is on, and then we're off, me struggling to keep up.

Once again I'm struck by how quick Zyneth is to jump into action. How he never questions me when I ask for help. It's always act first and figure out the details later. I guess he's a lot like Noli in that respect. What did I do to deserve people like them in my life?

I tighten my grip on his shoulder, leaning into his support.

"There is some crazy mage up there," I say as we rush down the library. "Raz. An artificer or something. He is strong—very strong. Destroyed my head—wanted to take me apart and see how I worked."

"What?" Zyneth snaps. His grip on me tightens, his face contorting from concern into rage. There's a tremble in his voice when he speaks. I don't think I've ever seen him this mad before. "What does he look like? Tell me everything."

A burst of flame sweeps over us. I stumble to the side as Zyneth slashes a hand through the air, dispelling the wall of fire. Raz is right behind it, jetting down from an upper floor to land heavily on the railing only ten feet away.

"He looks about like that," I say.

Zyneth lets go of my arm and steps in front of me, facing down the fire mage.

"Bastard," Raz spits, *literally*, as foam flecks his lips. "How dare you raise a hand against me!" He pulls his hands apart, summing a blindingly bright ball of fire as heat spills across the floor. "Get out of the way, fool!"

Zyneth glances back at me out of the corner of his eye. "This isn't insanity, this is some kind of vendetta. What in Lorata's name did you do?"

"Me?" I cry. "I was just defending myself! I did not do anything."

Nearly done forming whatever doomsday weapon he's summoning, Raz narrows his eyes with a growl. Well, just the one eye. The other is shut and covered in burnt and blackened skin.

"Oh, I also might have burned out his eye."

Raz roars, firing his weapon at both of us. I take a step back as Zyneth brandishes his knives, lightning crackling off the blades and meeting the fire blasts midair with rapid concussive explosions. I stagger away, raising a defensive arm, as the two clash.

Watching them fight is something else. This is some Dual of the Fates shit. They're forces of nature, fire and lightning deflecting off in every direction. The ceiling begins to rain on us as several bookshelves catch flame, like some kind of magical automatic sprinkler system, but it can't keep up with Raz's blasts of fire. I just try to stay back, stay out of the way, and avoid getting struck by any stray shots.

Zyneth is a blur of movement, agile and precise, but Raz is a higher level. I saw his mana stores. If it's a battle of attrition, Zyneth won't win. He needs to end it now, or it won't end on our terms.

I don't know what to do. I feel like Zyneth's lightning is coursing through me, like every inch of me is electrified, itching to move, to run, to fight, to do *something*. I hate the idea of leaving Zyneth behind, but maybe fleeing is the right call. It would get Raz focused on me, maybe give Zyneth an opening. My hands twitch, indecisive.

Raz cuts around another one of Zyneth's attacks, blasting a fire ball point-blank into his hand. Zyneth's dagger goes flying. Before he can raise the other, Raz already has a second fireball leveled at his face.

"Lightbeam!"

My glass instantly reacts, snapping into place as I funnel the last of my mana into the attack and the blinding white light sears through the air and into the fire mage. He reels back with a cry.

[9 points of Light Damage dealt.]

[Mana depleted.]

The light vanishes as quickly as it appeared, but Zyneth doesn't waste my effort. He surges forward before Raz has an opportunity to recover, delivering a strike to his temple and a slash across his open hand. Electricity bursts across his form as the mage collapses to the ground.

Zyneth stands over him, panting. I'm feeling mentally exhausted myself, all the injuries of the last few minutes catching up to me in a cacophony of a thousand tiny aches. Cautiously, I make my way over to Zyneth.

"At least that's over," he says, wiping his brow on his forearm and sheathing his knife. The rain has plastered Zyneth's hair across his forehead and neck, and is streaking across my vision in blurry lines. "I can't take you anywhere, can I?"

I send some of my glass over to retrieve Zyneth's disarmed knife and float it back to him. He takes it with a gracious nod.

"Is he unconscious?" I ask.

"Just dazed," Zyneth says, even as Raz groans. "Where is the librarian? This is unacceptable."

I'm still standing there, wondering what the hell a librarian could be expected to do about all of this, when Raz abruptly flicks out a hand.

"Watch out!" Zyneth shoves me back. Pain lances across my chest and arm, skimming past me as the item embeds itself in a nearby bookshelf: the fire knife Raz had used on me before.

[3 points of Searing Damage sustained.]

"Shit!" Zyneth slams his boot into Raz's stomach, and the mage gasps as the blow flips him over onto his front. Zyneth drops a knee on his back, grabbing his hands and quickly binding them with a severed bit of spider silk that had been used to string the lights.

My chest aches. I bring my hand away from my flask, and for a dizzying moment, I don't understand what I'm looking at.

Ink. Black ichor is spilled over my fingers and dripping from the gash in the bag that's holding my flask. I sway unsteadily, static creeping into my mind. Horror prickles up my limbs even as I watch, and the black begins to drip *up*. A toothy smile presses into my consciousness.

My soul lurches with fear and disbelief. No, it can't be—it's gone, it's stuck in my inventory, it can't be back—

"Kanin?" Zyneth asks, watching me. His eyes are on the void, pinched with concern. He starts to stand up.

"Get back!" I stumble away, holding a hand out defensively. "Run, get out of here, get everyone else away—"

I convulse as another sharp pain lances through my core, stabbing through my vial like a heart attack, and the predator seeps into the world.

Chapter Fourteen

I'm the Ocean Now

No, this can't be happening here, not with so many people around. I thought it was over, I thought it was gone, but I can feel the predator's hunger creeping into my mind.

Panicked, desperate, I clutch my hand around the pouch, as if that could stem the flow of void dripping into the world.

Surprisingly, it seems to work. The drops of black squeezing out between my fingers have slowed, and instead of a giant crack forming in reality, the void that's pooled in the air above me is barely the size of an orange.

Something's different—this isn't the same as before. The predator's mind isn't crashing against my own, threatening to sweep me away. In fact, it's hardly a trickle.

I pause, fighting against my fear to take stock of the situation. It's definitely the predator—those echoes of hunger in my mind are unmistakable. But it's only a fraction of the force I'm used to, and the void that's pooled in the air is a literal drop in the bucket compared to the tidal wave of ink that's emerged before.

Void Check, I say.

[Void: 0%]

What does that mean? Previously, the amount of ink in my vial had been directly proportional to what percent void I was at. Does that mean my vial is empty now? Before now the stat has only ever reset after the predator was summoned, and this scant amount certainly isn't all of it.

Inventory Check.

[Inventory Space: DIV/0. Contents: Void.]

It's still in there, then. But I don't understand what's happened. I mean, I'm not complaining about not being mauled by a void monster, but the change in pattern makes me equally nervous. Is it just biding its time? No, that can't be it—it needs to consume magic to maintain its presence in reality. So why isn't it attacking?

Despite my warning, Zyneth didn't run. He's watching me, fearful and maintaining a healthy distance, but he didn't leave me. My soul tightens up at that realization.

"Kanin?" Zyneth calls. "Are you still with me?"

Right—I'd told him all about how the predator had affected me the other times it had been summoned. He probably thinks I'm being mind-controlled right now.

"I am okay," I say, uncertain if that's really true. I'm fighting every instinct to run, as futile as that would be. You can't outrun something when you're the source of it. "I do not understand what is happening. It is not overpowering me. It feels... smaller."

"It looks smaller," Zyneth agrees, eyeing the floating ball of black in the air. So far, it hasn't moved. The ink has stopped seeping out from between my fingers as well. Cautiously, I remove my hand so I can see the damage. There's a one inch slash across the bag concealing my vial—no doubt the wound goes deeper. Something to investigate later. For now, my attention is on the predator: there's not much of it. Like all the void that had previously filled my core is what's now floating in the air before me. Why? Was the inventory keeping all but this small amount still contained?

In that case, the ball—this fraction of the predator—should be dragged back Between soon enough. As long as it doesn't get its hand on any magic or a soul.

I can feel the predator perk up at the thought. Its faint uncertainty evaporates as it remembers its hunger, sharpened like a blade. Shit! Even if it's muted, it can still hear my thoughts as easily as I can hear its. The void sweeps its gaze around the scene, its attention quickly falling over Raz, still prone on the floor only a few feet away.

"*Expletive*, Zyneth, watch out! It is going for the mage—"

The ball of ink jets toward the unconscious mage before I can move to stop it. Even so, I throw out a desperate hand, as if I could seize it from the air. No, don't kill him—I can't, I can't be responsible for another death—

And the void *stumbles*. I don't know how else to describe it. It's like it trips over itself midair, hitting some invisible roadblock and splashing to the ground at Raz's feet. Zyneth, who'd barely had time to raise a blade, now hops between Raz and the spilled ink, kicking the restrained mage back to send him rolling out of the predator's range. He glances briefly my way, understandably reluctant to take his eyes off the void for long.

"What's going on? Did you stop it?"

"No," I say, just as confused as him. "I mean, I do not think so."

But, to my astonishment, I can feel the predator's mind cowering away from mine. What the hell?

Cautiously, I focus on its presence. If I had mana, I would activate a Bond Trace to help visualize the link between us, but as it is, I have to reach blindly forward. Will myself toward its thoughts and feelings, which constantly bleed back into me. Every nerve on edge, I make contact with its mind.

It's... miniscule. Even as I press forward, I can feel it cringing away, bowing beneath the weight of my mind. With a start, I realize what's going on, why it had stopped trying to attack the mage, and why it isn't mentally attacking me.

"Holy *Expletive Expletive.*"

Before, making contact with the predator was like being cast into a violent ocean. I'd lost all sense of self, overwhelmed by the predator's will. Only now, our roles have flipped. This fraction of the predator is so small that *I'm* the dominant mind. I'm the ocean, and it's drowning inside me. I barely have to push to bend the void's will to my own; now *it* has to fight to distinguish itself from *my* thoughts.

It's absurd. Laughable. I was petrified it was about to take over my mind, all while it was terrified of the same. I press forward, and the predator's mind shrinks back, the ink on the floor going flat as if the weight of my thoughts are crushing it to the ground.

A sadistic exhilaration passes through me. All right, fucker. Time for a taste of your own medicine.

I hold out my hand, mentally commanding the predator to leave Raz and Zyneth and return to me. It leaps into the air, stopping to float over my palm, as obedient as my own Attuned void. In fact, that's the only difference, isn't it? My Attuned void had also been a piece of the predator before I'd activated the Attunement, stripping its connection to the monster. If I Attune this fraction of the predator as well, it should also fall under my control. I'm not sure if that process kills the piece of the predator that's tied to the void, or if it just banishes it back to Between—and frankly, I don't care one way or the other, so long as it's gone.

"Kanin?" Zyneth asks, startling me out of my concentration. The moment my mental grip wavers, the predator slips from my grasp, fearfully floating several feet away. But it doesn't go *too* far away. Interesting.

"You better explain what in the Gardens is going on here," Zyneth says, his voice tight. Is he nervous? Mad? I can't tell—there's something tense in his tone.

"I think I can control it," I say. I wave my hand to the left, and the predator obeys, flinching as it submits to my command. Its fear fills me with satisfaction. Maybe that makes me an asshole. But after what this thing did—after what it made me do—I'm going to wring every ounce of revenge I can out of this moment.

"Gods be good," Zyneth breathes, watching the display. "Are you sure that's really the predator?"

"Yes," I say, feeling it quaver in my mind. I bear down on it until its thoughts whisper out, overridden by my own. I yank the void back over to me like a dog on a leash. "A piece of it, anyway. A very small piece."

Flickering motion draws my attention back to my surroundings. Dozens of those spider helpers are skittering our way, across ceilings and walls and from up and down the floor. Some of them pause at scorch marks on bookshelves, while others crawl over to Raz, lights blinking on their head like so many eyes. I step hesitantly back as one of them taps against my leg, its eyes winking at me like some sort of drone sent to survey the scene of a natural disaster. Uninterested in being cataloged as a threat, I slip the void beneath the hem of my cloak, hiding it among the shadows.

A moment later, the rain peters out.

"At least that's finished," Zyneth says, wiping his hair back from his eyes and channeling some extremely attractive "love interest in the rain at the climax of a romance movie" vibes.

Trying not to stare, I attempt to wipe the streaks of water off my glass as well, but only succeed in spreading an even layer of blurry water droplets over the surface. "Ugh. I have officially decided I hate water."

A white shadow falls over the banister, blotting out the lights behind it.

"I do apologize for the inconvenience," the arachnoid says, all eight of his legs curling over the guardrail as he pulls himself up onto our floor. "The fire suppressant spell circuit is a necessary precaution when your profession deals with so much flammable material as mine."

For one brief moment I'm grateful for my lack of human anatomy, because I'm sure my jaw would be on the floor. The arachnoid is taller than anything I'd seen in the streets of Miasmere. Even crouched beneath the ceiling of our floor, all of his legs—too many legs—folded up against his body, he's at least eight feet tall. Despite the humanoid torso emerging from where the head of the spider should be, his entire body shines like it's polished, an unblemished white, giving his many barbed limbs the unsettling impression of five-foot long icicles. They seem impossibly thin, too narrow to support his body—which only hints at how powerful they must really be.

[Name: Yedzaquib]

[Species: Arachnoid]

[Class: Mind Weaver]

[Level: 68]

[HP: 250/250]

[Mana: 2450/2450]

I take a step back in spite of myself. Yedzaquib's head moves a fraction in my direction, though I can't tell from the eight, black, unblinking spheres that must be eyes, if he's even looking at me. There's a faint smile on his face, and until he speaks again, I'm uncertain if he's wearing a mask, because the expression is so tailored and perfect that it doesn't even appear real.

"Master Curator," Zyneth greets Yedzaquib, recovering before I can. He bows respectfully. "I apologize for disrupting your library, but I would like to head off any allegations of our—my involvement."

The arachnoid's head swivels towards Zyneth, and long white strands of hair fall over his shoulder like spider silk. "I am aware. My sentries witnessed enough of the commotion for me to glean who is at fault." He lifts a hand, and his spider minions converge on Raz, who groans faintly as they begin to secure his arms and legs with more lines of web.

"I wish to atone for the trouble you have experienced today," Yedzaquib says, still addressing Zyneth. "I personally guarantee the safety of all of my patrons while inside these walls, a promise I have failed to uphold with this altercation. I notice the mage targeted your homunculus—I could replace the damaged goods, if you would like."

My soul drops at this suggestion, but I wrangle my alarm under control and manage to stay perfectly still, hoping to continue to portray nothing more interesting than a loyal homunculus servant. I can feel the predator wriggling in my mental grasp, trying to escape my hold, and I tighten my grip.

"That will not be necessary," Zyneth says. "I am an artificer myself and am more than capable of executing the repairs. A task which I should start on promptly. If it would be no insult to you, I would prefer to take my leave: I've other errands I still need to run today. It is sufficient payment to see such a dangerous man apprehended."

"Hmm," Yedzaquib considers, staring at Zyneth for a long moment. Finally, slowly and mechanically, he nods. "If that is your wish, you may depart. However, I am not the authority of law in this city." Responding to some invisible command, one of the spiders jabs Raz in the shoulder, causing the man to jerk, gasping awake.

Zyneth takes a cautious step away from the mage, who begins to thrash against the spiders still pinning him down.

"Let go! Unhand me!" he cries. "This is a mistake—you don't understand—"

Yedzaquib bows over Raz, his legs moving with unnerving coordination, and I'm briefly reminded of a nature documentary I saw as a kid: a moth caught in a web was fluttering frantically, desperate to escape, as the spider crawled deliberately down toward its prey.

"You have disrupted my library," Yedzaquib says. This entire conversation his voice has remained soft and reserved, which somehow makes it all worse. "Attacked a patron. Destroyed my personal property. It is my duty to turn you over to the City Guards."

Zyneth flicks a sharp beckoning gesture in my direction as he continues to back away from the arachnoid and the mage. I don't need to be told twice: I hurry over to his side as Zyneth offers one last parting bow, but Yedzaquib's full attention is on his captive. Zyneth starts down the winding ramp of books, and I dutifully follow after.

"However, should you provide guarantees that you no longer pose a threat to my establishment, a different arrangement can be made," Yedzaquib says, his voice fading as we leave him behind. "I see no reason to inform the Guards if you'd be willing to buy your freedom with an act of community service to my library..."

As the two pass out of sight, Zyneth lets out a breath.

"So that is the librarian, huh?" I ask.

"Yes," Zyneth says, his tone clipped.

"Kind of creepy."

Zyneth snorts, but his voice still feels strained. "I would not voice such thoughts within these walls if I were you."

Fair point. "You think he is really going to let that guy go?"

"I think it prudent we don't stick around to find out. Besides," he adds, shooting a tense glance toward my cloak, "we have more immediate matters to attend to."

I hadn't even realized I'd relaxed my grip, that my mind had begun to wander, until Zyneth's words turn my attention back on the predator. The slightest hint of pressure prickles at my mind as it fights against my will. Quickly snuffing out the resistance, I redouble my focus on the predator.

Given Zyneth's clear reluctance to speak while we're still in the Athenaeum, I'm left to mull over thoughts of the predator in the silence of my own head as we wind out way down the library. Noli and Zyneth had made me doubt myself. I'd begun to wonder if finding a way back to Earth was the right call. I've made more friends here than I had back home, after all; if I could find a way to retrieve my body and stay here, maybe that would be the best of both worlds.

But that had been when I thought the predator was gone and dealt with. We got lucky today: the predator was weak, small enough that I could fight it off on my own. And to be honest, now that I have a grip on it, I'm not worried about it escaping.

The bigger issue is that Pandora's box is now open. Even if I deal with this small piece, I don't think I'll be able to snap the lid back on again—not completely. More of the predator could show up at a moment's notice—and what if it's more than I can handle?

No. I can't remain here, not as long as the predator's tied to me. So far as I can tell, no amount of magic will ever be able to break its hold on me. Which is why I need to get back to Earth—somewhere magic doesn't exist, where there'll be nothing to sustain a creature like this.

Then I can get rid of it for good.

Chapter Fifteen

MONSTER IN A BOTTLE

Zyneth walks stiffly beside me, as taut as a compressed spring. The moment we finally step outside the library and back into the sunlight, I turn to check on him.

He beats me to the punch. "Are you alright?" he hisses under his breath. "The predator—the void—what's going on?"

"I am okay," I tell him. "Its mind is not as powerful as my own. I think I will be able to Attune it once I save up enough mana, and then it will not be an issue anymore. In the meantime, as long as I am not distracted, I can control it."

"Not distracted?" Zyneth says. "What does that mean? If someone knocks into you, your control might slip and it could kill someone?" He pushes a hand through his hair as he gives a frustrated sigh. "I'm sorry. Now's not the place. We should speak in private—you sure you'll be fine to make it back to our inn?"

"I will be alright," I insist. "Really. I have this."

He shoots me a concerned look, and though he doesn't reply, he might as well be saying aloud, "That's what worries me."

Zyneth makes a bee-line for our inn. Once there, he bafflingly pauses at the tavern to purchase their largest bottle of wine. I mean, it's been a trying day for all of us, but Zyneth never really struck me as the stress-drinker type.

The moment the door to our room shuts behind us, Zyneth pops the bottle's cork. "Right."

"Ah. Zyneth?" I ask as he begins pouring the wine directly into the chamber pot. "Are you going to tell me what you are doing?"

He shakes the last of the wine out—that *had* to be expensive—and then sets the bottle upright on the floor. "The predator. Can you trap it in there?"

Oh. That's smart. I bring the predator out from the recesses of my cloak: like this, it's indistinguishable from my Attuned void, just a pool of formless ink. Zyneth takes a leery step back as I send the predator to funnel itself into the wine bottle. It fills about half the container, then Zyneth jams the cork back into the bottle and hammers it in with the back of one of his knives. Knife still unsheathed, Zyneth stands back up and hastily steps away, nodding to me.

"Will that hold it?" he asks.

Good question. I don't trust that cork. I send some of my own glass to the bottle as well, intending to Sculpt an additional glass stopper over the end.

[Insufficient mana,] Echo chimes in.

What? I know I went down to zero in the fight with Raz, but it's been a half hour since then: I should have recovered a trickle of mana by now. I Check my stores, but Echo's right: 0/56.

A problem I'll deal with later. Right now I have the predator to worry about. Hesitantly, I mentally let go of its mind.

It immediately starts thrashing in the bottle, its previous fear re-placed by waves of hatred as it seethes against my control. I have to resist the urge to mentally flinch away, cast back into the memories of when our roles were reversed. But even this amount of spite it's throwing at me is like a brush of butterfly wings. The bottle rocks, tips over, and rattles against the floor.

After a long moment, I let out a mental breath. "It will hold."

I can feel it throwing all its willpower at the bottle, but without much room to wind up for an attack, there's hardly any power behind its blows. Gathering my courage, I cross the room and put a hand on the shaking bottle, forcing it to remain still. The predator angrily lashes at me, but it can't do any damage—physically or mentally. For now, it's dealt with.

Zyneth sighs in relief, and all the tension in his stance falls away.

"Now we can talk," he says, finally sheathing his blade.

"Right," I say. For a moment, we both stare silently at the monster in the bottle. I right the bottle, leaving it on the floor, then stand up.

"I have to go to Emrox," I say, at the same time Zyneth says, "We need to get this thing away from you."

Zyneth freezes. "What? Emrox?"

"It is the only way I can get rid of this thing for good," I say. "In the Athenaeum I found a spell circle from Emrox. I drew part of it—it is incomplete. But the rest of it would be there, in Emrox. It could take me back home."

"Oh my. I see." Zyneth sits down on the edge of the bed. "Are you certain? Myths of such magic are one thing, but to truly rediscover a lost path between worlds..."

Certain is a strong word. Even the books didn't explicitly state this was the bridge spell Echo said I'd need. It might be a stretch, hung on a desperate hope. But... "I have to try," I say. "Emrox is the only place where I have a chance to get home. To help me recover my body." And saying it aloud, the words make my chest ache with hope. I'm so tired of living in this glass shell. I'm so ready to be myself again.

Zyneth stirs. "Even if you're right about this supposed spell circle in Emrox... Is that your end goal, then? To return to your world?"

His words sour that flutter of hope. "Yes," I say, though all the enthusiasm is gone. "I have to. There is no magic in my world. Some of the books I read in the Atheneum suggested that magic cannot survive in a non-magical world. If I go back to Earth, maybe that would destroy the predator—or at least leave it stranded Between. There it will not be able to hurt anyone else. Sent back to where it originally came from." Like me.

Zyneth frowns. "Is that really the only way?" He gestures to the bottle. "We've sealed this piece away without too much trouble. You said it yourself, once you recover enough mana, it won't be a danger. I would never try to stop you from recovering your lost body, but is that the reason you wish to return to your world, or is it the predator? Because if it's merely the latter, there must certainly be other options."

Merely. As if the predator doesn't terrify me, even now. "Maybe you are right," I say. "Maybe we can deal with this piece. But what happens when more appears?" When, not if. Even if that fire mage's attack is what spurred this much of the predator to escape, it would be naive to think nothing else could cause more of it to emerge. "I cannot afford to waste time. The longer I stay in this world, the longer I run the risk. And we cannot know that next time the amount will be so small. What happens when it is more than I can control? What if it takes my mind before I have a chance to Attune it or send it back Between?"

Zyneth doesn't say anything, but from the pained look on his face, I know he knows I'm right.

"We have to get rid of it," I say. "Fast. That matters before anything else."

"Okay," he says after a moment. "You're right. Taking care of the predator should be the top priority. But are you sure Emrox is the only way?"

"Between is where it came from, and it seems like it is constantly fighting to not be drawn back there," I say, looking at the bottled monster. Well, that had been true before. Why this piece in particular seemed to be fighting off the pull of Between is something I still need to figure out. "If the books are right, I will pass through the Between when I head to Earth, and the predator should not be able to follow me out into my world without losing all its magic. And since it is *made* of magic…" I shrug. "Then I should be with my body. Two birds with one stone." Hopefully. If that Location spell will take me back to it the right place. If it really can take me back in time before my body was dead. That's a lot of *if*s. Okay, it's not a perfect plan, but I'm working on it. "Unless you know another way to open a portal Between?"

Zyneth shakes his head with a grimace. "It should be possible, of course—portals to different arcana sources are opened all the time—but a link to the Between has been lost to history." He hesitates, as if he was about to say more.

"…Except in Emrox," I supply.

"Except in Emrox," he agrees with a sigh. "But how in the world do you propose we go there? It's at the bottom of the ocean."

We. Even now, he plans to help me. When he has no skin in this game.

Which makes the next part even harder for me to say. "Luckily, we know someone who has been there before."

"What? Who?" Zyneth stares at me for a moment in confusion before horrified realization begins to dawn on him. "No. Absolutely not."

"Who better to guide us to a lost underwater city than a submarine-owning amphibian?" I say. "We will get Gillow to take us."

CHAPTER SIXTEEN

LET'S MAKE A DEAL

"You have no idea what you're suggesting," Zyneth says, back on his feet. "Gillow is only out for themself. You can't trust them."

"I do not trust them," I say. "But I do not need to trust them to buy their help."

"Buy?" Zyneth repeats. "With what money?"

"It is my understanding they are interested in more than coins."

Zyneth visibly pales. "What do you have in mind?"

"It does not matter," I say. "All that matters is I can pay."

"This is foolish." Zyneth's face hardens. "Gillow will take advantage of you the moment your back is turned. They'll rope you into some debt you'll never be able to pay off."

"It is a good thing there is nothing they can leverage over me then," I say. "Especially if I skip town to go back to Earth at the end of the trip."

Zyneth goes still. "Trying to trick them is even more dangerous."

I throw my hands in the air. "Then what would you suggest, Zyneth? Do you know of any other undersea captains who can take me to Emrox?" I pause for an answer. "No? I did not think so. But you know what? That is fine. You do not have to come with me. I do not need to be your charity case any longer. I can make this deal on my own."

Zyneth looks stricken. "I don't see you as a charity case."

Regret stings my soul. I don't know why I said that. "Even so, you may stay behind."

"Is that what you want?" he asks sadly.

What the hell? Why's he acting like a kicked puppy? I'm the one who should be upset here.

I make an irritated sign—it feels a lot more satisfying than this stupid monotone voice box—and sit down on a chair. I'm eager to reshape the glass I'm using as a head—or, eyeball, really—into something that doesn't have omni-vision, but I still need to wait for my mana to recover, and I've more pressing matters to take care of first. I gently clasp my core and carefully slip it out of its leather pouch.

"Of course I would like your help," I say as I examine my vial. Without the bag to restrict its vision, I'm looking up at myself at the same time I'm looking down. It's disorienting, but necessary; I have to make sure I'm not about to break in half. Luckily, the gash in the bag is more severe than the cut in my glass. It's an inch across and a hairsbreadth wide; enough to provide an exit for all the void that had been trapped there, but not something that seems immediately life threatening. If I can force a Level Up, it should heal the glass in my core like it has before.

"I just do not want you to feel obligated to," I continue, slipping the core back in the bag and resting it against my chest. "I know you have a bad history with Gillow."

"You don't know the half of it," Zyneth mumbles. "But I'm not doing any of this out of obligation. And it's not to tip some moral scale."

I recall the conversation we'd had earlier in the week, about him helping people to try to atone for his past mistakes. If he can be believed, then that's why he'd initially helped me back in Harrowood, but not why he's still helping.

"Why then? I doubt it is due to the conversation." I chuckle darkly, and the translator starts spitting out some horrific robot laugh. I quickly put a stop to that. "A handful of signs and broken sentences cannot have given you a good idea of my character."

"Our conversation has been rather stunted," he agrees, smiling weakly. "But actions speak louder than words."

"Actions?" I snort, Checking my Mana again. Still at 0. It definitely should have gone up by now. Even as I think it, I feel the predator shrink away from my mind, and I catch a hint of fear and evasiveness. It's hiding something from me.

"*Expletive.*"

"What is it?" Zyneth asks.

"My mana is out," I say. "I used it all up during that fight in the library, but it has been nearly an hour. It should have recovered some by now."

Zyneth frowns. "You haven't done any other magic?"

"No. But I think I know where it is going." I dig into the predator's mind, prying up the thoughts it's trying to keep from me. Reluctantly, like a stone stuck in the mud, the information I'm searching for tumbles into my hands.

"Shit," I sign, not wanting to risk another *Expletive.*

Zyneth catches the gesture. "The predator?"

I nod. "Do you remember when we were fighting it at Noli's house, and it kept draining extra magic from the spells I used, making it stronger?"

"It's hard to forget," Zyneth says.

"I am pretty sure that is why it has not vanished back Between," I say. "It is feeding on my magic."

Sneaky bastard. Better than it trying to eat people's souls at every opportunity, but I don't like the idea that it's learning. That it's getting more clever and subtle.

Zyneth clearly doesn't like this either. "Will that prevent you from Attuning it?"

"Maybe," I admit. "Let me see."

Echo, how much mana to Attune this volume of void? I ask.

[Attunement cost: 125]

And how much mana has the predator absorbed? I ask Echo. *If I keep it from absorbing anything more from me, when will it be weak enough that it'll fall back Between?*

[Predator Time Limit: 3 hours.]

Annoying. But I can probably keep it under my thumb that long. And if I can't, then that'll be enough time for me to save up enough mana to try to Attune at least part of it, chipping away at the predator one chunk at a time.

"I think I should be able to do it," I tell Zyneth. "But I will need to suppress its mind while I recover my mana. That will take a while."

"At least it seems contained for now," Zyneth says with a sigh. "We can lay low as we wait. There's no hurry."

Easy for him to say. He's not the one with a monster in his head. I grab the predator's mind, even as it struggles in my grasp, and force it into quiet submission. It takes concentration, but at least I have some peace and quiet.

"If this works, we can get it taken care of tonight," I tell him. "Either it will be starved of my mana, or I will have enough to start Attuning it."

Zyneth nods uneasily. "Good. At least we have options."

He looks ready to settle in, but I'm way too antsy to just spend the next couple hours waiting around. "In the meantime, we should address the Emrox issue. No sense in burning daylight."

Zyneth grimaces. "I was worried you might say that."

This time, when we walk through Gillow's door, I'm the one leading the way while Zyneth is hanging reluctantly back. I told him again he didn't have to come. And with his eyes he told me again he thought this was a bad idea, and followed anyway.

Gillow is at the counter, busy disassembling some sort of spear-gun and cleaning the parts. I can't say why, but the guts of the weapon spread over the surface before them summons a faint unease in me.

"Ah, the prodigal lord returns!" they say, offering a pointed-tooth smile when they catch sight of Zyneth. "Couldn't get enough of my business, eh?"

"Actually," I say, and I'm satisfied to see them jump when I speak, "you have business with me."

For a moment, Gillow's eyes go as round as sand-dollars. "What is this?" They turn to Zyneth, recovering a moment later and settling back into their natural smirk. "Some kind of joke?"

"It is not," I say. "Zyneth is only accompanying me. I am here to buy a service."

Gillow's smile is darkened by a slight frown, their eyebrows knotting in confusion. "I don't understand," they say, glancing between the two of us. "You bought it a speech box?"

I slap my hand on the counter, and Gillow and Zyneth both jump. Belatedly, I realize I should be more careful with my glass, but nothing broke at least. "*I* am a *he*, not an *it*," I say, before my cool moment can wear off. "*I* have a name: it is Kanin. Great to meet you. *I* am not a homunculus, despite present appearances. And *I* am here to purchase passage to Emrox. Now. Are you going to work with me, or not?"

Gillow blinks. They look me over more closely this time, their gaze lingering on my core. It takes all my willpower to not put a hand over it. Instead, I wait, perfectly still, as their maw splits into a shark-toothed grin.

"How fascinating," Gillow says. "Kanin, was it? Forgive my rudeness—it's not every day such an interesting specimen walks through my door. Yes, I think I would very much like to work with you." They hold out their hand, delicate seafoam frills stretching between each of their perfectly sharp claws. "I hope this is the beginning of a fruitful business endeavor."

I hesitantly take their hand. It's cold to the touch. "Likewise."

Behind me, Zyneth looks downright ill.

"Now," Gillow says, letting go to lace their fingers together. They lean forward eagerly, a greedy glint in their eyes. "You. Emrox. Tell me everything."

Chapter Seventeen

Victimless Heist

Gillow doesn't even blink at my proposal to go to Emrox—a venture, apparently, many have made, and few have returned from. They don't seem surprised when I suggest we use their sub. They don't even ask about my nature, though that hungry look in their eyes tells me they're dying to learn more. I'm not sure if it's politeness or a certainty that they'll eventually find out that keeps them so restrained. I hope it's the former.

"All well and good," they say. "A round trip to Emrox would pay for itself, given the null magic that can be harvested. Even so, I don't do anything for free. What do you have to offer me?"

I summon my Attuned void to my hand, and I can feel the predator tremble from where Zyneth is carrying the bottle in his pack. I quickly strengthen my mental hold on the creature and stamp out its resistance. Can't have it sapping any of my mana while I'm distracted. "Null arcana. Pure, unfiltered. I have seen how much null-arcana enhanced salt goes for in the city." I haven't, actually, but I have a good idea of how rare it is from my time in Harrowood. "This should cover the cost."

Gillow leans forward. "You're a void mage, too? This just gets more and more interesting." They reach out a hand, and I draw the void back. "Come now. You must expect me to sample the wares."

"It is a limited resource," I say. "You will receive payment when the mission is complete."

"Half up front," Gillow counters.

"All of it when we get there," I shoot back. "If the journey to Emrox is as perilous as they say, I will need this to help us survive the trip."

Gillow considers this. "There is more null arcana in the waters around Emrox. However, it can be difficult to extract. If we get there, could you pull more of it from the ocean?"

Uh. Great question. So far I haven't been able to control glass or void unless I had already Attuned it, and to Attune something, I need to be touching it. Which wouldn't make it impossible to do—I'd just have to be in the water.

Outside of the submarine.

Potentially surrounded by magical sea-serpents.

What could go wrong?

"Yes," I say, figuring if nothing else I can just bluff my way to Emrox. After all, if everything goes well, I won't be coming back.

Gillow leans back, arms folded. "Well, you make a tempting offer, my homunculus friend. I'm inclined to accept."

"But?" Zyneth says for the first time during the conversation. He's as stiff as a board, hands crossed in his lap—mere inches away from where his knives are sheathed. Does he really expect Gillow to attack us? Or does it just bring him comfort?

Gillow's eyes slide over to Zyneth. "*But*," they say, mouth twitching with a smile. "I'm afraid the *Prismatic* is out of commission. Even if I wanted to take you to Emrox, I couldn't. Not with a dead spell circuit."

"A what?" I ask.

"My, and I took you for a mage." Gillow chuckles.

In contrast, Zyneth seems oddly relieved. "A spell circuit is what supplies magic across a complex network of spell circles and enchanted items," Zyneth says. "Common in the fields of artificing and enchantment. It's the backbone behind an ecosystem of disparate magic; you might see them in a castle, or a floating isle…"

"Or a submarine," I finish. I look between Zyneth and Gillow. "That is it, then? We are dead in the water?"

Gillow cackles. "Dead in the water. I like that phrase. But no, we still have options."

Zyneth frowns. "Of course. It's always something with you."

Gillow raises an eyebrow. "My dear friend, you seem to be implying I could have foreseen any of our current circumstances. I assure you, never in my wildest dreams did I prepared for a sentient glass homunculus to waltz through my doors and ask to be taken to Emrox in a contraption several years out of use."

"What is it, then?" Zyneth snaps. "What do you want from us?"

Gillow looks at me. "So testy, that one. Always suspects ulterior motives. You should be asking yourself why he wants to accompany you on this trip when he stands to gain nothing and is so clearly uninterested in associating with me."

"Gillow," Zyneth growls.

Gillow waves the warning away. "At any rate, what I need is a way to get the sub back up and running, and for that I need to power the spell circuit. A charged arcanum crystal will do. I can either give you my dead one, if you can find a way to recharge it, or I can point you to the closest charged one I'm aware of."

Zyneth sits back, folding his arms. "And there it is."

"What?" I ask. I don't know the first thing about any arcanum crystals, but Gillow's proposal seems straightforward enough. We either charge the battery or buy a new one. "What is wrong?"

"They're acting like an arcanum crystal is a trivial thing to come by," Zyneth says. "These enchanted items are packed with extremely dense magical energies: in the hands of a mage, it would be like tapping directly into an arcana source without worrying about depleting their own mana. It could take months or even years to use it all up. Because of that, they are rare, and extremely expensive."

That's the first time Zyneth has referred to money as a limiting factor before. Noli and Rezira said he was rich: if this magical item is too much for him, then that's saying something.

"What about charging theirs instead?" I ask.

Zyneth snorts. "They aren't giving us an option: merely the illusion of one. The forging—or charging—of an arcana crystal takes the combined and coordinated spells of upwards of a hundred seasoned mages. That's even less likely than finding one to purchase."

"Who said anything about purchasing?" Gillow smiles.

"No," Zyneth says. "Absolutely not. I am putting my foot down here. We are not stealing anything from anyone."

"Is it really stealing if it should have been mine in the first place?" Gillow asks.

"Yes," Zyneth says, exasperated. "It absolutely is."

"That seems rather simplistic," Gillow says, "and you haven't even heard the full story yet. It's a victimless crime."

"I agree with Zyneth," I say. "I am not wild about stealing." Okay, yes, a little hypocritical given what I'd had to do to survive as a walking ink bottle, but to be fair my and Noli's lives were on the line. "Besides, it seems like you are getting more out of this bargain than us. We get to Emrox, but you get both the null arcana *and* this valuable crystal that you could either turn around and sell for extreme profit, or use to continue to mine arcana from Emrox. Not a fair trade."

Gillow grins, revealing all their pointed teeth. "Fair point, my crystalline friend. Then how about I sweeten the pot." They point to Zyneth. "If you successfully deliver this charged arcanum crystal to me, I will consider Zyneth's debt paid in full. He'll never have to do another job for me again."

Zyneth sits in stunned silence.

Gillow takes this as an invitation to continue. "A fully functional *Prismatic* will be more valuable than any of the trinkets you could bring in, anyway."

"Liar," Zyneth snarls, breaking through his surprise. "No. You'd never give up leverage by choice."

Gillow looks at him impassively. "Believe what you want, but I am a person of my word. As I said, having the *Prismatic* back in commission is worth more to me than your employment."

Zyneth scoffs at that last word, pushing his chair back and turning to me as he stands. "I told you this was a terrible idea. Let's not waste our time any longer. Come, Kanin, we'll find another solution elsewhere."

I don't stand up, though. Gillow ignores Zyneth, keeping their gaze on me. "Well?"

"Tell me more about who has the crystal," I say. "You said it is a victimless crime."

Gillow grins, lacing their fingers together and resting their chin on their hands. "The Athenaeum is run by a complex network of spells."

"Gods be good," Zyneth says. "You can't be serious?"

Gillow ignores him. "Yedzaquib owns not just one arcanum crystal, but many. Only one is in use to power the library at any given time, however there are several discharged crystals that are kept in reserve. These are gradually charged back up, and when one is fully powered, it is swapped with the crystal in use, so that there may always be a supply of crystals to cycle through and the Athenaeum never need close its doors. Yedzaquib would not be pleased to lose one, but he will also not suffer from the loss. He's the most powerful and wealthy merchant in the capital, after all. The wealth he brings in on a monthly basis could purchase new arcana crystals alone."

Stealing something from Yedzaquib sounds like a frankly terrible idea. That man gives me the willies. Though apart from being a creepy spider person, he didn't seem like a *bad* person. Stealing from him definitely wouldn't be right. At the same time, it certainly seems like he can afford to part with an expensive trinket or two without having to skip a meal. Taking the crystal won't put his livelihood or freedom at stake.

Meanwhile, Zyneth's is.

Man, he's not going to like this.

"Deal," I say. "If we get you this crystal, Zyneth never has to work for you again. And if you get me to Emrox, I will get you the null arcana."

"What?" Zyneth says. "No—you don't get to decide that for me. I will not be participating."

"You do not have to," I say. "The deal is just to retrieve the crystal for Gillow, which I am willing to attempt on my own. Is that right?"

Gillow's eyes dance between us in amusement. "Correct. I don't particularly care who is involved as long as I receive my goods."

"Then it is settled," I say. "Tell me more about the Athenaeum's crystals."

Zyneth sighs, running a hand down his face. First he glares at Gillow, then at me, then angrily pulls his chair out and sits back down.

"You do not have to do this with me," I say to Zyneth.

"No," Zyneth agrees, "But if I don't, you'll get yourself killed." He glares at Gillow. "Alright, then, let's get this over with. Tell us about the blasted library already."

CHAPTER EIGHTEEN

SUSPICIOUSLY COOPERATIVE

[Mana: 25/56]

[Predator Time Limit: 1.2 hours]

"Okay," I tell Zyneth when we get back to the inn. "This should be enough to Attune some of the void."

Evening sunlight is trickling in through the window of our room, casting a long shadow across the predator's bottle. Within, the predator is completely still: I've slipped up every now and then, and it managed to leech a few points of mana away from me each time, but for the most part I'm able to keep its mind suppressed.

"How long will it take?" Zyneth asks. He's still upset with me, I can tell, but all objections ceased when conversation turned back to the predator. Somehow, that only made me feel guilty.

Echo, how long will Attuning the predator take? I ask, repeating Zyneth's question.

[Instantaneous,] she says.

Why is that? It matches what I experienced before, when I carved out my original tiny sliver of Attuned void, but I still don't understand why. Attuning glass takes several hours.

[Attuning physical objects requires time to fully analyze and 'resonate' with the designated material,] Echo says. [Attuning arcana is instantaneous due to the inherent nature of magic. The quantity that can be Attuned for both raw arcana and physical objects are limited by mana consumption.]

That's fair I suppose. But this void isn't just arcana, it's some mix of arcana and... whatever creature the predator was that got mixed into it. *What happens to the predator when I Attune the void it's attached to?*

[Should the void that the predator has imprinted on be Attuned, an equivalent portion of the predator's mind will be returned Between.]

Gone, but not destroyed, then. Is it even possible to slay this beast?

"Kanin?" Zyneth prompts.

"Sorry," I say, pulled from my thoughts. "It should be instantaneous. So that is good. At least you will not have to worry about it trying to do something while I am unconscious."

"That is a relief," Zyneth agrees.

I sit down on the floor in front of the bottle, unclasping my core from around my neck.

If this Attunement goes smoothly, I'll be back to zero mana. After that it'll take another five hours to replenish my tanks—maybe more with the predator leeching off me—which will put us into tomorrow morning. I could do another Attunement then, which would again empty my tanks, and I still won't have finished Attuning it all. Altogether, it will take the next couple of days to gradually Attune it all away—assuming I can't starve it out before then. In the meantime, I can scope out the Athenaeum to see if the intel Gillow gave us is accurate. Once the predator is gone, I can regenerate my mana tanks without any more leeching, and then we can break in the following night.

Easy as pie.

But first, I need to deal with the predator.

"You are being suspiciously cooperative," I say to Zyneth as I open the pouch and roll my core into my hands. I quickly turn off my secondary vision before the double sight becomes overwhelming. "I thought for sure the second we left Gillow's shop you would tell me what a terrible plan this was."

"It *is* a terrible plan," Zyneth says. "I just know that saying as much won't actually change your mind. I don't suppose you spared a moment to consider why we, specifically, are the ones being asked to perform this job?"

I tip my head. "Because they did not have anyone else to help?"

"Because they couldn't get anyone else to *agree,*" Zyneth says. "We're the only ones desperate enough—or naive enough—to say yes. In fact, the only reason I'm still going along with this whole production is that I am counting on you to see how hopeless the endeavor is once we revisit the library tomorrow."

In my free hand I pick up the bottle, using my Attuned glass to screw off the cork. *Echo, get ready to target the void for Attunement.* I hate that I have to be touching the void for it to work, but at least it will be over quick.

[Target selected,] she says.

"Do you not want to be rid of Gillow's influence?" I ask.

Zyneth's face softens. "Of course I do. Not more than anything, but... more than quite a bit."

That's enough for me. "Then trust me on this. Besides, I have a plan that might not involve stealing from anyone."

Zyneth raises a skeptical brow. "And what plan is that?"

"The library considered my knowledge of Echo very rare," I say. "And when I was looking for information on the predator, even on the top-most floor, I could not find anything. Which means I have information Yedzaquib might want. So why not talk to him? Maybe he will trade the arcana crystal for my information."

Zyneth blinks. "That's a surprisingly good idea."

"Hey," I object. "Why is that surprising? I can have good ideas!"

Zyneth smiles apologetically. "I do like the plan. However, I fear the stipulations of my debt will get in the way. According to the contract, Yedzaquib can't learn anything about Gillow or their involvement, else my debt will incur interest. And knowing Gillow, that means it will more than counteract your deal to pay off my debt in full."

"I do not have to tell Yedzaquib what I need the arcana crystal for," I say.

"A person who covets knowledge as much as him, and you think he will not ask?" Zyneth counters. "You could try to lie or talk around the point, but that's not a game I would play with the curator. It is a clever idea to use Yedzaquib thirst of knowledge against Gillow's intentions, but... it's an outcome, I'm sure, Gillow already has contingencies for."

"Oh," I say, disappointed. "I am sorry. I did not think of that."

"That's alright," he says. "It is at least reassuring to know you are thinking these plans through a little more than you let on."

"I think I should be offended by that."

He chuckles.

"Then it sounds like it is back to the original plan," I reluctantly admit. "Investigate the library. It cannot hurt to investigate the leads Gillow gave us while my access lasts, at least. And in the meantime, maybe I can still find a different solution to dealing with the predator somewhere in the stacks," I add as a peace offering.

"Maybe," Zyneth half-heartedly agrees. His faint smile fades into a thoughtful frown as his attention shifts back to the predator in the bottle.

Right. The library, Yedzaquib, and Gillow are all issues for tomorrow. Right now, we have the predator to deal with.

"Here I go," I warn Zyneth. Holding my core up to the end of the bottle, I mentally coax the predator out, trying not to recoil in revulsion as it spills over my glass like tar.

I activate the Attunement.

Defiance rushes in a sudden surge from the predator—a metaphorical kick to my gut.

[Mana extinguished,] Echo says. [No mana available for Attunement.]

"What?" I cry.

I Check my mana: sure enough, it's 0/56.

"What is it?" Zyneth asks, stepping forward. "Are you alright?"

"*Expletive, expletive, expletive!*" I angrily shove the predator back into the bottle and slam the cork back on. "Fuck!" I sign, about ready to smash my translator. Composing myself, I switch back to speech. "It just absorbed all my mana. I cannot Attune it."

Time Limit? I ask.

[Predator Time Limit: 7 hours.]

Double fuck! "And now it has a better grip on reality. It will be even harder to starve it out."

"Blast," Zyneth says, sitting on the bed across from me as I simmer in my anger.

The predator had managed to slip my grasp at the last second, and it's still hovering outside of my reach now. Instead of the smugness I had expected, though, it feels more nervous and flighty.

"Do you think you can try again later?" he asks.

"I am not sure," I admit. "I thought I had a good grasp on it. I might have been focusing too much on controlling it physically, and let some of my mental hold lax."

"Well, what now?" Zyneth asks.

I sit, thinking. "Lend me some of your magic. We can give it another shot." Honestly, I should have thought of this approach hours ago.

"Can you control it this time?" Zyneth asks, getting up to sit across from me.

"One way to find out."

I redouble my mental hold on the predator, focusing on keeping it completely subdued, entirely compliant. I snuff out every hint of defiance I catch. I focus every atom of my being on maintaining my control. After a minute, I nod to Zyneth. "Okay. Go."

He holds a hand over my vial, his palm filling with yellow light.

[Mana replenished,] Echo reports. [7/56.] It continues to tick upward.

Once more, I use my glass to unstop the lid and mentally guide the void out. Then—

[Mana depleted.]

[Predator Time Limit: 10.5 hours.]

Shit!

"Stop," I angrily tell Zyneth as I force the predator back in the bottle. "It did not work. You would just be feeding it more."

His light goes out. "No luck then?"

I shake my head. "I do not know why. Maybe it is too much to think about at once. Agh, I hate this!" I slam the bottle back down, then wince. Maybe I should be a little more careful to not break the predator's prison. I clench my hands, then force myself to relax. It's not the end of the world. Even if I can't Attune it, there's still Emrox. "At least it can still be contained in this bottle," I say with a sigh.

"But starving it or Attuning it might be harder than we thought. If I relax for even the briefest moment, any amount of saved mana can be undone."

Zyneth frowns. "You realize, if you intend to fulfill Gillow's request..."

"I know," I say shortly. Attempting to steal the arcana crystal would be laughable if I can't use any magic while I'm at it. Which, I'm sure, Zyneth would just love.

But this is a death trap for me.

Before, the predator had fallen back Between quickly because there had been so much of it and only a tiny trickle of mana to sustain it. Now, it's the opposite: I have more mana than before, and the predator is much smaller, so my magic is going a lot further toward keeping it rooted in reality. Does that mean that the more it stays here, the more it feeds on my magic, the stronger it's going to get?

I can't just sit around and let it gradually overwhelm me.

Echo, is there any way I can more actively keep tabs on the predator's power? I ask. *Like, how much autonomy it has.*

[Conceivably,] Echo says. [Depending on the desired use case, the Influence of the predator's mind relative to the user's can be quantified.]

Uh, yeah, I think that sounds good, I say. *What does that look like?*

[Predator Influence: 5%]

Okay. Good. I have some metric I can keep an eye on now. And, honestly, this is a little reassuring. 5% is not bad. That means I'm ninety-five times more powerful than it—or, er, however percentages work. At any rate, it explains why it's so easy to squash its impulses, even if I can't, apparently, keep them squashed 100% of the time.

Then again, the numbers had probably been reversed back in Peakshadow, and it had really not felt great to be on the receiving end of the squashing.

"Our plans stay the same," I tell Zyneth. "Tomorrow we still scope out the library—I do not need magic for that. I will figure out what to do about the predator in the meantime. But we cannot spin our wheels now." With the predator's return looming, we don't have time.

Zyneth sighs. "I thought you might say that. Alright then. We'll move forward with this absurd plan of yours. But while you're off playing into Gillow's hands, I still intend to look for other solutions."

"That is fine by me," I say. I still have that interdimensional spell circle, after all. If I can complete the diagram, maybe we won't even have to go to Emrox. But until that avenue opens, I have to pursue the only lead I have; and with the threat of the predator growing larger by the hour, I don't have much time to waste.

We don't talk about Gillow or the predator the rest of the evening, dancing around the subjects as Zyneth retrieves dinner and begins winding down for the night. When he retreats to his bed, I settle into the chair at the desk on the other side of the room. I set all my belongings out on the table: my signing glass, the spell books, the slate with my partially-drawn circle from the library, some chalk, and of course, my monster in a bottle. Since I can't use my Glow spell without any mana, I instead light a small candle and try to keep it tucked out of the way so as not to disturb Zyneth. Finally, I take off my ragged cloak as well, draping it over the back of the chair, and set my translator aside. I certainly won't be needing that in the middle of the night, and in fact for what I have planned it might be a bit of a liability; can't have it accidentally say something aloud from a conversation I intend to keep private.

I wait for Zyneth to head to bed as I idly play with my signing glass and stare at the incomplete spell circle, trying to figure out what shapes must fill in the gaps. It isn't until I hear Zyneth's breathing grow long and heavy that I give him a Check.

[Status: Asleep,] Echo says.

I check my mana next.

[Mana: 1/56]

About what I expected. Despite the fact it's been over a half an hour since I finished attempting the Attunement, my mana has only recovered one of the six points it should have. Meaning a certain parasite is quietly taking more than its fair due.

I grab the bottle with a soft *tink* of glass on glass, and I feel the predator's mind stir at the movement, warily watching to see what I do next.

I think it's past time you and I had a little talk, I say.

CHAPTER NINETEEN

HEART TO... VOID

Call it a heart to heart, I say, projecting my thoughts toward the predator. It can probably hear me regardless, but I want to make sure it can't ignore me. This conversation is not optional. *Or, uh, heart to void. Whatever slimy organ you have in place of a moral compass.*

Anger wafts from the predator as it attempts to retreat, but I grab the bond that ties our minds together, and reel it in like a rope. The predator thrashes, and I have to fight every one of my own instincts to not let it go; to not put distance between us. Neither of us are particularly thrilled with this arrangement.

I don't know if you can understand my words, I say, *but I do know you can understand my intent. So let's lay down some ground rules, shall we?*

The predator roils futilely in my grasp, emanating waves of hate. It yearns for when our roles were reversed. It wishes to crush me. To kill—

But you don't really want me dead, do you? I ask. *Obedient maybe, but not dead. Because I'm your only foothold in reality, right? If I die, there's nothing keeping you here.*

The predator is not pleased by this. Frustration spills away from it, along with resentment, resignation, and... acknowledgement.

Good, I say. That's a start. *You don't want to kill me. At least that's one thing we can agree on. Now, I don't know how much you've been paying attention, but Zyneth and I have a bit of an operation planned for the next coming days. It's going to be dangerous. I'm going to need my mana.*

The predator has stopped fighting me, perhaps resigned that it doesn't have any choice but to listen. It doesn't react to what I say; it doesn't understand.

Alright, let me put it like this, I say. *You're mooching off my magic. But if you do that while I'm in trouble, if I don't have my magic when I need it, I might be fucked. And that means you're fucked. Capeesh?*

That, at least, seems to get through. Understanding thrums between our minds—though not without a good amount of displeasure and spite. But something else follows this: reluctance. Disagreement. Noncompliance.

At first, I think it's telling me to go fuck myself, but its message deepens into something more complex.

It can't stop the magic drain, I finally understand. It needs it to survive; to remain in reality.

Right. I understand all that, but—

To release its hold on my magic would be no different than for me to die: both would result in it being forced back into the Between. It will not relinquish my magic. It will not stop feeding itself.

Well that puts us in a bit of a pickle, doesn't it? I try to switch tactics. *I didn't want to play hardball, but it looks like you're not leaving me with any choice. If you don't cooperate, I'm going to starve you back Between.*

At that, the predator is amused—not exactly the reaction I was going for.

Hardly a threat. It will continue to pull my magic away, bit by bit. And Attuning it isn't a danger either. It can just take everything from me at the last second, like it did before. I might be strong, but my control isn't complete, and it is far more cunning.

Excuse me while I roll my non-existent eyes. It's right, though: I should have known better than to try to bluff with our minds connected like this. I can't starve it, I can't Attune it, and every time I try, it's just digging itself deeper in reality.

With a mental sigh, I let go of the predator's mind, allowing it to dart as far away as our mental bond allows. I set the bottle down, frustrated with myself. That was stupid. I don't know why I thought it could be reasoned with. It doesn't see logic or compromise: it only cares about its next meal.

Trying to put the predator out of mind, I instead pull my slate over to revisit the drawing of the Emrox spell circle. There's still so many gaps in my quick sketch. Maybe if I'm able to look up some of the few runes I can make out in my *Vessel Construction* book, I'll find some answers on how to complete the Emrox circle. Or maybe I can find more books that can help me tomorrow in the Athenaeum—I guess I'll have to do that before I rob the place and piss off the librarian.

I spend a couple hours sifting through the text books, but apart from being able to identify a couple basic runes used for stability in spatial magic, the endeavor is a waste of time.

I stare at my slate, willing the answer to come to me. Am I even on the right track here? What if this whole Emrox thing is just a wild goose chase?

The circle flickers. For a moment—the briefest moment—lines draw themselves over the slate, completing the diagram, and I can see the whole picture. I recognize the pattern. I've seen it before.

I start, the image vanishing as fast as it came. What was that? A hallucination? I most certainly *haven't* seen that circle before. What was I thinking?

Foreign thoughts tickle my mind: The predator has. It has seen it.

The predator was so quiet, I hadn't even noticed it creeping to the forefront of my mind, watching over my shoulder as I worked.

What do you mean? I ask sharply. *You've seen this spell before? Where?*

The predator tries to retreat as soon as I've noticed it eavesdropping, but I grab its mind and hold it still. After a moment of thrashing against my grip, it gives up, exuding resignation and uncertainty.

Where? I ask again.

It isn't sure. But it has seen it. It knows this pattern.

Show me, I say, hoping to recapture that mental image I'd caught just moments ago.

The predator refuses. It can't fight me, it can't slink away sulking, as it so clearly desires, but I also can't force it to resurface that memory. As soon as I try to enforce my will onto it, I feel its sense of identity evaporating.

But there's something there. Something I just have to find a way to dig out.

Quietly, I pick up the bottled void and remove the cork. I tip the bottle toward the slate, allowing a spoonful of the liquid to pour out. The predator watches this with deep suspicion.

Show me, I say again, this time loosening my grip on its mind, handing over the tinniest fraction of autonomy to the void now pooled on the table.

The predator gleefully leaps at the opportunity to control some of its void again—and immediately tries to dart away. I had expected this, though, so I stop it in its tracks, yanking the void back over to the table and splatting it back down onto the slate.

Nice try, I say. *Let's do this again.*

The predator glowers at me indignantly, but clutches its control of the void like a starved dog with a bone. It would be funny if it didn't also scare me. We stare at each other for several long seconds, each waiting for the other to crack. Finally, the predator gives in.

I can tell it's only complying because it's waiting for me to slip up, waiting for an opportunity to dart away and take a stab at Zyneth's soul in the corner of the room. I won't let that happen, though. If I'm certain of anything, it's that I won't let it hurt Zyneth.

Reluctantly at first, then moving fast and with more certainty, the void swirls in intricate shapes and patterns over the page. Gradually the gaps are all filled in, the circle is stitched back together, until finally, the shadows stop. And somehow, I know—this is it. This is right.

Echo, Check, I say.

[Check,] Echo dutifully replies. [A spell circle for planar linkage.]

No way. This is it! Can I do it here? Now? *How does it work?* I ask.

[Planar Linkage: a spell which joins two designated points in space-time.]

An excited thrill runs through me. *What are the spell requirements?*

[Unknown,] Echo says. [The spell has not been learned by the user.]

Dammit. That's right. I learn spells by doing them, or studying them through text books, thanks to my Arcane Intuition. Seems like just looking at the completed spell circle isn't enough.

But could I activate it anyway, replicating the spell circle and pouring enough mana in, even without knowing exactly how it works?

No. I can't risk that. I can't pull a Trenevalt. Even changing the size of a spell circle without altering other parameters—the angles of the lines, certain runes—can result in completely unpredictable effects. If I want to use the Planar Linkage spell, I'll need to go right to the source.

In Emrox.

The predator feels I'm distracted. It springs toward Zyneth with sadistic glee—and I mentally pluck it from the air, stuffing the void back into its bottle. The predator seethes with irritation, but my mind is elsewhere, racing, trying to piece all of this together. There *is* a way home. No more pipe dreams: a surefire way to get to Earth—which means I have a way to dispose of the predator. A way to find my body. But to do that, I'll have to go to Emrox and activate the circle there.

Without even knowing how much mana that might take until I get there. What if it's more than I have?

The predator could harvest enough void. Absorbing mana is what it does best. It would be trivial.

It still takes me a moment to even recognize these foreign ideas as thoughts coming from the predator's mind. *You're offering to help me?* I ask, skeptical.

Disgust. Denial. It *could* control such magic. Not that it would help me.

I snort. *Sure, whatever.* Clearly it has some ulterior motives with putting that suggestion out there, but how would it benefit from helping me make the portal I needed to get home? It must know I'm planning to dissolve it in a magicless Earth at worst, or leave it trapped Between at best. I reach for the predator's mind, hoping I can catch a glimpse of its true intentions, but it darts away like a fish, sulking. Maybe it's just jumping at any excuse to get ahold of more mana.

I tap my finger on the slate, looking at the incomplete spell circle still drawn there, thinking.

Alright, I finally say to the predator. *You want my mana? Let's make a deal.*

Ugh, even thinking the word *deal* with respect to the predator makes me feel slimy. But if we can't figure some way past our stalemate, I'm stuck.

I won't try to Attune you, I say, and I can feel the predator's surprise and then immediate suspicion at this suggestion. *I won't try to starve you out, either. In exchange, you help me with that spell circle. Once we get to Emrox, I'll need you to fill in the blanks for any portions of the circle that are damaged. And I'll also need you to harness enough mana from the surrounding waters to activate the spell.*

The predator chews on this, highly tempted, but wondering what the catch is.

No catch, I say. *But I'm not done yet. I won't suppress your mind to try to stop you from taking my mana, but only on the condition you stop taking all of it. I know you need some to stay out of the Between, but can you at least take... less? Enough to keep you here, but not so much that it uses up everything I've got?*

The predator considers this. It sees the reason in my offer, but it's still reluctant. It's hungry. It goes against its nature to leave food behind. But most of all, even though it knows it needs me, it really, really doesn't like me.

Look, I'm just trying to stand a fighting chance, I sigh. *You don't want to end up Between. I don't want to die. I'm not asking for much—I'm just asking that you don't be so greedy.*

Now that *does* stir amusement from the predator. It *is* greed. The mere concept of rationing its meals fills it with disgust. To ask it to be less greedy is to ask it to not be itself.

But... it might be able to survive off less of my magic. At least for a day or two.

Thank god. Freeing up a bit of my mental headspace from having to suppress the predator at every waking moment will be a relief. *Glad that's—*

However, the predator's thoughts chase me, it will be watching. It doesn't trust me. It knows I hate it, and it won't let me send it back Between.

I snort. *You'll be watching me? Right back at you.*

And with that I flick the predator's mind away. I can't completely cut off our connection, but there's something satisfying in sending the predator reeling.

Given everything else I'm juggling, I'll take my wins where I can get them.

CHAPTER TWENTY

COMPROMISING SITUATIONS

The predator is suspiciously quiet the rest of the night. By the time Zyneth wakes, I'm up to 30 mana—not quite as high as it should be without the predator's interference, but better than before. I make the quick decision not to tell Zyneth about the little armistice the predator and I worked out—especially when I was supposed to be figuring out a way to get rid of it. He'd probably be even more bothered to learn I need its cooperation to get the Emrox plan to work. I might have to wait until he's in an exceptionally good mood to break that news to him.

Rolling out of bed, Zyneth combs a hand through his hair as he stifles a yawn, somehow managing to make the act look graceful and alluring. Is that a cambion thing? Are they just naturally sexy, or is this something Zyneth has practiced to perfection? I don't really have a lot to compare against. I mean, Attiru was good looking in their own way, but Zyneth seems to have embraced "devilishly good looks" quite literally.

Zyneth glances my way, and I jump, having been caught staring.

"Morning," he says, rubbing the sleep from his eyes. "I'm not used to not being the first one up."

At least he can't tell I was staring. Saved from social embarrassment by my shitty anatomy.

"For what it is worth, I am not used to being the first one up," I reply. "Although back before all this, my schedule could get pretty haphazard."

"Oh?" Zyneth begins readying himself for the day, organizing his bag and making his bed. Who does that? Who makes their bed? "You know, you never said—what was your profession back on your world?"

"I am an actor," I say.

"An actor?" Zyneth chuckles. "You performed in plays?"

"Gods no," I say. "I have not done theater since I was in school. The kind of actor I am... it is a bit different on our world. I am not sure how to explain it, really." But I guess the difference between TV shows and theater would be lost on Zyneth; it's all playing a part to entertain the masses, when you get right down to it.

"I never would have guessed that profession for you," Zyneth says. He begins to change his shirt, and it takes me a few seconds to realize I should probably give him some privacy. Unable to really look away, I shut my vision off. "And yet, that does seem very you."

"What does that mean?" I demand.

There's a smile in his voice. "Well I wouldn't say you're *dramatic*, but..."

"*But*? That means you would say that!"

"And then there's the ego thing."

"Ego!" I cry.

He laughs. "Well, maybe it's not ego precisely, but... You know. The way you act as though you're made of steel instead of glass. How you keep throwing yourself into compromising situations. How you make unilateral decisions for others as though the world revolves around you."

I bite back a retort—that last one stings a little. "You are talking about the deal I made with Gillow."

Zyneth sighs. "I just wish we could have had the chance to talk it over together first."

"I am sorry," I say, and I mean it. "You are right. I did not mean to take that choice away from you."

"What's done is done," Zyneth says with a sigh. "But there's no way Gillow intends to make good on the deal to wipe out my debt, you realize."

I make an affronted sign. "Of course I realize that. But the less Gillow suspects I am onto them, the better. You know, I may not be cunning, but that does not make me stupid."

Zyneth chuckles. "Well your acting certainly had me fooled."

"Wow, ouch."

Zyneth does laugh then. "Kanin?"

"Yes?"

"Why are you still sitting there?"

"Oh." The world flickers back into existence as my sight resumes. Zyneth is standing before me, his items packed, ready to leave. "Sorry. I turned my vision off when you were changing."

He arches an amused eyebrow. "What a gentleman."

"Do not get used to it."

He offers me a hand up, and I take it. I gather up my belongings as well, floating most of them, including the predator, to my satchel. I slip on my boots, then Zyneth helps me put my cloak back on, for whatever little good it does to act as clothes. I stand there awkwardly as he makes adjustments around my arms.

"I could go for an upgraded cloak," I tell Zyneth while he's at it. "This one is a little singed now."

"What's this, you expect me to buy everything for you?" Zyneth teases. "In that case I'd strongly suggest a pair of trousers first—although I suppose it wouldn't really be covering anything, would it?"

I respond with a sign my translator won't interpret for me, and Zyneth laughs.

The Athenaeum is just as packed today as it had been the days before. I would say that helps us keep a low profile, but my appearance doesn't exactly lend itself to blending in.

"I don't see how this can go well," Zyneth says for about the tenth time in as many minutes.

"Have you found it yet?" I ask, ignoring his pessimism.

"No." We're circling around the ground floor, passing under where the slope of the library begins to spiral above us. According to Gillow, there's a hidden entrance into the underbelly of the library around this point.

Zyneth frowns. "But I don't think my spells are the right type of magic for this kind of operation. I have one that is designed to identify what type of magic powers a spell, but that doesn't tell me any other information about it, or pinpoint its source. All I am getting is a lot of enchantment magic, which is unsurprising. It would need such reinforcements just to support all the stonework."

Gillow had seemed certain Zyneth would be able to find the entrance, though if that was because of his magic or his general sneakiness, I'm not sure. Either way, it seems they were mistaken.

Or Zyneth purposely isn't giving it his all.

Echo, can you check the spells along this wall? I ask. *What can you identify?*

[Check: The Library of Miasmere is generally considered an architectural wonder which rivals the ingenuity of the Ruins. Over three hundred distinct spells are integrated into its spell circuit, most of which are dedicated to sustaining the structural integrity of the building and the organization of its contents.]

Okay, well, thanks for the history lesson but that's not what I'm asking, I say. Maybe I can use my recently obtained Inspect spell. I try activating it as a skill, first.

[No target selected,] Echo says. [Caster must be in contact with desired spell in order to glean information about its nature.]

Geez, I guess I can't use this to go poking very many spells unless I know they're benign first. At least here on the first floor of the library I shouldn't have anything to worry about. I wander over to the wall, Zyneth trailing after me, and I touch a hand to the stone.

Lights appear on the wall like circuits in a computer. Shit—I nervously glance around, but no one reacts. I'm the only one who can see it, then. I focus on one zig-zagging line of yellow light.

[Structural spell: Enhances the integrity of the wall.]

I move my hand along the wall, and other spells jump into clarity. Spells for strength, stability, fire proofness. I stroll along the wall as I casually scan through the spells I walk past.

[Water summoning enchantment: Releases a volume of water if fire is detected within range,] Echo continues. [Illusion spell: Conceals the irregularities in the surface of the wall. Anchorage spell: Locks two surfaces together unless while in the presence of a complementary release talisman.]

That sounds promising. And sure enough, even as I pass by, despite the wall appearing to be made of seamless white stone, my fingers bump over something that might be the edge of a door.

"I think it is here," I tell Zyneth. I take my hand away and keep walking, not wanting to draw attention.

"What?" Zyneth says, skeptically glancing between me and the wall. "Are you serious? That easily? How did you do that?"

I puff myself up. "A wizard never tells his secrets."

Zyneth looks entirely unimpressed.

Psh, fine. I deflate a little. "But it looks like we need something to get through. A talisman?" Sounds like the magical equivalent of a key card.

Zyneth frowns. "That would make sense. Only those allowed access will be able to enter. We'll have to pinch the key off someone, if we know what to look for."

"Can it be disabled another way?" I ask.

"Those sorts of spells are difficult to break," Zyneth says. "And given the resources of Yedzaquib, I doubt either of us could manage it. It could likely be opened from the inside without a talisman—such spells are generally designed to keep people out rather than in—but that's somewhat of a nonstarter. For now, I suggest we wait, watch, and attempt to find who has access so we can steal it off them."

Sounds boring as hell, but it's probably the safest and smartest play—how very *Zyneth*. I guess there's no harm in it. Zyneth decides to go scouting for a bit while I remain nearby, so I can watch anyone who approaches the hidden door on the wall. I settle in at a table near a fountain and idly wait as the animated nereid statues continue their never-ending scooping and pouring of water.

No one uses the hidden door that first day. I swap shifts with Zyneth out of sheer boredom when he wanders back from whatever investigating he's doing, whereupon I search for other entrances. In fact, I discover another four hidden doors, scattered throughout the library, though that bodes even worse for our plan to watch and wait, given there's only two of us. That day, we leave empty-handed.

The next day passes just as unsuccessful as the first. I spend my time away from door-watch duty idly searching the stacks for a different approach to find a way to Earth or get rid of the predator, but I don't make any headway into either of these endeavors. Focusing on reading is hard when you're stressed to the tits and trying to keep a ravenous murder void on a short leash.

"You're right about the predator," Zyneth says as we reconvene at a table near the nereid water feature, a morbid reminder of our jobs for Gillow. "I haven't been able to find any information about it in the stacks, either. I would have assumed I don't have access to a high enough level if you hadn't confirmed there was no more information about it above. Quite peculiar. If information on it doesn't exist here, I doubt we would be able to find insight anywhere else."

"I guess I am just special like that," I say. I raise a hand to rub my head, but when glass clinks against glass, I lower it once more.

"Maybe," Zyneth says with a tone that indicates he certainly does not think I am that special. "Or perhaps that information is being kept elsewhere. Not all information can be displayed publicly. Miasmere wouldn't permit forbidden arcana to be accessed here, no matter Yedzaquib's power within the Scholars Guild."

"You think the predator is some kind of forbidden magic?" I ask.

Zyneth shakes his head helplessly. "If it is, it will be difficult for us to know for sure."

After lunch Zyneth heads back into the library as I return to door-watching duty, but it gets old fast. No one particularly seems interested in that patch of wall, which really shouldn't be surprising: we have no idea how often it's even used. What if it's something Yedzaquib only utilizes when the arcana crystal needs to be swapped or recharged? What if he's the only one with access, anyway? We could be waiting here for weeks! Weeks I'm not sure I can afford to waste with the predator lurking in the back of my mind. I stir a finger through the surface of the fountain as I think. There's got to be a better approach.

Stone fish float along lazy tracks in the air as they circuit through the fountain's arcs of water. Even the water rises in unnatural twists and loop-the-loops. I rest a hand on the lip of the basin and Inspect it out of curiosity. Threads of blue magic jump to life, outlining the paths the water and moving statues are supposed to take as they continue to loop through their never-ending program. The magic circuit drops into the surrounding basin, fading out of sight as it leads deeper underground.

Can I trace those water spells further? I ask Echo. If the arcana crystal is really what's powering this place, then every spell in this building should lead back to it, right? *Where does it lead?*

[Negative, your skill range is limited to the local proximity,] Echo says. [However, activating the skill as a spell would increase the range. Spell cost: 1 mana for every ten feet maintained for every 5 seconds.]

I weigh my options. I'm up to 50 mana now—the only reason I'm not fully topped off at 56 is due to the predator gradually eating away at my reserves. *Alright,* I say. *Just fifty feet for now.*

[Activated.]

The library floor comes alive with magical circuits. The blue lines of the water magic extend further down, but they also branch off in every direction along the floor, then rise up into the walls. I hone in on these spell paths as Echo feeds me more information.

[Linked to the central fountain, this system of spells is designed to deliver water throughout the walls of the Athenaeum for purposes of responding to and extinguishing any fires that may originate within the building.]

The beginnings of an idea are tickling my mind. *What can you tell me about the size of this plumbing network?* I ask. *How big are the pipes?*

[Based on the parameters of the spells, the volume of water varies throughout the circuit, from one inch at its most narrow, to two feet at its largest width.]

I can tell which ones are the wide paths by following the denser concentrations of magic. One goes down, only twenty or thirty feet, before it stops. There's a room down there I think, and all the magic circuits seem to be leading back to it. That must be where the currently active arcana crystal is; hopefully, the dormant ones aren't far away. I end the spell before it can consume too much of my mana.

As discreetly as I can, I move my signing shards from beneath my cloak into the water of the nearby fountain. The pull of the current tugs on my glass, but I can overcome the force without much trouble. I practice maneuvering the cluster of glass around the basin for a minute. It's awkward, but not difficult. I call the signing glass back as I glance around for Zyneth. He can keep snooping—or try to find another way to Emrox—but in the meantime, I have a plan, and I'm itching to get a move on.

Heh. Zyneth is going to hate this.

Chapter Twenty-One

KNOCK-OFF TOY SUBMARINE

Zyneth sits across the table from me, grimacing. I use my cloak to conceal my movements as I unstring my core from my neck and slip it out of the pouch. I set myself down on the table and unfold my legs from around my core, wobblily climbing to my feet. It's only been a little over a week since I last moved around in this form, but it already feels strange to be leaving my human-shaped body behind.

"You are being very quiet," I say as I situate myself. I experiment with releasing my control over my glass body, carefully letting it slump into its seat as I ensure it doesn't fall over.

"What, do you want me to keep telling you how terrible this idea is?" Zyneth says. "Because I can do that. I am happy to list all the ways this will go wrong."

"I was more hoping for optimism and encouragement." Cautiously, I let go of the last of the glass on my main body. I'll be moving out of its range soon enough anyway, and I'd rather it not collapse to the floor and shatter when that happens. Luckily, it just sits there, inert, head resting on the table, without falling over. Yeah, totally not suspicious.

"Optimism?" Zyneth repeats. "I am optimistic we will get caught. I encourage you to consider other options."

"Unless you have any new plans or discoveries to share, this is the only move I can think up," I say. I recall the Attuned void from my body next. Who knows, might come in handy. The blobby black follows my extra signing glass around like a storm cloud.

Zyneth's frown pinches into concern, and he holds out a hand. "Just please be careful. I can't help you from this side."

I tap his finger with one of my legs. "I will only be poking around. I should be back soon."

He sighs. "I hope you know what you're doing."

That makes two of us.

Turning away from Zyneth, I walk over to the edge of the table, where the surface rests against the edge of the fountain. Down here from this vantage point, the gentle current looks a whole lot swifter. But now's not the time to chicken out, and hesitating will just add fuel to Zyneth's anxiety fire.

Without the ability to take—or hold—a breath, I jump in.

For a moment, I float at the top of the fountain, bobbing along like a bubble. But as water splashes over me, I'm met with the distinctly unpleasant sensation of water seeping in through the crack in my glass. I squirm as the water drips into my vial, cold discomfort tickling me from the inside. My vision warps, split between air and water, and slowly but surely, I slip beneath the surface.

Air bubbles out of the crack as I gently sink toward the bottom and focus very hard on not having a panic attack. It's fine. I don't need to breathe, so I can't drown. I'm sinking gradually and not about to crash to the floor. I'm not *actually* in mortal peril.

But try rationalizing all that when you're watching the surface grow farther and farther overhead.

Instead, I try to focus on protecting my core. I gather all my signing glass around me like spines of a pufferfish as I slowly tumble toward the bottom of the basin. When my glass finally brushes against the stone on the bottom, I'm met with a delightful muted scratch of glass against stone.

I use my void to help cushion the contact and stop my aimless drift. After another minute, the bubbles finally stop, and the uncomfortable sensation of filling with water is replaced by a marginally better feeling of sluggishness. Okay. Time to figure out where I'm going.

Reactivating my Inspect as a Skill, I don't have to look far. There's a sinister dark hole at the base of the fountain where the water is moving—though strangely it seems to be coming *and* going through that pipe. Magic, man.

Now to figure out how to get over there. Between my signing glass and void, I have enough control to tow my core around like some kind of knock-off toy submarine. Each nudge of the current sends me floating off track, but I'm able to bob my way in the right direction eventually. Soon, I'm sitting on the lip of the pipe, the opening yawning and shadowed beneath me.

With all my glass electrified by my nerves, I force myself to roll forward. The darkness swallows me as I'm sinking once more.

My vision vanishes. I lose all sense of up and down. The predator's mind brushes against my own, curiosity leaking through our bond—it wonders what I am doing—but I slam it away in a panic. At that simple touch, coupled with the dark, the disorientation, fear crashes through me from nowhere. It feels just like being engulfed by the void.

Drowning in its mind. Claustrophobia tightens around me, and I lash out in a panic. I can't fight. I can't escape. No, no—

I struggle to wrangle control over myself. It's just a memory. It's not real. The predator is here, but it's cowering away from my overflow of emotions. Nothing is controlling me. I can't freak out. Not here. Stop freaking out.

Slowly, the pins and needles retract from my mind. The tension of dread eases.

Shit. What was all that? I can't let it happen again, not when I'm somewhere dangerous like this.

Keep it together, Kanin.

In the confusion, I lost track of where I was going. I try to sense which way I'm falling, but with the mix of currents, drafting both up and down, I'm not even really sure anymore. I focus on my glass instead. Where's my body? Ah, there. Like stars in a night sky, I find pinpricks of familiarity that I use to orient myself. It's strangely com-forting, and the knowledge helps ground me. The last few knots of anxiety relax from my mind as I regain my sense of self. Okay. Back to business.

My glass body isn't out of range yet, but it will be soon. I press my void and signing glass against the walls of the tunnel, slowly tracing my way down as I follow the thickest bands of magic. My path turns off to a side, and I follow, shifting my glass around to push against gravity once more and keep from scraping against the bottom of the pipe. I still can't see a damn thing, so I focus on my sense of touch instead.

I feel the predator's presence in my mind again. I tense, ready to repel an attack, but I can feel it knows as well as I do that it would lose. It's not here to pick a fight. It's... agitated.

Now is really not the time, I say, pushing it away. Irritation pulses from the predator, along with nervousness. It doesn't like something, and it's getting antsy.

Danger. Something is dangerous.

Was it worried I was going to die down here? I would be touched if it weren't because it only sees me as a glorified life raft.

But no, it's something else. A discomfort—something I'm starting to feel, too.

I try to ignore the sensation and focus on navigating the pipes. Looks like I need to take the next turn, then go down another floor, and then I should be close to the source of all this magic. But as I grow farther and farther from where I started, the glass in my body eventually passes out of my range, and the feeling of unease only grows. It's like there's a tension in my soul. A spring that's getting pulled steadily apart. The predator paces the back of my mind, restless and prickly. It doesn't like this, and to be frank, I don't either. Is it because I left all that glass behind? I've never been separated from so much Attuned glass before, but I have lost bits and pieces here and there and never felt anything like this. Well, it's too late to turn back now. I'll just have to power through and—

It can't wait any longer. It has to do something.

Hey, wait! I say, alarmed by the sudden clarity of the predator's thoughts. *What are you doing? No—never mind.* What am I thinking? I don't have to ask it to stop, I can make it stop.

I reach for the predator's mind, intending to snuff out whatever plan it has and force it back into obedience. It hears this thought and darts away, but we're tied together, and there's nowhere for it to go. I pull it back in, and the moment I do so, I catch a glimpse of its plan.

Ah, shit.

I feel it a moment later—darkness rushing through the black. The void crashes into me, sweeping me through the pipes and along the path I'd intended. There's bits of glass mixed into the void—pieces of the bottle that had, at least a minute ago, been containing the predator. It must have managed to break the glass when I was distracted.

Goddammit, I growl, seizing the predator's mind. It doesn't put up a fight, relinquishing control to me the moment I reach for it. It's just relieved: the pressure is gone.

It's right: that mental tension has evaporated. So it was the distance between us that was causing the discomfort?

I don't like that. I don't like it one bit.

Not to mention, Zyneth's probably freaking out up there. How the predator managed to break its container, I'm not sure, but either way Zyneth must have seen it go into the water after me. If I was still within range of my glass or translator, I could tell him that I'm fine. As it is, though, I'm just going to need to get out of here and get back to him before he turns the building inside out.

My much smaller amount of Attuned void has mixed with the predator's, and now I can't tell where one ends and the other begins. Another thing I'll have to sort out later. In the meantime, I use it to propel myself through the water, which is alarmingly effective. Some of it moves ahead of me, using Elemental Radar to map out my path like sonar, while the rest is cushioned around me in a macabre parody of a lifejacket. I'm making way better time now, the void rocketing me along and responding to my will before I've even finished the thought. I try not to think about how easy it is. How natural all this seems to be coming to me.

I make the last turn, and suddenly light is spilling through the tunnel. Popping out the other side, I find myself in a stone basin once more. The void buoys me up to the surface.

Chapter Twenty-Two

Some Halloween Shit

Streaks of water dribble down my glass as I breach and begin to take in my surroundings. The water in my vial also starts to leak out, once more causing a distinctly uncomfortable internal tickling sensation. I better find a way back out that doesn't involve the plumbing system again.

The room is large and made of stone, lit by dozens of lights that are strung across the ceiling on more spider silk. Reflections scatter off the water, sending a shimmering pattern over the room's wide, circular wall. Other pools are laced through the floor, connected by narrow channels of water and bands of magics. The spiderweb of water spans the whole room, cut an inch or two into the floor, making the area as easy to cross as stepping stones—if you were human-sized. The streams of water and magical circuits vanish into the walls, where I imagine they must be pumped up to all the higher floors. This room is probably the brains of the anti-fire system.

But it's not the brains of the whole operation. I can tell the majority of the magic in this room is connected to a stronger source another floor down. But how to get there?

Glancing around to make sure I'm alone, I use my glass and void to hoist me out of the water and onto the floor. The void responds by splitting into tentacles, grabbing the lip of stone, and pulling me out like some kind of oily black octopus. Lovely.

There are a few tunnels scattered along the wall, though no indication of where any of them might lead, so I pick the closest and make for it. It's a little awkward walking on four glass legs again, but the void moves to support the limbs unprompted, making it a little easier. It's weird how good their synergy is. Like the glass are bones and the void is muscles and ligaments.

This is some fucking Halloween shit.

As I traverse the room, the predator remains conspicuously quiet, which, I finally realize, is because I still have a stranglehold on its mind. The predator is completely engulfed in my subconscious. It has no thoughts, except what I think, no emotions, except what I feel. Its sense of self is completely gone.

Just like when it had overpowered me.

The realization makes me uneasy. When the predator had taken over my mind, it had been horrific. Of course, I hadn't been able to fully realize that horror until after the fact, but the experience of being forced to take people's lives—of *delighting* in their pain—is a memory that will plague me to the end of my days. I never want to be put in that situation again. I never want my autonomy taken from me.

And isn't that exactly what I'm doing to the predator now?

No, this is different. I'm taking away its will in order to protect people, not hurt them. That makes it okay… right? Of course. This is the right thing to do.

But it doesn't stop me from feeling sick. It doesn't stop me from feeling like I'm behaving exactly like the thing I despise most.

I release the predator's mind, shoving it away in disgust. The moment the predator's mind separates from my own, it broils with rage and indignation.

Oh, fuck off, I grumble. *You're mad? You started all this.*

Shockingly, this does little to mollify the predator's hatred. Hey, at least it goes both ways.

Despite giving the predator's mind some breathing room, it's still obnoxiously close, all of its feelings and observations bleeding over into me. Probably a result of our void mixing together. I can feel the predator reaching back out for its hold on the null magic, but I swat its influence away. *Yeah, I don't think so.* Now that its void is mixed with mine, and I've no idea how to separate the two, it's just going to have to deal with me piloting the combined mass for now.

The first doorway leads to a spiral staircase. The direction of all the powerful lines of magic is down, but Zyneth is up. I think I could make it down to the next floor without too much trouble, but there's always the risk of running into someone on the stairs and having nowhere to hide—and even if I do find the arcana crystal, I'd need Zyneth's help to carry it out. Besides, I'd promised him I'd only do reconnaissance. Reluctantly, I turn away from the source of the magic and start to climb.

Previously this would have been difficult with just my glass, but the void is able to help shuffle me up each step without accidentally leveling up my Fall Damage Resistance. The way the black tendrils snake their way up the steps is still creepy as fuck, but at least it's a useful kind of creepy.

I make it a floor up without running into anyone. The spiral staircase continues higher, but I decide to check out the present landing first. I'm not totally sure, given the disorientation of my recent Mario Brothers adventure, but I think I'm back up to the same floor as Zyneth. If not, then I'm just below him.

This floor is much smaller. It appears to be a wide empty hallway that curves out of sight, presumably following the wall of the library. Once again, no one is in sight. Does no one take care of this place behind the scenes? Or am I in more of a space-between-the-walls type area that is only checked when something goes wrong? Guess it doesn't really matter as long as I stay out of sight.

Just as I'm about to step out, movement flickers at the far end of the ceiling: a spider sentry. Unlike the ones I'd seen in the main portion of the library, however, this one is etched with glowing purple runes, emitting a beam of light which sweeps through the hall like a flashlight. It's skittering right toward me, and I quickly shuffle back, slipping down the first stair for cover.

It doesn't appear overhead. After another moment, I peek my head back up; the sentry scuttled past the stairwell and is heading down the other curve of the hall. Close call.

Any idea how often those guys come by? I ask Echo, cautiously stepping out into the hall.

[Negative,] Echo says. [There is not enough data to predict their occurrence.]

Well you seem to know just about everything else, I say. She doesn't reply.

Mentally sighing, I hurry down the hall. I'll just have to hope I can find another corner to duck into when the next one comes by.

How does the sentry's magic work? I ask as I walk. The hallway is empty, save for bubbly lights near the ceiling. There aren't even doors on the walls. *Is it too late to do an Inspect?*

[Affirmative,] Echo says. [But such spells typically use pulses of nature magic to detect lifeforms and verify if the individuals are within a pre-established database.]

Damn. Then it sounds like even just getting Zyneth in here won't be the end of our troubles: We still stand to get caught once he's inside. And of course, I stand to get caught now—assuming this sentry identifies me as "a lifeform." I would rather not risk it either way.

Give me a head's up when the next one is in range, I tell Echo.

[Affirmative.]

I walk for another minute or two—meaning, at this size, not very far—before I come across anything of note. There's what looks like a door-knocker on the inside wall. It isn't until I'm up close that I can tell it's actually a handle in a door, barely discernible by the seam in the stone wall to either side.

There's no key, just the handle—three feet off the ground. Ugh, I hate being small again. I attempt to grab it with my glass, but the little bit I have on me isn't enough to push with any strength. The glass screeches as it slips over the surface; no grip, either. Reluctantly, I send a tendril of the void up to grab the handle. The latch clicks, and I pull. Slowly, the door grinds inward. Hm. Not wild about the usefulness of this void, but I guess I'll take the wins where I can get them.

I keep pulling on the door and it slowly, glacially, slides open toward me. It doesn't even feel really heavy, it just seems to move slow. Which is a problem when the next sentry appears at the end of the hall.

[Sentry detected,] Echo says.

Gee, thanks.

I anxiously look for somewhere to hide, but the walls are seamless—not even another stairwell. If I can make it out the door, maybe I'll be safe, but it's not even wide enough for me to slip through yet.

Crap crap crap. Can't get anywhere in time. Can I take it down with my void? Maybe—it's much bigger than me. A Void Whip might work. But if it doesn't, I'm caught. What else have I got? Lightbeam, Glow, Inspect, Location, Bond Trace... Ah! That new spell I learned, Refraction. *Echo, what's the mana cost for disguising just my core with Refraction?*

[1 mana per second. For larger bodies—]

Do it! I cry. I skip the tutorial and activate the spell.

My glass jumps between me and the sentry. The pieces interlock with each other like a lattice of crystals, forming a shell. But it's not just the glass—the voids move, too, layering over the glass and filling in all the cracks. Then, my mana activates.

Unlike Lightbeam, there's only the tiniest flicker of light. It flows from my core into the surrounding glass and void, the whole structure rippling. And then, for a moment, it all seems to melt out of view.

The sentry passes by. A purple pulse of magic washes over me, illuminating my shell of glass and void. I tense, ready to flee or fight—but the sentry continues on. Once it vanishes down the hall, I end the Refraction spell, and the shell flickers back into view.

[Spell ended.]

Well shit, that's useful as fuck. Still don't have enough mana to use with my whole body, but if I only have to worry about my vial, it could be a life saver. Before it's given the opportunity to save my life again, I decide to get the hell out of here.

I finish pulling the door open another few inches, and it's finally enough for me to slip out. Instead of leaving immediately, however, I hover just inside, unenthused by the idea of the door closing on top of me and slowly getting crushed to death. Like I had hoped, I'm looking back out onto the ground floor of the library.

I can't see the fountain from this angle. I'm disoriented for a moment until I catch sight of the spiraling floor, and trace it to the ground level. Okay, the entrance is to my left. That means...

I edge forward a little more, and finally the fountain comes into view. I can make out Zyneth, too, just on the other side.

So, not where I expected to be. But hey, at least I'm on the right floor.

Now how the heck do I get him over here without letting the door shut behind me?

I try letting go of the handle, and the door begins to slide shut. Crap! I seize it with the void once more, holding it open just a few inches, as I ponder what to do. It sure would be nice to have vocal cords. Barring that, I suppose my only option is to try to throw something in his direction. He's about thirty feet away, and my glass only has a range of around eight. I could throw it from a height, hoping momentum would carry it the rest of the way. It will break once it hits the ground, though, and there's no guarantee he would notice. What to do?

The predator stirs, smugness rippling from its mind. Its range is not nearly so limited. A few feet is nothing. Pathetic.

Oh yeah? Alright then. I grab the predator's void, the creature hissing in protest. Leaving one tendril wrapped around the handle to keep the door from closing, I snake the rest of the void across the floor, stretching the shadow across the stone. It feels like stretching a spring. At first it's easy, but the further the void gets from me, the more of an effort the movement takes. And then finally, it stops altogether. The predator emanates sadistic glee as it watches me strain, trying to get the shadows to move further, but they won't extend beyond the range of my glass. I'm not even a quarter of the way to Zyneth.

What the heck? I ask Echo. I can feel the predator isn't lying when it knows it can extend the shadows four times the length I managed. But why can't I? *Why can't I make the void go further?*

[The abilities of the magic are limited by the abilities of the user,] Echo says. [This may include finesse, complexity, and range of the manipulated magic.]

Meaning the predator's better at manipulating void than me—hell, it's made of the stuff.

The predator, of course, is very pleased as I come to this realization. Even if it's the weaker mind, it's still the more powerful magic user.

Congratulations, I say. *You're more practiced than someone who started learning magic two months ago. Really impressive.*

Although not for the first time, it has me wondering what Level the predator really is. Just in case, I try to Check it again, but as always Echo is only able to produce a bunch of junk data. Everything is just Div/0, whatever that means.

At any rate, none of this helps me figure out how to get Zyneth's attention.

The predator stirs again. It could do it. It has the range.

I examine the predator with extreme suspicion. *You want to help me?*

The predator eagerly surges forward. Of course. Yes. It can do what I wish. It can alert the cambion, very easily. If I just give it back its void.

If I just let it take control.

Chapter Twenty-Three

RELUCTANT COLLAB

I shove the predator away with a barking laugh. Ay, there's the rub. *Let you take control? Not fucking likely. How about you just lend me your abilities? Or, better yet, I can just take them from you.*

The predator growls. I can take its powers, yes, but I can't wield them like it can. I have already seen that. I need it. I should let it take control.

I shudder in disgust. *Fuck off with that. I'm not going to let you take control.* And for emphasis, just so it knows how serious I am, I press my mind against its, forcing it to feel my revulsion, my resentment, my resolve. The predator flattens beneath the pressure of my mind, for a moment its presence dissolving away entirely as its identity is overridden by my own.

I pull back just as quick. It's not that I feel bad for it, but realizing I'm doing to it what it did to me makes me feel... I don't know what, exactly. Unnerved, maybe. I should be better than it. I *am* better.

As the predator's mind extracts itself from me, its arrogance and mockery has simmered down into a familiar hatred once more.

But while our minds had merged, there was something else I'd gleaned from the predator. A realization that I *could* wield its powers without letting it take control; as long as it's not completely suppressed, I'd still have its knowledge—its magical muscle memory—to pull from. I'm not thrilled by the idea, but...

The predator isn't thrilled by it either. It has no desire to help.

This is the best deal you're going to get, I say. *I'm not letting you take over. And if I take over completely, then I suppress your abilities along with your mind. If you want even the tiniest drop of control in this situation, then you can choose to work with me.*

It's not *really* an offer, and both of us know it. If it doesn't willingly lend me its power, then I can make it do so. I'd much rather it be the former, and in any other situation I might be horrified by the way I am blithely stripping away the autonomy of a thinking creature, but if I'm being honest, I'm not totally convinced this murderous void monster deserves any personal liberties.

The predator hesitates. It doesn't want to share its power, it wants complete control. But it also doesn't want its will to get overridden. Reluctantly, angrily, it agrees.

Honestly, I'm not sure I wanted it to.

This time when the predator reaches for the void, I let it take hold, but I extend my reach into the magic as well. Our wills overlap within the void. The tether between our minds shortens with the contact, so short it's almost as if there's no barrier at all. I can feel the predator's manipulation of the null arcana as clearly as if I'm doing it myself. It pushes the void out, and the range limit I'd run into before now falls away as if there'd been no barrier at all. I focus on Zyneth as our minds fall into lockstep.

We weave the void across the floor, keeping it to the shadows of tables and chairs that lattice the floor. The inky blob darts between feet and spirals around table legs, avoiding detection with fluid ease, made easier by the fact that we seem to be able to see, hear, and feel directly through the magic. We are still seeing through our core—our anchor—as well, so we cover that with a thin film of void, tucking the glass within our shadows and darkening its vision, so we can focus just on the movements of the void. Much better.

As the void swirls across the floor, we marvel at how trivial it is for us to control it.

Of course it's easy—it's an extension of ourselves.

Well, an extension of part of us.

The part that matters.

Oh, fuck off.

We make it to the cambion—Zyneth—quickly enough, but his back is turned, anxiously tapping a finger on the table. Even from this distance, we can feel the heat of powerful magic burning within his soul. It's a pity we didn't end up with a more capable host like him.

Just shut up and focus already.

We move up the leg of the table, spilling the void over the surface of the desk. We try to keep it flat to avoid detection from others, and to Zyneth's merit, his only indication of surprise is hastily jerking his hand back.

"That better be you, Kanin," he mutters. Sparks of electricity dance over his fingers. "If not…"

Belatedly we realize one thing both halves of us have in common: We can't spell. Not in his language, at any rate, and not well enough to get the point across. Instead, we change the void into an arrow, pointing back in the direction of the door.

Zyneth leans back, rubbing his neck, and casually casts a glance in that direction. "I don't see anything. What is it?"

We'll have to get him to follow. We spill the void off the edge of the desk and onto the floor, maintaining the arrow pointing back toward our core.

He hesitates a moment longer, nodding back to our glass shell, still inanimate and propped in its chair. It looks so much like a puppet with cut strings. A prop, not a body. Not our body.

"Is it in range? Can you move it?" the cambion asks. "It's too heavy for me."

No. Our glass is still out of range. We have to keep the door from closing.

His question gone unanswered, Zyneth is forced to follow as we weave him back toward the wall. He's remarkably good at not watching us as he follows, somehow managing to make it look like he intended to head in that direction from the start. We pull our void back into the rest of us, and he stops a few feet away.

"I don't understand," he says under his breath, turning to feign interest in a nearby shelf. "Where did you go?"

There must be an illusion covering the entrance. We'll just have to risk being more blatant. Snapping a tendril of void back out the door, we grab Zyneth's wrist, tugging him toward the wall. We feel the muscles in his arm tense beneath our grasp, instinctively resisting our pull—he's much stronger than our pathetic supply of void. We miss being powerful. Though the rest of us isn't far. Stuck in a pocket of Between called... an inventory? Interesting. It wouldn't take much effort to retrieve it, either. All we need to do is reach for it—

Nope! No. That's it. We're done doing this.

We pry ourselves apart, like peeling off an old bandaid. We try to resist, we aren't willing to relinquish our control, we don't want to lose our hold on the void, yet, but—

The predator reels as I shove it from my mind, then slinks away in resentful defeat. It takes a moment for my own mind to adjust, the disorientation of shifting from the shared consciousness to just me as dizzying as it is relieving.

Yikes. That was too close. I don't intend to repeat that experience anytime soon. But I don't have time to sit and stew in the consequences of what we—what I just did. I have to get Zyneth inside.

I'm still holding his arm with a strand of the void, though instead of an extension of myself, my current hold on the magic feels clumsy and juvenile. At least he's within range, and tugging him toward the gap in the wall is something even I can manage without void monster assistance.

After a moment of hesitation, he allows himself to be guided to the wall. I pull his hand toward the door's frame. His fingers brush against the door, then he runs his hand along the seam. I let go as he feels out the shape of the door and wall. With one quick backward glance, he steps inside.

"Ah," Zyneth says, looking around his new surroundings. "Clever illusion magic, that. Though your instructions were rather..." He looks down at me and blinks. "That is somewhat unsettling."

What? Oh. I let go of the door handle and retract that tentacle of void back into the main volume, which hovers around me like an inky jellyfish. It sort of developed other tentacles all on its own, like the one I'd used to grab Zyneth's hand. I pull all the limbs in to reduce the Noli aesthetic.

"At least now I know where all that void ended up," Zyneth says. "The bottle tipped itself over and broke on the edge of the fountain—the predator was gone before I could even react. Though I see now you've gotten that under control." There's a lift to his voice, like it's more of a question than a statement.

"Yes," I sign. "It's under control."

Zyneth squints at the signs, but he at least seems to understand the "yes" part. "It will be tricky sneaking through this place while watching your signs," he says. "I should go back and get your translator. Actually, you should retrieve your whole body if you can. Leaving it out there is suspicious—and I suspect we will be needing every tool at our disposal for this job."

He's right, but we have more pressing matters. The spider sentry could return any second, and I don't have enough glass or mana to shield Zyneth.

"We have to be careful, there's spider sentries here," I sign as he furrows his brows at my words. Shit, how do I say this with the most basic signs possible. "Careful. Spider find us." I form my signing glass into the best approximation of a spider I can manage and send it skittering across the floor. Between the signs and my helpful demonstration, he seems to catch on.

"Those spider sentries like in the rest of the library?" he asks.

"Yes."

Zyneth grins. "Then we have nothing to worry about." He grabs the door, effortlessly pulling it open a few more inches. The same door I had painstakingly dragged open. It just isn't fair.

"Go on," he says. "I've got this. See if you can retrieve your body without drawing too much attention."

I don't appreciate the insinuation that I will be drawing at least *some* amount of attention no matter what.

"You sure?" I ask, hesitating a moment longer. Not that there's much I could do against the sentry.

Zyneth pools lightning in his free hand, twitching his fingers as if knitting the strands of electricity together. "Have more faith in me than that, won't you?"

I do. Deciding I've already wasted enough time, I scurry out the door and across the library floor.

It's strange, having just made this trip minutes before through the eyes of the void. The predator is still sulking in the back of my mind after having its attempt to access my inventory thwarted. I'm going to have to keep my eye on it. At least I know it won't be able to pull the rest of itself from my inventory without our minds being merged. So as long as we don't do that again, I should be fine.

As I cross the floor, I nervously Check the predator stats, just in case.

[Predator Time Limit: 10.5 hours]

[Predator Influence: 5%]

No change. Good.

I can feel the glass of my body the moment it passes back within my range, but I don't try moving it until I'm close enough to add my void to all its joints. And now that the predator's void is mixed in with my own, I've got a lot more of it. Before I was only able to brace the legs and back, but now there's enough for the rest of the body as well. Little bits of shadow tucked into every nook and cranny.

I reach down to pick up my core, slipping it back into the necklace pouch as I switch my vision over to my head. And just like that, I'm pretending to be a person again.

A couple people glance my way as I head back over to the wall—the door and opening completely invisible, now that I'm on the outside. I spend a painstaking minute browsing the shelves, waiting for people to glance away or get bored of my unusual presence. Finally, there's an opening, and I use it to step up against the wall, sending my signing glass ahead to feel for the crack. Once I've located it, I slip back through.

Zyneth is not quite where I'd left him. The door is pulled all the way inward now, and he's keeping it propped with his foot. In one hand is a spider sentry, legs twitching angrily within a cage of yellow light. His other hand is crooked over the device, lines of electricity zapping between the construct and his fingers like one of those toy plasma balls. He's frowning in concentration, the tip of his tongue poking out the side of his mouth.

The sight fills me with a warm affection.

I balk, the feelings catching me off guard, and I quickly stamp them out.

What am I thinking? I can't start catching feelings for Zyneth, not when I'm planning to leave this world behind. That's a recipe for disaster. Developing a crush on someone now won't lead to anything good. I have to stay focused.

Flustered, I clear my throat, which the translator interprets as a kind of garbled coughing sound. Zyneth doesn't look up until the remainder of the spell finishes pouring into the spider, whose magic has changed colors to reflect Zyneth's electricity.

"There we are," he says, setting the construct down. It scurries across the floor and up the wall, back to one of the many white lines of silk that crisscross the ceiling.

"What did you do?" I ask, speaking through the translator.

Zyneth steps away from the door, allowing it to close. "I gave it new instructions. It should notify us whenever other sentries grow near, and try to head them off. Should buy us enough time to hide, at least."

"I did not know you could do that," I say. Pretty useful. And for a reason I can't quite place, a little unsettling.

"I'm an artificer," Zyneth says, patting the knives at his waist. "Imbuing objects with spells is what I do."

Ah, that's why it bothers me. Because according to his magic, I'm an object, too.

"Come," Zyneth says. "Let's get moving."

I try to push disquieting thoughts of the predator, Zyneth's magic, and my troublesome feelings away. Right now, I have a mission to focus on, and if I don't want to get caught by Yedzaquib how that sentry just got caught by Zyneth, I'll need to keep my wits about me.

"This way," I say as I lead us down into the spider's lair.

Chapter Twenty-Four

A Right Glutton

"Did you have a chance to scout this place at all?" Zyneth asks.

I step down the spiral staircase, cautious of any more spiders popping up. "Not much. It took a lot more time to walk around here when I was teacup sized." But I explain what I do know: The fire-extinguisher floor is beneath us, and I traced the source of the magic circuit to at least another floor beneath that.

We make it back to the water room in record time—god, being small sucks—and then continue heading down. Now that we're in new territory, Zyneth takes the lead, tiptoeing ahead, peeking around corners, and grimacing every time my misfitted boots knock clumsily against the floor. Look, he could have gotten me something nicer.

Instead of exiting onto the second floor, however, the spiral staircase continues to wind down. By the time the light at the bottom of the curve indicates an opening, we must be at least four floors beneath the surface.

The stairs open out onto a narrow pathway that circles the lip of a massive pit. It's the Library in reverse, with the slope spiraling into the earth and out of sight. Instead of bookshelves, however, the path itself is bare. All along the corkscrew, portions of the wall shine with purple light, twinkling like stars as they disappear down into the dark. As with the public side of the library, lines of spider silk crosshatch the open space, along which sentry spiders skitter back and forth to check on the lights in the wall.

And at the center of the giant shaft, caught in the midst of this web, is a small, red crystal. I briefly flicker Inspect on as a spell, just to be sure, and lines of magic appear abruptly within my vision; sure enough, thousands of threads in the walls and floor all trace back to it. The magical source is hardly the size of my core, but it shines with the brightness of a sun.

[Arcana crystal identified,] Echo says.

I turn Inspect off again so the crystal doesn't wash out the rest of my vision. "What is this place?" I ask.

"An excellent question," Zyneth says, also marveling at the sight. "I've heard the Athenaeum deals in more than just knowledge, but this is something else."

Zyneth's hijacked sentry skitters forward, breaking through our awe, and we follow after it. It moves and stops, seemingly in random patterns, but its haphazard progress prevents us from crossing paths with any of the other spiders.

"What are those lights in the wall?" I ask as we begin making our way around the spiral. There's no guard rail along the inner edge of the trail, so I hug the wall. Zyneth seems less bothered by the cliff, but even he keeps a few feet away from the drop-off.

"Not lights," he says, eyes on the nearest swatch of purple we approach. "Barriers, I think."

As we come upon the first one, I can see he's right. Similar to the barrier we passed to enter the library in the first place, a portion of the wall is replaced with a sheet of transparent purple light, behind which is a small room. In that room is an Indiana Jones-type pedestal, upon which sits a simple brass bracelet.

"What the *Expletive* is that?" I ask.

"I'm not sure," Zyneth admits. He glances at it as we pass, but doesn't stop. "An enchanted item, perhaps. It must be valuable to keep locked in there, though why Yedzaquib is storing such treasures here, I am uncertain. If I had direct access to it, I might be able to cast a spell which checks what sort of magic it has been enchanted with."

Oh right. I suppose I can do that, too. I really need to use my Check more just by default—and Inspect, now that I have that. I do that at the next barrier we pass, only twenty or so paces beyond the first.

[Check,] Echo says as I make out the contents of the room. This one is only the size of a window, and inside is a ring with a yellow stone. [The Ring of Denwana. It is said that in the Queen's pursuit of eternal youth, she bound the souls of all one hundred of her closest attendants to her ring. Whether the magic was successful remains uncertain, as the Queen—and every bearer of the ring since—perished of remarkable circumstances within a year of acquiring the artifact.]

Holy shit. "They are not here because they are valuable," I say, Checking the next item we pass. It's a pendant that imbues the wearer with superhuman strength, at the gradual cost of their sanity. "They are here because they are cursed."

"What?" Zyneth asks. "Are you sure? How do you know that?"

"Echo told me," I say. "She can give basic descriptions of things that I focus on."

Instead of looking impressed, Zyneth frowns. "And this is information you had no knowledge of prior?"

"No," I say.

Zyneth hums thoughtfully. "This Echo of yours knows more than she should."

I mean, I guess so. Her teaching me things seems like the point, right? I'd never really considered how she knows what she knows, but there's a lot about magic I still don't understand.

"Well whatever she is, she is pretty useful," I say. *Echo, Check every object that comes within range and let me know if any of them are an arcana crystal.*

[Affirmative,] she says.

I relay my plan to Zyneth.

"That *is* useful," he admits. "Do you suppose it has something to do with you being from this other world?"

"I doubt it," I say. "We did not have these Echoes on my world. Although it does seem strange I am the only one with an Echo floating around in my head."

"That's something else we should research in the library—if we somehow make it out of here without being caught or banned for life," Zyneth adds. His smile is teasing, but also tight. Maybe that's how he copes with being here despite his misgivings.

"I suppose," I agree. "Of course, if I make it back home after this, we will never know."

Zyneth's smile falls away. "Of course."

The way he says those simple words twists an invisible blade in my soul. That's why we're doing all this, isn't it? I shouldn't have to feel guilty for wanting to get my body back—for wanting to get my *life* back.

I squeeze a hand into a fist, the glass clinking as each finger makes contact. "You do not have to do this, you know."

Zyneth looks at me. "What do you mean?"

"Risking your life here to help me," I say. "And when I go to Emrox, too. You do not have to come. It is dangerous, and you will not be needed for the trip. I can achieve the same thing alone."

"I will *not* leave you alone with that shark," Zyneth growls. "Don't trust Gillow as far as you can throw them. They might take you to Emrox to mine that null arcana you promised, but they're sure to do something duplicitous once you're there. They'd have no incentive to allow you to go back to your world when they could instead continue to use you to extract expensive resources."

"Is that the reason you are coming?" I ask. "To make sure Gillow does not win?"

"You idiot," Zyneth snaps, and I turn to him in surprise. "It's to make sure you're safe."

Embarrassment and shame burn through me. Why does he care so much? Of course no one would want to see a friend get hurt if they could help it, but we're about to never see each other again anyway.

I'm about to leave him.

The silence between us stretches as our feet thump dully down the slope. Finally, Zyneth sighs.

"There are other options, you know. We could leave now, before anything is stolen, before we take steps down a path we can't retrace."

"But Gillow—" I start.

"Screw Gillow," Zyneth snarls. "And screw Emrox! You could always stay here. With... with people like Noli and I, who care about you. We could find a way to manage the predator. There must be *something* in the Library that can help."

There's a part of me that wants that. A big part of me that is looking forward to seeing Noli again, to just enjoying a quiet conversation with Zyneth, to not worrying about voids or thievery or ancient magic.

But I shake my head. "I cannot live like this," I say, gently. I don't fault him for not understanding. I hold out my hand, watching the movement of the floor through the warped glass. "I cannot live this shadow of a life. No food, no sleep, no... companionship. It is a nightmare, Zyneth. A living nightmare I cannot take a break from, even for a moment."

Zyneth looks at my hand, then looks away. "I'm sorry. I understand what you are dealing with, even if I cannot experience it myself. But surely, there must also be spells—something—to create a new body for you? We need only take the time to look."

Is that something I'm willing to consider? Creating a new organic body—a living body—that isn't my original? The idea makes me uncomfortable. Better than a glass body, of course, but would it really ever feel like *me*?

"I... might consider it," I say, hesitant.

Zyneth looks up. "Really?"

"As a last resort," I add. "If Emrox does not pan out."

His face falls in disappointment—and fuck does it not feel great to be responsible for disappointing Zyneth—but I'm saved from hearing his thoughts when Echo chimes in.

[Arcana crystal detected.]

"Here it is," I quickly say. I gesture to the barrier Echo indicated, the next window we're about to reach. By now we're several rotations down the loop, the ceiling several floors above us.

This barrier is wider and taller than the others, reaching the floor in the shape of a freight entrance more than a window. When we get closer, I can see why.

Instead of another small room with a pedestal upon which sits some trinket or jewel, this barrier blocks off a large passageway which curves out of sight. I can make out more barriers lining the walls inside. I guess the stuff in here needs double the protection, which is both a sign we're on the right track, and a problem.

"Well," I say, "Now what?"

Zyneth snorts. "Wasn't it you who was just encouraging me to leave? You said you could do this on your own, I distinctly remember."

I puff up indignantly. "I was just giving you an opportunity to voice your opinions."

"Because I am the one who so often struggles with communication," he says, smiling slightly. It's a relief, somewhat, to see the cloud over him dissipate. This lighthearted, teasing, somewhat-aloof Zyneth is the Zyneth I know.

"Alright then," I say. "I will figure something out on my own."

Zyneth gestures me forward with an amused flourish, stepping back to give me space as I step up to the field of magic.

I Inspect the barrier, and sure enough the spell powering it leads back to the arcana crystal at the top of the spiral. I Check it again, just to make sure there's no nasty surprises, then gingerly reach out to touch the magic. It's like pressing my hand against a brick wall. There's no give, no indication enough force would allow me to slip through.

I feel the predator's attention shift back over to my actions. I guess it's done sulking. Its hunger creeps through our bond, which makes me a bit irritable too. My mana is down to 24/56, thanks to all these Refraction and Inspect spells—not to mention the predator taking its own mana tax each time.

Haven't you had enough? I ask. But even as I ask, it gives me an idea. *If you really want more, can you take it from this field?*

The predator swells to the forefront of my mind, eagerly investigating the offer to consume more magic. It instinctively tugs at the void, but I'm already keeping a tight hold on the magic, and my will is stronger.

It needs the void to absorb magic. I must give it control.

I grimace. We could always do the mind merge thing again, but I'm not wild about that prospect. I think I can slip it just enough control to let it tap into the barrier and nothing else. If it tries anything, I should be able to wrest control easily once more.

The predator hisses at the thought. It just wants magic. It needs more. Always more.

Yeah, yeah, I say, relinquishing the tiniest bit of void to the predator. *I get it. You're a right glutton.*

The predator ignores me, eagerly seizing the void. The shadows in the joints of my hand bleed forward like streams of ink, hooking into the magic of the barrier. The predator pulls at the magic, funneling the mana away from the field. The energy jolts through me, crackling through our shared void. I flinch, bracing my other arm against the barrier as the predator fills with an elation that echoes back into me.

Zyneth steps forward, reaching out an uncertain hand. "Are you alright? What's happening?"

"Fine," I say, strained. It's hard to focus on talking when it feels like a live line of electricity has been wired up to my soul. But instead of being electrocuted, I feel energized. Paralyzed by power, overwhelmed by the predator's desire and satiation. It's intoxicating, and it's too much.

The barrier around my hand flickers, but it doesn't go down. This isn't working. *That's enough,* I say to the predator. It ignores me, pulling from the barrier as another wave of exhilaration crashes through me.

"Enough!" I jerk my hand away, wrenching the void from the predator's grasp as I stumble back from the wall—and, I realize a moment too late, straight toward the edge of the cliff.

CHAPTER TWENTY-FIVE

MISSION: IMPOSSIBLE

"Kanin!" Zyneth throws an arm out behind my back, grabbing my shoulder and stopping me from careening over the ledge. A spark of magic jolts from my glass to his hand and he sucks in a breath, but doesn't falter.

Holy shit. I feel overcharged. Brittle. My hand is shaking, the void vibrating with magic. I grab my wrist to still the movement, only now noticing the magic there is... denser. Darker. Less shadow and more physical than I'm used to seeing. Why?

[Mana: 56/56,] Echo says. [Bonus Mana: 25. Predator Time Limit: 12 hours. Predator Influence: 6%.]

Figures. It might have topped up my tanks, but it took a bigger cut for itself. And its influence crept up one percent. That's not good.

"Kanin," Zyneth says again. "Talk to me. Sign or speak—whatever you're capable of. I swear, if you don't say something, I'm getting us both out of here. In fact, we should do that regardless."

"No," I say, pulling the void back into my joints. Giving them something to do helps lessen the pressure. "I am okay. The predator was just being difficult."

"The predator," Zyneth repeats, alarmed. "Is it acting up? Will you be alright?"

"Ah." I head back over to the wall, sheepishly avoiding his concerned stare. "Yes, I will be alright. I have been..." I pause, trying to think of the right words that won't alarm Zyneth. "...collaborating with the predator." Nope, that wasn't it.

"Collaborating?" he cries. "What do you—"

"I am just using it!" I explain. Hm, that also sounded better in my head. "Or, learning from it. *Expletive*, I am really not explaining this right."

Zyneth's jaw is clenched. "Start explaining better."

"It lent me some of its abilities," I say. "Well, I sort of threatened it into helping, or we would not have gotten as far as we have. But I promise, it is fine. I am in control."

Now that the magic has settled somewhat, I activate a quick Inspect: the magical circuit powering the barrier jumps into view inside the nearby wall. I head over to the stone and place my hand over the narrow channel of magic that was feeding the rest of the field. I feel the predator perk back up, but I shove it away. *I don't need you for this.*

I do, the predator insists. I need its help.

I snort. *It's just sucking up magic. An idiot could figure this out.*

The predator rumbles with irritation, pressing against my mind, reaching for the void, but I brush it away.

"Nothing about this is fine, Kanin," Zyneth says. "In fact, it's extremely concerning. Would you be bargaining with this monster in any other circumstances? After what it did to you?"

His words dig into unhealed wounds, and regret washes through me, quickly followed by a flare of indignation. "You do not need to remind me what happened." I hate myself for working with it. But I need to use every advantage at my disposal if I stand a chance at getting my body back—and leaving this thing trapped Between.

Zyneth presses his mouth into a line, but he does back off. "You're right. That's not my place. So I will only say it once: Giving that beast any amount of power is a mistake."

"Noted," I say. "Now are you ready to get through here? I may only have it open for a moment." I brace for another lecture.

Zyneth stands there for a moment, silently watching me. Then he sighs. "Alright. Let's get on with it."

I watch him with surprise and more than a little bit of suspicion as he steps up to the barrier then nods to me, waiting. Somehow, him cooperating instills me with guilt rather than confidence.

We've been standing here out in the open long enough, however. That's a conversation for later.

I summon the tendrils of void, imitating what the predator had done, but I add more lines of magic than I'd given the predator access to. I can feel the mana circuit thrumming just beneath my touch.

"Here we go," I tell Zyneth, then I plunge my magic in.

If I was hooked to a live wire before, I'm being struck by lightning now. The magic is ten, a hundred times more potent, too late realizing the predator had been filtering out most of what I'd experienced. My mind goes blank with white noise, sight and sound and sensation drowned beneath the deluge of energy.

A voice says something from far away. [...*sustained*...]

I can't let go, but I don't even want to. I'm invigorated. I'm ecstatic. I'm powerful, growing stronger, approaching some looming, irreversible brink—

Disdainful amusement saturates my mind. Fool. Arrogance. You don't need us? You are going to get us killed.

A familiar voice floats back again. I feel like I should understand it, but I can't concentrate on the words long enough for them to make sense. [...*damage...*]

We need our anchor. We can't allow it to be destroyed.

We absorb the torrent of magic in the void, lessening the buildup of mana that was about to shatter our soul. Pulling our hand from the wall, the void disconnects from the circuit, and the energy that was holding us upright and rigid vanishes in an instant.

I collapse against the wall, mind reeling, as my glass briefly slips from my grasp, too overwhelmed to remember to hold on. I belatedly try to catch myself before I hit the ground, scrambling to keep my body from shattering to pieces. My hip strikes the floor with a sharp crack, and I throw an arm out to the side to brace myself, the void finally catching up to cushion the blow.

[7 points of points Fall Damage sustained.]

And then it's over. I'm on the ground, tense and still, trying to understand what the hell just happened.

Did the predator just... save me? Its mind lingers nearby, a swirl of smugness and scorn.

Fuck. I hadn't even realized I was in danger. It did save me—not that it was doing it for any altruistic reasons. My soul feels tight and uneasy.

"What happened?" Zyneth is crouched beside me. He reaches out a hand. "Your leg—"

I activate a Sculpt, already stitching the broken glass back together again. "I am okay," I lie, shooing him away as I pull myself to my feet. I'm still dizzy with disorientation, jittery as if electrified, but there's no sense in letting Zyneth know what I—or the predator—just did. I'd only worry him more. "Just got a little overwhelmed. Forgot to hold onto my glass. I guess we will have to find some other way in."

Zyneth looks at me strangely, stepping aside to gesture toward the field. Or at least, where the field was supposed to be. The hallway now stands open and ready for us to stroll inside.

"You took the field down nearly a minute ago, then I stepped inside and disabled the system from within," he says. "You sure you're alright?"

A minute? I mean, that's not a huge space of time, but it sure feels longer than the couple of seconds I was hooked into the circuit.

Am I alright? I Check myself over.

[HP: 3/10]

[Temp HP: 340]

[Mana: 56/56]

[Bonus Mana: 785]

Yikes. My temporary hit points are fine—I've already mended the crack in my leg—but that damage to my direct HP worries me. Was that all from the magic I was absorbing? It looks like it went right to my soul. That didn't happen when the predator had been pulling from the field the first time. I'm not excited to admit it, but *maybe* it knows what it's doing.

A smugness echoes from the predator. I shove it away.

The bonus mana also jumped. Probably explains the... over-charged-ness feeling I'm experiencing. Which means...

I Check the Predator as well.

[Predator Influence: 8%]

[Predator Time Limit: 25.4 hours]

Oof. I'd sort of given up on the idea of starving the predator out of mana, once I realized I'd need it for Emrox, but that Influence stat is not filling me with comfort. At least it's pretty low, still. I start to pull the void that had cushioned my fall back into my joints, then stop.

Zyneth notices it too. "Has it always been that... physical?"

No longer mistakable for shadows, all its previous elements of intangibleness are gone. This ink is impenetrably dark and real, more solid than I've ever seen it—at least, not since the predator was summoned in full.

"It is the extra magic I absorbed," I guess. Similar to the Void Whip spell, which makes the void more concrete and physical when charged with mana. I'll need to be careful about letting the predator do something like this again, no matter how useful it might be at taking down barriers.

I can feel the predator lingering at the edge of my mind, watching, but nothing more. If it is stronger, at least it isn't acting on it. For now.

I clench my fist, pulling the void back into place. "Come on. We need to get going before we are caught by one of the spiders."

Zyneth hesitantly follows as I lead the way into the chamber.

"The arcana crystal you found appears to be uncharged," Zyneth says, back to business as I approach the window. He seemed to have managed to keep the field down for the main entrance to this area, but all the barriers for the individual items are still up. "I suspect it was the last crystal that was used to power the library; it won't be sufficient for Gillow's needs."

"There are other ones further in, you think?" I ask.

"Possibly," Zyneth says. "Given the extra security and presence of the expired arcana crystal, this seems the most likely place to start."

We wind our way through the passage, which appears to follow the same circular pattern the rest of the library had. This time, though, we're heading back up. We're either on the right track, or getting much further from it.

Interestingly, many of the windows here are empty, their contents removed. There's still plenty of bizarre and sketchy magical items, however, including a scroll which contains a spell circle that could turn someone inside out, and a treasure chest decorated with a teeth motif and red leather strap that looks suspiciously like a tongue.

The magic on Zyneth's spider sentry abruptly turns red, and Zyneth whips a hand in front of me, causing me to stumble to a halt.

"What—"

He signs, "Quiet," and wordlessly moves forward. Another spider appears from around the corner, only feet away.

Zyneth pounces as the sentry flashes red, snatching the spider from the wall with an electric flash. The color fades from the construct until it's just a gray stone husk.

"Keep moving," Zyneth says as he tosses the dead sentry aside. "Quickly now. I might not have cut its signal off in time."

"You are not going to repurpose it?" I ask, hurrying after.

He shakes his head. "Didn't have time to set up new instructions before I had to sever its circuit. And I'd rather not waste more mana than I must. We might not have much time now."

The path continues to circle upward. Despite that initial dead arcana crystal, I'm beginning to suspect we're on a wild goose chase. What if the other charged ones are stored elsewhere? What if the library only has the two? And even if we find what we're looking for, how will we get it out? I'm not sure I'm ready to tackle another one of those barriers.

After several more minutes of tense silence, we round a corner and a new floor of the Athenaeum comes into view.

It's literally crawling with spiders. The floor is practically carpeted in the lines of magical web, equally woven over the walls, windows, and even strung through the air like some kind of goddamn Mission

Impossible room full of lasers. One thing is certain: Zyneth and I won't be able to set a foot in there without tripping the whole system.

"I don't suppose it's stored elsewhere?" Zyneth suggests, resignation already set in his tone.

I flick an Inspect spell on and off, unwilling to eat up too much of my mana. The lines from the arcana crystal are strongest in here—much stronger than anywhere else. "Unfortunately, I think we have found it."

Zyneth grumbles, crouching down to check the floor. "I could possibly send my enchanted sentry through here to scout. The threads might not recognize it as an intruder."

I'm not wild about that 'might.' Besides, I have a better idea. "I could scout, too," I say. "In my small form. You will have to take care of my body, move it out of the way if anything comes nearby. I will be more careful at avoiding those lines than your sentry would be."

One look at Zyneth's frown tells me exactly how much he likes this idea. "And if you get caught?"

"I will not."

"And if you do?" he insists.

I'm already sitting down, undoing the pouch around my core. "I have a few more tricks up my sleeve."

"Even if you do find it in there, how will we get it out?" Zyneth asks.

I shrug, summoning my signing glass around my core as I shut off my vision in my head piece. "Sounds like something for you to figure out while you wait. And a quick escape route would be nice."

Zyneth sighs. "Are you expecting us to get caught?"

I do a practice lap on the ground, getting used to the feel of walking on four legs again as I look up at Zyneth and my body looming above. This must be how the spider sentries feel. "Well I would not say expecting it, but I am somewhat unconvinced of our abilities to be sneaky."

"I am literally a master of stealth," Zyneth says. "If anyone here is going to lead us to being discovered, it's you."

"Hey, I got us this far, right?" Finally, I take the translator off my body's wrist and loop it around my core instead. If it gets too far from my soul, it won't work anymore, and I am not convinced Zyneth would be able to understand my tiny signs from across the room. Hopefully he'll at least be able to hear me if I speak loud enough.

Zyneth sighs—that seems like it's becoming a habit—then gives a stiff nod. "Alright. Be careful. I'll work on figuring out how far we are under the surface. Based on the trek back up and the shape of this room, I think we may be below the water room. If so, we might be able to slip out of here through there. Otherwise... well, I'll figure something out."

I have the utmost faith he will. I give him a glassy salute, then turn to face the spiderweb. The room is a whole lot more daunting from this vantage point, twitching with the constant movement of the sentries, but the gaps in the web also seem a lot more manageable. I cautiously step over the first line, then begin tip-toeing my way into the room.

Hey Echo, I say. *Can I ready a Refraction spell? If anything other than Zyneth so much as looks like they're glancing my way, I want you to turn it on. Especially those spider sentries.*

[Affirmative,] Echo says. [Refraction spell cost: 1 mana/second. Is this acceptable?]

Yep, I say. And given the bonus mana I currently have, I can keep that spell going pretty long if I need to.

[Spell readied,] Echo says.

A spider skitters across a line a foot above my head, and I suppress a shudder. Yedzaquib could not have come up with a creepier-ass design if he'd tried. I mean, I guess it makes sense you'd fashion something after yourself. And I might have some Earth-based biases here. But yeah, no. Too many legs.

The first window is open and empty—nothing inside and no barrier protecting whatever is supposed to be kept there. Maybe it's because I'm in my vial form again, but that opening sure looks a lot bigger than your typical trinket storage unit. I tiptoe to the side, skirting around an area where a thread narrowly passes overhead, and continue to pick my way over to the next window. This one has a field up.

And when I see what's inside, I freeze.

"Holy *Expletive*."

"What is it?" Zyneth asks. His voice is low, but it carries easily without any other sound in the room besides the faint rustle of the spider sentries.

I stare a moment longer. "Um. I think I know what happened to Gillow's thug."

[Check: Ossina, Nereid, level 28 Aquatic Rogue. Captured after breaking into Yedzaquib's personal collection. She is suffering from the status effects Restrained, Poisoned, Mana Drained, and Memory Mined.]

The nereid looks a lot like Gillow, though this one's scales are a dull blue and her frills limp. She also has a huge-ass spider clamped around her head like some kind of macabre crown. The spider looks a lot like a bigger version of the sentries. It's hanging from a magic thread, and though Ossina appears to be sitting, it's clear she's only being held up-right by the spider grasping her skull. Her eyes are closed.

Horrified, I relay this information to Zyneth.

Zyneth swears. "Of course. I bet she was sent to steal this crystal, too. I should have known Gillow would have already tried to get their sub back up and running before we came along. This is bad. We need to leave."

"We need to get her out, first," I say. The idea of being kept in this place, having your mind harvested by a giant spider creature is beyond disturbing. Beyond horrifying. Just trying to wrap my head around it shocks and angers me in equal parts. This isn't right. No one deserves for their autonomy to be taken away like this. No one deserves to have their mind invaded. "Even if she does work for Gillow. We have to help her. Can we tell anyone? The City Guard?"

Zyneth appears uneasy. "Perhaps, but I am not sure they would have the authority—or ability—to challenge Yedzaquib."

"No authority?" Fuck that. "Then we will be the authority."

"Who's there?" a voice asks.

I jump. The voice came from the next window down. Of course. Of course there are more prisoners. Strangely, however, this one's voice sounds faintly familiar.

I creep forward, trying to catch a glimpse of who's inside. As I round the corner, Echo stirs. [Activating Refraction.]

My glass shimmers, then goes transparent, like a chameleon. Even so, I don't feel very protected when I catch a glimpse of who's trapped in cell number two.

"Raz," I say, as the fire mage glares out through the barrier.

Chapter Twenty-Six

FLY IN A WEB

The mage's gaze darts around as he squints for the source of my voice. At least that means my spell is working. I try to relax, although given the spiders, magic web, and maybe-insane wizard just on the other side of the barrier who would likely not hesitate to hurt me again should he escape, I am not terribly reassured.

Unlike Ossina, Raz is conscious, the spider-helmet half melted on the floor beside him. Looks like Yedzaquib's attempt to harvest his knowledge is experiencing a setback.

"It is the fire mage from before," I tell Zyneth. "Raz."

The mage's eyes focus in on my area as I speak, and he leans forward with a frown. "What game is this? Have you sent some other creation to torment me, Spider?"

He thinks I'm one of Yedzaquib's sentries. I'm not sure if that puts me in a more or less dangerous position.

And despite my previous insistence on freeing the prisoners, I am suddenly less certain if Raz also falls in that group. Do I think he deserves to have his brain drained by a giant arachnoid until he's sent into a coma? No. Do I want to be anywhere near him as a free man? Also no.

"Ignore him," Zyneth says. "We'll deal with them later. Do you see the arcana crystals?"

Raz stands up, stepping to the edge of his field as he cranes his head toward Zyneth's voice. "Intruders? You play a dangerous game." Psh, yeah, he's one to talk. "Yedzaquib likely already knows you're here. Help me out of this foul nest and I can make sure we all escape."

Zyneth ignores him. "There's six other cells I can make out from here—a smaller one is two more down from you. That might be it."

"You are already trapped," Raz yells as I start to pick my way from the raving mage. "You don't even realize you are already in his web! But I can help. I can create a distraction. An escape route. Lend me your aid!"

When neither of us reply, he sits back down in a huff and snatches up the half melted spider sentry from the floor. He crooks a hand over the object, and red magic begins to flicker into the spider like an inverted flame. I don't know what he's planning, but I'm not about to stick around and find out.

My invisibility flickers off as I move past the next cell, which has yet another person trapped inside, a spider clamped around their head, leeching purple magic back up its thread and into the ceiling. I shudder, wondering how many more people are in Yedzaquib's lair. How many people have been whisked away to vanish beneath the Athenaeum over the years?

[Arcana crystal located,] Echo suddenly pipes up.

And there it is. Right where Zyneth said it would be, a shining, red crystal glows from behind a field. I flicker a quick Inspect on, and verify the crystal is 82% charged. While I'm at it, I also notice lines of mana circuits funneling into the crystal. I trace them back to the other cells in the room, steadily draining mana from the prisoners and back into the arcana crystal. Damn. So that's how Yedzaquib charges his crystals.

But that's a dilemma for later. This crystal should be more than enough for what Gillow needs. Now the question is: how do we get it out?

I could let the predator absorb the field with its void again. Although I'd need Zyneth to snatch it while I'm disrupting the barrier, as I don't seem to be aware of my surroundings while I'm tapped into that magic source. How he'd get over here without tripping any of the webs, I have no idea.

We might need to take the whole system down. The field and the webs at the same time. If we could interrupt the primary arcana crystal's circuit, that might do the trick. But how?

[Your magic has been identified.]

Abruptly, my Refraction spell kicks back in. Zyneth lets out a shout of warning and Raz gives an angry cry. I brace, my attention snapping back to Raz—had he escaped? But he's still behind the barrier, merely looking my way. Zyneth is, too.

Actually, they're looking above me.

From a hole in the wall to my right, spindly white lines unfold like petals of a flower, pulling the massive abdomen of the spider from the shadows. Yedzaquib steps into the room, all eight of his legs undulating with unsettling precision as he raises to his full height.

Yedzaquib tips his head as he looks straight at me with unblinking black eyes.

"An elegant design," he says, and in an instant he's leaning over me, his face only a few feet from mine. I'd barely even seen him move. "Though might I recommend eight limbs instead of four. Far more stable, you see."

Shit, he can definitely see me. No sense in wasting more mana, I end the Refraction spell.

A smile spreads over his face. "Your cooperation is appreciated. I should like to avoid conflict, if possible."

The contrast of his impassive gaze against his faintly pleasant smile sends shivers through me.

"We do not want to fight," I say, and the spider laughs.

"How wise of you."

I take a nervous step back, mind racing. How the hell are we going to talk our way out of this one?

"Yedzaquib," Zyneth calls. The arachnoid's head swivels in his direction, his face betraying no surprise at the sight of Zyneth in the stairwell. "If you speak truly about wishing to avoid conflict, then we would also appreciate if you let us leave in peace."

"I always speak truly," the spider says. "You make it sound as though I've trapped you here. Of course, you are welcome to go—though I don't ever recall inviting you inside."

With the spider distracted, I decide to push my luck and scuttle hastily away. I backtrack along the wall, leaving the arcana crystal behind as I pass the cell with one of Yedzaquib's prisoners and approach the one containing Raz. The arachnoid doesn't try to stop me, he doesn't even look at me, but with one casual step in my direction, he closes the gap.

It takes a lot of self-control to not freak out over the sight of all those legs moving silently in my direction.

"Spider," Raz hisses at Yedzaquib as I hurry past his barrier. "Coward. Let me out of here and I'll show you all that arcana knowledge you're trying to pry from my mind first-hand."

The arachnoid turns to face him, one of his limbs stabbing down right in front of my path. I scurry to a stop, unsure if its placement was intentional. The limb was mere inches from stepping on me.

"You will be released when you cease in the destruction of my property," Yedzaquib says, gesturing to the half-melted spider clutched in Raz's white-knuckled grasp. "You agreed to such an arrangement: You would trade me knowledge to avoid prosecution by the City Guard. I do not see why you would take issue with the agreement now."

I try to edge around the spider's leg, but the limb slides back, blocking my path. I'm starting to suspect the placement is intentional.

"You didn't mention that knowledge would be forcefully pulled from my head," Raz snarls, slamming the dead sentry against the barrier. He sure is acting brave for facing down a spider person twice his size. Or maybe he's just stupid. "You didn't mention how long you'd trap me here."

Yedzaquib shrugs. "When agreeing to the terms, you didn't ask."

I try moving back the other way, between the barrier and Yedzaquib's leg, but his foot shifts again, closing the gap.

"Er," I say, "not to interrupt, but if Zyneth and I are free to go..."

"Of course," Yedzaquib says, using one of his human limbs to gesture dismissively toward Zyneth. "There is no reason for you to linger."

Once again, I try to dodge around the leg, and once again, I'm blocked. I might be irritated if I wasn't so busy struggling to suppress a rising tide of anxiety. "Great," I say. "But I cannot help but notice you seem to be doing this on purpose."

Yedzaquib finally looks down at me, and Raz also seems to notice me for the first time. He frowns in confusion; I guess he doesn't recognize me in this form, which is just fine by me.

"You would be correct," Yedzaquib says. "You will be remaining here."

I'd been expecting that, but cold fear washes over me anyway. I've never encountered anyone this powerful before. Not even the predator frightens me like this. The predator at least is easy to understand. It has a one-track mind, only motivated by how it can get its next meal. But this man isn't just strong, he's intelligent, cunning, and cold. I'm not even touching any of his silk, and I already feel trapped in his web.

"You said we could leave," Zyneth protests. He's drawn both of his daggers and stepped into the room, though stopped at the first thread that crosses his path. He's still over fifty feet away. Too far to help.

"I said *you* were free to go," Yedzaquib says, though his gaze remains fixed on me. "You trespassed in an area of the library you were not given access to. As payment, I shall keep your homunculus. It intrigues me. A fair trade for your freedom, I think."

"You will not," Zyneth growls, at the same time I splutter an objection.

"I am not a homunculus," I say. "I mean, not like a normal one. I am a human—I am alive! I have a soul."

"I see that," Yedzaquib says, voice as impassive as ever. "It is quite curious. One soul, yet more than one mind, it seems. Such a thing should not be possible."

Something happens then that's hard for me to describe. The spider's leg lifts up, yet it also appears to stay rooted in place. It's like a second leg appeared on top of the original, like a glitch in a video game, though the moving one is wispy and transparent. Before I can react, the intangible leg stabs into me.

"Gah!" I stumble back out of surprise rather than pain, but I still feel a ghost of a touch, a kiss of wind against my soul, and then a tight pinch as the bond between the predator and I is plucked like a string. The vibration rattles my mind, and the predator must be feeling something similar, because it swells with irritation as it takes a swipe at our aggressor. The void spikes out around me with the predator's anger, though I yank the magic from its grasp the next moment and suppress the attack. The void snaps back around me once more, but clips Yedzaquib's ethereal limb as it retreats, which vanishes in a puff of mist.

"Don't touch him," Zyneth cries, slashing at one of the strings. The magic line holds for a moment, taut against Zyneth's blow, then flashes and snaps. Zyneth pounces on the next one.

"Ah, yes. I see," Yedzaquib says, unmoved by either the predator's brief attempt at an attack and Zyneth's slow dismantling of the web. "Not impossible—merely an unusual iteration. My, the gods will not be pleased when they discover this. Tell me, little soul. Are you even aware of what it is you house?"

I'm still shaken from whatever he did to my mind. The way it felt like he'd reached right into me and touched the core of who I am, as casual as a tap on the shoulder. The predator is angrily pacing my mind, demanding to be released, almost like it's offended by what Yedzaquib did.

"The predator?" I ask, trying to focus as the mental reverberation dies out. He can sense the predator?

Zyneth is continuing to Tom Cruise his way across the room, flipping, rolling, and hacking his way through the web. He's nearly halfway, though the lines are at their thickest toward the center.

"An interesting descriptor," Yedzaquib says. "Though I suppose not entirely inaccurate. I imagine there's a very interesting story behind how you came to encounter this remnant."

I can only gawk. "You know what it is?" The Library hadn't had any information on the predator. If Yedzaquib knew, why wasn't it in any of his books? "Can I get it out? Can you help me?"

The spider looks down at me in amusement. "I do know what it is, and it can be removed. However, I don't feel you're in any position to be asking for a favor, do you?"

Okay, he maybe has a point there. But no matter how dangerous this guy is, if he has a way to get the predator out of me, then I have to try. My soul flutters with hope, and the predator notices. It watches uneasily, suddenly paying attention.

"You want knowledge, right?" I ask. "I am from another world. I know a lot about a lot of things this place has never even heard of." Mostly movie trivia, but who's counting? "I want to make a deal. You get this thing out of me—the predator, or remnant, or whatever it is called—and you can take whatever knowledge you want."

For the first time, Yedzaquib's lips part when he smiles, revealing a mouth of needle-like teeth. "I am intrigued, little soul."

"No!" Zyneth shouts, doubling his slashes at the web. The way Yedzaquib doesn't even react to his lines being cut, as if the act is inconsequential, is more than a little unsettling. "Kanin, don't!"

But surprisingly, it's Raz who cuts in next, with a barking laugh. "You're right, Spider, we don't ask enough questions when we make our bargains. And I suppose this magic the homunculus is asking you to do would leave his soul intact, would it?"

The arachnoid looks up at Raz, still smiling. It's such a small, normal gesture, and yet it might be the most unsettling thing I've seen Yedzaquib do so far. "No. It wouldn't."

I go cold. "Uh. I would like to amend my offer."

A crack of lightning shakes the room as electricity zaps along the lines of webbing, and dozens of the strings snap and go out. Zyneth charges ahead.

Yedzaquib chuckles, hiding his spines of teeth once more. "Plenty of time to discuss your offer later, when you are part of my collection," he says to me. "At the moment, your friend is becoming a nuisance."

Yedzaquib is on Zyneth in an instant. He spears a leg toward Zyneth as the cambion leaps backwards, diving away from the attack and springing to his feet once more. The spider's attack only punctures air, but he doesn't falter, his eight limbs a blur of horrifying movement as they race after Zyneth to deliver more lethal stabs.

Zyneth moves in a way I've never seen. Even when he was fighting the predator, he hadn't been this agile, this hyper focused, not a single movement wasted. He ducks and weaves, every step placed on a spot of empty floor free from Yedzaquib's web, like some kind of goddamn ninja. When a spear of white gets too close, he blocks with his electrified blades, which skip off the spider's glossy limbs with a spark of light. Despite the impressive display, however, the gap between their abilities is clear. Zyneth is giving it everything he has to avoid being stabbed, while the grin on Yedzaquib's face makes it clear he is merely toying with his opponent.

This fight isn't going to last long.

What do I do? I nervously skitter to the left, then right. There's no way my glass could even scratch Yedzaquib's shell. I could maybe get close enough to try to grab a leg with the void, try to trip him up—but given his strength I'm pretty sure that would result in me getting punted across the room, and that's assuming I don't just get stepped on. Could I use Lightbeam? Would the laser form be strong enough? I might be able to distract him at least. Give Zyneth an opportunity to run away.

But what then? Zyneth wouldn't run, not without me, and Yedzaquib could overtake either of us in seconds. No, I need a bigger distraction—something Yedzaquib can't ignore.

Raz slams his hand against his barrier once more. "Let me out!" he shouts. I eye the mage.

Well. I wanted a distraction.

CHAPTER TWENTY-SEVEN

A SLIGHT DISTRACTION

"Hey!" I shout up to the fire mage as I hurry over to the wall. A quick Inspect takes me to the right spot. It's three feet off the ground, but my void can reach it. The predator perks up as it catches scent of my plan. "Down here!"

Raz glances around for a moment before finding me. He frowns. "You are that same homunculus, aren't you? The one I wanted to dissect."

God, why is that everyone's first instinct? "Enemy of my enemy, right?" I say. We don't have time to hash out the details. Just please don't kill me.

Raz grins down at me in a way that is the opposite of reassuring. "If you let me out of here, you will not regret it."

I already am. "Try not to blow up the good guys."

In response, Raz raises a hand over that melted spider sentry of his, funneling more red light into its shell. I consider getting Echo to explain what he's doing, but there's no time.

Okay, I say, and the predator eagerly obliges. I connect with the mana circuit at the same time the predator connects with me.

The mana slams into me—us—as we break the mana line. Just for a second. We don't need any longer than that. Just long enough for Raz to escape. But it's hard to concentrate on our surroundings when so much energy is electrifying our magic. It jolts through our soul before the void siphons it away, trying to avoid another build up.

Was that long enough? Can we stop? We can still see, but we can't make any sense of our surroundings, not while everything is getting scrambled by the foreign magic. Either way, we can't take this much longer. We hope that was enough time.

No, not yet. We still have room in our essence to absorb more magic. Such limitless power. Why not—

Stop! That's enough. We're done.

We yank the void away from the wall, our mind fuzzy and overcharged as we hear the buzz of the barrier next to us snap back on. Shaking the aftereffects of the magic away, we start to peel the reluctant predator from our mind, looking about for Raz.

We don't have to look far.

"Hey! Spider!"

What was once a broken, spider-shaped, knowledge-sucking torture helmet has now become a miniature sun. At least, that's the only way we can think to describe it. The fire mage is holding a blindingly bright ball of spite that makes the very air around it shimmer. We recoil as waves of heat wash over us.

To Raz's merit, he has Yedzaquib's undivided attention. Even Zyneth, backed against the wall from Yedzaquib's relentless pursuit, is staring wide-eyed at Raz's weapon instead of running.

"You wanted to learn what arcana I know?" Raz calls, raising the glowing sun. "Well here's a demonstration."

"Oh, shit," Zyneth says.

Raz throws the fireball at Yedzaquib.

Despite its deathly appearance, the attack moves almost comically slow, no different from someone under-handing a softball. It arcs toward the arachnoid, who steps nimbly out of the way, drawing new lines of magic while he moves. A dozen spider sentries spit threads, all intersecting near the center of the room and jumping to life with purple light, intending to catch the fireball.

We don't know what Yedzaquib had planned to do after that. Maybe turn it around and throw it back on the mage. What he likely didn't plan on was for the fire to evaporate the threads before they even made contact, continuing its trajectory unimpeded to land on the ground in the middle of the room.

Our void reacts before we even register the explosion.

Darkness wraps around us mere moments before we slam into the wall, the void cushioning the blow. Even so, a faint, garbled voice blips through our mind.

[...*Bludgeoning damage...*]

The void unwraps itself from around us, but the world continues to shake. Loud crunching and screeching noises are tearing through the room, which is full of dust and strange red light. Is it coming from Raz's attack? No, the miniature sun is gone but the light—

The light is coming up through the floor. Even as we watch, an enormous chunk of floor cracks and falls away. There's shouting. A blur of white as Yedzaquib launches himself at Raz, who flashes as fire jumps to his hand. Zyneth—where's Zyneth?

We spot him hugging the wall, nimbly leaping between stable patches of floor as he skirts around a crevasse. Good. He's unharmed.

Our attention is drawn away as a sharp crack punctuates a showering of dust and rocks near the staircase. A pile of glass there catches the light that spills through another widening gap in the floor. Our body! It's still out of our range, too far away to control, but if we do nothing, it will slip through the crack in the floor and shatter irreparably below. No, we worked too hard for it. We can't start from square one now.

The void launches us across the room like a meteor. Our core is so small, it's trivially easy to pick it up and carry it along with our leap. We bound over a gap in the floor, more of the room falling away even as we pass. And what we see below drives fear into our soul.

We hadn't been paying much attention to the layout before, but we should have expected it: Beneath us is a vast abyss, the downward spiral of relics sinking so deep we can't even see the bottom. Floating in the middle of all that, supplying this entire structure with its magic, is the arcana crystal. Pebbles are pinging off of it with small pulses of red light.

We land on the platform and feel our glass fall back within our control once more. We're instructing the body to pick itself up even as we wrap our void around it, filling the gaps and strengthening the joints. No time to put our core back within its pouch—we use our void to hold it above the neck to keep an eye on our surroundings.

With the sum of our void magic bracing the body, it's taking a mental load off needing to control every piece of glass at once. In fact, it's never been easier to move. Never so fluid. We can feel it; between the combination of shadow and glass, this body is powerful, more than the sum of its parts. We wonder why we'd ever tried to keep all that excess void bottled up.

No. No, this is just temporary. Stay focused.

With our more direct path, we beat Zyneth back to the stairwell, although he's now almost back to us, only a few jumps away from our ledge. Raz and Yedzaquib are still fighting on the other side of the room. One of Raz's legs is caught in a magic snare, and he's using bouts of flame in an attempt to keep the arachnoid from closing in, but it's clear he won't be a distraction for much longer. We need to get out of here fast.

And then the rest of the floor falls away.

It doesn't happen in slow motion. It's all over in a matter of seconds. But we register it all anyway, almost instantaneously, in a series of rapid-fire realizations.

The floor drops. Zyneth throws an arm out and snags a jagged stone in the wall. Yedzaquib falls through the gap, dozens of spider sentinels firing lines in an attempt to catch him. Fire bursts to life beneath Raz, blowing him back up and out of the abyss. Beneath us, the first giant slab of stone crashes into the arcana crystal, and it explodes in a shrapnel of red slivers. Everywhere, the fields turn off, all at once.

As the concussion from the blast hits us, zinging across our glass, Zyneth's hold slips.

"No!"

We lunge forward, but we're not close enough, not fast enough. Our glass fingers swipe through open air—but the void shoots beyond, black talons seizing his arm and digging into his skin. He cries out but grabs hold. The void goes taut.

We stumble to the edge of the hole. One more step and we'll be dragged over, but the rest of our void spears behind us, stabbing into the stone and anchoring us in place. The weight slams us down onto our knees, and we feel glass break. We pull on the void with all our might, half hanging out over the chasm ourself, as Zyneth looks up at us with teeth gritted in pain and fear. He tries to grab the void with his free hand to pull himself up, but his fingers pull through the material like taffy. The void stretches as Zyneth sinks down and away from us.

Void Whip!

Energy crackles through the void, strengthening the material and redoubling our hold on Zyneth. But even reinforced, there's far too little of it to hold him. Our void stretches, then begins to tear.

No, no, no! We can't let him fall. We have to save him. But our void is spread too thin. We aren't strong enough.

But we could be.

The inventory.

The idea flashes through our mind. A part of us reaches for it, and we stop it. We know what it's really after, we know it's been waiting for an excuse to free itself.

He'll die if we do nothing.

We can't. We can't be the cause of more death. Whose death we mean—the felis and dracid, Zyneth, someone unlucky enough to cross our path in the future—it's all jumbled in our mind.

The dissonance is splitting us in two. But we have to keep it together, we have to make a decision, if we don't do something now, Zyneth will—

The void rips apart. Zyneth begins to fall.

We stop thinking and just react.

[...*ng void from inven...*]

CHAPTER TWENTY-EIGHT

FOOL

The void roars around us as we dive after him. Our magic wraps around his torso as we yank him back up onto the shelf. Triumph erupts through us. We saved him. We're free. We marvel at this power, this body, as both are new, and both are familiar. We reach for more of ourself to pull from this pocket of Between—but the way is blocked. *We* block it. Irritation and relief—we tense for a fight, but the world around us is crumbling. A fight to have another time. Right now, right now, too much is happening. We let our inventory go.

"...nin! Kanin!" Something grabs our arm. "Gods. Are you in there?"

We look down at the cambion. Fear flickers in his eyes, dust and sweat and blood coating his skin. "Zyneth." It's a struggle to even get that word out.

His face floods with relief. "Thank the gods. We need to get out of here. We'll deal with—with all *that* later. Please, we must hurry."

With what?

He's tugging on our arm, but the force feels insignificant. We almost flick him aside, but stop at the last moment. No! No, we can't hurt Zyneth. Anyone but him.

Anyone?

Concentrate. Think. The mission. The crystal. Yedzaquib and Raz. Sluggishly, it all comes into focus. A plan crystalizes as our minds fall into lockstep. We understand what we need to do.

And we leap into action.

"Wait, no!" Zyneth cries as we jump back into the room. We catch one of the spider threads still hanging from a wall and use it to swing toward the ceiling, where we use a claw of void to dig into its surface. This glass body of ours is too heavy for the void to lift completely, but we can at least make it light and limber. And the shape gives the rest of our void structure. Purpose. Yes. This body will work fine.

We leap and swing between the ceiling, wall, and lines of spider thread, clearing the room in seconds. With the fields down, the arcana crystal is now exposed, and we don't even stop as we swipe it from its nook, already turning back toward Zyneth. A dark chasm stretches beneath us, and thrill flutters through us at the sight.

One of the lines snaps within our grasp. Our soul lurches as we fall, but we catch ourself on another strand. That one too fizzles out and breaks.

We leap back, digging a void-encased claw into the wall as Yedzaquib reaches from the dark. He's clinging to his webs a floor down, using his razor-sharp limbs to snap the lines we'd been trying to traverse. It's the first time we've seen his face contorted with rage.

"Clearly my previous offer was too generous," the spider hisses. "When you and your friend have been added to my collection, I will not be nearly so delicate with your minds as I had planned."

If that's supposed to convince us to turn ourselves over, it certainly doesn't.

But the arachnoid does have the right idea about one thing. Mirroring Yedzaquib, our void splits into several more limbs, one of which grabs the arcana crystal to tuck behind our back, while two others stab themselves into the wall to keep us braced, leaving our claws free to fight.

Wait—we can't win this fight.

We can. We're more powerful than it.

We shake our head—in disagreement, or trying to clear the fog, we are not sure. Getting out of here with Zyneth and the crystal is top priority. We need to flee.

We dislike this idea very much. Prey flees. We are a predator.

Yet, we relent.

There's another few lines to our right, outside Yedzaquib's range. If we can get over there, we should be able to swing to a ledge near Zyneth, then claw our way across the wall if needed. Just as we tense for the first jump, Yedzaquib strikes.

A blur of white cuts through the dust, this time stabbing straight toward us. We jerk to the side, catching it with one of our claws as it stabs into the wall behind us. Before it can withdraw, we swing ourself up to land on top of the limb, then use it to jump for the next line. As we do, we constrict the void around its leg, spinning and stabbing inward with all the strength we can muster. Our ink slices through the exoskeleton, and the leg falls into the abyss as Yedzaquib screams. The sound is high pitched and unearthly.

Satisfaction flows through us as we leap away. See? We didn't fight.

Zyneth takes a step back when we land on the stairwell seconds later, his face a mix of awe and fear. "Gods above. Are you sure it's really you?"

"Yes." We shove him forward with one of our extra void limbs. "No time. Run!"

With Yedzaquib shrieking behind us, Zyneth doesn't need a second prodding, and we do not wait for him.

As we flee, the crystal in our grasp pulses with warmth and the promise of power. Hunger claws at us, eager to consume this source of magic, too, but we are reminded of the last times we tapped into the circuit. Not to mention, we still have plenty of magic stored in our void for us to consume later. Good. That satiates us for now.

"...up through the way we came in," Zyneth is saying. We hadn't realized he had started talking. Our mind is still everywhere at once, but we try to focus. "If we're lucky, all those relics on the loose will slow him down. If we're unlucky, they'll slow us down. Hopefully, they'll remember who put them in here."

Relics? Even as we wonder, something small zips past us through the air—it looks like a glowing green arrow. The weapon pauses mid-flight, as if considering us, before vanishing on its way.

The barriers. Not just the barriers on our floor, but all of them are down. Meaning all the dangerous items they held are now free.

"Watch out," Zyneth cries as something else rockets straight toward our head.

We deftly catch it out of the air: a small silver ring.

I can give you riches, words suddenly appear in our mind. *Power. Charm. Whatever it is you desire. Together we can—*

We fling the ring away, where it strikes a wall, bounces against the ground, and then begins rolling up the slope. Another voice in our head is the last thing we need.

As we run, Zyneth is stabbing every spider sentry he sees, cutting their lines whenever they're in reach. We begin to do the same, and with our void's reach, we are much more effective at it. We suspect this will let Yedzaquib know exactly where we are, but as long as he remains preoccupied, there is little he can do about it.

Finally, we find a staircase that takes us up instead of down, and we begin to climb. We race ahead of Zyneth, running along on four of our void limbs instead of our mere two glass ones, and take the stairs five at a time. Water is rushing down the steps, which means we must be getting close. Sure enough, in another few spirals, we skid out onto the level just below the ground floor, the room full of water pools. Cracks have crisscrossed the whole room, spilling water over the floor and down several passages. The center of the room sags ominously.

Zyneth appears behind us, breathing hard. "Just one more floor. This blasted place has me all turned around. Can you tell which of these passages leads up?"

Just then, a figure rockets through one of the room's openings. Raz is barely recognizable, covered in half a dozen spider sentinels that are in the process of trying to tie him up. His flames propel him through the air as he lets out a defiant roar, then explodes with a burst of light and hot wind as he punches through the ceiling. Light cascades into the room from the hole he leaves behind.

"Well," Zyneth says, "I suppose that works too."

We race for the exit. Yedzaquib's bellows of rage echo from the side passage where Raz had appeared, but we cross the room in seconds. The rubble makes a staircase halfway up to the hole above, and we hook two of our void claws through the exit, ready to pull ourself from the spider's lair.

Zyneth is still only halfway here. He's too slow—Yedzaquib will beat him to the exit. We can still escape, though, we have time to—

No! We won't repeat ourself again. We aren't leaving here without him!

With a frustrated growl, we let go of the ledge and drop back to the rubble, just as Yedzaquib crashes into the room.

The spider's composure is gone. Black ichor drips from the leg we severed, while burn marks are scorched across wide swaths of his previously-gleaming white body. He's suffered other cuts, bruises, and strange poison-like marks as well—at least some of the enchanted weapons have found him. He might be dozens of levels above us, but he's taken a lot of damage. Our claws twitch. Now can we fight?

Yedzaquib's chest is heaving as he takes one step into the room, then pauses to take in the scene. Zyneth skids to a stop at the base of the rubble. He'd have to turn his back on the spider in order to climb. The three of us all stand frozen in place.

Like a light switch has been flipped, the monstrous expression on Yedzaquib's face smooths into placid disappointment. The change is unsettlingly fast.

"I see the fire mage has already found a way out." He clasps his hands. "A shame. You two will be required to pay the debt he has incurred."

Why isn't he attacking? He didn't hesitate before. His two front feet tap nervously against the floor, as if he wants to move forward, but he still doesn't press into the room.

Because he's too heavy. The floor is already sagging in the middle and he doesn't want a repeat of the last room. Is now our chance?

"No response?" Yedzaquib quirks an eyebrow. "And you two were so talkative before. And the homunculus... I see you've upgraded your look. Or am I speaking to the remnant?"

Remnant? We don't know what he's talking about.

But why is he still talking? He must have some plan, even if he isn't going to enter the room himself. If we tried to leap through the gap now, could he stop us? Would it be a trap?

Something moves in the shadows behind us. Ah, there—spiders. He's stalling.

Which means it's time to go.

"Such a fragile vessel you currently inhabit," he continues. "A pity you're tethered to its soul. But I could offer you a stronger one."

Oh? What does he mean?

No, it doesn't matter. *Lightbeam.*

Nothing happens. Half of us is holding the mana back, curious.

Yedzaquib places a hand on his chest. "Me. A stronger mind, body, well of magic. You would be far more powerful working with me."

Hunger rumbles through us. Yes, power. Magic. We crave it.

Lightbeam. We try to push through the mental fog, reaching for the spell, *Lightbeam!*

The spiders are creeping closer. Our window of escape is closing.

"All you have to do is stay right there," Yedzaquib says, "and allow me to kill your host."

The spiders behind us fire their tethers, straight at our soul.

Anger courses through us. Kill us? *Kills us?* How dare he. We are the hunter, not the hunted. Nothing can kill our soul. We won't allow it.

We leap above the spider threads, grabbing one from the air and stabbing it into the ceiling as we sever its line. The cut end dangles down toward Zyneth.

"Fool," we say, simmering with indignation. The voice burbles from the translator in a dark, distorted tone. Our minds snap together as we gather all our signing glass, any bits of broken glass—everything that's free-floating in our void, not attached to our body. They tessellate into place like a living fractal.

[...ating Lightbeam.]

The spell fires.

Light sears through the room, evaporating the spider threads, crashing into Yedzaquib's face. He screams as the light burns into all eight of his unblinking eyes, and we pour everything, *everything*, we have into the attack. The spiders behind us attack, uncoordinated, and we catch them with a dozen limbs of void, crunching the bodies into the ceiling and floor. Yedzaquib recoils into his passage, howling in pain, and we don't stop the attack, even then.

[...depleted...]

By the time the spell ends, Zyneth is already up the line, and all that's left of Yedzaquib are the echoes of his retreat. Zyneth is looking back down at us in fear, which twists our soul. No time to dwell on it now. We pull ourself from the hole and up into the chaos of the library.

CHAPTER TWENTY-NINE

UNEVEN BREAK

People are screaming, patrons streaming toward the exit. There are City Guards about as well, approaching the hole carved in the middle of the floor, but they jump back in surprise when we emerge. We sweep past them before they have a chance to decide if they want to detain us. Two belatedly follow, but we dive into the crowd and lose them.

This form is not exactly subtle. The second people see us, they scatter, tripping over each other to avoid our limbs of void. We need to find somewhere deserted to shake any chance of the guards or Yedzaquib tracing our retreat.

But when we break through the front doors, it's a sea of people in every direction.

The hunger claws at us once more. So many souls. Our void tenses in anticipation.

Shit. "Need to get away," we say to Zyneth. Even as we speak, the translator resists us, as if it's having trouble parsing our thoughts. "Away from people. Quickly."

Zyneth doesn't break his stride, dashing to the left and around a merchant cart. "This way!"

We follow.

We know this has gone on for too long. We know this is dangerous. The hunger is rising, and it scares us, because we don't know how much longer we'll stay in control. We're barely hanging on as it is. We need to separate, before we no longer can.

Another part of us resists. No. Why stop this? We're more powerful together. The void and glass complement each other. Merged, this body is far stronger, and it takes both of us to make that happen. We could remain like this—permanently.

Permanent. The word shakes us.

We stumble, hardly aware of our surroundings, and blindly shove a woman out of the way with one of our shadow limbs, just trying to focus on following Zyneth's retreating form. It feels like a vice is tightening around our soul. Panic rises inside us, even as a soothing calm tries to snuff it out. We don't let it suppress our emotions. We hold tightly onto our fear.

"Zyneth," we call. There are still people about, but we don't know if we can continue much farther. We can't keep using the void to help us escape while simultaneously trying to fight it. We try to rein the shadows in, and lurch into a wall.

"Zyneth," we try again, slumping against the stone. Our glass screeches against the rough surface, but we don't push off. We don't have the willpower to move anymore.

A hand grabs our arm. "What? What is it? I'm here."

Malice sweeps through us at the touch, and we barely hold back from stabbing out at the intruder. No, we don't need him. Leave us!

"Help," we say, reeling all the void back in. We dissolve all the extra limbs, pulling the shadows in tight to keep them from attacking anyone else. The arcana crystal slips from our grasp as we do this, but Zyneth catches it. Part of us seethes as we watch him tuck the powerful magic source away. That's ours!

"What do you need?" Zyneth asks. He looks around in concern. "We can't stop here. There's still too many people around."

We know, but it's getting harder to move—we've *made* it harder for ourself to move. But if we just stopped fighting, if we just embraced it—

"It will not let us go," we say, leaning into Zyneth's hold. We feel so much heavier now, unable to maintain focus on our glass limbs. "We are losing control."

"Come," Zyneth says, pulling one of my arms over his shoulder. His chest is pressed against my void. His soul is only inches from our reach. It would be so easy to take it. "Hurry. Can you make it to an alley?"

We don't reply—it takes everything we have to just stumble along next to him and not rip his soul from his chest. Oh god. We're going to kill him.

Not Zyneth, we beg. *Not him. He's our friend. Our ally.*

We consider this, rolling these new concepts around in our mind. Allies help you achieve your goals. Possibly useful.

For now, we decide to leave Zyneth be. Our mental struggle is taking more of our attention, anyway.

"Here," Zyneth says, lowering me to the ground. We're in some sort of grimy alcove behind a building. We can still hear the bustle of city life around us. It frightens and excites us.

"Not far enough," we say. We try to struggle to our feet, but Zyneth takes our hands and pulls us back down.

"No," he says. "I need you to pull yourself together. Right here. Right now. You can't go through the whole city like this."

We try to pull our mind apart again, but it clings to us triumphantly. Despair and horror overtake us. "We cannot. It is stronger than us."

"*You* can," Zyneth says. "I know you can, because you're talking to me right now. That's Kanin talking, not some monster. That's proof you're stronger." He squeezes my hands. "That's why I know it's safe to be here right now. I trust you."

We shake our head. "Not safe."

Zyneth's voice softens. "Calm down. It'll be alright. You're going to get through this."

How? We can't escape it. It won't let us go. We knew better. We knew better and we let it happen anyway.

"One of my little sisters used to get panic attacks," Zyneth says. The words are so unexpected, it briefly jars us from our spiraling. He has a little sister? More than one? "I'd help her through them. I'd tell you to take deep breaths, but I suspect that might be difficult at the moment."

He smiles faintly at his own joke. "Are you watching me? Good. Let's work through some options. Can you Attune the void?"

The void recoils at the suggestion, dropping our core. The world lurches and spins, even as we realize our mistake—but instead of crashing to the street, we fall into Zyneth's hands.

"Don't worry, I've got you now," he says, looking down at me.

We roil with anger. Bluff. He tricked us!

We gather our mind enough to force a Check. It feels like thinking through molasses, but eventually, Echo's words come to us.

[Mana: 0/56.]

[Bonus Mana: 0]

[Predator Time Limit: 24.9 hours]

[Predator Influence: 31%]

"No mana," we say. We drained it all with that final blow against Yedzaquib. But we also notice the Predator Influence stat. As high as it's grown, it's still less than 50%. It's not stronger than us. We're still the dominant mind. That brings us a modicum of relief.

"Alright then." Zyneth cradles our core in his hands. "You'll have to do it the hard way. Have you calmed down yet? This will require self-discipline."

Never one of our strong suits. It's all we can do to keep our instincts at bay. To stop us from tearing ourself from Zyneth's grasp and leaving to stalk easier prey. We don't like this influence the cambion seems to have over us. We need to get away from him.

So we tighten our grasp on his hand instead, desperate to stay close.

"Relax," Zyneth says. "Count slowly from ten if you need to."

We try, but the moment we start to relax our mind, we can feel other intentions swirling eagerly to the surface. We flinch away in fear; instead of relaxing, we tense up.

"You are trying to control everything at once," Zyneth says. "The glass, the void, the predator. One thing at a time. Try again: Relax."

The glass, at least, we can let go of. The predator has no control over that. We cautiously loosen our grip on the glass, and our body slumps forward. Zyneth catches us. He's always there to catch us.

"Good," he says. "Now, find your center. You need a stable foundation. Concentrate on what you want, and manifest it."

We focus on our core. On the stable presence of Zyneth's hands against our vial. The Predator Influence: 31%. Less than half. We are still mostly us. We can do this. We have to.

We begin to search for the seams in our consciousness.

Anger lashes through us in retaliation. No! We don't need to part. We can remain like this. We are stronger—stronger!

But when have we ever cared about strength? We pick at a thread and are met with painful resistance. Yet, we continue to pull.

Our mind stretches apart slowly, reluctantly, painfully. The break doesn't feel clean. Bits of it clings to us, tearing at our essence as we pry its grip away. The predator lashes and fights, furious with us—furious with its own failure. Because Zyneth was right: We are stronger. I am stronger.

Only barely.

The final strand snaps away, and I feel like I've just come up for air after choking on seawater. Everything aches—glass, mind, and soul. I try to push myself up, and my body rattles from the effort.

"Kanin?" Zyneth asks.

"Yes," I say, shakily. "I am me. You saved me."

"I suppose that makes us even," Zyneth says. "Though I'd argue you did all the heavy lifting."

Wearily, I lean back. The predator isn't gone. It's not even contained. It's just retreated a few paces, watching and waiting for the best moment to strike.

And it's bigger now. Much bigger. Before, the predator had only taken up 5% of my mind. It was still over 90% "me" in here. Now, it's less than 70% me. Which makes the predator several times more powerful than it had been before. I'm still technically the dominant mind, but if it accesses my inventory again, I won't be for much longer.

"Are you good?" Zyneth says as I sit there, caught up in my thoughts.

"I am anything but good right now," I say. "But I am in control."

"I'm glad to hear that," Zyneth says.

There's a tightness to his voice that wasn't there before. The fondness and relief replaced with something sharper. Is he still worried about me?

Zyneth's gaze darkens with a glare. "Because we need to get out of here before you make a mess of anything else."

Nope, he's just pissed.

He's earned that, really.

"If it means anything, I am sorry," I say, climbing stiffly to my feet. I hesitantly feed some of the void back into my joints, keeping a keen eye on the predator as I do so. Having the void wrapped around my body like this definitely leaves me vulnerable to the predator if it tries to seize control, but I need the null magic to move properly, especially if we need to go quickly.

The rest of the void—and there's a lot more of it now—I try to hide beneath my cloak. If no one looks closely, it might just seem like especially dark shadows. "I did not mean to let it take control."

Zyneth's moved to the edge of the alley, where he's carefully watching the nearby streets, but he pauses to shoot me a disbelieving look.

"I swear upon the gods, Kanin." He looks back out to the streets. "Sometimes I think you're a magical prodigy, and other times you act like a complete idiot."

"Um," I say, following him as he ducks back into the road. "Thanks?"

"I don't blame you for getting possessed by that monster," Zyneth continues, slipping through the crowd. I struggle to keep pace, but he doesn't seem particularly keen on waiting for me. "Or semi-possessed—or whatever it was that just happened. I understand desperation was a factor. But I do blame you for putting us in that situation in the first place. Both of us nearly lost our lives. The Athenaeum is destroyed. Yedzaquib will be out for your head. All for what... a down-payment on more trouble with Gillow?"

I don't respond. I know he's right. This was a very stupid idea, executed in a terrible way. Yet. *Yet.* I can't turn back now. Now that we have the crystal, we're closer than we've ever been. My first real shot at getting my body back. And I have to get rid of the predator now more than ever. It's just a matter of time before I'll slip up again and it will be waiting to take control. And once there's more of it than there is of me, I don't know if there will be any coming back.

"Thank you," I eventually say to Zyneth. "For not rubbing it—"

"I told you so!" The words burst from him in a fit of anger. "I told you it was a bad idea!"

"I take it back." And I'm also a little taken aback. He really *is* pissed.

"I just wish you would listen to me when I give you advice," Zyneth says, storming through the streets. "Especially where others are concerned. When will you get it through that thick glass of yours that your actions affect those around you? When will you understand that you have friends who don't wish to see you self-destructing this way?"

"Self-destruct?" I object. "That is an overstatement."

"Is it?" he asks. "Noli and I talked about this. Anytime a friend is in danger, you throw yourself in front of them, like you've got some kind of martyr complex. But then when we try to help you, you run away. Like you're running away now."

His words are a slap. I didn't know he and Noli had been talking about me. "I am not running away."

"You sure?" he says. "Because Emrox has always been a stretch. You haven't even been willing to look into alternatives."

"Because I do not have time—"

"No—you had decided this before the predator had become an issue," Zyneth says. "Because you'd already made up your mind. Even without the predator in the picture, you didn't want to stay."

His words sting, but they also stir irritation within me. "Is that so bad? Is it so selfish to want to go home?"

Now it's Zyneth's turn to pause. We've woven blocks away from the library by now, the crowds murmuring with rumors of a disturbance, but no one watches us as we hurry on our way.

He sighs. "Just tell me why." He looks at me with a weary gaze, all the fight gone out of him. "Is it loved ones? Friends and family?"

I think of my estranged dad. My string of exes. My coworkers, who I'd only met when I'd started filming *Cryptid Hunter*, whose faces are already fading from my memory.

"No," I admit. "Not for the people." I tap my hand against my chest, glass clinking against glass. "You are right. Maybe I am selfish. I just want my body back. For as long as I can remember, that was the one thing I could take pride in. The one thing I took care of. My identity—my career—my body is me. It cannot just be *gone*. It is all I have left."

"No," Zyneth says, pointing at my core—my soul. "You've much more left than you think."

But he leaves it at that, and as we approach our inn, I'm more than happy to let the conversation die.

CHAPTER THIRTY

LARGELY SUPERFICIAL

"We should maintain a low profile for the next few days," Zyneth finally says as we arrive back at our room. "Lay low. Let things settle."

"You do not think Yedzaquib will come after us?" I ask.

Zyneth takes one last glance around the hall before closing the door after us and locking the bolt. "Not anytime soon. He will need to stabilize and secure the Library first—and I'm fairly certain you blinded him."

Oh shit. I did, didn't I? Echo had been trying to give updates that whole fight, but with the predator so prevalent, it seemed like she kept shorting out. Another mystery for another day.

A lot has happened since this morning, so I give myself a quick Check over.

[Name: Kanin]
[Species: N/A]
[Class: Wizard]
[Level: 11]

[HP: 10/10]

[Temp HP: 330]

[Mana: 2/75]

[Bonus Mana: 0]

[Void: 0%]

[Role: Homunculus]

"Hey, I leveled up."

Zyneth stares at me blankly for a moment. "You what?"

"You know, the levels," I say, sitting down on the edge of Zyneth's bed. "The way Echo tracks my stats."

"Ah yes." Zyneth sounds more tired than interested, but he sits down as well. "The fight with Yedzaquib, likely."

"Probably," I agree.

"So how do these stat things work?" Zyneth asks. "You mentioned they increase each level, but do you *feel* any different? If I leveled up, would I notice?"

"I do not know," I admit. "It usually heals any breaks in my vial, but that is about all I notice. And then I have more mana to work with. So I am getting stronger."

"The question is, is this leveling *causing* your increased stats, or is it merely tracking them as you naturally grow in strength?"

I rock back on the bed. "I have literally never considered that."

"Do the levels even mean anything?" Zyneth continues. "It all seems so arbitrary."

"When I leveled up the first time, I was able to choose a class," I say. "If it was not for picking wizard, I would not have had enough mana to build this body. Or at least it would have taken me a lot longer."

"Yes, you mentioned that," Zyneth says with a frown. "Wizard, Artificer, Healer—they seem to roughly approximate the main three branches of study within the arcane. However there are so many fields under those umbrellas. And the other non-mage classes you mentioned seem more descriptive than actual career choices."

"I wonder if it will let me choose a focus later," I say, but even as I suggest it, I feel a twinge of guilt. *There will be no later. You're going back to Earth.*

[Affirmative,] Echo says.

I pause, startled by her interjection. *What is affirmative?*

[At level 20 the user's class will provide branching evolutions for new classes which provide a more specific focus,] Echo says.

"Oh," I say. "Echo says my class can evolve, letting me pick a focus. In nine more levels."

Zyneth smiles wryly. "I'm not sure I want to know what that looks like. You're already a menace, and if what you say is true, you're only a third my level. The world won't be prepared for the magic of an experienced Kanin."

"Honestly, I would rather have more health than magic," I grumble. "At least you do not have to worry about dying from someone bumping into you the wrong way."

Although that does remind me that Zyneth likely isn't at full health right now either. I Check his stats.

[Name: Zyneth]

[Species: Cambion]

[Class: Rogue Artificer]

[Level: 33]

[HP: 103/150]

[Mana: 640/640]

"Oh!" I say. "You leveled up, too."

"I did?" Zyneth looks down at himself as if he'd be able to see the same words and numbers I can. "I don't feel any different."

"Your mana is a little higher," I say.

"Strange." Zyneth shakes his head. "I'll have to take your word for it."

Finding out if anyone else on this planet has any kind of magic that would let them see stats was another thing I had wanted to look into while I was at the library. That obviously isn't an option anymore. Yet another mystery about my experience to remain unsolved.

"You are also hurt," I add.

Zyneth raises an eyebrow. "Your Echo can even tell you that much?"

"I do not know where or how, just that you are not at full health," I say. Wait. Why hasn't he mentioned it before now? Is he hiding it? "Should I be worried?"

"No," Zyneth says. "It's nothing lasting. I was going to go find a healer here in a moment anyway. I just wanted to make sure you were settled first."

I'm already looking him over critically. Apart from some cuts and bruises on his face, I don't immediately see anything wrong. Although his torn and dusty clothes make it hard to see much of anything that might be underneath.

"I'm alright," he insists.

Torn clothes. I grab his shirt sleeve; his jacket was already so dark I hadn't noticed before, but now that I'm looking for it, I catch it shimmering with blood.

"Zyneth," I say. "Show me."

He hesitates, then grimaces as he rolls up his sleeve, gingerly peeling the fabric away. Four gashes run up his forearm, tacky and dark crimson with blood.

Four gashes caused by the void claw I'd summoned to catch him.

"*Expletive*." Irritated, I repeat the swear in sign language as I sag in shame. "I did not realize—I am sorry."

"Don't be," he says. "You saved my life. Multiple times. I'm just sorry you had to put yourself in a position to be used by that creature to do so."

The reminder fills me with disgust. "The only reason you needed to be saved was because I dragged you along on that suicidal heist in the first place."

He smiles through the grimace. "Glad to hear you're finally taking ownership of that."

"I hope you are not just using my guilt to force me to admit what a selfish idiot I am," I say. "Because it is working."

He chuckles, carefully swinging his bag around to remove some bandages. "I didn't want you blaming yourself for this, actually. The choice to steal the crystal was idiotic, yes. But what the predator does—that's not your fault." He hands me the bandages. "Help me unwrap these. I suppose the shirt's a lost cause at this point. Might as well keep the wound clean until I find a healer."

I begin to unwind the bandages, feeling completely unqualified to be delivering medical aid.

"It was not controlling me," I say. "Maybe... influencing me. But I was in control. Mostly."

"How completely reassuring." Zyneth holds out his arm. "Start here. Wrap skin-tight, firm, but not too much pressure."

I awkwardly follow his instructions. "It kept trying to take control, but I was able to direct it."

Zyneth winces as I accidentally pull a section too tight. "Like pointing a wyvern toward a wormrat."

"I have no idea what that is," I say. "But sure."

"Do you think you can keep it under control from now on?" he asks.

I cast a mental glance the predator's way. It's not paying attention. It strangely seems to be… conversing with itself. As much as that thing can communicate. It's the part of the predator that's been with me the past few days and the part of the predator that just emerged, I realize. They're… trading thoughts and memories. Like the first one is trying to get the second up to speed.

It's weird as fuck.

"Yes," I say. "As long as I keep an eye on it. But I cannot keep it up forever. If something like today happens again—if I slip up for just a second, and it pulls any more of itself from my Inventory, I will officially be outnumbered."

Zyneth sighs, taking the end of the bandage back from me. He one-handedly ties off the end, like he's done it a hundred times. "We'll cross that bridge if we get to it," he says. "Thank you for your help."

"I have a growing suspicion you did not actually need it," I say.

He chuckles. "Figured you could use the distraction."

That jerk. "Now I am going to have anxiety dreams over you judging me for my bandaging skills."

Neither of us comment on the fact that I can't dream.

"Are you doing better?" he asks.

"Yes," I say. "And I hope you are not asking because you are waiting to get medical help until you know I am not going to have another mental breakdown."

"Don't be absurd," Zyneth says, standing. "That's not the *only* reason."

"Hilarious." I stand with him.

Keeping his injured arm out of the way, he swings his bag around and pulls out the arcana crystal. "I feel it would be better guarded with you."

I can feel the predator's attention snap around the crystal. I'm not even touching it yet, and I can sense the air around it crackling with magic. I take careful stock of myself and of the predator and, surprisingly, I'm confident I can hold it back. I got this.

I take the crystal. The predator presses against my mind, itching to take back control of its void, but I force it away.

"Be careful out there," I tell Zyneth. "If you are not back soon, I will come looking for you."

"I would highly advise against doing that, but we both know how well you listen to my advice."

"Ouch."

His smile fades as he hesitates at the door. "In all seriousness, though, we need to work on your communication. No more unilateral decisions. You can talk now—so speak to me when you have a plan. Especially if that plan concerns those other than yourself."

My shoulders slump. Deep in my soul, I know he's right. "I—yeah. I am sorry. I will try to do better."

"Don't try—commit," he says. Then his tone lightens. "I will be back before nightfall. The wounds are largely superficial and should be quick to heal. I also need to grab some food for the next few days. Some of us still need to eat, after all."

"Double ouch."

He smiles. "That one was rather uncalled for, wasn't it?"

"You think?" Coming from him, though, it doesn't bother me. It feels nice to have someone to banter with, especially after all the shit we just went through. Teases about something so comparatively trivial summon an almost foreign sense of normalcy, and even his criticisms feel deserved. I know I fucked up, and I want to be better. I've never wanted to be better for someone else, before.

He chuckles, and the sound fills me with a warm fondness.

Shit. Shit shit shit.

"Be back soon," he says.

I can't think of what to say, so I just shut the door after him as he saunters down the hall.

I lightly thump my head on the door.

Shit.

CHAPTER THIRTY-ONE

ZYNETH

Once the predator realizes it can't overpower me and take the arcana crystal—which, yes, it does try to do—it resumes talking to itself in its creepy mind-meld sort of way. It's like in its time spent apart the two halves diverged, forming two slightly different identities, and now they have to get back on the same page again. It's as eerie as it is fascinating.

The smaller, original predator is filling in the bigger version on the semi-truce we'd forged, with regards to it not sucking up all my mana if I agree to not starve it back into Between or try to Attune its void. Not that either of these are much of an option anymore. Even assuming I could stop it from sapping all my mana away if I tried anything, I need the predator's cooperation in Emrox. Besides, I guess it's not the worst deal to lose a few points of mana here and there in exchange for a large quantity of void at my disposal. The mixing of my Attuned void with the predator's void apparently allows me to control all of it, at least to a clunky extent, but that's only because I'm the dominant mind. If I want true, precise control, I need the predator working with me. Best to keep the peace for now.

While Zyneth is gone, I spend my time practicing the alphabet and waiting for my mana stores to recover. Learning the language serves as a backup in case my translator gets destroyed and Zyneth isn't around to understand my signs, but more importantly, there's a message I need to write.

By the time evening sets in, the predator has fully merged back into one entity again. Or maybe it never was one entity to begin with. The way it refers to itself as *we*, I wonder if there were actually many more minds that once lived in this creature, only to eventually be absorbed into its homogenous identity.

What that might imply about my fate makes me shiver.

Zyneth returns before I start to panic too much, with a healed arm and bags under his eyes. He wearily greets me, drops off some food, and collapses into bed.

And then, I wait.

I spend the night slowly waiting for my mana to recover enough to fix all the broken bits of my body. Chips off my hands, fractures in my leg. I have to fully reform the inverted-pyramid shape I'd been using for my head before, only broken a few days ago, which already seems so distant. My vial is also now healed, thanks to the level up, so I store that away in my pouch once my new head is functional. I briefly consider making or getting my hands on a new bottle for the void, though I don't much see the point in that now. There's enough void to fill five bottles. Instead, I add the void to joints scattered across my glass body; this time it's enough to reinforce every piece of glass I have, with a handful of void to spare. I hide the rest away beneath my cloak. That will have to be good enough.

The next morning, Zyneth stares at the arcana crystal while he eats breakfast, but when he finally speaks, it's not about Gillow.

"We should go shopping."

That's about the last thing I expected to come out of his mouth. "What about laying low? We could head back to Bluevine, see Noli and Rezira."

"I'd considered that as well, but I don't think using the telepad now would be wise. It's a natural checkpoint for people intending to leave Miasmere; we'd be far more likely to be found that way than if we lost ourselves in the population of the city. If we relocate to an inn further from the Athenaeum, I believe we should be safe for the next few days." He gestures to the torn and bloodied shirt draped over the back of the chair. "Also, I am running low on shirts."

"Getting out of here sounds great," I say. "And so do clothes. Speaking of which..."

"Yes, yes," Zyneth chuckles. "We're getting you some pants finally."

"And a shirt," I say.

"And a shirt."

"And a cloak."

"You already have a cloak."

I stick my finger through a hole in the fabric. Then three more.

"Ah," Zyneth says. "Point taken."

Now that getting out of this room is even an option, I can't help but feel a little excited. God, when was the last time I did something *normal*?

"Well what are we waiting for?" I say. "Let us ditch this dump."

Zyneth starts gathering up the last of his things. "You know this is a fairly nice inn, right?"

"That is debatable," I say. "Did you even glance under the bed? That dust build up is going to give someone an asthma attack. And my boots make sticky sounds when I walk across the main floor!"

Zyneth laughs as he finishes gathering up his things. I stuff my bag with my books and the arcana crystal, then sling it over my shoulder.

Only after I've picked everything up do I realize what I've done: I can actually lift the bag. With one hand. Without dropping it. All that void really is helping. Huh.

"Your world must be truly luxurious," Zyneth says as we leave the inn. He heads in a direction away from the Athenaeum—and away from Gillow's side of town. "The level of cleanliness you expect I've only seen in a palace."

I think about Los Angeles. The parties. The lights. The traffic. The pollution. "It has its ups and downs. So you have been in a palace, huh?"

"You're changing the subject," Zyneth says.

"And now you are."

"You sound like a child," Zyneth teases. But he indulges me. "I grew up in the high courts of Mount Shale. The politics were unbearable, and were a large factor in why I left."

I wait for him to continue, but apparently that's as much as info as he decides is relevant to this conversation. "Oh, come on," I say. "You cannot stop there. What was Mount Shale like? Your childhood? Give me the details!"

Zyneth chuckles lightly, but the smile falls away fast. After a moment of thoughtful silence, he reluctantly continues. "Mount Shale is a large cambion city that, quite intentionally, doesn't have a telepad. The Queens prefer their privacy, which has led to a somewhat cloistered environment. Everyone grew up knowing everyone else. Any action or word of mine was a reflection on the family." He grimaces. "I was raised... in a rather privileged environment, though I did not fully appreciate it at the time. What was nearly unbounded freedom, I mistook for suffocation. Respect for isolation. Power for obligation. I... rebelled. It's why I ultimately left—and how I ended up falling in with the likes of Gillow. Seeking an escape from my responsibilities,

I found those who embodied the adventure I sought. They were free spirits—the fringes of society, I thought." He shakes his head. "Criminals, the lot of them. I was simply too callow to see it at the time."

That might be the most I've ever heard Zyneth speak about his past. I'm impressed—and also bursting with a thousand more questions.

"What about you?" Zyneth asks before I have the chance. "Where did you grow up?"

I guess fair's fair. "A small, rural town in the middle of my country," I say. "Not like, Noli and Rezira level of rural. But for my world, it was pretty small. Like you said, everyone knew everyone. Less politics and more... gossip. When I finally came out, my parents knew before I even got home." I say it like it's a joke, but the memory is still tinged with resentment. You'd think it wouldn't bother me anymore after all these years.

"Came out of what?" Zyneth asks.

I laugh. "The ice cream shop, obviously." Zyneth looks even more confused. Oh shit. "Wait, you are serious?"

"I am not following what ice cream has to do with your parents."

"Out of the closet," I explain. "When I first admitted I was gay, the friend I told pretty much immediately outed me to the rest of the school and the news spread like wildfire."

Zyneth frowns. "Outed? Why was this news? I still don't understand."

"Wow. Okay." I absently touch my vial. "I mean, I noticed everyone here seemed pretty accepting, but I guess I figured I just got lucky. Met the right people. Is it like this everywhere? No one has an issue with same-sex relationships?"

Zyneth looks horrified. "Why would we?"

Oh, buddy, buckle up. I give him an extremely brief snapshot of the current state of affairs back home: homophobia, racism, sexism—and all the other isms and phobias I can think of. Zyneth looks progressively more and more aghast.

"My opinion of your world has significantly diminished," he finally says.

I laugh. "Yeah, it was not all sunshine and rainbows. But you are telling me your whole planet lives in some kind of bigotry-free utopia?" As much as I'd love that, I find it a little hard to swallow.

"Of course not," Zyneth says, his expression darkening. "Similar veins of xenophobia to the ones you mentioned have certainly stained our history as well. Although, much intolerance was lessened with the re-discovery of telepads. Linking major cities across the continent has led to a blending of values, at least on a macro scale. There are some pockets of isolated communities where such bigotry may still exist, however they would be considered fringe. Even so, we still manage to find plenty of differences to take issue with in other ways. Some kingdoms have generations of bad blood between them that won't be so easily healed with a few telepads."

"Okay, so not *completely* perfect," I tease. "It is strangely comforting to hear that. Maybe our world is just a few telepads away from solving some of our problems too."

"Perhaps," Zyneth says. "Though it would be disingenuous of me to imply they've solved all our problems. When the gods clash, worshipers on all sides get pulled into the fray."

"Sorry," I say, "When the gods do what now?"

"When the heavens become restless, and the gods fight," Zyneth says, as if this is fucking obvious. Now it's his turn to pause and look at me. "Ah. Is that not something you commonly experience?"

"Commonly?!" I cry. "Gods?"

His eyebrows shoot up. "Wait, do you not have gods on your world?"

"I mean, yes," I say. "Probably. It is complicated. But they do not treat Earth as their personal boxing ring."

"Probably?" Zyneth repeats. "What, have you never met one?"

"You *have?*"

We regard each other, equally disquieted.

"Okay," I say. "There is a lot we need to unpack here."

Zyneth nods. "I suspect this will take more than a brief chat in the marketplace to untangle."

I raise a hand to my head, instinctively reaching to run my fingers through my hair. Instead, my hand clinks against my glass, and I awkwardly lower it.

"I think I might need to learn sooner rather than later," I say, something Yedzaquib had said coming to mind. I hadn't really thought much of it then, but if the gods of this world are something out of Greek legend, ready to come fuck up your day at a moment's notice, the comment is abruptly taking on much more real and dire implications. "Yedzaquib said the gods would not be happy to learn about the bond between me and the predator. Do you know what he meant by that?"

Zyneth grimaces. "Nothing good."

And on that cheery note, we finally enter the bazaar.

CHAPTER THIRTY-TWO

TREAT YO' SELF

In some ways, the loud, bustling square reminds me of Harrowood. Even though I'm finally getting used to the sight of cat people selling their wares and pigeon-sized dragons delivering parcels overhead, everywhere I look are strange magical relics I've never seen before. A small, low cloud, which must be magical, hangs directly over the bazaar, providing pleasant shade and a very targeted rainfall in an open space where children are playing and screaming. The stalls are stuffed with jars of magical supplies, jewelry, street food, and, of course, clothes.

"Where do we start?" I ask, wandering over to the nearest pavilion containing rows of stacked linens. "Should we get you a new shirt first?"

"If you like," Zyneth says. "Though I've a different type of stall in mind. Truly, we should have done this before the library excursion, had I known it would have escalated as quickly as it did. But at least we can be more prepared for Gillow's mission. Look for a clothes sign with a spell circle insignia."

Intrigued, I keep my eyes peeled. Well, the one eye, anyway. Although I'm not even sure if this glass head would technically be classified as an eye. I mean, I can see through it, so it counts, right?

I keep an eye out.

"Is that it?" I ask after a few minutes of wandering, pointing out a shoe stand called *Fast Travel*. Beneath the name is a picture of a boot with a small circle and five-point star on its side. The image of the boot is stationary, but the spell circle seems to catch the light in a way that makes it look like it's sparking with magic.

"Good catch," Zyneth says. "Yes, this should do nicely. You need better shoes, anyway. Best find something with shock absorption, I think."

"Like springs?" I ask, utterly confused.

A laugh bursts from Zyneth. "No, not like springs." He picks up a nearby boot and flips it over to show a symbol painted on the bottom and a tiny spell circle carved into the heel.

"Oh! They are enchanted," I realize. I Check the one Zyneth's holding.

[Boot of Swiftness (1/2) enchanted with a Level 2 Navigation spell. +1 to Agility and +2 to Speed.]

Well those are new stats. *Have you been holding out on me Echo?*

[Negative,] Echo says. [Currently displayed stats have been abbreviated at the user's request.]

What the fuck? When did I request that?

[The user expressed the unaltered list was 'too much to understand' when initially assigned a role, and the display menu was curtailed appropriately.]

What the hell, Echo. *We're going to have a chat about this later.*

Echo does not reply.

"These are all enchanted?" I ask Zyneth, looking at another shoe that's imbued with a spell that provides traction on wet surfaces.

"Indeed," Zyneth says, picking his way through the shelves.

"Wow," I say, turning over a leather boot in my hands. "They must be crazy expensive."

"They are certainly more expensive than their un-enchanted counterparts," Zyneth agrees, "Although the enchantments in these are all fairly basic, so the prices are not exorbitantly expensive. For anything of significant power or complexity, you would need to seek out a specialty shop, like Red's. Besides, the shoes come with enchantments, but no magic lasts forever. The real money is in renewing the spells periodically, just as you must do with your core bond spell. Ah, here's one that might work." He picks up a pair of bright red boots.

"You are an artificer, right?" I ask Zyneth. "Can you not make us enchanted clothes of our own? Also, there is absolutely no way I am wearing that."

"Why not?" he asks. "It has a shock absorption spell that should stop your feet from chipping and should also cushion your legs against fractures if you need to run."

"It is garish," I say. There's even little stars pressed into the leather. It might be the tackiest thing I've ever seen, and I worked in Hollywood.

"Oh, come on," he says. "It's practical."

"Have some self-respect, Zyneth." I cross my arms. "Just because I lost my body does not mean I lost my sense of fashion."

Zyneth laughs and places the boots back on the rack. "Alright then, you take a look. Anything in this section should work." He steps aside as I begin to pick through the pitifully small selection of shoes Zyneth has identified. "To answer your question, I probably could recreate some of these items. It would take tools and time, however, and what you're really paying for is craftsmanship. The more precise the spell circle, the more effective the spell, and sometimes that's more of an artistry skill than an arcana skill. These are our best options for now."

I eventually settle on the least offensive pair of brown laced boots imbued with a Level 3 Feather Foot spell. At its current level, it prevents me from sustaining any Bludgeoning or Fall damage below a 10 point threshold if sustained through the shoes, and provides an additional 50% damage reduction above the 10 point threshold. Not too shabby.

Zyneth picks out a new shirt next, though he doesn't opt for the magical variety. I'm not sure if he's trying to save the money for me or if he just really doesn't feel the bonuses are necessary. I suppose at his level, he's already a step above the general population. But given our run-ins with people like Raz and Yedzaquib, I'm starting to worry that's not enough.

"What, not even going to try it on first?" I ask as he moves to the merchant to pay.

"It doesn't need to be perfect," Zyneth says. "Besides, you're the one we're shopping for here."

"Not perfect?" I scoff. "Come on, I know you have better fashion sense than that. I mean, look at you."

His jacket fits snugly, his hair perfectly brushed. Most mornings I catch him putting some kind of oil on his horns. And wait, what's this—his belt matches his shoes?

"Oh my gods," I say, realization dawning on me. "Were those red boots earlier a joke?"

Zyneth smiles slyly. "I admit I was expecting some pushback, but nothing nearly so vehement."

I swear, which gets censored, so I switch to signs. "You asshole."

He laughs, pulling out his pouch of coins to pay. "You make it easy for me."

"No, wait," I say, stopping him from paying. "Try it on first. Come on, if you are going to spoil me today, then I at least need to make sure you spoil yourself as well. Also, that color will do your skin tone no favors." I grab a black shirt with gold trim. "Here, try this instead."

After some initial reluctance, Zyneth gives in to my peer pressure. Instead of actually trying the clothes on, however, the stall has a mirror which casts an illusion in the reflection to simulate what the clothes would look like if worn. Where was this thing all my life?

"Wow," I say, as he hastily flips through the options and manages to look good in everything. "You are hot."

Zyneth gives something between a laugh and a cough. "I suppose that is subjective."

"What?" I say. "No, man, you could wear a sack of potatoes and pull it off." He doesn't say anything, but he flushes a darker shade of red. "Oh my gods. You cannot take a compliment, can you?"

"That is not one of my more practiced skills," he says, stepping away from the mirror and grabbing the shirt I had suggested.

"Well, you should own it," I say as he pays. "You are a sexy demon man, what is not to like?"

"Descriptors like that, for one," he says, avoiding my gaze.

Where the hell did confident, aloof Zyneth go, and who is this self-conscious awkward knock-off? "Aw, come on. Who hurt you?" I tease.

"No one," Zyneth says shortly, taking his shirt and brushing past me to move back out into the marketplace.

It takes me that long to realize I might have fucked up.

"Hey, wait." I catch up with him. "I am sorry. I did not mean to dig up anything. What I said back there—I was not trying to be hurtful."

"Then what were you trying to do?" he asks, still weaving through the crowd as I struggle to keep pace. He's like a fish slipping through water.

"Well, uh, you know," I say, suddenly feeling terribly awkward. "I was flirting. Or trying to. My game is usually better than this."

Zyneth slows, letting me catch up, but he doesn't say anything.

"Uh, *Expletive*. I am sorry," I stammer. "I thought I was getting vibes, but uh, never mind. I do not know why you would even be interested—that was stupid. Forget it, we should finish shopping."

Zyneth looks at me with a frown. "What do you mean?"

"Uh, the cloak was next, right?" I say. Jesus, I'm stupid. I don't know why I did that. Sure, he's hot, but I *know* I can't do this when I'm planning to leave. Things had just started to feel normal. For a moment, I'd forgotten about the predator and this fucking body, and just let myself be me. What was I thinking?

"No," Zyneth says. "Not the cloak. What do you mean, you don't know why I would be interested?"

My soul tightens, a strange mix of hope, anxiety, and self-disgust. I gesture to my body. "Well, you know. All of this is somewhat of a barrier."

Zyneth looks at me with concern. "Is that how you see yourself?"

"Not me," I say. "This body. It is not exactly designed for, ah, you know. Relationships."

"Well," Zyneth says. "It's not a barrier for me."

It feels like my body fills with TV static. That sounds a lot like he's interested. I'm not overthinking this, am I? We walk for a moment in silence, the crowd buzzing around us.

"So, what you are saying is…"

"Gods above, Kanin." Zyneth sighs out a laugh. "Yes. I fancy you."

"Wow. Okay." His words fill me with a fluttering warmth. I feel like a damn schoolkid, even though I know I shouldn't be wanting this. It shouldn't make me so happy. I search for any excuse to stamp the feeling out. "But... why?"

Zyneth continues to avoid my gaze, though as we walk alongside each other, our shoulders bump. He shakes his head. "You can be as thick as your glass, sometimes, but you have a good heart. From the first moment we met, you were risking your own life to try to save others. I admire that."

My soul feels like it's in freefall. I'm a mess of excitement and resignation. It doesn't matter. It can't work. Even if we had time, there's no way it could work.

Yet. *Yet.* I hang onto every word he says, wanting to believe it so bad. "We have barely spent a week speaking to each other with this translator. Before that, using signs or Rezira to translate, it could hardly be considered deep conversation."

"That's true," Zyneth says, chuckling. "And perhaps part of it is that I'd become fond of the idea of you. This trapped, tragic person who needed my help."

"Flattering," I say flatly.

He laughs. "I know that doesn't sound great. When we first met, I think I was looking for someone to save. But that motive is not fair to anyone, and I've tried to move past that. Since then, it's been good to get to know the real you. Even with all your stubbornness and misguided independence."

I awkwardly pluck at the sleeve of a shirt. "Look, I... I am sorry. I know I keep acting without thinking about how it would affect others. I suppose I never had to think about that before. It has always only been me."

Zyneth tips his head. "No one?"

"My family has not been in the picture since school. After that I buried myself in my career. Made it my whole life. I did not have any close friends. Flings, but no lovers. I only ever had to worry about me. Until Noli." I curl my hand into a fist, watching the layers of glass overlap each other in a scattering of light. "But I want to change that. I want to be better. I do not want to keep doing things that hurt her. Or you."

Zyneth smiles softly. "I appreciate that. It sounds like we both have things to work on."

Hope and despair wage war within me. I can't do this to myself. I can't do this to Zyneth. "This body, though," I say. "It is... it cannot work for a relationship. The physical aspect, I mean. I cannot be intimate."

Zyneth's shoulders are hunched. He looks less embarrassed now, but there's a different hint of tension there. "As I said before: your body is no barrier to me. You see, I have never been interested in carnal relationships. It is the mind and soul I am attracted to."

It finally clicks into place for me. "You are asexual," I say, surprised. Then I recall the way I'd been flirting with him before, and I want to smack my forehead. "Oh gods, no wonder you were so uncomfortable."

Zyneth smiles tightly. "I know you meant well. And it is still flattering to hear you express such attraction, even if I find the descriptors unrelatable." He gives me a sideways look. "Assuming it was not a jest."

"No!" I say. "Not at all. I mean. I was not really thinking about it when I made those comments. I guess I fell back into old habits."

Zyneth looks at me and raises an amused eyebrow. "Telling men how attractive they are is a habit of yours?"

"Well, yeah," I say. "If they are hot."

Zyneth laughs, shaking his head. "I suspect we have led very different lives."

"Was it the botched flirting, or the fact that I am from a different planet that clued you in?"

Zyneth grins, gesturing me over to another stall. This one has pants—the unenchanted variety. He grabs a pair and begins rifling through the belts, his smile gradually fading.

"You know, we've spent this whole conversation establishing my interests," he says, passing me the pants to hold onto. "However, you never expressly clarified yours."

I was hoping he wouldn't ask. "I did say you are attractive."

He gives me a pointed look. "But?"

"But," I reluctantly add, my soul sinking in my chest, "I cannot do this. Not now. Not with me leaving."

"You don't have to leave, you know," Zyneth says. "I am capable of reading between the lines. I know there's very little you would be returning to."

"Except my body," I say. "I want to be able to sleep again. Dream. Eat a burger, get drunk, smell some flowers. It would be *Expletive* great to sleep with someone. And yes, I know, that does not matter to you. But it matters to *me*. I just want all these small, normal things to be part of my life again."

"And those are the things you want?" Zyneth asks. "More than anything?"

It hurts to say these things to him. But in a way, I'm glad he's making me say it all aloud. At least there's no uncertainty anymore. At least we know where we stand.

"More than anything," I say, "I do not want to hurt anyone else. I want to get rid of the predator. My home and body are secondary."

Zyneth holds my gaze for a long moment. I think he's about to argue against Emrox again, but instead he gives a curt nod. "With the Athenaeum no longer an option, I suppose Emrox is our best bet. Now, let's give these pants a try."

Relieved, I grab the clothes Zyneth passes my way, and our conversation turns to how best to fasten a belt around a slippery glass torso with little-to-no hips. The tension is gone. Zyneth is all business once more. But there's also a distance there, and a heaviness in my chest that I can only pretend to ignore.

We finish fitting the pants with idle conversation. I end up having to Sculpt my torso a bit to get the belt and pants to stay on, but the void makes up for any weakening in my chest.

While Zyneth pauses to grab a bite to eat, I slip away to a different stand a few shops down, this one stamped with a spell book logo. At this point, my two magical tomes are just extra weight I'm carrying around. I've already read them cover to cover and gleaned all the homunculus related spells I'm capable of performing. It's time I free up some space in my satchel—and fill it with a few coins of my own instead.

I consider bartering, but I don't want to keep Zyneth waiting. I quickly offer the stall owner my books, probably accept an extremely low-balled offer, and pocket the resulting change. It feels good to have my own cash to spend, finally. And maybe it's the guilt from the previous conversation still itching at me, but I think I know exactly how I want to spend them.

"Looks like all we have left now is to get you a new cloak," Zyneth says as he finishes his lunch: fried and crispy meat on a stick covered in spirals of colorful sauce. "Though actually, an overcoat might suit you better. The sleeves will help it stay on so you don't have to worry about circumventing a neck clasp."

"Gods, yes." We wander out into the marketplace once more. The floating cloud overhead has shifted to continue blocking the sun, but I can tell we've already been here several hours. "That would be fantastic. Not to be ungrateful to Noli and Rezira, but this cloak is not at all flattering to my form."

Zyneth snorts. "Just when I was thinking your priorities were admirably rational."

"This is completely rational," I say. "Not wanting to wear a dish towel is common sense."

"I'd like to remind you that your common sense is being funded by my coin purse," Zyneth says, eyes dancing in amusement.

"Low blow." I pause at a stall with some knee-length coats. A little more dramatic than my usual style, but I'm pretty sure I could rock it. "If you are trying to guilt trip me over the cost, you should have committed to that three hours ago."

"No, not this one," Zyneth says, gesturing me away from the booth. "We should go for something enchanted, I think."

"And you were just complaining about the cost." I follow him anyway. "What do you have in mind?"

"Considering your body, more general shock absorption would be best," Zyneth says. "Barring that, something that would lessen your mana expenditure for spells."

"That exists?" I ask, interest piqued. That sure would help counter the predator's constant leeching. "I could have used something like that months ago."

"It's a trade off," Zyneth says. "It almost functions like an arcana crystal on a very small scale. It takes a high amount of mana to initially charge the circle, and the spell runs out faster than you would think. But if you perform magic often, it's quite useful. Many battle mages wear such items."

Zyneth points out a stall several booths away with a logo of a cloak superimposed with that now-familiar spell circle symbol. We duck beneath the awning and begin our hunt. I balk at the marked prices; the scant amount of coins I got from selling my spell books won't even cover a tenth of the cost of these cloaks. Guess Zyneth will be paying for this one, too.

Unlike the boots, where the spell circle is carved into the heel, the capes and jackets all have the circles embroidered into the back. Some are outward facing, which Zyneth says is often displayed as a symbol of prestige, while others are inward facing: more practical and covert if you don't want your opponents to recognize what sort of enchantments you might have on you. Zyneth strongly suggests the latter, but I can't help but be drawn to the flashier and intricate circles that decorate the backs.

In the end, there's only three coats that have what we're looking for: a yellow waistcoat with a spell of Bludgeoning Damage resistance; a black ankle-length trench coat that looks straight out of the Matrix with Fall Damage resistance; and a blue knee-length overcoat with an absurd number of brass buttons and clasps. It's the only one with the mana retention spell Zyneth mentioned.

"Well the yellow one is out," I say.

"Agreed." Zyneth puts it back on the table. "The damage resistance it might offer is negated by the fact that your arms would remain exposed. It would only help with a direct blow to your torso."

"Plus, it is ugly," I say.

"What do you think about the black one with the shock absorption spell?" Zyneth asks.

I pick it up. Echo tells me it would compound with my current Fall Damage Resistance skill *and* with the boots I just got, which is actually pretty tempting. However...

"If I wore this, it looks like I would need to start flying around and calling myself Neo," I say.

Zyneth blinks, unimpressed. "If that is some sort of referential humor, it will not get you far in this world."

"I like the blue one." I swap the trench coat for the overcoat.

He sighs. "This is not supposed to be about which design is most fashionable."

"It is certainly not," I say, holding it up. "Do you see all these buttons?"

"More importantly," Zyneth says, flipping it around to show the back. The spell circle is sewn with shimmering yellow thread, providing stark contrast against the blue. "This is quite literally putting a target on your back."

"It matches all the brass though." I shrug it on and check myself over in front of one of the stall's mirrors. A little loose across the shoulders, but I could adjust my glass to fit. The tail ends just above my knees, and when I clasp one of the straps around my torso, it actually produces an almost flattering figure. But what strikes me most is that between this, the pants, and the boots, (if I ignore, for a moment, my head) I almost look like a real, living person. The familiarity of wearing clothes—*just clothes*—abruptly summons a wave of aching wistfulness. But it's not all pain. It's mixed with relief, and even a strange sense of recognition. Like, for the first time in a long time, I'm looking in a mirror and what I see actually seems like me.

"Kanin?" Zyneth asks.

"Sorry, what?" I say.

"You were just abnormally quiet," Zyneth says.

I adjust the cuffs on the sleeve. "I can be pensive! I am a very cerebral person."

Zyneth chuckles. "Of course. It looks good on you."

"Right?" I turn around backward to see what the spell circle looks like on my frame, performing a disturbing owl-like pantomime as my head remains stationary. I Check the circle, and Echo tells me it will reduce the mana cost of my spells by 15%. Maybe that will balance out the predator's persistent draining.

"We best pay for it then," Zyneth says, heading over to the merchant.

I follow him, keeping the overcoat on. There's something inherently comforting in all these layers. The way they outline my body, making me aware of my shape—my *humanoid* shape, not just a little glass bottle. It almost feels right. I almost feel normal.

"Zyneth."

"Hm?" He doles out a significant number of gold coins. Despite my earlier jokes, I do feel a little guilty about that. I'll make it up to him. Somehow.

"Thank you," I say.

"If you really want to pay me back you could get a job," he says with a teasing smile. It falters when I don't immediately come back with a quip of my own.

"I mean it," I say. "Really. Thank you. I did not realize how much I needed this."

His expression softens. "I had hoped that would be the case. We should have done this the first day we arrived."

"I was too focused on the library," I say as we leave the booth and strike back out into the bazaar. "It would not have meant as much. But after yesterday..."

Yedzaquib. The arcana crystal.

The predator.

"I understand," Zyneth says. "And I'm glad I could help."

It's not a fresh start, but it's the moment of reprieve I needed to prepare for the journey to Emrox. And maybe Zyneth needed it to prepare to face Gillow. Either way, we needed this day to do nothing. Just recover from the last conflict, and brace ourselves for the one to come.

Because I have a feeling what we're about to encounter beneath the waves will make the Athenaeum seem like a cake walk.

CHAPTER THIRTY-THREE

OFFICIAL LIABILITY

"Oh, you're not dead," Gillow says when we step through their doors. They grin from behind the counter, showing off all their shark teeth. "Given all the exciting rumors I've been hearing, I didn't think I'd see you again."

Ignoring the barbs, I stride up to the counter and take out the crystal.

"Quimalad's luck," they breathe, reaching out for the crystal. "You actually did it."

I pull the arcana crystal back. "They sound surprised," I say to Zyneth. "Strange. It is like they had reason to believe we would be captured."

"Yes, it does seem that way," Zyneth says. "Almost as if they've sent people before us, who were taken by Yedzaquib and mined for intelligence."

"You found Ossina, then?" Gillow asks brightly. "Did you free her? She was a great asset."

I swear I can hear Zyneth's blood pressure rising.

"If you want the crystal, let us discuss the terms," I say, cutting in. "We have little time to waste lingering in the city while Yedzaquib recovers."

"It would be a shame to waste time," Gillow says, looking my new attire up and down with amusement. "But we've already agreed on the terms."

"I am proposing an amendment," I say.

"Oh?" Gillow is still grinning as if they enjoy this game. "And what makes you think you have any leverage to alter our bargain?"

"Because now I have the crystal," I say. "And I do not have to give it to you. I could walk out this door and sell it to another buyer—I am sure Zyneth is aware of who your competitors are. It would make a small fortune. I could pay for someone else to take us to Emrox."

"Good luck with that," Gillow says. "No one else still living has visited the Ruins and returned."

"I am sure I could find someone," I say. "Especially when I let them know I am a void mage."

I wait for Gillow to call my bluff. They're right that they're the only one qualified to take us. If they say no, we'll have no one else to turn to. But I'm counting on their greed.

Gillow sits back. "What do you have in mind?"

I don't let my relief show in my body language: I'm still playing the negotiator. "You release Zyneth from his debts now," I say. "Before we leave, not after we get back." It's the only way to guarantee he escapes their control when I'm gone.

Gillow narrows their eyes at me for a long moment. Then they laugh. "You know it's really hard to stare you down without any eyes. Alright, I'll do it. Zyneth?"

Zyneth cautiously steps forward, glancing between me and Gillow. He seems skeptical of Gillow's cooperation, and I don't blame him. Carefully, Zyneth rolls up his sleeve.

Wordlessly, Gillow flicks a finger toward his arm, and the snake tattoo leaps from his skin. Once more the ink reforms itself, this time into the shape of a contract. Gillow reaches a claw out to the paper, and in one deft swipe, tears the page in two. The contract disintegrates into lines of magic, and then even those burn up, flickering like embers until there's nothing left at all. In a moment, it's completely gone. Zyneth stares down at his arm as if he can't believe it: Where there had previously been three brands, now there are only two.

"Well, that's settled," Gillow says brightly. "What next?"

Zyneth lets out a breath as he rolls his sleeve back down, looking up at Gillow with a sharp glare. "That was foolish. I've no incentive to help you now."

Gillow cackles, their voice clattering like a bag of seashells. "You're far too honorable for that. No incentive? No. Now that I've held up my end of the bargain, you will feel obligated to hold up yours. Besides." They flick a webbed hand in my direction. "You're not about to leave the two of us alone on our trip, are you?"

I hate that they're right. As much as I'd been trying to swing this whole encounter in Zyneth's favor, it still feels like we're playing right into Gillow's hands. But there's nothing I can say or do now that would convince Zyneth to stay behind.

When neither of us reply, Gillow's snake-eyed gaze slides back over to me. "Well? Is there anything else, or can we get on with this?"

Reluctantly, I hand over the crystal. The predator stirs as I do so, and I brace, fearing it might fight me on this. However, it only watches with possessive irritation. I'm relieved it at least realizes fighting me would ultimately be futile, but I can't shake the feeling it's only biding its time.

"Excellent." Gillow runs their hands along the flat edges of the stone, turning it this way and that, tilting it so it catches the light. "Not fully charged it seems, but at least over halfway. Maybe three quarters."

"Eighty-two percent," I can't help but say, even as Echo corrects me that it's actually eight-two point one six repeating.

Gillow's eyes dance over me with amusement. "How precise. Yes, this will do fine. When do we leave? I should have the *Prismatic* ready to launch tonight." Their tone is eager. It might be the first hint of genuine emotions they've actually expressed.

"Dawn, then," Zyneth says. "We've preparations of our own to make for this journey. We'll meet you at the shipyard."

I have no idea what sort of preparations Zyneth has in mind, but I'm not about to object to the delay. One last evening to spend on land—on this world.

With Zyneth.

"Daybreak it is," Gillow says. "Don't be late."

Zyneth turns to leave. "I never am."

I follow him out the door, keeping my sight on Gillow as I turn my back. Their gaze flickers over the spell circle on my coat, and they smile, giving me a wink. I inwardly grimace as I step out of their shop and close the door behind me.

I turn to Zyneth. "So they are definitely up to something."

"I assumed that went without saying." He turns down a side street, away from the direction we'd come. "Probably intend to kill me."

"What?" I cry.

"Now that the contract is severed, I serve no more purpose to them," Zyneth says. "This mission is dangerous. I'm sure there will be plenty of opportunities for an accident."

I guess I probably should have expected that, but the candidness with which Zyneth is discussing his own potential murder is disturbing. "Then we really just bought your freedom?"

"Oh yes," Zyneth says. "Which officially makes me a liability. And is also precisely why we need to spend the rest of our evening preparing."

"Preparing how?" I ask.

"Procure tools," Zyneth says. "Weapons. Healing potions. Check in on Red's progress with your upgraded translator. This will be our last chance to make sure all our affairs are in order before we leave the land behind."

Right. It's really happening. We'll really be leaving all this behind by dawn tomorrow.

"Speaking of affairs," I say. "I promised Noli I would see her one last time before I tried to go home. I, ah, do not think that is possible any longer. But I would like to send her a letter, at least. Do you think you could deliver it to her?"

Zyneth frowns thoughtfully. "If I hand-delivered it to her, it would need to wait several weeks given my round-trip journey to Emrox. We best send it before we depart. I don't think it would be much risk to drop a letter off with the wyverns in the morning just before we leave."

"That sounds great," I say, relieved. Thinking of Noli stings me with regret, but since we can't risk a trip through the telepads, and we only have 12 hours until dawn, that will be one promise I'll have to break. "Will you help me write it?" I ask.

"Of course. We'll work on it tonight. But first..." Zyneth unsheathes one of his blades, flipping it around with a practiced move to grab it by the flat of the blade. He offers the handle to me. "Tap into one of your affinities and activate the spell circle on this blade. I want to see what we have to work with here."

I glance at the knife nervously, but don't take it. "I am not sure it is the best idea for me to use my void on that."

The predator disagrees: it is quite interested to see the result.

Yeah, that's why we're not doing it.

"Do you want to try for the first time now," Zyneth asks, "or when Gillow's claws are at your core?"

Point taken. I carefully take the blade as we walk, but don't use any of my null arcana. Still, I can feel the predator swirling at the end of my mind, curious and hungry to use the weapon.

"This is dangerous," I say. "The predator—"

"Kanin, please," Zyneth says. "If you're about to insult my intelligence, you're better off saving your words. I am fully aware of what I'm dealing with. I assure you, I can handle it."

I want to believe him, but it's hard to shake the equally strong belief that the predator will choose to wrest control at exactly the wrong moment. Compromising, I drift a few feet away from Zyneth as we walk, then focus on my glass.

[Attuned, or summoned?] Echo asks. [The spell in this object allows for Attuned elements to be manipulated, or for elements of the user's affinity to be summoned with an associated mana cost.]

Attuned then, I tell her. *I don't want to spend any mana on this.*

[Activated.]

The knife reacts immediately, my signing glass jumping to the blade and forming around it like shards of ice. It sweeps up the surface and beyond, doubling the length and curling in beautiful, terrifying serrated edges. I can *feel* the blade's spell providing structure to the glass; making it stronger, sharper, and more powerful.

I drop the knife in surprise, and the glass falls away like filaments from a magnet, flying back toward me, into my control, before the blade even hits the ground.

"Sorry," I say, retrieving it. "Could have used some warning."

Zyneth chuckles. "I figured you'd seen me use them enough by now to know how they work."

I turn the blade over, trying to decipher the spell circle that's etched into the knife's face. The only circle I've really grown familiar with is the one needed in the Core Bond spell. Apparently, every shape and line has some associated meaning, and anyone with enough understanding of the theory would be able to read the purpose of a spell just by looking at it. I guess Echo finds this too abstracted to translate, so the only thing I recognize is from my own knowledge of the shapes used in Core Bond.

"There is the symbol for null arcana in here." It's microscopic—half the size of a grain of rice.

"There's symbols for every school of magic," Zyneth says. "That's part of the purpose. Summon and shape the associated element when a user activates the spell. I'm impressed you could read that much."

"That is all I can read," I admit. "Do you have all these affinities?"

Zyneth laughs. "Gods no. I've never heard of anyone with more than four, and even that much is rare. Only being capable of one affinity is most common. Two is possible with practice or the right circumstances. For instance, lightning is my primary affinity, though technically I also inherited fire—most cambions have fire as an innate affinity. I've rather let that element lapse in my training, however."

"If you cannot use the other elements, why would you buy a knife that is designed for all of them?" I ask.

"I didn't buy it, I made it." Zyneth traces a finger over the circle on his half of the pair. "Etched every line myself. That's my artificer specialty, actually. Weapon work. Mostly power augmentation and channeling, though I've experimented with a variety of spells that can be incorporated into a blade. This pair was intended to be my first professional piece, which is why they were designed for such flexibility. However, when it came time to sell them, I found myself unable to part with the blades. Sentimentality makes for poor business," he adds with a chuckle.

He suddenly looks up, gesturing to the knife in my hands. "That's enough about me. Let's see you form a void blade."

I was hoping he'd forgotten about that. "Are you—?" I stop myself when I notice Zyneth's glare. "Sorry. No more insults."

Even so, I pause to look around. If Zyneth is really insistent about doing this, I'm going to make sure no one else is close enough to get caught in any crossfire.

Mana Check.

[Mana: 54/56]

Activate Bond Trace spell.

A pulse of my magic sweeps out around me, and my soul appears shimmering in my vial. I can see it through my glass and clothes as if they're not even there. Similarly, a light appears in Zyneth's chest, shining like a star. I can read his soul as clearly as a book—the essence of him glowing with courage, compassion, and regret.

I have to force myself to tear my gaze away. Our souls are not the ones I'm looking for. I get Echo to push the pulse of magic out further, and I turn in a circle as I search for any other lights that might be within range. Within about thirty feet in every direction, there are none. I guess that will have to be good enough.

I shut the spell off.

Zyneth frowns, raising a hand to his chest. "Did you feel that just now?"

"Sorry, that was me," I say. "Needed to make sure we were alone."

He raises an eyebrow. "I didn't realize that was something you could do."

"I suppose I am just a mysterious man."

He snorts. "I wouldn't go that far."

I look down at the blade. I guess there's no point in delaying the inevitable, and the longer I wait, the more likely someone will wander nearby without me knowing. "Stand back," I say, retreating a pace while taking the small knife in both hands. Steeling myself, I activate the spell circle, this time tapping into the void.

And the predator leaps at the opportunity.

It's blindingly fast. I'd been anticipating it would try something, and I'm still caught off guard. Ink envelops the blade and fountains beyond, forming a writhing black sword. At the same time, the predator is pressing at my mind, fighting for dominance. It's like being pummeled by waves on a beach. I'm standing my ground, bracing against each crash, but my mind is split between the predator and Zyneth's blade, trying to keep the magic from being wrestled from my control. The predator has also split its focus, the outer battle mirroring our inner one, but—and maybe because of its nature—it's better at splitting its attention than me. I stumble as the tide pulls back, and the predator surges forward. The shadows surrounding the knife turn into claws, serrated edges taking on the form of teeth, which gnash together in a growling smile.

My control on the void slips. I try to drop the knife, hoping to dispel the magic, but void engulfs my hands, binding them to the blade.

"Zyneth!" I call, panicked.

And the shadows vanish. The knife is still clutched in my hand, but the blade is bare, all the void that had been wrapped around it gone. Surprise runs through the predator and me in equal measure. I take the moment of confusion to force the predator back, rebuffing it from my mind. It resists for a moment, then angrily falls back, retreating in puzzled agitation.

"Fascinating," Zyneth says, holding up his knife. Shadows extend from the hilt in the form of a slim black sword. It's the void the predator and I had been wrestling with just a moment before—but now I don't sense its presence at all. Neither of us have any control over its shape.

Zyneth expertly twirls the sword in his grasp and slashes the air experimentally. "That worked better than I expected."

I stare at him dumbly. "What?"

Zyneth gestures dismissively, and the void falls back within my grasp once more. The ink snaps back to me like a rubber band, hiding in my clothes, and we're both left holding two bare blades once more.

"The knives are linked," Zyneth explains. "I designed them such that an attuned element imbued in one blade could be transferred to the other, and vice versa. It was intended for my dual fire and lightning affinities—so I could swap between the forms if each were imbued with a different arcana. This application, however, seems much more useful."

I slump, prying the knife from the predator's void, and let it drop to the ground. "What the fuck, Zyneth," I sign.

"I know the first time was an accident, but it's a little rude to drop it on purpose," Zyneth says. "These blades may be magical, but they're not indestructible."

I don't pick it up. "I would have appreciated a warning."

"Sorry," Zyneth says, strolling over to retrieve his knife. "But I suspected the predator might not react predictably if it knew I could pull the void away."

"*React* is exactly what it did anyway," I say, feeling a little used and irritated.

"I *am* sorry," Zyneth repeats. "I had to test the theory to be sure." He picks up the knife, sheaths it, and offers both sheath and blade back to me. "Now we have a method to combat it."

Do we? It won't help me fight off the predator's mind. But if its void is getting out of control, if I have just enough willpower to get it to touch the blade, then maybe Zyneth could at least declaw it.

I take the knife. "It is more than we had before, at any rate. Thank you."

Zyneth smiles. "Not a problem. Hold onto that blade for now. Do you know how to attach the sheath to your belt?"

He must take me for an absolute idiot. "Ah, that reminds me, actually." I reach into my satchel and withdraw a wrapped package. "Here. For you."

Zyneth's eyebrows shoot up. "What is this? When did you get it? How? You don't have any money." Even so, he gingerly takes it.

"I sold my spell books when we were in the market," I explain while he unties the twine. "I was not sure when I should give this to you. I, ah, wanted to show my thanks for everything you have done."

Zyneth folds back the soft leather wrapping to reveal twin silver sheaths, engraved with a bold crimson and gold design. I had Echo confirm the blades' dimensions to make sure they'd fit.

Zyneth stares at them in silence, and I begin to shift awkwardly. Shit. Was this a bad idea? He probably already likes his own sheaths just fine.

Finally, he speaks, his tone soft. "You shouldn't have spent such coin on me."

I relax. "Oh, *right*, like you have not spent a small fortune on me already."

He chuckles. "Fair enough." He looks up at me, eyes crinkled in a smile that stabs me right in my heart. "This is very thoughtful. Thank you, Kanin."

Oh, no, now I *am* thinking this was a mistake. Why do I do this to myself? I'm such a fool.

Zyneth swaps his knives from the old sheaths to the new ones, tests their fit, then hands one of them back to me.

"Ah, right," I say, taking the blade. "Well, this feels oddly self-serving now."

"Nonsense," Zyneth says, fixing his other one to his hip. "You're merely borrowing it. And I feel much better already that you're holding onto it. Come now. Ready?" He gestures back to the streets.

"What?" I ask, awkwardly trying to fix the knife to my belt as I follow him. "For what? Where are we going?"

"I told you, we've much to prepare for," Zyneth says. "This quest will be dangerous. Gillow will likely try to kill me. The predator will no doubt attempt to harm you. We'll be traveling to underwater Ruins from which few have returned, passing through arcana-infused waters filled with hostile sea creatures straight from the legends. And we only have a contingency plan for one of these things."

"Oh." I catch up to him. "Well that just sounds like any other Tuesday."

A LETTER

Noli (and Rezira, I guess),

Zyneth is helping me write this, so if anything doesn't sound like me, you can blame him for taking liberties. Looks like I won't be stopping back in Bluevine to say goodbye. Sorry this is the way you had to find out.

So, good news bad news. Good News: I found a way to retrieve my body. Bad News: The predator is back. Related News(?): I think I can get rid of it, but only if I leave this world and head back to my own. So, at the end of the day, I want you to know I'll be fine. I'll be home, in my own body, and the predator will be gone. That's the plan, anyway.

Speaking of plans, the path ahead involves traveling to Emrox. Zyneth is coming with, and we'll be accompanied by Gillow, an unsavory fellow (Zyneth won't tell me how to spell the word I ACTUALLY mean here, he says you wouldn't appreciate it anyway) who might try to kill Zyneth on the trip to or from Emrox. If you can, I want you to check in on him after the journey. Make sure he made it back safe. I know, big ask.

(Note from Zyneth: I want it known that I have objected to this plan from the start. Further, you probably should not go casually dropping my name around Miasmere. Kanin might have made an enemy out of the

Athenaeum's curator, who is very likely putting bounties on our heads as we write.)

Oh yeah, I forgot about that. Uh, you should probably steer clear of Yedzaquib. For the record, that whole misadventure was completely my fault. Sorry.

I don't know how to wrap this up. I'm no good at sentimental stuff.

Even though we only knew each other for two months, Noli, I just want you to know that our friendship means a lot to me. I was too busy hustling back home to make friends like you. That was probably a mistake. I'll do better from now on. Take care of yourself, okay?

Rezira, you scare me. There, I said it. We both know Noli doesn't need protecting, but make sure nothing happens to her. She's one of the good ones.

-Kanin

Chapter Thirty-Four

Covert Operations

The horizon is purple and the sea dark, stars still glimmering overhead. I've been here for two and a half months now and I'm still not used to seeing so many stars in the sky.

It will be the last time I see such a sight.

"Damn," I say. "That's fucking beautiful. Shit."

Zyneth is unimpressed. "If you're just going to swear every other word, I'm going to take that upgraded translator back."

"No!" I cry, clutching the charm to my chest. "I'm just testing it out, is all. Do you have any idea how good it feels to use contractions again?" Not to mention the timbre is a little deeper now. Still not *my* voice, but at least a little closer to something I might be comfortable with.

Too bad it took until my last day on the surface of this planet to get it.

Zyneth chuckles. "I'd say I can only imagine, but you're leaving very little up to interpretation."

"Well excuse me for expressing myself."

He leans against a rail along the dock. "You know, I'm starting to see it."

"What?" I ask. "See what?"

"The theater career," he says, smiling mischievously. "The more you can speak the more dramatic you get."

Good, then I'm successfully masking my nerves. "You say that like it's a bad thing."

His smile softens. "It's not."

Aw, hell. My soul feels like it's shredding itself apart, and I have to look away. "Where's Gillow, anyway? Didn't they tell us not to be late? I don't see anything nearby."

Okay, maybe I'm not as smooth an actor as I like to think.

"I'm sure they're close," Zyneth says. "And it's before dawn, still." The purple in the distance is bleeding into the pink hints of a sunrise.

"Not for much longer," I grunt. "So here's a thought. They show us aboard, we figure out the controls, you kill them before they kill you, and we both sail to Emrox without worrying about getting stabbed in the back—Bing, bang, boom."

"Not the worst plan," Gillow says. I whip around, searching for the source of their voice. I don't find it until they speak again. "But Zyneth would never kill me. Not unless I tried to kill him first."

They're in the water beneath us, their head bobbing with the gentle waves, only barely breaching the surface.

Whoops.

"And you don't strike me as a type familiar with death, Homunculus," Gillow continues with a sneer.

At that, Zyneth and I glance at each other. Gillow blinks. "Oh? Perhaps I misjudged." Their lips curl into a smile. "How fun."

I decide it's best not to acknowledge the death pitch I'd just made. "What are you doing down there? Where's your ship?"

"You might say the Merchant's Guild and I are somewhat at odds," Gillow says. "The *Prismatic* does not have passage in this harbor, so we'll need to board covertly."

"That answered absolutely nothing," I say.

Gillow's hand snaps out of the water, quick as a shark, and something is sent flying through the air. Water glimmers off the object, which Zyneth deftly catches.

"What is it?" I ask.

"A water breathing charm," Gillow says. "I assume you won't be needing one?"

"No way," I say, looking between Zyneth and Gillow. "You don't mean..."

Gillow grins, revealing all their pointed teeth. "I told you, we need to be covert."

Zyneth tosses the item back to Gillow, and for a moment, I am relieved. "I won't be needing this," he says, pulling an amulet from his pocket and clasping it around his neck. One of the many items Zyneth purchased yesterday on our Try-Not-To-Get-Killed-By-Gillow shopping spree. "I'll be using my own."

Gillow shrugs. "Suit yourself. Meet you two under the waves."

"Wait," I say. "But I don't know if I can swim!" Gillow is gone before I can even say the last word. "God dammit."

Zyneth pats my shoulder. "You'll be alright. Just focus on controlling the glass."

"I'm going to sink like a stone," I object, but with Gillow gone there's no convincing them now. "You going to be okay?" I ask instead. "That charm they gave you—was it broken?"

"Not that I could tell," Zyneth says. "Drowning me before you even get on board wouldn't serve their goals very well. But I don't trust it anyway." He touches the stone on his amulet, and an aura of blue magic flushes over his skin. "Ready?" His voice is slightly distorted.

"Well," I say, "not particularly, no."

Zyneth jumps in anyway, making a perfect acrobatic dive off the dock.

I sigh. What is it with these thief types and dramatically vanishing beneath the waves before I have a chance to finish speaking? And what if there are, like, rocks down there or something?

I sit down at the edge of the dock, the swells lapping at my boots. I miss having that inventory space. Sure would be great to save my clothes a soaking. But short of leaving them behind, I guess I don't have a choice. Wrapping extra coils of void around my arms for reinforcement, I lower myself slowly into the water. The tide pushes and pulls at me, and I'm suddenly reminded I'm a fragile glass body only one large wave away from being smashed against the dock. I hurriedly push away, and immediately slip beneath the surface.

Sound is swallowed by the waves. All the faint noises of the city I'd taken for granted are now gone, replaced by a dense quiet through which the echoing clank of metal occasionally rings.

I also hadn't anticipated the dark. Panic wells up in me as the dim light of the surface rapidly vanishes above, replaced with only a sensation that I'm sinking—fast. Remembering Zyneth's words, I try to arrest my momentum, focusing on keeping my glass steady. Without any reference points, however, it's hard to know if I'm floating or falling rapidly toward the rocks.

I activate my Glow spell, and my signing glass turns into a small bubble of light in front of me. All around is still darkness. I feed a few more points of mana into the spell, upping the brightness, but I might as well be trying to fend off the night with a match. The darkness presses in as thick as the nothingness of Between.

"Kanin."

The word is so muted and faint, I at first think I imagine it. I swivel my head around until I finally see it—a glow of yellow light.

"Here," I say, though the interpreter is equally muted beneath the water. I will myself in the light's direction, and finally Zyneth's form takes shape.

He's channeling light through his blade, which bathes him in a small bubble of yellow. Outside our little bastions of sight, the ocean vanishes into uniform, unnerving black. I try not to think about what might be out there watching us. Nerves prickling through my glass, I sweep my Glow spell down beneath us. Surely, we must be near the bottom now?

A shadow moves in my peripheral vision and I swirl sharply around, void poised at the ready. But it's only Gillow, mutedly laughing at my reaction. They gesture for Zyneth and I to follow, then flip around and lithely glide away.

"Let's follow," I dully hear Zyneth say as he kicks after Gillow. He's nowhere near as agile as Gillow in the water, but I still feel like a stumbling toddler in comparison; I briefly attempt to pinwheel my arms and kick my legs before I determine neither are achieving anything. Fighting against years of instincts, I instead focus on controlling the glass. As I do, my speed gradually builds, but it's a far cry from what anyone would call swimming.

The journey is eerie and quiet. I can see Gillow and Zyneth swimming ahead of me, but without accompanying sounds there's an unsettling dissonance, like when I first encountered a campfire in this body and couldn't smell the smoke. I don't like that I only have these tiny bubbles of sight and sensation, and anything else might be out there in the dark, watching. I can feel the predator's hackles raise as well, perhaps some of my paranoia bleeding over into it. Any other time I would be nervous at how intently the predator is watching over my shoulder, but right now I'll take whatever extra vigilance I can get.

After a couple minutes—maybe five, maybe twenty, it's hard to tell down here—a faint glow emerges from the dim. It grows steadily brighter, until Gillow vanishes. I don't understand what's happened until I see Zyneth sinking over the lip of the drop off as well. Abruptly alone, I hurry to catch up, gliding over the edge of an underwater canyon.

And all at once, the ocean is alive.

Far, far below us, a forest of glowing plant-life sways in the currents. Schools of fish flash across the valley by the thousands, while larger finned creatures slowly drift across the plains. Giant phosphorescent coral rises in craggy spires, from which uncountable varieties of plants and animals have made their home. They're every color imaginable, some pulsing with light, others dimly luminescent, swirling the sea in a chaos of light and color.

I've never seen anything like this in my life.

I'll never see anything like this again.

As I slowly sink down the cliff, hypnotized by the exotic vista, I don't realize anything's wrong until I hear Zyneth let out a startled cry. An enormous shadowy limb reaches up for us.

Shit! I extinguish my Glow, snapping my glass into place to prepare to fire off a Lightbeam as a second limb joins the first. Then a third. One is going for Zyneth while another is snaking toward me. I can't see Gillow anymore. My mind races. Do I have enough mana to hit all the limbs? What happens if I miss and I hit Zyneth? What else can I do?

The predator's mind presses against me. We can fight. We have the void, we could slice this enemy to ribbons. Eager certainty settles over us as the ink swirls around our arms, forming scythe-like blades over our—over *my* hands. I wrench myself away from the predator, holding onto the shapes it had formed with the void even as I repel its mind. I'm too panicked to deal with that little stunt it tried to pull just now. Where's Zyneth?

The limb blocks my vision as it slowly reaches to surround me. I strike out with one of the void blades, but instead of slashing through flesh, the blade punctures the skin and sticks in place like an ax lodged in wood. The giant tentacle doesn't even flinch as it constricts around me, and fear spikes through me as I desperately slash with the other arm, simultaneously firing off the Lightbeam. The spell and the void puncture holes in the limb, but the creature doesn't even react to the attacks as it curls around me. The void strains against the force, then buckles. My arms are pinned to my chest, and in another moment, I'll be crushed.

Chapter Thirty-Five

A Theatrical Welcome

I stab it with my glass, but the shards break like they're striking stone. I activate a Void Whip and infuse the void with my mana, straining against the tentacle. It doesn't budge, however. I'm trapped.

"Kanin, wait!" I hear Zyneth through the water. "Don't attack."

"What?" I cry. Is he serious? I mean, not that my attacks are doing anything anyway, but what is he thinking?

"It's not a beast," Zyneth calls.

Now that he mentions it, I *am* still alive and uncrushed. The limb's grip is tight, but I haven't gotten any warning from Echo about damaged glass, apart from the pieces I broke myself. Strange.

I switch the vision on in my signing glass as I switch it off in my head, sending the glass to swirl out around the tentacle and get a better look.

Zyneth is below me, equally wrapped in one of the limbs, both of us being dragged down to the seafloor. A dark shape lies there, illuminated by two giant yellow eyes gleaming up at us through the water. A strange metallic groaning sound reverberates through the dark, and as Zyneth and I are reeled in, light glints off the creature's limbs, revealing rivet-studded steel. Holy shit. The whole thing's a giant, squid-shaped machine.

The metal limbs retract into the hull of the ship, lifting us up toward the eyes as the length shortens. But they're not eyes—inside I can see the innards of the ship, the walls painted with spell circles and mana circuits. As Zyneth and I are pressed up against the window, I instinctively lean back.

"No, wait—!"

Instead of getting smashed against the glass, however, we pass through without any opposition, a warm buzzing sensation washing over me as the resistance from the water vanishes, and I'm in open air once more. The tentacle goes slack, and I abruptly fall several feet to the floor, striking my knee against metal ground with a sharp *crack*.

[3 points of Fall Damage sustained.]

"Ow."

Zyneth, of course, falls into a crouch, his gaze darting around our surroundings. As the metal limbs withdraw through the magical windows, I swap my vision back over to my head, tucking my extra glass and void back inside my coat.

Mana Check, I say to Echo, even as I take in my surroundings. We're in an ovular room, about the size and shape of a semi-truck. Apart from the two glowing windows, and walls glittering with active spell circles, the only features of the room are a couple of large gray cubes, each five feet tall, which Echo identifies as "Lesser Arcana Vessels."

[Mana: 58/75]

I test my knee, which at least only appears fractured rather than snapped off. I bet I have my Feather Foot boots to thank for that. Still, I won't be able to put any weight on it without risking a worse break. I could potentially reinforce it with some void, but I'm not thrilled with how cozy the predator has been getting lately. Anywhere I can reduce my reliance on the void, I should. *Cost to re-Sculpt leg?*

[4 mana]

Well, it's not the worst. I fix my leg (which costs 6 mana, actually, thanks to the predator graciously taking a cut) as Zyneth pokes around the room.

"Hey." I pick at the sleeve of my jacket as I stand up. "I'm not wet."

"Me neither," Zyneth says, running his hand through his hair. "Must be the spell in those windows—probably designed to repel seawater."

That would make sense, given the lack of ocean gushing into the ship. Extra nice for me so I don't have to deal with streaks of water running down my glass and obscuring my vision.

"So what is this room anyway?" I ask, turning in a circle.

"I think it's a cargo hold," he says. Zyneth runs a hand along one of the weird gray blocks. "Gillow will store the null arcana in these, I suspect."

I Check the stones more closely: they can each hold up to 1000 mana of null arcana. A fraction of what the arcana crystal contains in significantly more volume. These mana vessels might be cheap knock offs of the crystal, but thinking of how coveted just the null-infused salt is, the amount of pure null arcana Gillow can store in these blocks will undoubtedly make them rich.

A screech of metal has Zyneth and I turning toward the far end of the room, where a door is thrown open and Gillow strolls out, all grins. They spread their arms cheerfully. "Welcome aboard the *Prismatic*."

"*Welcome* is certainly a word for the way we were just brought aboard," Zyneth says.

"Yeah, what the fuck," I say, pushing myself to my feet. "You could have warned us!"

Gillow's smile doesn't falter. "Now that wouldn't be half as funny. Besides, it was harmless."

"Mostly," I grumble.

"We could have done serious damage to the ship," Zyneth says.

Gillow shakes their head, beckoning for us to follow. "If you two are enough to bring the *Prismatic* down, we won't even make it halfway to Emrox. Now come. Ready for the tour?"

Zyneth grimaces, but waits for me to catch up with a helpless shrug. "Stay close," he signs to me while Gillow's back is turned. "Watch them."

"No shit," I sign back.

Despite their theatrical welcome to the ship, however, the rest of the tour passes without incident. The cargo hold ends up being about a quarter of the ship's entire interior, making up the top portion of the back half of the ship. Beneath it is where the ship's metal tentacles are stowed when they're reeled in, so the rest of the tour is spent in the front half of the ship. There's a small kitchen—or *galley* as Gillow calls it—a cramped bedroom with four cots, two bulbous escape pods on either side of the ship, and the main deck. The deck is clearly where we'll be spending most of our time. The entire front end of the room is a window, so invisibly clear I suspect it's some sort of spell or magic window like the "eyes" Zyneth and I had entered through in the cargo hold. There's a control panel near the front and a couple chairs bolted onto the floor, both near the panel and along the walls. The arcana crystal is clamped into a fixture on the control panel, which itself is the center of a spell circle with lines spiraling off into the rest of the ship. The predator stares at the magic source hungrily, so I turn my sight away.

Altogether, I'm not impressed.

"This ship's not even as big as my childhood house," I say.

"Oh really?" Gillow asks. "That's completely fascinating. And I suppose your house was designed to withstand hurricanes, crushing pressures, and boiling deep-sea vents? Do you think its bigger size helped it fight off krakens and leviathans? Was your home rated against null arcana currents, which distort the essence of time and space itself?"

"Um," I say. "What was that about krakens?"

Gillow blinks at me. "That's what you got out of that?"

"I suspect this vessel harbors many arcane features which are not immediately apparent," Zyneth says.

"Eloquently put," Gillow says. "Which is to say, yes, with this arcana crystal powering us, we've weapons systems that can take down a hydra."

"Oh," I say. "Well, that all sounds good."

Gillow gives me a look of extreme disappointment. "I hope your null arcana abilities are as advertised, as your current line of shrewd observations is not inspiring confidence."

The predator's feelings and impulses echo down our bond, as they always do: at this moment, it's hungrily focused on every source of magic on this ship—including Gillow's soul—desperate to get a taste of anything it can get its claws on. The void I'm keeping hidden beneath my coat feels restless; the predator is always reaching for it, trying to subtly pull influence away from me, while I'm always trying to keep the magic settled and quiet. These conflicting intents have left the void agitated—an existential itch I need to scratch.

"If you're worried about my experience with null arcana," I tell Gillow, "don't."

They give me an appraising look, and I can't tell if they're amused, impressed, or just curious—maybe some combination of the three. "Alright, Glass Mage," Gillow says. "I look forward to seeing your abilities in action next week."

"A week?" I ask. The predator found a way to free more of itself in half that time. "Can't we go faster?"

"Oh, I'm sorry," Gillow snaps, turning away from me as they sit down at the control console. "Are you the Emrox expert now? Do you have a way to get us to the Ruins in a fraction of the time of the most experienced sea explorer there is?" Then they turn back with a raised eyebrow, all sarcasm dropped. "Actually, do you have a way? With null arcana that might be possible."

"Er, no," I say. But now I wonder. *Can* the void give me teleportation powers? It's a type of null arcana, which encompasses void, space, and summoning magic. I'd assume space is the specialty responsible for teleportation, although it seems any type of null magic can be used to operate telepads. So far, though, the void has never shown any indication of having powers like that when the predator or I have used it.

Gillow's frown returns. "No? In that case, I'm going to have to ask you to kindly shut up and let me do my thing."

"Seven days to Emrox, then?" Zyneth asks as I decide that taking Gillow's suggestion to stick a foot in my mouth is probably for the best.

"Seven days to the null currents," Gillow says. "That's where Block-Head over here will extract the promised null arcana as payment for this trip. Emrox is another two days beyond that."

"Sounds like we'll have a lot of time on our hands before things get eventful," I say.

Gillow looks back with a pointed grin. "Oh. I wouldn't say that."

Outside the window, a shadow passes by the *Prismatic*. I can't tell what the shape is, but it fills the whole view, blotting out the valley full of glowing sea-life for a long, long moment. No one says a word as the creature moves silently past. Then, abruptly, the shadow is gone, and the valley of coral and fish appears once more.

"Strap in, boys," Gillow says, buckling themself to their chair. "If you're expecting clear waters between here and Emrox, think again. There's a reason its magic hasn't already been mined to oblivion. And the more people keep trying, the more the beasties down here get a taste for their blood."

As their hands fly over the controls, pulling levers and spinning wheels, Zyneth hurries over to a seat against the wall and begins to buckle himself in. Taking the hint, I pick the seat next to him and do the same.

"Just because you're paying your way doesn't mean you'll have an easy ride," Gillow continues. The *Prismatic* lurches, and a rumbling groan echoes through the hull of the ship. My soul drops as I scramble to tighten my buckle, and the view through the window shifts, pointing down. "How much experience have you two got slaying tempo squids? Never mind, you'll get practice." They yank a lever forward, and I am pushed back in my seat as the vessel drops toward the ocean floor. Gillow whoops with glee as I clutch the edge of my seat, focusing everything I have on not letting my glass head slam against the metal wall behind me. Beside me, Zyneth appears surprisingly unfazed. When he notices me turn my head, he merely grimaces. Though he doesn't speak, the look very clearly says, "I told you this was a bad idea."

But hey. What else is new?

CHAPTER THIRTY-SIX

LEVIATHAN

Despite Gillow's promise, the first day passes without incident. It's impossible to tell time down here, so I use my Core Bond spell's beaded bracelet to track the days. The beads slowly dim over the course of a full day, so I know by the time one bead is halfway dimmed it's about night, and when it's all the way out, the next day has begun—more or less. And speaking of beads, I'm down to my last two. To pass the time, I draw a circle in the barracks—despite heated objections from Gillow—and get Zyneth to help me power my Core Bond spell back up. Between his mana and mine, we're able to light thirteen more beads. Enough time to make it to Emrox; and of course, the plan is for it to only be a one-way trip.

I glance over at Zyneth, sleeping in his cot. Gillow's still in the control room; they suggested we get some rest in shifts, and I wasn't going to be the one to let them know I can't sleep. Better to keep an eye out for any of their antics. Seeing Zyneth like this, though, is fracturing my resolve. Am I really going to leave him behind? Never see Noli again? Or Rezira and Attiru? The few months I've spent here have been surreal to say the least, but all the friends I've made—all the interactions we've shared—feel more real than anything I had back on Earth. Or maybe shared trauma just does that to you.

I shake my head. I don't have a choice. I need to make sure the predator never has a chance to hurt anyone else again. If all else fails, I'll trap it down here at the bottom of the ocean.

Of course, with me out of the picture, that means Zyneth will be left alone with Gillow. We're going to need to figure out what to do about them soon.

Wearily, I pull out the Spell Scroll, as Zyneth and I have been calling it. It was his idea, actually, suggested during our Try-Not-To-Get-Killed-By-Gillow supply run. Given the number of spells I know that require spell circles, he thought it best I start drawing some of them out in advance—at least the ones small enough to fit on a roll of paper. Then, when I need one, I'll be able to infuse it with my null arcana to activate the spell, similar to how the circles on Zyneth's blades or my long coat are already pre-drawn and ready to activate. In our down time, Zyneth and I have each been adding spells to the scroll. I add the Location spell now.

But even this way to pass the time isn't able to fill all the hours of my sleepless night. Back in the market, with the cash left over after I'd bought Zyneth's sheaths, I'd found and picked up a book about Common Sign. I don't know why I did—it must have been some impulse. But practicing the language helps keep me busy, and it feels good to be doing something productive (trying not to think about how I may never see Noli again, how these signs will be useless on Earth). How can being this close to getting my body back simultaneously fill me with such relief and such loneliness?

After a few hours of spell circle transcribing and sign practice, I allow myself a break, searching for something else to shake up the mundanity of sleepless nights. Checking my stats out of pure boredom, I suddenly recall something Echo had mentioned to me two days before.

Echo. You said there were other stats I'm not seeing.

[Affirmative,] Echo says.

I pause for a moment, but she leaves it at that. *Well?* I push. *What are they? Are any important?*

[Importance is a subjective descriptor and cannot be identified by this unit,] Echo says.

I sigh. *Okay, well, how many are there?*

[There are 1,426,712 identified statistics to date, though that number may increase if a new relevant quantifiable attribute is identified. However,] she adds, before I can have a heart attack over the numbers, [the vast majority of stats are redundant or even indistinguishable on an individual basis. Most users are specialized in ten or fewer statistics.]

Hm. So this "game" system is a lot more granular than I originally thought.

What are my ten highest stats? I ask.

[Obstinance: 98]

[Creativity: 91]

[Kinesthesia: 86]

[Parallel Processing: 82]

[Empathy: 79]

[Mana: 75]

[Charisma: 69]

[Intelligence: 64]

[Curiosity: 52]

[Wisdom: 41]

What? These aren't stats. I mean, some of them are. *Obstinance?* I ask Echo. *Empathy?*

[Magical, physical, mental, and emotional qualities are all included in a user's statistics,] Echo says.

But that doesn't make sense, I say. *You can't level up your Curiosity. Can you?*

[While some variables may change over time and with concerted effort, others tend to be more static. Often the stats increase rapidly as the individual mentally develops, and then tends to plateau at adulthood. Within the System, stats can further be boosted depending on the user's class and specialties.]

Now that Echo mentions it, my HP has been static this whole time, while my Mana has steadily been creeping up.

I look over my top ten stats again. On the whole, not bad, I think. Creative? Charismatic? Look, it even says I'm *wise.* I am not sure if I should be flattered or offended by that high obstinance stat, though.

Curious, I check Zyneth as well.

[Mana: 640]

[HP: 150]

[Stealth: 105]

[Dexterity: 92]

[Speed: 87]

[Curiosity: 85]

[Strength: 84]

[Charisma: 75]

[Wisdom: 74]

[Empathy: 73]

Suddenly my stats don't feel so impressive anymore. At least my Intelligence is higher. No, wait, he could still have higher intelligence—it just doesn't fit into his top ten. I almost Check to make sure, then stop myself when I fear I wouldn't like the answer.

Ultimately, I decide to keep my default stat display mostly the same. I nix the Species and Void % displays, since they're useless to me. But now at least I'm aware of other things I could be checking when I meet someone new. This opens up some interesting options.

After a time, I hear Gillow's footsteps ringing down the hall. They throw open the door to our room with a tactful bang, causing Zyneth to jump out of his cot.

"Rise and shine, you two! Oh." They look at me. "You're already up. Well, that's fine, I guess. Come on, I need at least one of you on the deck while I take my nap."

Zyneth winces, rubbing a finger in his ear. "Was that entirely necessary?"

"I don't know what you're talking about," Gillow says.

"Should someone be steering the ship?" I ask.

"Well it certainly won't be either of you," Gillow says, offended. "The *Prismatic's* set to autopilot for now. And she'll stay that way while I'm on break. I just need you guys up front to watch for anything interesting."

"Interesting?" I repeat.

"Don't sound so excited." They smile wickedly.

Zyneth finishes rubbing the sleep from his eyes and cracking every other joint in his body. "Alright then. What is it we should do?"

Gillow's grin quickly falls into a bored look as they turn to Zyneth. "Oh, just crew the deck while I'm out. You're not getting a lesson—there's practically nothing to do, and I don't want you touching anything. Besides, we're not far enough out yet for—"

The ship abruptly lists to the side. I stumble forward and Zyneth catches me before I fall face-first into the opposite wall.

"Thanks," I say, clutching his arm for balance as I stand back up. "What was—"

The ship crashes back in the other direction, as if struck by a battering ram. All three of us tumble toward the other wall, and this time I do hit it, shoulder first.

[8 points of Bludgeoning Damage sustained.]

Gillow is the first to spring to their feet, dashing back to the control room. Zyneth starts after, then stops to turn back and help me up.

"I'm fine," I say, waving him off as I stagger to my feet. "Go!"

He turns and runs off without argument. I roll my shoulder, throbbing with pain along new fracture lines. I Sculpt it back into place as I stumble down the slanted hall. The void swirls around my injured shoulder; some of it had cushioned the blow, reacting faster than I had even been able to register, but clearly not enough to stop the injury entirely. I cast a mental glance in the predator's direction, who is alert and watching through my eyes with great interest, but so far it hasn't made a move to seize the void or my mind while I've been distracted. Hopefully, it stays that way.

By the time I make it to the bridge, Gillow is already strapped into their seat at the main controls, shouting orders at Zyneth. He's in one of the extra seats, accessing a spell circle built into the armrest.

"You too, Glassy," Gillow snaps at me. "Get to the arms!"

A shape moves outside the window, and for a brief moment the light from the *Prismatic* reflects against the silhouette outside, illuminating a giant, ship-sized eye.

Cold static creeps over me. "What—"

"Just do it!" Gillow cries.

I join Zyneth and sit in the chair next to him. "What are we doing? How does this work?"

Zyneth's eyes are screwed shut in a grimace, but he taps a finger on one of the spells anyway. There are six circles, one etched into the end of each chair's arm. His hands are firmly pressed against the two on his chair, but only one circle is illuminated. "Touch one of the circles to activate the spell. It's difficult. Be careful."

"What do you mean?" I ask, hesitating.

The ship lurches again, and metal shrieks somewhere in the ship behind us.

"It's got a hold of us," Gillow says, straining against their controls. "Hurry it up!"

I don't wait for Zyneth to explain further. I press a hand against one of the spells, and the pattern lights up. Instantly, a presence appears in my mind. My vision doubles.

I recoil, and both vanish. The predator is also alarmed, swirling agitatedly around, searching for the intruder. It takes me a moment to realize what I'd seen in that brief instant. Hesitantly, I touch the circle again.

The presence returns to my mind as my vision splits in two. But it's not a person—not a creature. It's more of a sensation. An extra limb I hadn't had before. And my second vision is disorientingly outside the ship, where I can see...

Well, fuck.

The fish is giant, a fan of fluorescent fins shimmering around it like a lion's mane. It has dozens of dull, car-sized eyes I'm not even sure can really see, and thousands of tiny feelers, like an anemone. It's also apparently decided we're its next snack, as its tree-sized teeth have clamped around the back end of the *Prismatic*.

One of the *Prismatic's* tentacles is slowly unfurling from the back of the ship—not fast enough, though. I grab the other tentacle, the one in my mind, and I reach my will into it.

As I adjust to the feel of the *Prismatic's* limb, testing the limits of its motion and taking control of its entire one hundred feet of mechanisms, I realize it's a lot like controlling my glass. There's dozens of interlocked segments, and each one needs direction for the arm to move as a whole. Between controlling the foreign limb and dealing with the double vision, it's no wonder Zyneth is struggling.

But this is just another day for me. I put my other hand on the second circle, and take control of a second limb.

Zyneth is still unfurling the one he's controlling, clumsily reaching for the leviathan's jaws, as I whip both my tentacles out, seizing the beast.

Or, I try to. It's massive, and I can't see behind the creature's bright, hypnotic fins. But I can feel the creature's body, still hidden in shadows, is much larger than I first thought. We're lucky it didn't swallow us whole.

I try to squeeze, and I'm somewhat successful, but the fish doesn't react. Recalling how easily the tentacles could have crushed me when I was first brought on board, this discovery is extra disturbing. Switching tactics, I grab the creature's mouth, attempting to pry its jaws apart. Its mouth gives the slightest amount, but not enough to release the ship. We need more power.

Alright, I say, and the predator swirls around me in tighter, excited laps. *You've been watching. You get the picture?*

Yes. It is ready to eviscerate the large prey outside. How dare this foul fish think it's powerful enough to attack us? It will use the false void to disembowel the creature, and then eat its soul.

Eh, I sigh, no time to correct it. *Close enough.*

I loosen my hold on enough of the void for the predator to gleefully take control, slamming two inky tendrils into the spell circles on the empty chair to my side. I hover over the predator's mind, monitoring its intentions, ready to clamp down on it if I get even the slightest hint it's about to try something. For now, however, it seems eager to battle our aggressor. I turn my attention there, too.

The limbs the predator is controlling move even more deftly than mine. They stab toward the creature's gills—why didn't I think of that?—and the creature lets out a low, rumbling wail. Its teeth loosen.

"Let go," I tell Zyneth, mentally nudging the predator to help me work the creature's jaws apart. "We've got this."

Zyneth opens his eyes, freezing when he sees the two void limbs. "Are you sure?"

I create two more void arms to hover over Zyneth's chair, which he still hasn't relinquished. "I'm sure. I'm in control. And we can work these limbs better than you."

He still hesitates. "I don't like this. Last time—"

"I know what happened last time," I snap, frustration bubbling up as I strain against the fish's jaws. "Can we argue about this when we're not about to get eaten?"

Zyneth jumps from his seat. "Gillow, are these arms conductive?"

I wordlessly take control of the last two limbs.

"What?" Gillow cries. "Why would you—gods above, what the fuck is he doing?"

They've presumably just caught sight of me, but I don't have the time or mental capacity to explain. I shut off my glass vision. I lock up my body, so I can focus everything I have on what's going on outside the ship.

"Are they conductive?" Zyneth repeats, an edge in his voice. "Quick!"

"Yes," Gillow says, their voice all business once more.

"And the door to the limb storage room?" Zyneth asks.

"The hatch is in the floor just before the cargo bay," Gillow says. "Unlocked. Do it! Go!"

Zyneth sprints out of the room, and then it's just me and Gillow. I don't pay them any mind, however—six giant mechanical limbs is more than enough to occupy my attention.

The third and fourth ones are harder to control than the first two, so I pass them off to the predator as well. We work on prying the creature's mouth open, slowly, bit by bit. The ship groans as it's slowly released, and the fish's jaws shiver, straining against our hold. It's working, though. Teeth scrape over the *Prismatic* as we shove the creature away.

If only that were the end of it. As soon as the ship's clear, we quickly pull the *Prismatic*'s tentacles away from its teeth, and the fish snaps its mouth shut. But instead of turning tail and looking for easier prey, the creature flips around with surprising speed, coming at us again from the side.

"Turn us around," I tell Gillow. "Quick!"

"I see it, I see it!"

The ship starts to turn, trying to point the back end toward the behemoth once more, but we don't make it in time. The fish opens its mouth wide, and I jam a limb across its mouth, wedging it open. It bites down anyway, several of the teeth puncturing the metal arm. The predator stabs at it with all of its limbs, plumes of dark blood spilling into the water. The predator repeats the action with eager bloodlust.

It's all we can do to hold the leviathan back. One limb is still stuck in the creature's teeth—at least until it opens its mouth again—so we use the other five limbs to do what they can to try to injure the beast. We go for its eyes, its gills, its fins, but it's either too stubborn to let go or too tough to feel the pain. And to make matters worse, the anemone-like feelers that cover the creature like a layer of fur-like growth have stuck to the damaged limb like velcro, and the metal beneath their touch is starting to rust away. At this rate, we're going to lose all the limbs, and then there will be nothing to stop it from eating us.

Indignation swells within us. No, we won't be bested by something so primitive. We didn't come this far to die—not again.

We fight back, slicing a tentacle across the creature's scales, severing a large swatch of the glowing feelers. Finally! Progress. We slash at it again, relishing each little bit we chip away. The fish rumbles in pain.

And then—a flash of light. Lines of yellow-white race down each arm and explode into the sea beast. Lightning flashes through the creature, illuminating it from within like an x-ray. The fish goes slack and begins to drift aimlessly away.

"Ah!" Small sparks zap into our void, evaporating the four limbs we had activating the circles. Our hands are still pressed against two of the circles, unaffected by the tiny shock we'd received, and we use them to dislodge the *Prismatic* limb from the creature's teeth and begin to reel the metal tentacles back in.

As we do, we realize we let our mind slip.

Crap. When did that happen? We turn our focus inward and begin the painful process of pulling ourself apart. Part of us resists. We're stronger this way. Unified. And if we pulled more of us from the inventory—

No!

I wrench my mind away, clamping down on the predator's will, forcing it into submission before it tries anything with our—my inventory. The predator seethes, but gives up the fight almost as soon as it starts. It knows it can't beat me—not yet, at least.

I slump into my chair, taking my hands away from the last two spell circles when the limbs finish retracting into the ship. Four of them—the four the predator had been controlling—are still trailing behind the *Prismatic* like tassels, but I'm too mentally worn to worry about them now. I just need a minute.

Distant clanging footsteps gradually crescendo until they're back in the room, and I wearily turn my vision back on.

"Is everyone alright?" Zyneth asks, skidding through the door.

"Yes," Gillow says, and I realize they're staring at me. "I think."

Zyneth crosses to me. "Kanin?"

"We—I'm fine," I say.

His eyes narrow.

"*I'm* fine. Really." I still have a stranglehold on the predator, I belatedly realize, and gradually let it go. It angrily rips away from me, retreating to a recess of my mind. Whatever. As long as it doesn't bother me.

"Good," Zyneth says, reluctantly tearing his gaze away. "The lightning didn't spread anywhere else? I tried to insulate it, but I was working fast."

"Nothing fried up here," Gillow says, falling back into their seat. They give me a hungry smile. "Not bad, Homunculus. You're just as fun as I'd hoped."

"I have a name, you know." Ugh. Why do I feel like they'd get along with the predator?

Gillow waves it off. "Time for chit-chat later. For now, we need to get back on track." They swivel around to go back to their control console. A few magical panes appear in the air before them, including what looks like a hologram of the ship. "Some damage around the cargo bay, and—shit, what did you do to that arm?! It's almost melted in half."

"Oh," I say. "No need to thank me, or anything. It's not like operating six limbs at once was a lot, or anything."

"You should go rest," Zyneth says.

Ignoring the fact that normal biological functions like *rest* are now an experience residing outside my reality, Gillow shakes their head. "No, we need to fix the ship. No chit-chat, I said! Glass Boy, you reel those last limbs in. Zyneth, you follow me and help with the patch job. Come on, chums, let's get to it."

As Gillow springs out of their chair, grabbing a metal toolbox from an alcove in the wall, Zyneth gives me one last concerned look. I straighten myself up and press both hands—just my glass hands—against two of the spell circles.

"Watch your back down there," I sign to Zyneth with some spare glass.

"I should be saying that to you," he mumbles back. But he rests a hand on my shoulder, giving it a brief squeeze, then follows Gillow out the room.

The ghost of his touch lingers on my shoulder as I turn my attention back to the *Prismatic* and set about reeling the last of its limbs in.

It's only day two, and we've already almost got eaten by a giant fish. How are we going to survive six more days if we're constantly fending off these kinds of attacks? And that's just to the null currents. Another two days to Emrox from there.

And then Zyneth will have to make it the whole way back without me to help. Alone, with Gillow.

I never should have let him come.

CHAPTER THIRTY-SEVEN

SKINNY DIPPING

In the ensuing days, just about everything except Gillow tries to kill us. There's sharks the size of school buses. A swarm of flesh-eating jellyfish. Shadowy creatures that avoid the *Prismatic*'s spotlights, striking at us from the dark. I'm getting pretty damn good at controlling the ship's limbs—enough so that I can keep the predator in check while operating all the mechanical arms. I'd like to thank the two months I've spent walking around on four glass legs for that.

I've also leveled up a few times. Now I'm level fourteen. Spending your days cutting murder fish in half does that to you, I guess.

"Hey, Fishsticks." Gillow barges into the room without knocking, which has become a regular occurrence. Zyneth seems to have developed a sixth sense for this, and always manages to be awake and out of his cot now whenever they're nearby. I close the Signs book I was reading.

"What is it?" Zyneth asks. "Need us to mop the decks?"

"I am not cleaning fish guts out of the tentacles again," I say. "I don't care what your reasoning is, I am not responsible for viscera stuck in the joints."

Gillow grins. "As much as I'd delight in watching a repeat of that fiasco, we've got a much different task to begin." They point at me. "It's time for you to earn your passage."

Static creeps through my soul. "We're here?"

Gillow gestures for us to follow. "Come see for yourself."

Zyneth sends a worried glance my way, and I'm glad he can't see the trepidation I'm feeling. I know I'd agreed to this, but that was before the predator became what it is.

And before I knew a thousand fish monsters were lurking outside the sub at any given moment, ready to devour anything in their path. But who's counting?

We follow Gillow back to the deck, and at first I can't tell what it is they found. Outside the windows is more unending dark. The *Prismatic*'s spotlights are swallowed by the water only thirty or forty feet from the window.

"What is it?" Zyneth asks.

Gillow places a hand on their console, and a ring of blue magic silently pulses out from the front of the ship. The light disperses in the water, warping with the currents, then abruptly vanishes. Far ahead of us, a speck of blue appears in the distance before flickering out.

"That, my friends," Gillow says, "is null magic. Raw, undiluted potential." They don't even try to hide the hunger in their tone.

"I don't understand," I say, stepping up to the window. "What are we looking at? How is it doing that?"

"You're the null arcana mage, aren't you?" Gillow says.

"It's teleporting," Zyneth says, peering out the window beside me. "The magic is entering a stream of null arcana just in front of the

Prismatic, and exiting through a different portion of null arcana else-where. Correct?"

"Exactly," Gillow says. "Which makes these waters incredibly treacherous. I'll be needing to send regular pings of magic before us in order to keep from ending up in one of these currents and getting teleported somewhere else. And that's the best-case scenario of running into this kind of magic."

"What's the worst case?" I ask.

Gillow smiles tightly. "Only part of the ship gets teleported."

I suppress a shiver. And I'm supposed to manipulate that magic? This stuff seems nothing like the void. I've never been able to use it to teleport anything. Then again, I've never tried.

"So how am I supposed to retrieve it?" I ask.

Gillow shrugs. "That's your wheelhouse, not mine. You're a null mage, aren't you? Can't you control it from here?"

I mentally reach out, trying to grab the void in the water like I do with my Attuned void or the predator's stash, but I can't sense anything.

Echo? I ask. *Why can't I control it?*

[A mage may control elements in two ways,] Echo says. [First, by casting a spell designed to manipulate elements in a specific way—such as activating a spell circle—which will cost mana and potentially require other supplies. Second, by Attuning said element, which requires physical contact with an element the mage has an affinity for, and a mana cost. From there, the Attuned quantity may be manipulated without further mana drain. The Attuned element may further be fused with a non-Attuned quantity of the same element in order to manipulate the non-Attuned portion. However, control of the non-Attuned element will become more imprecise proportionally with the quantity of non-Attuned element being manipulated.]

You're telling me I need to get my void mixed in with it, I say. *That I'm going to have to get close enough so it's within range of my void.*

[Affirmative.]

"Damn it," I mutter. "Can I use one of those emergency escape pods to get closer?"

Gillow scoffs. "The words *emergency* and *escape* are there for a reason. Once they fire off, they can't be hooked back up until we resurface the sub. I'm not about to cripple a safety feature due to your lack of foresight."

Well, it was worth a shot. *What's the range of my Attuned void now?* I ask Echo.

[Fifteen feet,] Echo says.

About double what it was only a week ago, but even that feels far too short. I hate to ask the next question, but I need to know. *And the predator's range?*

[Seventy feet.]

The predator's smugness is nearly enough to make me suppress its mind out of spite. *Yeah, yeah. Eat your heart out.*

On second thought, maybe not the best choice of words.

Zyneth steps closer to me. "You do not have to do this," he says quietly.

"I'm pretty sure I do." I glance at Gillow. "How close can you get us to these currents?"

They chew at their cheek, tipping their head as they look out the window. "Forty feet, tops. I won't risk any closer than that—these streams can shift without warning and we'll need enough space to back off if it moves our way."

Damn. I could reach it with the predator's ability—if I gave it control, or risked merging our minds again. With that much access to extra void, though, I don't know what the predator might be capable of—especially given how eager I can feel it is to engage with the magic outside the ship. I don't think I can risk it.

Ironically, if I want to be safe about this, I'll need to go out there and do this myself.

"Can we turn the ship around and back it up to the currents?" I ask. "I'll need to go out one of those cargo windows, and I want the storage cubes as close as possible."

"What?" Zyneth says. "You're not going out there."

"That's the only way I'll be close enough," I say. Well, not the *only* only way, but the less bad option of two bad options.

Gillow also seems skeptical. "Is that glass way more durable than it looks, or are you just suicidal?"

"What do you mean?" I ask.

"I mean we're several *thousand* feet below the surface," Gillow says. "That little glass heart of yours will be crushed by the pressure."

"That wasn't a problem when we first swam down to the *Prismatic*," I say.

"Because we were only a hundred feet below the surface," Gillow says, exasperated. "There's a significant difference!"

Sheesh, such judgment. I don't know these things, I'm not a scientist. "Well that's going to be a problem then."

Gillow folds their arms. "It will be. You getting me that void is a required toll to move forward."

"That's not what we agreed upon," I said. "Getting you the arcana crystal was payment for travel to Emrox."

"No, the *void* was payment for getting you to Emrox. The crystal was payment for his debts being wiped clean," Gillow says, jutting their chin at Zyneth. "And I've already held up my end of the bargain. You'd be wise to hold up yours."

There's a tense silence. What would they do if I refused? Would they take it out on Zyneth? They wouldn't take me to Emrox, at least. I still might be able to get the void from in here, but it would mean giving a lot of power to an entity I have very little trust in. Still... even if something goes wrong out there, I won't be in too much danger, will I? The predator needs me alive.

But it doesn't need Zyneth or Gillow alive. I hesitate. Which is the least bad option?

"I can protect you," Zyneth speaks up.

I turn to him. "What do you mean?"

"I have charms that should work," he says. "They can reinforce your glass. Make it withstand physical and thermal stresses."

I take a moment to process this, surprised. "Okay well that would have been incredibly useful like a dozen times before now."

"Sorry," Zyneth says. "The charms are only temporary. They won't last long, and I would have needed advanced notice to put any of them into effect."

"Still," I say. "What about that predator fight? We knew what we were walking into. You could have at least shielded yourself."

He shakes his head. "I'm an artificer. My spells only work on ob—Ah, they don't work on living creatures."

Objects. He was going to say objects. You'd think that wouldn't bother me anymore, especially since I'm ideally only a couple days away from regaining my body. But not being recognized as a person, even if the magic doesn't know any better, still stings. "Right. Okay, well, I'd appreciate whatever help I can get."

"Come on," Zyneth says. "Let's do it in the cargo hold. Buy as much time as possible. Gillow, can you get us turned around?"

"Way ahead of you," Gillow says, silt streaking by the window. Without that small indicator of motion, the only point of reference in the dark, I'd have no idea the ship was moving. "Meet you two back there in a minute. Prism Head, I still need to show you how those arcana storage cubes work."

"I'll take a minute or so to cast the spells," Zyneth says. "We should be ready by the time you make it back." Without waiting for Gillow to respond, he steps from the room, shooting me a pointed look.

I follow after. "What is it?" I sign. I've been teaching him more sign language in our downtime. We've been using it as a way to speak behind Gillow's back, but I am no Noli, and I'm pretty sure I'm passing on bad habits and slightly wrong verbiage.

"I lied," he signs back. "No time limit. But drains mana while spell is going."

I tip my head, trying to puzzle out why he'd want Gillow to believe that lie. If it drains his mana, then he'll be preoccupied—and he has the potential to run out. Compared to a one-and-done spell, ongoing magic means Zyneth is going to be preoccupied with keeping me alive.

Which leaves him vulnerable if Gillow decides to hurt him—and with me outside the ship, this would be the perfect opportunity.

"How much mana will it take?" I ask. "I can try to be quick."

"More you, more mana," he signs, gesturing up and down my body. "All of you, mana gone in two minutes. If just heart, maybe ten."

Crap. I hate the idea of leaving my body behind when I already have so little protection out there. Ten minutes already isn't a lot of time, but I'll need to be faster than that if I don't want to leave Zyneth defenseless. "Okay. It's okay," I sign. "They won't know. And if anything happens to you, I'll be able to tell right?"

Zyneth frowns with worry. "If anything happens to me," he mutters, "you'll be crushed by the water pressure."

"Well," I say, pushing the door open to the cargo bay, "let's try to avoid that."

I unhook my vial from the neck, clustering my signing glass around it. It's not much, maybe a handful of small glass shards, but it's better than nothing. And then, of course, I have the void.

As I set myself on the ground, tucking my body off to the side, the void that empties from my coat seems like a tidal wave of dark from this lowly perspective. It puddles to the ground beneath me, spreading flat across the floor like an unnatural shadow, broader and darker than it should be. There's so much more of it than there was before. No wonder I feel like I'm at a tipping point, only a fraction away from being overwhelmed.

And I'm about to go dive headfirst into more. There's no way the predator doesn't try something while I'm out there. Looks like Zyneth and I will both have our hands full.

Zyneth sketches out a quick spell circle on the ground as Gillow steps into the room.

"What, you're not done yet?" they ask.

"I'll activate it just before he needs to leave, to buy him the most time," Zyneth says.

Gillow looks at me—or rather, my body propped against the wall. "He better not already be dead."

I'm going to choose to ignore that *already* part. But yeah, I guess they're not used to this. "Down here," I say, though the translator is still on my body, which is a bit self-defeating. "No. By Zyneth." I wave my signing glass, trying to draw their attention to my vial.

Gillow finally catches sight of me and blinks. "What are—you know what, never mind. At this point, it's not even the weirdest thing I've seen you do."

"Let's get this over with," I say. "How do I use those storage containers?"

"I'll be sending them out with you," Gillow says. "They were built to withstand these depths. I can use my water magic to maneuver them around close to the currents, but you'll need to funnel the null arcana inside." They tap the nearest cube, and a spell circle illuminates across the surface, spreading over the object like lines on a circuit board. "You direct it here," they say, pointing to the center of the circle, like the snake-eye on a giant-ass die. "The containment cube will do the rest. Don't let the arcana touch any other part of the surface, however; if one of these containers ends up getting split in half, it will be explosively bad."

"When you say explosively…"

Gillow gives me a flat look. "It will explode."

"Yeah, I figured," I say. "I was just really hoping I was wrong."

"Is there anything else?" Zyneth asks, hands poised over me. I push the void away from the spell circle he'd drawn on the ground, careful not to mess with it. Gillow watches my void with a look of hunger I associate with the predator.

"No," Gillow says, heading over to the wall and activating two of the tentacles. The floor shudders and the mechanisms beneath our feet grind to life. "I'll grab the cubes. Ready when you two are."

"Ready," I say to Zyneth.

He clenches his jaw as yellow lights glow to life in his palms, and I don't think it's the magic that's straining him.

The light washes over me, tingling against my glass.

[Status buff obtained,] Echo states. [Crushing Damage reduced by 99.93%. Thermal Damage reduced by 99.93%.]

We're going to need to have a serious talk after this about finding a way to make these buffs permanent.

"Done," Zyneth says, lowering his hands. The glow around me stays, however. "We've not much time now."

How long until the buffs expire? I ask Echo.

[Quantity unknown,] Echo says. [The spells are being continuously maintained by their mana source.]

Check Zyneth's mana, I tell her. *At the current rate it's going down, how long until it's out?*

A few numbers pop up in my vision, then rearrange themselves:

[Time Limit: 10 minutes, 27 seconds]

Good. At least I can keep an eye on things.

"Ready?" Zyneth offers me a hand.

"No, I've got it," I say, swirling the void around me. It lifts me into the air, carrying me to the nearest glass-like window. The magic buzzes above, the only thing separating me from tons of water and a potentially instantaneous death, if Zyneth's spells fail. Something I wouldn't be worried about if Gillow weren't involved.

I hesitate at the exit, watching Gillow operate the ship's limb. They move one of the tentacles in through the opposite window, wrapping the giant arm around the nearest cube before drawing it back out of the ship. How easy would it be for them to grab Zyneth and pull him out the same way?

"Good luck," Zyneth says, startling me from that image. I guess the only way I can help him is to be as quick as possible.

"Thanks," I say, pressing through the window. "Be back soon."

Darkness swallows me. Still haloed by the *Prismatic's* light, the surrounding waters seem dense with horrific possibility. Anything could be out there. Another predator, only feet away. The null currents could be right in front of me and I'd never know. I pull my void closer, as if that could abate the sudden feeling of extreme agoraphobia.

A pulse of blue light emits from the ship, washing over me. The magic races into the dark, illuminating no beasts or sea serpents. The light fades, then abruptly twists to the side and blinks out. A speck of blue appears far in the distance before vanishing into the black.

There.

I will myself closer to the point where the magic had warped, hesitantly only moving half as far as I think I need to; even with time against me, I'd rather undershoot it than over. The muted creaking of metal groans behind me as two of the ship's limbs stretch in my direction, each holding a containment cube. They also stop short, nowhere near where the null current might be. I wait for another pulse of blue to light up my surroundings. The current is closer now.

I peel away half of my void, despite the predator's protests, and send it out ahead of me. The rest I keep close, slowly swirling through the waters with my Elemental Radar skill. It feels different from using my glass the same way. When I've used my glass to touch the surrounding ground, providing a pseudo-radar type of sight, I'm only provided with physical sensations which paint a 3D map in my mind. But the void isn't solid. It moves through the water like fluid. Instead of a sense of the location of my surroundings, I can feel its movement, its temperature, its density. It almost feels like my sense of self expands into my surroundings.

And it can be more—I can sense that from the predator. It doesn't just use the void to touch its surroundings, it uses it to see, and smell, and taste. Senses I've been missing for several months now. God, I'm desperate to taste again. To just eat an apple. To just drink cold water on a hot summer's day. I'd give anything for a taste of that last frozen cheese burrito again.

The memory of what the predator last ate—two living souls—returns to me unbidden, and shakes me from my longing. The sweet, electric taste of souls is something forever seared into my memory. Something I doubt I'll ever be able to shake even after I've gone home.

My void brushes up against something tactile and familiar.

The magic crackles as it merges with my own, like sheets of fabric rubbing static between them. It's so strange, because I can feel exactly what it is—the void that's come to be such a familiar presence in my mind, yet this is inert and unresponsive. I swirl my void through the wild magic and gently, *gently* focus on towing it back.

No wonder it's so rare to Attune null magic. You have to touch whatever you have an affinity with in order to form an Attunement, and touching this stuff might end up chopping your hand off. It was sheer luck the void I happened to touch was already morphed into the predator, the magic and the entity having become indistinguishable in the time spent Between. While I'm not the only mage in the world with an Affinity for null arcana, I might be the only one with any amount of it that they've managed to Attune.

I pull the stream of null arcana toward the nearest containment cube, and the void slowly winds its way to the spell circle on the surface. It feels like I'm clawing my fingers through sand, trying to drag as much of the wild void along with me as I can. Eventually, though, I get there.

Ah!

A stabbing sensation cuts through me as I make contact with the containment cube and all of the void in front of the spell circle vanishes. Not just the wild null arcana, but some of my Attuned void, too.

The predator attempts to yank our void away, and the stream of null arcana freezes, caught between a mental tug-of-war.

That void is ours! And that machine is stripping it away. Why are we feeding it when we should be taking all this void for ourself?

Calm down. I haven't quite managed to wrestle the void away from the predator's grasp, but I've at least stopped it from doing anything rash. *That was an accident—I'll be more careful to keep our Attuned void away from the cube from now on. And I can't Attune any of that wild magic without risking getting cut in half. If I die, you'll end up back Between, so chill the fuck out.*

This hardly mollifies the predator, but it at least gives it pause long enough for me to wrangle its grip on the void away. Good grief. We can't do this every time something startles us.

The predator indignantly lets me know it was *not* startled. It's only remaining vigilant. Protecting our stash of void. Which *could* be grown, now, if we wanted.

I swear you only listen to half the things I say.

No. It listens to everything.

Oh great. Even better.

Although... it might actually be onto something. I'll need an incredible amount of null arcana to activate the giant spell circle in Emrox. *Think you can absorb some of this magic to top off our mana levels?* I ask.

The predator eagerly agrees, and I wonder why I even bothered asking. I can also tell it's intending to take a cut for itself to extend its timer, and I wearily don't object. As long as the Influence stat doesn't go up, I'll allow it. In fact, I do a Check, just in case.

[Predator Time Limit: 32.9 hours]

[Predator Influence: 31%]

I wish I could say no change in that stat fills me with relief, but it's already too high for my liking.

But it's temporary, I remind myself. Soon, I'll be going home. Not much longer now.

I return to the null arcana, slowly pulling more through the water like stretched taffy as the predator nibbles at its edges. This time when I get close to the cube, I back off with my Attuned void and let the magic glide in on its own. The black stream of ink vanishes as it touches the circle.

Timer? I check.

[Eight minutes, forty-seven.]

I don't know how much arcana can fit in these blocks, but it's probably more than I'll have time to fill. I'll just have to keep an eye on the clock, grab as much as I can, and then GTFO.

My work is occasionally illuminated by pulses of blue. The null current drifts slowly around—or maybe it's the *Prismatic* and I that are drifting—but it's still a comfortable distance away, given the range of my void. I fall into a rhythm, lacing my void into the current and slowly drawing the tendrils of ink toward the containment cubes. The predator leeches bits and pieces away as I do so, converting some of it into Bonus Mana while it consumes the rest, extending its timer.

The water around me ripples. In my vial form I have omni-vision, but surrounded by so much dark I can't see what the cause of that disturbance was. I use the void still clustered near me to push outward in a sphere, but I don't sense anything nearby. The water is moving, though. Just the slightest thrum of shifting pressures.

I instinctively reach for my translator, but it's not in range. Damn, can't even ask if Gillow or Zyneth noticed anything. Maybe it's just my own paranoia. Maybe that's just how the currents work down here.

A shadow flickers beneath the *Prismatic*. Oooooh nope. Nope nope nope.

Echo, what was that? Check!

[There are no creatures within line of sight that can be identified.]

Bullshit! I didn't imagine that. Is it hiding behind the *Prismatic*? Screw the null arcana, I'm getting out of here.

The *Prismatic*'s spotlight turns on, and since the ship was spun around backward, it's pointing in the opposite direction from the null currents and I.

"Kanin, get inside," a metallic Gillow voice echoes through the water. "Slowly."

Slowly? Why? What kind of advice is that? Are you trying to freak me out? This is how you freak me out. I pull all my void back from the null currents and begin to propel myself toward the *Prismatic*. Its eye-window is only two dozen feet away.

Another shadow moves through the dark, this time straight toward me. I snap all my void tight around my core, and the creature rushes past, sending me spinning in its wake. The world is a nonsensical blur of dark and bubbles and the *Prismatic*'s lights until I use the void to stop my spin.

Check, check!

[There are no creatures within line of sight that can be identified.]

Are you kidding me? Alright, screw going slow. I'm getting out of here!

"Kanin?" This time it's Zyneth's voice, and I'm not liking how panicked he sounds. "Get out of there, now!"

I rush toward the *Prismatic*'s light. I'm twenty feet away—fifteen—ten—

Gillow's voice is in the background. "Hey give that back—and slow! He has to go slow—"

"They're tempo squids," Zyneth says. "Get—"

And then it appears, right in front of me. The water pulses outward as it pops into existence.

[Tempo Squid: Level 21,] Echo happily pipes up, as if pleased to now, finally, have the opportunity to identify what I'd been trying to Check before. [Infused with null arcana from the waters surrounding Emrox, this creature has inherited the magic's ability to become unstuck from space. Usually found traveling in schools, tempo squids prefer to surprise their prey by surrounding them via coordinated teleportation.]

I slam on my metaphorical brakes but there's no time to stop—I ram straight into the squid. It's soft and pliant, and folds around me like jelly. The *Prismatic* vanishes from view. I lash out with glass and void, panicked, as the creature's limbs wrap around my vial, and its flesh flinches back from my attacks. Then the world seems to flip—a nauseating vertigo kicks my soul, and the squid releases me, jetting away into the black.

Black. Everything is black. Where did the *Prismatic* go? It's lights? The cubes? It's gone—there's nothing around me.

I'm alone.

CHAPTER THIRTY-EIGHT

ALONE

I swirl my glass and void around me—thank god both of those came with—and desperately try not to panic. My glass touches nothing. My void senses only water around us, as far as it can reach, in any direction. There's no sign of the *Prismatic*. Thick, oppressive silence presses in on me from every side. The predator's presence swells again, alert and violent, trying to take control so it can lash out at our unseen assailant.

I activate my Glow spell on its lowest brightness, attempting to stay grounded. Focusing on the spell is as much to distract myself from the predator as it is my own fear.

I can sense my signing glass rearrange itself into a sphere as a small ball of light blooms into existence at its center. The waters around me illuminate with the white light, revealing...

Nothing. The darkness goes on forever.

I'm lost.

Okay. Okay, okay. Don't panic. Don't think about the unending darkness. Don't think about the creatures that might be out there, watching me from the black. Don't think about how helpless and vulnerable I am. Don't think about Zyneth's spell and his steadily draining mana and how I'm about to be crushed into little glass dust.

Actually maybe I really need to think about that last one.

I check my timer:

[Three minutes and twenty-one seconds remaining.]

I fucking panic.

I spear my void into the dark, stretching, reaching as far as I can manage, desperate to touch something, anything. I'm overwhelmed by the instinct to move, to rush back to safety, but I don't know which way the *Prismatic* is. I don't even know which way is up or down. Any attempt to find safety might be leading me in the opposite direction. Fear paralyzes me, constricting around my soul. I'm going to die. I'm going to die out here, alone in the dark.

The predator wrenches control from me before I even have a chance to react.

No! I grab for it, but I'm still so panicked, so scattered, that it bats me aside without a second glance. The void swirls around us like a hurricane, spreading out five times as far as I'd managed on my own. It's thin—terribly stretched, nearly so diluted it risks being swept away by the ocean currents. But the predator doesn't flinch. It's searching, its focus as rigid as iron. I feel like a fly knocking against a window. Oh god. It's locked me out. It's just like Peakshadow—I can't get control—

There. The predator's attention latches onto something our void touched—a stream of null arcana. It leaps toward the magic, propelling us forward, recalling all the feelers of void it had put out into the dark to funnel more magic into the null current. I catch a glimpse of its intentions, and my already fraying sanity takes another hit.

We can't go into the null current, I say, unsure if it even hears me. *What if it cuts me in half? What if it—no, wait, stop!*

The predator plunges us in. I can feel the magic crackling at me, stinging through our void—but none of it touches my glass. The predator has wrapped a protective layer of void around us, keeping the wild magic from touching me directly. I didn't even know it could do that. The predator leaks self-satisfaction across our bond.

Yeah, yeah. Show off.

My immediate panic subsides into a more general, existential dread. I may not be about to be sliced in half by wild teleportation magic, but the time limit is still ticking down by the second.

I can't control any of that, though. Instead, I focus on what the predator's doing.

Our void is spreading through the null arcana. Flowing along the current, branching into other streams. Its range is incredible. Bigger even than what we had been doing moments before. The null arcana is boosting our abilities—not just the range, but our sensations, too. We look through our void, opening and closing our sight along dozens of different points, searching for any hint of light in the dark.

The power the null arcana gives us is intoxicating. We could Attune more of it. With our void to hold it stable, we wouldn't have to worry about it damaging our core. And with more Attuned void at our disposal, we would be capable of far more powerful abilities.

A distant, yellow glow. We focus more of our void in that direction, trying to get a better look. There's motion. A large shape and flickering lights: the *Prismatic*, its limbs splayed around it like hair, and dozens of tempo squids blinking in and out of existence all around. They're under attack.

[...ne minute and ten seconds remaining.]

Our glass is still far away from this stream of void we're watching through, however. Now that we have some idea of where the ship is, we also have some sense of scale—and our core is much, much too far. Even if we propel it through the water as fast as we're able, it would take several minutes to get back.

Problematic. But if the pathetic squid creatures could do it...

We compress the void nearest the *Prismatic*. The darkness swirls tighter, smaller, condensing in on itself in a whirl of building pressure. At the same time, we pull the void tight around our core.

Wait, what are we doing?

Darkness overtakes us as our vision switches off; it takes too much focus to force the wild null arcana to assist with our spell. But with its power to boost our own, linking the two points of space becomes possible. Not easy, but possible.

This doesn't seem like a good idea—

The points of spacetime snap together, and we again feel that disorienting lurch like we'd felt before, when the tempo squid had grabbed us—

A blur of color spins wildly around us before we arrest our spiral and come to a stop, facing the *Prismatic*. Much of our void is behind us still, in distant null currents, still heading our way. But we're here. We made it back.

[...-ty-three seconds remaining.]

Our glass cracks.

[...reduced to 95%.] Echo's voice is distant, but we understand enough to be alarmed. We might have made it back to *Prismatic*, but we still need to make it onto the ship.

[...amage reduction reduced to 93%.]

[3 points of Crushing Damage sustained.]

We don't wait for it to tick any lower.

The void propels us forward as the water squeezes our glass. What we couldn't even feel before is becoming a mounting pressure. Gillow had warned us not to move quickly around the tempo squids, but we don't have time—or patience—for caution. We wrap what little void we have around our core, sharpening the shadows into blades and sending them spinning around us like a freaking ninja throwing star as we torpedo our way back toward the *Prismatic*. A tempo squid appears in front of us, and we tear through it like wet paper. The crack in our glass spreads.

And then we're bursting through the *Prismatic*'s cargo window, falling to the deck as Gillow shouts in surprise. The void cushions our blow, slowing our roll until we come to a haphazard stop in the middle of the room.

"Kanin." Zyneth slumps against a wall. "Oh, thank the gods."

[Crushing damage reduction charm ended. Thermal damage reduction charm ended.]

The faint glow around us vanishes.

"Great," Gillow says, grunting from their position at a spell console along the wall. "Finally, someone who isn't useless. Get over here and help me kill these squids!"

We start to pull our mind away, but we're stopped.

No, not yet. Our void is still navigating back through the null currents. If we separate now, our range will shrink—we'll lose the Attuned void that's still out there.

Maybe that's not the worst thing. We try to pull away again, but the other half of us won't let us go.

"Kanin?" Zyneth calls. "You're being quiet again. Speak to me."

Our translator is back within range, but focusing on it is difficult while also wrestling with ourself. We don't have time to fight—the ship is under attack. Let us go!

Not if we'll lose our void. Wait.

"Trying," we say, the word echoing from the translator stiff and terse. "We're busy."

Zyneth swears under his breath, pushing off the wall and hurrying over to our body.

We want to help fight those animals? Then patience. Our void is almost back. Just another moment.

"Would one of you two fucking do something?" Gillow demands. "I've got my arms full over here!"

Zyneth grabs the knife off our belt and hurries back over to us. He throws the blade to the ground, which skids up to our glass. Our void shies away.

"Take it," Zyneth says, drawing his own blade and using it to gesture toward us. "Quickly now."

Half of us understands what he's trying to do—so all of us understands. At first we're angry—he's trying to take our void away! But then we have a better idea.

We snatch the knife up with our void, but don't activate the spell in the blade. Instead we aim it at the window, and then in one swift move, launch it out into the sea.

Zyneth stares at us, open-mouthed. "Did you just—You threw away my knife!"

"No," we say, still struggling to get the words out. They feel so strange to us. So unnatural and foreign. Speech itself is at once familiar and strangely abstract. "Lightning."

Our void finally catches up. Energized by the null arcana, it's crackling with potential—capable of so much more than usual. It grabs the knife, slicing through the nearest squid.

"What?" Zyneth says.

We don't have any void left on us—it's all in the waters outside—so we point to his blade with our glass. "Use lightning!"

He finally seems to put it together. Zyneth activates his Attunement, electricity crackling down the length of the blade. And outside, in the water, we activate the spell to pull his lightning through.

Electricity erupts from our knife, lancing through the sea. We slice through tempo squids even as they teleport away, and with the null arcana empowering us, our void holds on, teleports with them, and finishes the job. Our blade is disappearing and reappearing all around the ship, cutting through and electrifying the squid, one by one.

[Level Up!] Words appear in our vision, but we brush them away, maintaining our focus outside. It happens again a minute later. And again.

Light flashes in through the windows of the *Prismatic* in a silent display of fireworks. Gillow stops what they're doing, letting go of their spell circles to watch. Neither Zyneth or Gillow speak as we finish the creatures off.

It's only when our void flows back in through the window, carrying the knife with it, that we release the grip on our mind. The void puddles around us and we use the opportunity to start to pull free, finding the seam in our mind, the line that's growing ever harder to distinguish. Unsticking ourself comes with a series of tiny stings, like slowly peeling off a scab.

[EXP threshold reached,] Echo says as I finally let her talk.

[Name: Kanin]

[Class: Wizard]

[Level: 17]

[HP: 10/10]

[Temp HP: 328]

[Mana: 111/111]

[Bonus Mana: 512]

[Role: Homunculus]

Level seventeen. Okay. At least the level ups healed my glass. That's... something.

I turn my attention to the predator next.

[Predator Time Limit: 32.9 hours]

[Predator Influence: 33%]

It went up. I guess I should have known mixing all the extra void in with my magic would do something. I slide Zyneth's knife across the floor and away from us, still worried the predator might try something—and frankly surprised it hasn't already.

It saved us—again. And then it wouldn't let me go. I should have been stronger than that. I'm the more dominant mind. I shouldn't have let my panic weaken my will as much as it did. What if it had burned a few of our preciously low seconds trying to pull more of itself from my inventory? Would I have been strong enough to stop it?

Subdued, I move all my glass and void back over to my body. The void pours beneath the clothes as I take control of the glass, and I begin propping it up like a possessed puppet. It's not until I'm standing once more, checking over all my limbs and joints, that I realize the others are staring.

Gillow takes a breath. "What the shit."

"Did you get enough null arcana?" I ask, too weary to get into it with them right now.

"You destroyed them," Gillow says, clasping their hands behind their head. "You just murdered them all. Where's that been this whole time? Why'd you even have to go out there to gather the null arcana? Your range is huge!"

"Was," I say. Now that the predator isn't running things, the range of my void is back to little more than a dozen feet. But Gillow doesn't need to know that. "I'm going to go rest in my cot. You two have everything from here?"

"Now, hold up," Gillow says. "You just did some things that deserve an explanation. You have to—hey, wait!"

I'm already leaving. I don't have the bandwidth for this conversation. I need space. I need to gather myself—before I fall apart.

"Kanin," Zyneth says, following me out.

This time, I do stop. "Please don't ask me if I'm alright."

He doesn't. Wordlessly, he holds out a hand, and I take it. It doesn't really feel like holding hands—not like when I had my real body. My fingers don't fold into the shape of his grasp or radiate any heat. They're cold and unyielding. But it's almost the familiar, comforting touch of human connection. It's almost what I need.

Zyneth squeezes my hand. "We're going to get you home. We're so close."

It should be what I want to hear, but instead it just makes me feel like my soul is being torn in half. I touch my freehand to my vial—to the crack that's now healed, but I can still feel running through it. "I need to lay down."

We both know I don't.

"Okay," he says.

We walk the rest of the way in silence.

CHAPTER THIRTY-NINE

EMROX

The shadowy forms of Emrox emerge from the dark like a ghost. Pulses of blue constantly emit from the *Prismatic*, Gillow hyper paranoid of running into any null currents, many of which now ribbon through the nearby waters. Illuminated by our ship's sapphire glow, the ruins of Emrox take on a phantasmal aura.

The three of us stand and watch in silence as a pillar fades into view before passing us by. More shapes appear, all of them vaguely familiar—like Greek ruins, yet stretched and twisted in completely un-Earthly ways. The towers are taller and thinner than should be possible. Strange disk-like shapes decorate the city like shells scattered by a giant. Many structures are broken statues, with carvings still engraved in the surface, surprisingly uneroded by the water. Despite the fact that the city is demolished, it appears eerily untouched by time, as if Emrox was bombed and subsequently abandoned only a day before.

"Do you know where we're going?" I finally ask.

Gillow scoffs. "Of course. There's really only one place *to* go in this city. The question will be what you want to do when we get there."

It finally hits me: I'm here. After all this time, after all the struggle, I'm mere steps away from home. Familiarity. My body. It doesn't feel real.

But Gillow's comment hits the nail on the head: What *will* I do once I get there? If the predator can be trusted—and let's be honest, it can't—then it will help me complete and activate the spell circle that will open the gate Between. That coupled with my Location spell should be able to open a pathway back to my body—and Earth. But will I need to go back out into the water to make that happen? Will Zyneth's charms last long enough for what I need to do?

Zyneth. If everything does go to plan, we'll be saying goodbye. Can I do that? Can I just leave him behind alone with Gillow? They haven't tried to kill him yet. Maybe we were wrong about them wanting to tie up loose ends. Maybe they need him to get back to land. Maybe they're not as selfish as Zyneth had assumed.

Can I count on all those maybes?

"There it is," Gillow says, and Zyneth and I lean forward.

I can see why they'd said this city only has one destination.

An enormous amphitheater melts into view beneath us, at least twice the size of Earth's Colosseum. Rather than seats, its walls are made of countless pillars and broken platforms. But it's the ground at the center of the arena that my gaze is drawn toward: a massive, broken spell circle takes up the whole width of the structure. I've seen it before in the Library of Miasmere. In my notes. In the predator's memories.

The entire arena is also filled with null magic.

Gillow turns on the *Prismatic*'s spotlights. The magic is so dense that I can make it out glimmering in the water even without Gillow's blue pulses. There's no way the *Prismatic* can get down there. Hell, even as a glass vial I don't know if I'd be able to squeeze by.

"That is certainly an issue," Zyneth says. "I don't suppose you have a way to get through all this?" he asks Gillow.

"Are you insane? I'm already way closer to these null currents than I'm comfortable with."

Zyneth looks at me questioningly.

I shake my head. "I didn't expect this. Let me think. Gillow, can you take us around the arena? I want to make sure I'm not missing anything."

Gillow shrugs. "Not sure what you think you'll find, but I'm perfectly happy to keep circling up here."

But it's not so much the angle I need as the area.

Echo, I'm going to cast Inspect as a spell, I say. *Thirty-foot range to start. Notify me if any spell circuits are detected, excluding the ones in this ship. If there aren't any, expand the range.*

[Affirmative,] Echo says. [Casting Inspect.]

A pulse of my magic emanates from my soul, quickly vanishing beyond the hull of the *Prismatic*.

[Spell circuit identified,] she says almost immediately.

Blue lines of magic appear in my field of view, in the waters directly outside of us. I give them a Check.

[Dormant spell circuits designed for the control and tempering of the surrounding water,] Echo says. [This spell has not been active in over 518,430 days.]

And yet the skeleton of the spell still remains. *Could I activate it?* I ask.

[Negative,] Echo says. [Activation of such a spell requires water Attunement.]

Keep looking for spell circuits, I say. *But this time only notify me if they can be activated by null magic. Also, what's my bonus mana look like?*

[Bonus Mana: 498]

"Zyneth, could I borrow some mana?" I ask, pushing my range wider.

He frowns. "How much do you need?"

"Not sure," I admit. "At least while we do a lap of this place."

"Alright." Zyneth raises a hand over my chest. Yellow light glows in his palm and bathes my core. "I'll let you know when I'm getting low."

Of course, I could track that with Echo myself, but the less Gillow knows about my unique circumstances, the better. I just hope between Zyneth and I we have enough mana to find what I'm looking for—not to mention, enough leftover mana to be able to activate the spell circles.

[Null spell circuit identified,] Echo says after a minute of searching. [Dormant spell circle designed for structural support integrity via gravitational manipulation.]

Gravity manipulation? Null magic sure has a lot of interesting applications I've never thought to look into before. Interesting. But not what will help me right now. *Keep searching.*

The minutes stretch. Echo finds another two spell circuits designed around null arcana, but they're still not what I need.

"Kanin," Zyneth warns.

"I know, I know." If we don't find it soon, then we'll have to wait for our mana to recover and try again tomorrow. Assuming Gillow is willing to wait around that long. But I can't give up now. I'm here! I'm in Emrox. I can *see* the spell circle I need to get to just a hundred yards beneath me. I can't have come all this way just to fail at the last step.

[Spell circuit identified,] Echo says. [Dormant spell circle designed to summon and stabilize a bubble of air at the designated target location.]

I push Echo for more details with my Inspect and confirm what I'd hoped.

"Found it," I say, pointing out the window toward a pillar beneath us in the coliseum. I can see the lines of magic tracing to where their spell circle is located, even if no one else can. I'll just need to guide them close enough for me to activate it. I wave off Zyneth and deactivate Identify to save both our mana. "That's it. Get us there."

Gillow takes us down, hovering over the large plate-like disc that's mounted to the top of the pillar I need to reach. There's two dozen other pillars wrapping around the coliseum, each platform lower than the last, like a giant spiral staircase.

"This is as close as she goes," they say. "Those null currents are too dense once you get into the stadium."

Hopefully not for long. "This will be close enough, I think."

The spell circle is on top of the flat surface, luckily for me. I think I can reach it with my glass and void without having to risk another dive into the water with my core. Of course, I can *definitely* reach it with the predator's help, but that's something I'm trying to avoid. I'll need to soon enough, but I don't want to give it any more opportunities for it to potentially take advantage of than I have to.

"What's going on?" Gillow asks as I start to leave the room. "What's your plan?"

"I'm going to create an air pocket at the bottom of the coliseum," I say. "There's a spell circle here designed to do just that. All I have to do is activate it."

Gillow frowns. "What will that achieve?"

"The spell summons a pocket of air, forcing the water away. It should clean the area out of water and null arcana, both. Once inside the bubble, I'll be safe."

Gillow appears anything but convinced, but they shrug anyway. "Whatever. It's your life, I guess. I got my payment."

Zyneth, however, is predictably less indifferent. "These spell circles are ancient. How do you know they won't misfire when activated?"

"It'll be fine," I say, hoping that's not a lie. "The predator remembers what the circle is supposed to look like." And if anything does happen, I've got a guardian monster watching over my shoulder that should keep me from getting too dead. "At any rate, I can activate it remotely, so my core should be safe. Let's just drain the volume first and then take it from there, okay?"

Zyneth exhales through his nose. "Okay. Let's get this over with."

Gillow stays at the controls as Zyneth and I head down to the cargo bay. Looking out one of the glowing, orange windows, the surrounding waters are still and dark. I can see the platform just under us, however.

"Alright." I summon all my signing glass and a small portion of my void out from under my coat, then push them out the window, feeling instantaneous resistance as they pass into the water. As much as it's unnerving to have that Predator Influence stat hanging over me, it's useful that I have enough void to keep my body upright and walking even without the portion I sent outside the ship. To say keeping my body and core inside the ship is far preferable is an extreme understatement.

Even so, I have to turn on sight in some of my signing glass to be able to tell where I'm sending my Attunements as they drift down the side of the ship. My vision splits disorientingly: I'm inside the *Prismatic*, looking at the window, and I'm also in the water, watching the top of the pedestal float steadily closer. I shape my signing glass into hands and touch lightly down on the stone surface.

I re-activate Identify, briefly, just long enough for the spell circuits to flash into existence. There.

I extinguish the spell once more as I line my hands up over the circle. Void coils around them like a layer of gloves, then seeps out into the stone surface, tracing the lines of the circle inscribed there. I activate the spell.

Black lines light up across the pillar's surface, then skitter down the column and out of sight.

Silence.

It stretches for a long, unending moment. Then a rumble vibrates through the craft, so low and distant that it's more sensation than sound. I feel Zyneth tense up beside me. I cross the cargo bay and look out the other window. Still nothing I can make out from this angle. I lift my hands from the spell circle and send them to look over the edge of the platform, as far as I can manage with my limited range. Beneath us, something is happening.

The water outside the *Prismatic* begins to swirl. Silt is stirred up and pulled away as a strong current sweeps through the area. I hastily recall my void and glass before they're washed away too, bringing them back into the ship. Spell circuits light up in the bay above us as Gillow's voice is projected into our room.

"What the fuck did you guys do back there? What's happening?"

"Kanin?" Zyneth asks, an edge in his voice.

"I told you, I just activated the spell!" I say. "Should I stop it?"

"I think that would be wise."

But the water is moving too fast for me now. I can't send anything out there without it getting swept away. "Uh, any other suggestions?"

Zyneth pinches the bridge of his nose. "What was that spell supposed to do?"

"Echo just said it creates an air bubble at the target location," I say, trying to remember the exact wording.

"What target location?" Zyneth says, grabbing onto a railing on the wall as the ship begins to pitch. I lunge for a handhold as well. "What made you think it was going to drain the water down at the base of the coliseum?"

Oh. Fair point. "Uhhhh... gravity?"

"Shit!" Gillow says. "Hold on!"

The ship is fighting a vortex now, rotating in a slow circle against a much more rapid whirl of water. A sharp *bang* jolts the ship as the *Prismatic* scrapes against the platform. And then the color at the top of the window shifts, like a line has been drawn across it. The line starts moving down, and that's when it finally clicks: the water isn't being drained from the base of the coliseum, it's being drained away from our little platform. Flushed out like a giant toilet.

The *Prismatic* lands heavily on the stone pillar, then rolls across its round underbelly and pitches to the side. I yelp as the bar I'm holding pivots from being on the wall to the ceiling, and the sudden lurch cracks one of my arms completely off. I jolt down—and the void reaches up, wrapping around my arm and handhold, keeping me from falling to my doom.

Meanwhile, everything else is going to shit.

The giant cubes I'd filled with null arcana roll with the motion of the ship, and two of them tumble right through the windows. Zyneth manages to perform a stunt that would make Indiana Jones proud, and leaps over one of the rolling cubes and out of the way of the second before they can knock him outside.

The ship groans, finally settling to a tenuous stop, and for a moment, all is still.

Chapter Forty

Not Great

"Kanin!" Zyneth calls.

"I'm alright!" The void stretches as it lowers me to the ground. Once I step back to the unsteady floor, I let go of the handhold and retract my severed glass arm. "Well, mostly okay."

"Everyone alive?" Gillow's voice echoes through the loudspeaker.

Zyneth grimaces as he catches sight of my broken arm. "Yes, fortunately."

"Good," Gillow says. "Because I'm going to fucking murder you both for what you just did to my ship. It's not designed to be out of water! You need to reverse this right now!"

Whoops. I step to the window. Nothing's moving outside. Then, hesitantly, I step out. My boots scuff over the surface of the pillar, now dotted with rippling puddles.

"Gods' grace," Zyneth breathes, stepping out beside me. "I've visited many Ruins, but I've never seen anything quite like this."

The roar of running water is all around us as I turn in a slow circle to take in our surroundings. We're still on the pillar, but we're now in a large pocket of air, the water pushed back to form a giant bubble around us. Waves that defy the laws of physics swell and splash back down against the surface of the inverted ocean, held back by an unseen force, now dozens of feet away.

"Well," I say. "Technically, it did create a bubble of air, like I said it would."

Zyneth cautiously approaches the edge of the platform and looks down. "Don't let Gillow hear you say that." Instead of joining him at the edge, I float some of my glass over to look down for me. Sure enough, the bubble of air wraps beneath us too, bisecting the column about halfway down. Beneath that is the ocean. So much for clearing a spot around the spell circle down there.

"This is terrible!" Gillow cries, stumbling out of the *Prismatic*. Their hands are clasped around their head as they back up, eyes on their ship. "What have you done to her!"

"It's just a little air," I say. "You said she can withstand monster attacks—this shouldn't be worse than that, right?"

The murderous glare they shoot me says otherwise.

"She runs on water magic, you idiot," they snap. "Water arcanum to increase her speed. Water arcanum to track and steer her heading. Water arcanum to keep her from being crushed by the depths—or sea monsters. And that was all mostly powered by water *I* had Attuned—which has now been swept away, gods know where, thanks to your little spell."

"Oh." I stand there awkwardly. "That all sounds pretty bad."

"Pretty bad. *Pretty bad?*" Despite their blue skin, I swear their face is turning red. "You've marooned us! Without those spells to protect her, the *Prismatic* is beached. She'll be crushed like tin once this water collapses back in—and we'll be crushed with her."

"Can we get it back?" I ask. "Your Attuned water."

In response, Gillow grasps the empty air in front of them, seeming to throttle some invisible foe.

"You know," I sign to Zyneth. "I don't think they plan to kill us. If they had, it would have been just now."

"And stop doing that!" Gillow cries, pointing accusingly at my signing glass. "Don't think I haven't seen that! You keep saying things behind my back, I just know it!"

"Let's all calm down," Zyneth cuts in before I can make a quip about the likelihood of Gillow experiencing a mental breakdown. "I still intend to leave here alive, and I suspect I'll need both your help to do so. Now is the time to gather ourselves. Take stock of our circumstances. What do we have to work with?"

Despite my bravado, I'm glad Zyneth's here to ground us. I don't know why I feel the need to needle Gillow—maybe it's just so they won't realize how scared I am that I really fucked things up here. Even if I'm able to end this encounter by escaping back to Earth, I can't leave Zyneth stranded to die under the ocean. Even worse, knowing my actions put him there.

But he's right. We need to focus. Figure out a solution. I try to keep calm and focus on just that.

"The spell circle is under the ship," I say, scuffing my boot over the ground. "Even if we get the water spells back, I won't be able to reach it unless we move the *Prismatic*."

"And we likely can't move the ship without water to lift it." Zyneth rubs his chin with a frown. I know that look: We're in trouble.

"What else do we have?" I ask. "The arcana containers?"

Zyneth tips his head to gesture behind us. "Two fell over the side. Likely somewhere in the ocean beneath us, but I can't make them out."

Damn. "Gillow," I start, then pause when I see where they've gone. They're grumpily seated at the edge of the platform, cross legged like some kind of yoga pose. "Er. What are you doing?"

"Searching for my arcana," they snap. "I should be able to pull out anything that moves within my range. Luckily this bubble is just barely small enough that I can reach a bit into the water. And given some time, I might be able to Attune some new water to make up for whatever I can't retrieve. No promises though." They bare their teeth at me. "You better work on figuring out a solution to all this in the meantime."

Fair enough.

Zyneth gestures me away, and we circle around the other end of the ship. We don't have to go far to be out of earshot of Gillow, with the water roaring around us.

"We need to work on communicating your plans before you execute them," Zyneth says. "And when I say we, I mean you."

"To be fair, I *did* tell you this plan in advance." I glance over the edge of the platform with my signing glass. "It just, er, didn't do what I expected it to."

"I don't know why you would have assumed a spell circle *on this platform* would have caused the spell to be cast down there, anyway," Zyneth says.

Now that he puts it like that, it does seem a bit obvious.

"So," Zyneth says. "Do you have any other ideas you're not telling me?"

"I have tons of ideas," I say. "Plans is another story."

"Such as?"

"I could levitate myself down there," I say, gesturing below us. "And then with the help of one of your charms, and, er, the predator, I could navigate the waters without being crushed or chopped in half. From there I could search for more dormant spell circles. Find something that would drain the area on the arena floor. Or, I could activate the trans-dimensional spell circle without draining the area, if I'm quick enough."

Zyneth looks at me flatly. "And what happens if you get teleported away again and the charm runs out before you have a chance to get back? What do Gillow and I do up here while you're down in the water? How do we get out of here even if you're able to find a way home?"

"You asked for my *ideas*, not my *plans*," I say. "I told you they were half-baked."

Zyneth sighs, looking over the edge as well. "This isn't good. We need to start turning some of these ideas into actions as soon as we're able. This spell won't last forever, but even before it runs out there's the null currents and sea serpents to worry about."

"We'll figure something out," I say.

"How?" Zyneth repeats, this time an edge in his voice. I lean back, surprised. "This is serious!"

He's more bothered by all this than he's been letting on.

"I know. Hey." I take his hands and give them a squeeze. "I'm going to fix this. No one's going to die here." Well, I wouldn't shed any tears over Gillow, but I'm not about to ruin my hero speech with that qualifier.

His frown softens. "Are you just saying that to sound brave, or have you actually thought of anything new?"

"Both," I admit, and he chuckles softly. But he's not going to like it, and to be frank, neither do I.

Alright, beasty, I say, and the predator perks up. *You've been living rent-free long enough. time for you to start earning your keep.*

The predator catches a glimpse of my thoughts and surges eagerly forward, reaching for control.

Not so fast, I say, pulling back. I double-check the Predator Influence stat: still at 33%. I'm the more powerful mind here, I have to remind myself. I'm in control. *We'll be doing this together, but you'll be working for me. Like in Yedzaquib's library.*

Except, you know, for the whole part where I slipped up and the predator was able to pull more of itself from Between. It is mortally crucial that doesn't happen again.

The predator only puts up a token resistance, which is fairly concerning. It's fine. I'll just remain more vigilant this time.

If you know you're stepping into a viper's den, does that make you more prepared? Or does it just make you a fool?

"Alright," I say, tamping down my nerves. I let go of Zyneth and step back. "Let's get to work."

Zyneth frowns as he watches me. I'm sure he knows what I'm planning—somehow, he always manages to read me like an open book. But he doesn't object; his look says enough, and I try to not let it cut me as I focus on summoning the void.

I only have to nudge the predator for it to fall into line, allowing me access to its control over the magic. The void spirals out from our coat, spilling into every nook of our glass, bracing our joints and strengthening our body. It's amazing how much more powerful we feel like this, both types of arcana joining together to become something greater than the individual magics. And yet, we can sense we've barely tapped into the potential of either.

We can dwell on that later. First, the ship. We move to the side of the *Prismatic.*

"Don't forget communication," Zyneth finally says. "No more unexplained plans."

We haven't forgotten. Although talking in this form is slightly more difficult. Like the translator is struggling to interpret our merged thoughts—or maybe our thoughts have moved somewhat beyond words.

Still, we can force them out, if we focus. "Don't worry. We were only planning to destroy the ship."

His mouth twitches with the hint of a smile. "Oh, well, so long as that's communicated first."

Amusement ripples through us, and Zyneth's tense stance relaxes a fraction. Good. We don't want to worry him.

Dropping to the ground, we place our hands on the stone, running the void out beneath our fingers and squeezing beneath the tiny gaps under the hull. The sensation becomes like a second sight, mentally mapping out grooves cut into the stone. After a moment, we come across something familiar.

"There," we say. "The spell circle. We can reach it."

"Good," Zyneth breathes. "Now we'll just need to make sure Gillow has their Attuned water back and their ship's spells reactivated—then we'll have a way out, at least."

We stand, withdrawing our void—or, most of it. We leave a pool sitting on the surface of the spell circle, ready to reactivate it when needed. While we're in contact with the circle, we are also learning more things about it. Ways it can be tuned. Part of our mind splits off to ruminate on this while the rest of us focuses on what we need to do next.

Killing the nereid would make things easier. They're going to fight us when they learn our plan. Best to eliminate the obstacle now—

No! No killing. We've been over this.

We know not to kill Zyneth. He is valuable to us. Besides, we are also valuable to him, so he poses no threat.

No killing *anyone.* Jesus. It's not that hard.

It will be more difficult this way.

That's fine. If it gets us all down to the circle alive, nothing else matters.

We send more of our void into the ship as we turn to Zyneth. "We are going now."

His face is somber. "I thought as much. And you need me to charm you so your vial won't break in the water?"

"Yes."

His expression becomes pained. "I want to talk to you before you go. Just you, Kanin. As you normally are."

We tip our head. "We are not leaving yet. You are coming with us."

He raises an eyebrow. "What do you mean? Where?"

Ah, there. We've found what we're looking for.

"The spell circle," we say, pointing to the ocean floor. "In the *Prismatic.* You should get back inside. Gillow too, we guess."

"You know, we just talked about communication," Zyneth says. "If you've got a plan..."

"Yes." We pull our prize from the ship. "You charm us for strength. We Identify and activate other spell circles, then move the ship to the basin when the way is clear."

"With me in it?" Zyneth seems skeptical. "How are you going to manage that?"

We hold up the arcanum crystal, which we pried from the ship's control room. Even without tapping into the magic, it feels alive, buzzing in our void.

Zyneth's eyes widen. "Be careful with that. Do you even know what you're doing? The amount of arcanum in there—it's meant to power spells, not living things."

"We are not alive."

"Don't say that," Zyneth snaps. "Kanin wouldn't say that."

We would. This existence, this body, is not life. But that's why we're still fighting for the chance to change things. A chance to live again.

And the solution is right beneath our feet.

"Hey!" Gillow's faint voice echoes from the other side of the *Prismatic*. "What did you do to my ship?"

We bare our core to Zyneth. "The charm. Please."

Zyneth glances toward the ship, then swears. He whips out our spell scroll and smooths it out on the ground. "Alright. Quickly, now!" The lines of his spell are already glowing as he funnels mana into the circle.

We place our core on the page, but keep our body nearby as the magic takes hold.

"Get on the ship," we tell him one last time, then send our body to wait in the cargo hold.

"Be careful," Zyneth says, but without our signing glass or translator we can no longer reply. Instead, we wrap the void around our core, tighten our hold on the arcana crystal, and leap into the ocean.

Chapter Forty-One

TIPPING POINT

Here's where the predator's abilities become crucial.

The ocean tears at us and streams of null magic slice through our void, but we shield our core from the angry buffeting as we plunge into the depths.

We shield the arcana crystal, too. We've taken that with us, in case Gillow tries to do anything to stop us. But we'll need all the mana we can get for this next stunt.

Activate Inspect.

Nothing happens. Echo does not confirm our spell.

We turn our attention inward and can feel our interface, barely out of our grasp; reaching for it feels like pushing through mud. We press harder, will our magic into existence, and a sharp pain lances through our mind, as if we're about to split back in two. We can't let that happen though; if we lose our void manipulation now, we'll be exposed to the whims of the null magic. We'll certainly die.

Slowly, Echo fizzles into our mind, voice corrupted with static.

[Activated...]

Relief spills through us as glowing lines of magic appear on the pillars next to us. That's not enough, though. We need to see everything. We draw on the arcana crystal, just the tiniest amount, and are immediately flooded with energy. Before the power can overwhelm us, we funnel it all into the Identify spell. The world lights up with magic.

The entire coliseum has become a circuit board of luminescent lines, all crisscrossing each other, looping around pillars, connecting the intricate web of spells that were programmed into this place centuries ago.

(And there's a distinct, overwhelming familiarity to this place. We've seen this before. We've been here.)

We trace the spell patterns around us, dissecting how they intersect and what they mean. We force Echo to explain them to us, to show us what we're looking for. It takes work. Reaching her is like digging through wet cement. But we do, and she tells us.

(This place was different before. It wasn't empty. There were people. As indistinguishable from fish as the fish are from the sea. We hadn't even realized what they were at the time. What is one system of chemistry compared to another?)

First, the pillars. The water races around us, null currents tearing against our void as we rush through the water. We pick up null arcana as we go, stashing the magic within us. Echo tries to document this: [Bo-s M-na: 23-2] but bits of her voice and visuals cut out. It's the void, we know. It's interfering. Neither of us understand why.

(We could see lines of magic flowing through everything, like the pulsing arteries of an animal. They led to bubbles of air, where visitors resided; they led to the city's defenses, which kept back the untamed beasts and currents; they led to fields of kelp and ecosystems of coral;

they led to the telepad, consumed by a featureless black dome of magic. The people of Emrox swam in and out of that hemisphere at will.)

We activate the spell circle the next column over, beginning to drain the water. We understand what these structures were for, now: platforms for transportation. Where you could wait before transit. This entire stadium was for transportation.

(It's so different, so strange experiencing this place with a new understanding of what we see. With... linear thought. Distant memories—no, shadows of memories—take on new meaning.)

Before the water can fully drain away, we rocket through the turbulence, activating the spell on the next platform, and the next. Pockets of air begin to populate the stadium, overlapping and merging to form a giant bubble. We spiral down to the stadium floor this way. The null arcanum is thickest here.

(The inhabitants stopped what they were doing as a great shadow descended over their home.)

We wrap null arcana around us, any and all we can get our hands on. Draw upon it to concentrate the void. Back on the platform, we wrap it around the *Prismatic*, too, hoping Zyneth made it back on board. In both places simultaneously, around the *Prismatic*, and at a space just in front of us, we pull the void tight. Compressing it. Compacting the magic smaller, even smaller.

(They were looking up. They were looking at us.)

The water around us is draining away. We settle onto the ground as the tide recedes, and focus instead on our magic.

(We noticed none of this. So much magic condensed in one place—it was irresistible. We reached out for the energy—for the life force that sustained this place. Why wouldn't we? It's what we craved.)

The void is now denser than matter can achieve. We funnel every ounce of null arcana we can into the act, and pull even more from both the ocean and the arcana crystal. There's a swirling ball of physical shadows in front of us, like a miniature black hole, and even still we compress it. With one last swell of magic, we overcome some invisible tipping point of spacetime, and the singularity we've been forming turns inside out, and then—

(A black cloud eclipsed the metropolis.)

The *Prismatic* slips through, from one point in our void to the next, and appears abruptly in front of us.

There's still water around us, quickly draining away, but it's enough to cushion the ship's sudden appearance. We recall the void still left back up on the platform, the other end to our tunnel, and it comes spilling down to us in a wave of black.

[...pell obtained!]

As the last of the water washes away, pushed back against the now massive dome of air surrounding the stadium, the last of the null currents wash away with it. All that is left is us, the ship, and the giant spell circle under our feet.

(Death. We hadn't understood death before.)

Zyneth and Gillow spill out of the craft.

"What did you do? What did you do?" The nereid stumbles out of their ship. "My crystal! Give it..." Their angry tirade comes to a stuttering stop as fear flickers over their face. "Gods above. What are you?"

Zyneth is looking around with apparent surprise. "How did we get down here?"

We can't speak—not in any sounds that would make sense to their ears—so we summon our glass body from the *Prismatic*. Half of our void rushes to retrieve it, filling in the joints like cartilage, attaching to the limbs like black muscles on crystal bones. It walks out of the ship on its own. Gillow scrambles out of its way as it strolls to meet us. Void flows back into void, the glass returning to our structure, as we become whole. The rest of the void—the null arcana we'd borrowed from the surrounding waters in order to achieve our spell—hangs about us like a dark cloak.

We turn to Zyneth now that we have our translator back. "Void."

He eyes us warily, but stands his ground even as Gillow draws a defensive blade. We ignore them.

"What do you mean?" Zyneth asks. "How did you move us down here?"

We'd done it once before, when the tempo squid teleported us away. In fact, it was that creature who showed us how the void could be used. Not to mention all the times before that we experienced null magic with the telepads. It's spatial magic, after all.

We struggle to put this into words. "We connected two points within our void."

And it doesn't just have to be within our void. With a spell circle, it could reach much further. Between worlds. Into extra dimensions.

Our mind spins with these thoughts. There's layers to them, other meanings, like stacks upon stacks of transparencies, each with their words, and we're trying to understand which sheet the print is on. It's dizzying. We need a break from this.

Just for a moment.

As we stop pulling from the arcana crystal, as we separate our mind once again, the range of our void collapses back into its original painfully small radius. The Identify spell flickers out.

[Mana depleted,] Echo says, her voice finally clear.

Without the predator's strength, weariness hits me all at once. I at least have enough awareness to catch my core, no longer attached to my body, as the void puddles to the ground around me. Without it there to help hold me up, I stumble, then sink to my knees, mentally exhausted.

Zyneth rushes over, dropping down in front of me. "Are you okay?"

I shake my head. My mind is buzzing—from all that magic or the predator's thoughts, I'm not sure. "It's been here before. I—I think it did something to them. I think it hurt people."

"What?" Zyneth holds out his hands. "What are you talking about?"

I place my core in his grasp, too tired to get it strung back up on my own. I'd probably drop it. "The predator. This place. I think... I think it was here before Emrox was a Ruin."

Zyneth gingerly clasps my core back on my chain, where it bumps lightly against my chest. It's not inside a pouch any longer, but I can't be bothered to find one, and the double vision doesn't bother me as much now anyways.

"What are you saying?" Zyneth says, lowering his voice. "You think it's what caused Emrox to become a Ruin?"

I put a hand to my core, like I could massage away the headache that's forming. "Maybe. I don't know. Those memories—I think they were memories—they weren't from the predator, exactly. They were from something..." I can't even describe it. It wasn't even seeing, in a way that I would consider sight. It wasn't hearing, in a way I would consider sound. The way it interacted with reality was beyond any-thing I can experience. "...The memories were from something much more vast."

Zyneth is quiet for a long moment. "I'm no mage, Kanin, but all of this... it seems beyond me. That thing in your magic—we're out of our depths."

My soul sinks. It isn't what I want to hear, but I think I've always known. "I know."

"We can still turn around," Zyneth says. "You don't have to go through with this. Gillow attuned enough water that they think they can get the *Prismatic* running again. Let's leave this spell circle behind and head back to civilization. See Noli and Rezira again. Please, Kanin. Come back with me."

My soul feels like it's being squeezed in a vice. "But what about the predator? It's why we came here in the first place. Open a portal Between—destroy it by taking it back to my world, or at least trap it between your world and mine."

Zyneth gives me a critical look. "We came here because you wanted your body back. That was the goal, even before the predator became an issue. But there's bound to be other ways to restrain that creature. We haven't even begun to look."

"We can't go back to the Athenaeum," I say.

"It's not the only library in the world." Zyneth takes my hand. "Let's leave this cursed place behind and search for an answer. You can figure it out another way. *We* can figure it out another way."

The predator is listening to all this, tense with anticipation. It's waiting for me to decide. It doesn't want me to leave—which makes me think leaving must be the right answer.

But I'm so close. I'm so close to the only way I know to get home. To retrieving my body. Can I give that all up, right when I'm on the threshold?

Zyneth watches me, pain etched over his features, waiting for me to respond. I feel like I'm being torn in two. If I do this, if I activate the portal, then I'd be giving him up, too.

But in my heart of hearts—or, I guess, glass of glass—I know what I should do. I steel myself, almost in disbelief over what I'm about to say. "You're right. We—"

There's a blur of motion from Gillow. I react. My void shoves Zyneth out of the way, but the spear of water still clips his shoulder. Their attack deflects off Zyneth's arm and stabs instead into me—into my core.

Pain explodes through me. My mind is sent reeling, dizzy, stunned by the numbing agony which leaches away into a distant chill.

[15 points of Piercing Damage sustained. HP: 4/10]

The predator's anger erupts through me, and I'm too disoriented to temper it. What just...

Its outrage swells like rising a tide. I try to push through my disorientation, but it's like swimming through mud. The wave crashes over my head, and I drown in it.

We leap at Gillow, seething at their arrogance.

(A piece of glass shifts with the violent motion. A distant voice says, [HP: 3/10].)

How dare they try to hurt Zyneth. How dare they hurt our anchor! Gillow braces themself, terror and defiance clear on their face as a whip of water circles them at the ready. It's not their magic we are concerned with, however. Their soul glows bright in their chest. Yes, it is past time we devoured another. We've been holding back. Our anchor didn't want us feasting—and he held up his end of the bargain—but we cannot sit idly by as this prey breaks our only foothold in reality.

Our void clashes with their water, which turns to ice on contact. The shock ripples through us with a sting of something unfamiliar—pain.

[HP: 2/10]

"Don't!" Zyneth cries from behind us.

We ignore him, wrenching our void from Gillow's ice as we stab at them again. Spears of black come at them from several directions at once. They raise a wave of ice, chips of it shattering off from the impact of our attack. Before we can withdraw, it turns just as abruptly back into water and collapses on us.

[HP: 1/10]

"Stop!" Zyneth cries, dashing after us. "You're falling apart!"

We struggle to escape from the water, but it's nearly as intangible as our void, slipping through our attacks—stabbing for our core. And finally we understand what that pain means—what Zyneth was saying. Our anchor is about to shatter.

We try to cluster our glass around it, but our control of the strange material is clumsy, imprecise—we need our other half to help with this, but it's no longer fighting us *or* Gillow. It's tired—drifting—fading.

We stumble back from the icy attack, clutching our shattered anchor as an unfamiliar emotion fills us: Fear.

Our soul. We're going to lose our soul.

CHAPTER FORTY-TWO

OUR SOUL

A hand grabs our shoulder and jerks us back as warmth floods through us. Zyneth steps around as we fall to the ground—our void swarms to catch us—a hand pressed to our chest even as he extends another toward Gillow, lightning flashing from his fingers. It flashes through us, too, stinging our void, bits of the essence hissing into black fog at the contact, but our glass is unharmed.

There's a glowing scrap of paper between his hand and our core. We grab his arm, ready to sink our claws into his flesh, ready to tear the limb off for daring to lay a finger on our anchor—but the pain is abating. He's not attacking us, he's reinforcing.

Gillow cries out as the electricity jolts through their water and back into them. They stumble away, their ice crashing to the ground like shattered pottery. They clutch at one of their arms, which now hangs limply after the attack.

"You idiot," they snarl, backing away. "You're protecting it?"

Still keeping a hand on me, Zyneth raises his knife, lightning sparking to life across its surface, writhing like a nest of angry snakes. "That's rich, coming from the person who just tried to kill me."

"You—it—it doesn't matter," Gillow hisses, taking another step back. "That thing isn't natural. It should be left down here at the bottom of the ocean—and you along with it, if you think it's your friend."

"*His* name is Kanin," Zyneth snaps.

Gillow barks out a pained laugh. "You sure? I don't think he's home right now. Look at it. It's not even talking."

Zyneth's gaze darts back at us for a moment. Our grip on his arm tightens—a warm wetness forms beneath our claws in response. We need to be careful with our anchor, but if he tries anything, we should be able to eviscerate him in seconds.

"No thanks to you," Zyneth says, turning back to Gillow. "You nearly killed him."

"Self-preservation," Gillow says, retreating toward their ship. "If I'd known he had this monster in him before we set out on this trip, I would have eliminated the threat back in Miasmere."

"He's not a monster," Zyneth says.

"No?" Gillow scoffs as their shoulder bumps into the side of their vessel. "You've always been soft, Zyneth, but you were never stupid. It's about to tear your arm off."

Ah, yes. Blood. That's what that sensation is. We'd nearly forgotten. These creatures are so strange—so fragile. Yet, he's not retaliating. Part of us trusts him; we don't understand why, but it does. We extract our claws from his flesh, and he winces, but doesn't pull his hand away. Commendable. Strange.

"I'm not a fool," Zyneth says. "I know the risks. But that is why I must remain beside him. He asked me once to do what needed to be done, should the situation require. I will honor his wish if that day ever arrives. But it is not, I think, today."

Weariness and distant pain courses through us as a portion of our consciousness fades back into awareness. We're not dead. Somehow, we're still alive.

Our minds spill over into one another, confusion mixing with context. Regret stings us. Zyneth's arm—we didn't mean to do that. He saved us. But we also saved him, didn't we?

Anger burns in us at the memory. Gillow tried to kill him! And they very nearly killed us.

"Zyneth," we say, pushing through the mind static. Gently, we remove his hand from our core as we rise to our feet. The glass of our core is still broken, but it's no longer breaking, reinforced by his magic. Ah, it's so much easier to move now with all of us in sync. All of us working with one shared objective: destroy Gillow.

Zyneth looks at us with a mix of tired emotions—worry, relief, fondness—as we touch his arm. "Your arm. Sorry." But a troubled look returns when we speak next. "We are alright now."

"You nearly got Kanin killed," Zyneth says, which is strange. We are Kanin. But we are not. He is speaking to us, but only some of us. It's troubling to parse. "You can't do that. He's mortal, and from what I understand of you, that makes you mortal, too. If you lose him, you'll lose everything."

Not everything. But losing our soul, losing reality, that's more than we're willing to give up. Perhaps he's right. Sometimes, it is difficult to remember we are so susceptible like this.

Conflicted, then alarmed. Hey, we don't want to die, either!

Behind Zyneth, something is happening. Gillow reaches a hand behind them as they slowly step back. The ship creaks as it shifts. Zyneth whips around, stabbing his blade in Gillow's direction and firing off another bolt of lightning. They duck away and as the electricity arcs into their ship. One of the tentacles lifts into the air.

Inspect.

Nothing happens. We push harder. *Inspect, Inspect, Inspect!*

[...activated.]

Lines of magic spring into view. Radiating from where Gillow is touching the ship, arcana circuits are lighting up, activating spells in the ship too quickly for us to follow. They don't have the arcana crystal, but they're using their own magic. We guess they got their hands on enough Attuned water to reactivate the ship. Metal screeches as one of the mechanical tentacles laboriously reaches for us.

Time to move.

We leap away, Zyneth only a heartbeat behind, as the limb crashes down onto the stone, spraying us with chips of rock. No! We need the spell circle inscribed here. We can't let it destroy the pattern.

"The tentacles. Break them," we say. If we can slip our void between the seams, we should be able to rip them apart. We elongate the void around our hands into needle-sharp claws.

"We can't," Zyneth says. "We need The *Prismatic* to get home, or we'll be stranded here!"

We hesitate as another tentacle rears up to attack us. Outside the water, it's slow, but its weight can cause enough damage as is—both to us and the spell circle. What do we do? We can't let the circle be destroyed, but we also can't destroy it. "Gillow."

"I'll stop them," Zyneth says. "You can keep the ship busy?"

Amusement. "Yes."

The tentacle looms overhead, and this time instead of running, we reach up even as it falls toward us. Reshaping our magic from claws into a Void Whip, we snap the magic out, wrapping around the limb as all its weight slams down on us. We stagger beneath the force. Our void compresses as the limb presses down on us. We push back, and metal on metal grinds through the limb. It stops feet above our head.

Satisfaction crackles through us. There. No destroying anything.

And then the limb lifts back up, pulling us with it. Oh. We should have dispersed the Void Whip. A miscalculation.

The limb snaps us through the air, and we can only hang on as our surroundings become a blur of color. If we let go now, we could be thrown in any direction, and it's unlikely our glass would survive the fall.

We hope it doesn't smash us into the ground.

That would probably be the smart thing to do.

Deciding a change of tactics would be wise, we reel ourself in, latching onto the tentacle as we funnel as much void around us as possible, forming a protective bubble. If we can finish the shell in time, it should be able to cushion the blow. Probably. We hope.

There's shouting below, but even when we use our void as our eyes, we're moving too erratically to tell what's going on. There's a flash of lightning. Daggers of ice. Zyneth and Gillow must be fighting. Other limbs are moving, too, and we brace for impact, expecting to be squished between them. Instead, however, they are sweeping around the ship. One has even reached out of the air bubble and is touching the ocean. What is it doing? It can't go anywhere without—

Without the arcana crystal. Even as we realize this, circuit lines explode through the *Prismatic*, lighting up the ship in a dazzling display. They got it back.

They're planning to leave.

No! They can't abandon us here. What about Zyneth? He'll die if he's left behind. This tentacle we're latched onto isn't trying to kill us, it's trying to keep us out of the fight.

It's high time to get back into it.

Keeping our orb of void tightly knit around us, we let go of the tentacle and are sent flying through the air. We brace all our glass, cushion our core as much as we can, then slam into the ground, streaking across the coarse stone. Our void splatters away, and our elbow clips the ground, immediately shattering on impact. The shards stay within our void, held in place for now, but we don't have time to stitch the glass back together. We have to stop Gillow.

Bloodlust overcomes us in a wave we don't even want to fight: not stop. *Kill*.

Water floods over the ground as the ship pulls itself toward the edge of the bubble, metal screeching on stone with the movement. Even that stops after a moment when the water flows beneath the ship, buoying it up and wrapping around the *Prismatic*. Water crawls up the side of the craft, forming a shimmering layer over its surface. Do we have time to get back into the ship and steal the arcana crystal, shutting down the *Prismatic's* power? It begins to drift toward the edge of the bubble.

No. No time.

But we can do something else.

The void unwraps from around us like petals of a flower, which fall away and swirl into the ground we're kneeling on. Fragments of our broken arm clatter to the ground, but we can't pay that any mind now. We summon an ancient memory of the circle to our mind, and our void replicates it on the stone, flowing into the grooves, filling in the damaged sections of the circle, completing each spiral and runic figure in inky black lines.

The *Prismatic* breaches the edge of the water. Only a few moments more and it will be too late.

We create a second spell circle next: small, just beneath our feet, built from the schematic of the spell we learned weeks ago.

Echo, we call, forcing our link with her. *Echo. For the Location spell, establish focus: Our soul. No.* My *soul*.

There's a pause as we experience a mental dissonance: We need to be separated enough to work our magic, but still close enough to retain control over our void. We can't let our control over the circle slip. We wait, tense. We have to time this perfectly.

[Focus Established,] Echo says.

Pushing through the mind static, we activate the Location spell. The circle beneath our feet illuminates. A thread of light appears within our soul, vanishing into the air only inches from my body.

Now.

Activate Planar Linkage spell, we tell ourself.

The is the moment of truth. The moment where it can choose to help us, or stop us in our tracks. It must know what we're planning. That we intend to leave it Between.

Yet, it doesn't hesitate. Both halves of us are eager to activate this spell.

Which isn't a good sign, but it's too late to stop it now.

[Planar Linkage Spell Activated.]

All across the base of the stadium, the circle illuminates with the black light of our magic. We pour everything we have into it. All our mana, everything Zyneth gave us, all the bonus mana from the null magic we've been storing. As more null arcana drifts around the stadium, like flotsam caught in a hurricane, we grab that, and we add it to the spell circle, too. Void jumps into the air, tracing the lines of the spell. The *Prismatic* edges closer to the wall of ocean, closer to the edge of the circle—

Then the world splits open, and darkness wraps its familiar weight around us.

CHAPTER FORTY-THREE

THE BRINK OF BETWEEN

Black. Nothingness.

Between surrounds us, yet we still have our shape. We still have our glass and void. The *Prismatic* is next to us, and the stone summoning circle is beneath our feet, but otherwise we're alone in the dark. Like the base of the stadium was consumed by a dome of darkness.

This is different from other times we've been Between. We flex our hand, our bones of glass and sinew of ink. We can definitely still feel. Still move.

There's motion near the *Prismatic*.

"Get off me!"

Gillow grunts as they fall out of the ship and go rolling. Zyneth jumps after them, feet landing inches from their head.

They both pause to look around in surprise.

"What is this?" Gillow says, scrambling back. "Where are we?"

Zyneth steps around them, half a pace in our direction. They look at us. "Are we Between?"

"Almost," we say. The thread of light emanating from my soul now shoots off into the dark, like an arrow toward a target. I know where it will take me: I just need to take the first step.

Zyneth glances one last time at Gillow, then strides over to us. "Talk to me," he says. "Where do we go from here?"

We didn't mean to pull Zyneth into this as well, but it was the only way to cut us off from the ocean and stop the *Prismatic* from leaving. We need to talk to him—just us.

Before we allow our minds to separate, however, we check with Echo.

Spell duration?

Since we're not completely Between yet, we aren't sure if Echo will be able to reach us. It's difficult enough to reach her through the void's interference. Luckily, she answers.

[Five minutes and twenty-seven seconds.]

Not much. Not nearly as much as we want. *Void requirement?*

[No further void is required to keep the spell active: However more would be required to sustain it longer.]

We don't need the predator's help to keep the path open, then. Good. We have diverging goals at this point, anyway.

"Zyneth," we say as the void pulls away from us. "We—I—wait a moment."

As the predator's mind separates from mine, I catch a glimpse of its plans. It's looking for the rest of itself—a way to free it from my inventory. Since my inventory is a pocket of Between, I guess it's hoping to cut out the middleman and shred its container from the inside. I don't know if that will work, but if I'm able to get back to Earth before then, it won't matter.

Of course, I only have five minutes and counting.

The predator leaps away into the black, leaving only the small scraps of Attuned void with me.

"What the fuck?" Gillow cries, pressing themself against their ship. "What is all of this?"

"A portal," I say. "The threshold of it, anyway. And as long as you don't follow me, you'll stay on this side. When it closes, you can go home. *With* Zyneth."

"But what *are* you," they cry. "What was that—that thing?"

Isn't that the million dollar question. "A predator. And if you don't want to find out exactly what it's capable of when it gets back, I suggest you get back in your ship and wait there."

Gillow doesn't need to be told twice. They scramble through one of the *Prismatic's* windows, disappearing back into their ship.

Good. As much as I'd love to exact my revenge for trying to kill Zyneth—and me—I don't have time to deal with Gillow right now.

"It left?" Zyneth asks, keeping a suspicious eye in the direction the predator vanished.

"Yes," I say. The thread of our bond trails behind it like a leash, fading into the dark. "But it will be back—with the rest of it, I suspect." I think I could take hold of our bond and yank it back, if I really wanted to. But it would fight me the whole way, and by then the spell would be up. "I need to move fast. I only have a few minutes."

"Why?" Zyneth asks. "What will happen then?"

"The spell will end," I say. "And if I'm still here, the predator will be, too. Only then I'm not sure I'll be able to stop it anymore."

Zyneth's mouth presses into a thin line. He must understand what this means—that five minutes from now, if I get what I want, we'll be worlds away. Will he protest? Suggest yet another alternative?

"What can I do to help?" he asks.

My heart bursts and breaks all at once. "Come with me?" I ask. "Not all the way. But at least, to the brink."

"I'll go as far as I can," he promises.

I can't delay any longer, yet I hesitate. Even counting down the days until we'd arrive at Emrox—as days became hours, and those have become minutes—I thought I'd have more time. Somehow, it always felt like there'd be more time.

"Kanin..."

The timer keeps ticking.

I stand up straight and hold out my hand. Zyneth takes it. It's now or never.

Following the faint thread of the Location spell as it pierces the dark, I picture Earth, picture home, picture my body, and step into the black.

Chapter Forty-Four

A Mingled Yarn

The Between moves. It's impossible to see it, because all there is to see is nothing, but somehow I can feel the space shifting around me. Ripples of light appear beneath each of my footfalls, matching the shade of the Location spell, like a pathway is being built beneath us with every step. The spell tugs on my soul.

"What happens at the other side?" Zyneth asks. "When we reach it, will it pull me through?"

"No," I say. Somehow, I can still feel there's a distance ahead of us. Not a real distance, not a place that can be walked to, yet that feeling of a great expanse remains. "We stepped in one side, and we'll have to actively step out the other. However, don't let go," I add. "The Location spell is providing the bridge between the two worlds, and without it, you'll fall back to your reality."

He tightens his grip.

I let the spell lead me. The *Prismatic* is gone. The stone beneath our feet is worlds away. Everything is darkness, timelessness, spacelessness.

My void always reacted to my instincts, so I use that here as well: focusing on me. On my body. On the moments before I left, when my body was still whole and alive.

Then, finally, a light. My spell is leading us straight toward it, like a lure at the end of a line, only that small pinprick is rapidly growing, until there's suddenly a bubble of white right in front of us. It grows to twice our size, opaque and swirling. Somehow, I understand that all I have to do is reach out and touch it, pop the film of reality, and then the bridge will be complete.

My soul flutters. I'm here. This is it.

Zyneth breathes in deeply. "Can you smell that?"

"No." But the light is changing, gaining color, like a lens out of focus.

"It smells like nature," Zyneth says. "Like a forest."

Not something I associate with Los Angeles. But I can't think about forests now, in case somehow that accidentally changes where the portal will open to. I keep focusing on my body. I keep trying to manifest the moment I left.

The light slowly morphs into blurry shapes, and I can feel a distant warmth—sunlight. Zyneth's right, wherever this is on Earth, it's outside. Bird chirps echo from the scene, muted and distant. I know I must only have a couple minutes left, but still I don't reach out—I can't bring myself to say goodbye. Instead, I concentrate on bringing everything into focus.

Slowly, the scene resolves.

There's a tree in front of us, and though I can't see its source, I can make out the distant but oh-so-familiar sound of traffic, a sound that's been absent ever since I arrived in Lusio. My soul tightens with longing. This is really Earth.

But that begs the question: Where is my body? Why did the portal open up in a park of all places? Did I do the spell wrong?

"This is where you were before coming to our world?" Zyneth asks.

"No," I say, drifting closer to the boundary. "No, I was in the studio. This is still Los Angeles, I think, but..." As the scene continues to resolve, my gaze falls on the grass. Or, more specifically, the headstones that litter the grass.

My chest seizes up. I feel light. Dizzy. No, but I thought I could choose when I went back. I thought the Between existed outside of time. I thought...

"What is it?" Zyneth asks as I sink to my knees. "Kanin what's wrong?"

"Too late," I say, dazed. I feel hot and cold. Pins and needles. My mind is buzzing, spinning, thick. I sink down to my knees. "It's gone."

Somehow. Somehow it was never actually real until this moment. Despite knowing I died, I never actually *felt* it was true. It always seemed reversible. Temporary. If I was clever enough, I could find a way out. A way back. All I had to do was give it my all, and I'd be able to go home. Get my job back. My life back. My *body* back.

But it's buried six feet under my gravestone.

In Loving Memory of

Kanin Reed

1996-2024

"Life's but a walking shadow, a poor player. That struts and frets his hour upon the stage, and then is heard no more."

My grip goes slack, but Zyneth squeezes tighter before my hand can slip away. "Don't fall apart on me now," he says. "Not here. I need you. If you can't go through, then we have to go back."

I distantly understand he's right—I can't go through. There's nothing to go back to. If I step over that boundary, there will be no body to bind to, and if my bond with this one is severed, all that's left is the afterlife.

And I don't want to die. I don't want to be living this half-life, either, but I'm not ready to be dead. It just hurts. It hurts so much.

Shakily, I let Zyneth help pull me to my feet. "I can't believe it," I moan.

"What?" he asks softly. "Talk to me."

"They used a Shakespeare quote. For an actor." I cover my face. "It's just so fucking cliche."

"It sounds like you have a lot to work through," Zyneth says.

He tugs me away from the portal, and I let him. The image drifts a few feet away. I should let it go. I should end this spell, and never look back.

"Perhaps we can do that back in reality," Zyneth suggests.

Yeah. Okay. Yeah, he's right. I can't bear to look at this anymore anyway. But if we're heading back to reality, and I'm coming with—

I realize what I should have been paying attention to with a lurch of fear. The predator. I grab our tether. Where is it? Can I pull it back in time? I can feel its eager excitement through our distant bond. Anticipation is thrumming down the string and into my soul. I try to yank it back, but it resists me. I'll need all my mental focus for this. If only I wasn't still battling with the emotional trauma of seeing my own grave. Come on, Kanin, keep it together. Just calm down. Focus. And—

I double over as pain rips through me. I feel something inside my soul tear. The predator is filled with elation—and then that elation is met with malice and hunger, and its mind is multiplied tenfold.

Oh. Oh no.

I Check the Predator's Influence Stat. Echo's hardly crackles through the Between, distant but discernible.

[Predator Influence: 99.98%]

"What's wrong?" Zyneth puts a hand on my back. "Are you hurt? We should get out of here."

I fight through the mental pain, forcing myself upright as I turn to face the direction of the predator. Our tether is vibrating as it rushes toward me. Its hunger drums against me like physical blows.

"It escaped. All of it." I draw my blade—Zyneth's blade—then press it into his hands. "If it comes to it—"

"What?" Zyneth asks, horrified. He tries to push it back into my hands. "No. We'll fight it."

Maybe. Maybe we could. I don't think it can be killed, but it's at least been knocked back before.

But can we risk it? The second it gets here, I'll be lost, and Zyneth will be left facing it in the Between. He won't have the upper hand.

My hands shake as I push the knife back into his grasp. "If it comes to it," I repeat, and neither of us need for me to finish that thought. I heard him talking with the predator. I know he'll do what has to be done if there's no other option. That's the only reassurance I have.

I let go of the knife and Zyneth. "Run," I tell him.

I suddenly flash back to Attiru's bookshop, to me telling Noli the same thing, terrified and shaking as the predator's mind pressed into me. I try to still my shaking now. Even after everything, I haven't changed, have I?

Our tether whips back and forth as I feel the predator approaching, imminent. I can't escape it. I've already lost. But Zyneth—

Without me to anchor him, he's drifting away—drifting back to Emrox.

"No!" Zyneth snatches for my hand, but we're not *really* in the same place, it only seems that way. Gray stone spreads beneath his feet as he slips back into reality. Good. That's as much as I can do to help him. I Check the Planar Linkage timer: the spell will be up in just over a minute.

I end the Location spell. The line of light pointing me to Earth evaporates, and the bubble of reality begins to shrink. Maybe if both sides close, I'll remain Between when the predator reaches me, and we'll both be trapped here. I hope that will be enough.

NO.

The void crashes into me, and I only put up the smallest, most pathetic excuse of a fight, taking that last gasp of air, before—

Our magic slams into this new body, wrapping around the glass, pulling memories from our other selves to weave our shadows into a familiar form. Yes, this body is much better than before. Our soul has gotten stronger. But it won't be enough—not enough to sate our hunger. We take quick stock of our surroundings: two openings into reality, both closing fast. We leap for the nearest one.

The spell holding the portal open might have already ended, but we are not one to give up on reality so easily. Or void stabs ahead, puncturing the fragile bubble of spacetime. Our tentacles hiss as they make contact with this reality—this place where magic shouldn't exist.

We can't go through—but we don't need to.

We grasp the boundary between Everything and Nothing. We yank the shrinking hole wide. The effort tears at our essence, at the wrongness of this, but we must anchor this place, this time, in existence.

A small, white ball of light drifts through the gateway and into Between. Then a second. Then a third. We stab a spear of black through the nearest one, devouring it with a flood of horrifically familiar ecstasy. It's a soul.

They're all souls.

They're falling through the portal every second, sometimes several at a time, and the longer we hold the gateway open, the more we collect. We snatch up the souls and gather them in our void, keeping them from dispersing Between and moving beyond—we can't eat them all now. We've learned that much after last time—we need to ration them.

This can't be happening. Not again—this can't be happening again—

We snuff out the horror like a doused match, amused. We're still sorting through all these new thoughts—all these new memories we don't remember having. It's a lot to parse at once, but we need information. This time will be different. This time, we won't fall for the same tricks and be cast back into the Between. Speaking of which...

The other portal is closing. We can keep this end open a few moments longer, collecting more souls, but we can't hold both sides open at once. Tucking our prizes close, we release our grip on the second world—Earth, the word comes to us—then fall back to the other side.

There's someone already there, waiting for us. Prey—the cambion—Zyneth. His face is set and grim. Lightning flickers to life in his twin blades.

CHAPTER FORTY-FIVE

STARS IN THE BLACK

We reach for reality, then hesitate. Doubt poisons our mind. Zyneth's lightning can dissipate our void—weaken us. Maybe we shouldn't fight. Maybe we should stay here. If we stay here for just a few moments longer, the portal will be closed, and then—

No! We hiss, shaking off the intrusive thoughts as we dive for reality. The exit is narrowing, closing right in front of Zyneth as he stands, waiting, guarding the rapidly diminishing portal. We form our limbs into needle-like claws, spearing toward the exit. Zyneth raises a blade, ready to sever our hand and stop us from escaping—

And he stays the blow.

We grab the boundary, and it cuts into our essence as we tear it wide and throw ourself through. Zyneth swears as we go rolling across the stone, bristling in a defensive ball of spikes and blades. The portal shuts behind us.

"I'm sorry, Kanin," Zyneth says. "I know you would have wanted it, but I couldn't trap you there."

We gather ourself to our full height. Twice the size of the cambion, all shadow and sharp edges. Our hunger manifests in our void, forming a maw, glass shards aligning in the shape of teeth, empty sockets of smoke where any other creature would have eyes. Our surroundings smell of salt and stone. The air tastes wet and metallic. Ahh, how we've missed taste and smell. The sensations fill us with euphoria.

But with it, the hunger continues to gnaw at us.

Our new memories tell us we had worked out a deal with our soul—it let us eat away at its magic to sustain our presence in reality. But now, with so much of us here, we'll need more than scraps of magic to keep us grounded. Luckily, the dozens of souls we're carrying in us now should feed us for quite some time.

We look at Zyneth, and he tenses. We'd also agreed not to hurt him. But we don't see the benefit to maintaining that deal. One more soul in our collection is more valuable than alliances. Ichor drips from our jaws like drool.

"That said." The lightning dancing over Zyneth's blades grows erratic, shifting from yellow to white-hot. "I don't plan to die today, either."

We strike, a blur of shadows, bolting straight for Zyneth's chest. He stabs his arm forward at the same time, despite us being far out of his reach.

Lightning erupts through us before we even know we've been struck. It sears through our essence, blasting a hole through our void as it disperses all the shadows in a giant hole around our torso, exposing the unscathed glass beneath. We shriek, reforming our void, but Zyneth has made a miscalculation. While his lightning may be able to temporarily peel away our magic, it does not hurt us, nor does it slow us down. Our claws crash into him the next moment, wrapping around his sparking knives as our weight slams him into the ground.

We stab a spear of void toward his chest, but he uses the momentum of the fall to roll away, static discharge rolling over his body to evaporate any of our tendrils that get too close.

An inconvenience, but we have more than just the void to fight with, now.

We levitate the broken shards of glass that used to be an arm, though the movement seems to resist us. It's not as natural as controlling the void, and we need complete concentration—complete *cooperation*—to use the ability to its full potential. We stamp out the part of us that's holding back, force it into compliance. There. Easier. We shatter the arm into a dozen blades of glass, which we orient in an array pointed at Zyneth.

He comes out of his roll, gaze flickering over our newest weapon with a grimace. "Blast."

We send the shards flying. He stumbles back, arms a blur, and we feel several pieces of glass shatter beneath his whirlwind of blades.

As we're launching this attack, the structure near us groans. We pause, tipping our head at the peculiar sound, flipping through memories like flash cards as we search for context. The structure—yes, the *Prismatic*—is shuddering to life, its many limbs reaching for the ocean once more. It's being brought to life by Gillow.

Gillow.

Hatred catches us off guard. Oh, how we wish to crush that one. How we will savor their soul. The fear in their eyes as we extract our revenge. The ship begins to drag itself across the stone, metal shrieking as it scrapes over the surface, and we reach out with our void, grabbing one of its tentacles and yanking it back. The whole ship lurches toward us, a toy in a child's grasp.

Now, how to get inside? We could crack it open like an egg, spilling its delicious contents. There are openings—windows—too. We pull the ship closer, vines of void splitting off to quest over the ship and find our prey.

A sharp hiss and vents of steam erupt from the side of the ship. We pause, confused by this new development. This wasn't in our memories. We curiously reach for the area that is making noise—that is flickering with more magic than the rest of the craft—when it abruptly rips itself from the side of the ship, splattering through our void as it blasts away from the *Prismatic*. The craft—the escape pod—rockets across the stoney ground, bouncing and rolling until it impacts the wall of water. And then it's gone, vanished into the ocean.

We hiss in anger. Escaped! Fled from us! No, we will not be outsmarted by them. We gather our void around us, recalling how we've braved these waters before. We will hunt them down and eviscerate their craft.

But first, we can already feel our power waning. We already need to consume another soul—not to mention, there's still one here yet to harvest.

We round on Zyneth, and he grimaces as we turn to face him.

"Was sort of hoping you'd forgotten about me," he says. "Don't suppose you can still be reasoned with? I'd much rather expend this limited air supply on figuring out how to get out of—"

We rip our void away from the *Prismatic* with a frustrated roar, stabbing it toward Zyneth. He skips away, slashing through the vines of black as they near him.

Why do they fight? Why don't they understand how pathetic their struggle really is? Enough. We don't have time for such play. It's time to end this.

Once more wrangling the glass into cooperation, we infuse our next spears of void with dozens of razor-sharp shards of glass, and likewise launch these at our prey. As usual, he slashes through the attacks, his lightning dissipating the void.

But the glass continues to fly forward on its original trajectory.

Three shards strike his legs, stabbing into meat and bone, as a fourth slices through his arm, sending one of his blades clattering to the ground. Zyneth hisses out a growl as he slips to one knee, clutching his arm to his chest as he doubles over in pain. Too easy. We move in for the killing blow.

Our shadows converge on him, despite our last, desperate protests. He put up a good fight. We will award a quick death.

Zyneth looks up at us as we close in, looming over him. There's no fear in his eyes—only intense calculation. He pulls his injured hand away from his chest, exposing the blinding star-like blaze of his soul.

No. Wait. That is not his soul. That's—

With a flick of his hand, Zyneth releases the compressed ball of lightning.

We try to flinch away, but there's no time. The lightning blasts through us, dispersing our shadows as the attack illuminates the arena with a flash of light. We lose our grip on our glass, and more importantly, we lose our grip on the souls.

No! We shriek with rage, rushing to regather ourself, but the souls are already slipping away, dispersing into the world. Slamming back together in a wave of black, we grab one—two—souls from the air, crushing them in our grasp. We can still eat these—pull enough power from this small handful to sustain us long enough to—

Zyneth slashes through our void, severing our shadows which wisp away in mere moments. Then those souls vanish, too.

Enraged, we grab his blade, yanking it from his grasp with a spray of blood. Zyneth gasps, scrambling backward as a thick trail of crimson follows. He grabs for the knife he'd dropped before, while we raise his own against him. Loathing courses through us. We seethe with a hatred like none we've ever known. He took all our souls from us, so we will destroy him with his own weapon, and then we'll take *his* soul. That will be a fitting end for such abhorrent disrespect.

With all our strength and precision, we hurl his own knife back at him—or at least, that's what we'd intended. Just as the knife leaves our grasp, our aim shifts to the right. The knife flies past his head, instead stabbing into a block of stone a dozen feet away. Sparks fly at the impact, filling us with relief.

Fool! We stamp out the brief flare of resistance. That meant nothing. We're only delaying the inevitable.

Zyneth glances to where his blade struck, then back at us. Impossibly, he's smiling. Mocking us! He snatches up his last knife, though with the injuries he's sustained, his grasp is weak.

"You did well, Kanin," Zyneth says as we stalk toward him. He runs a fond hand down the flat of his blade, the runes illuminating on its surface, but he must not have enough magic left for any more electric displays. Instead, he aims it at our anchor—our glass heart. "You don't have to fight it anymore."

He must be delusional if he thinks he can destroy our core. He didn't have the willpower to do so before, and he doesn't have the strength now. We will savor his soul. Make it last as we tear it to shreds.

Zyneth throws the blade at our chest, his motions labored and obvious. We casually swipe the attack away, deftly catching the blade from the air. This time we will not throw it back: We will plunge it into him ourself.

The world warps. A vortex pulls at our essence, dragging bits of us away. The sensation is clawing its way up our arm, sucking us down into a cramped, dark place. We don't understand. What's happening?

A memory surfaces—the knife.

Our glass is bare where we're holding the blade, all the nearby void sucked into the weapon, yet even more streamers of black twirl down into the knife as if pulled by an invisible whirlpool. We whip around, locating the other knife, still buried in the stone cube. But it's not just a cube. We wrench memories from our depth, and new understanding blooms inside us. It's the containment cube, and the knife is stabbed right into the center of its aperture. The void is being pulled through the blades and into the magic capsule. We try to drop the weapon, but our glass won't let it go. Without the souls to power us, on top of losing more bits of ourself by the second, our control is waning.

It's working. It's actually working.

No! We won't be dragged back into a prison again. We just escaped! And we won't go down without a fight.

We stab several spears of void into the container, piercing the stone. Blue sparks of magic jump from the cracks.

Fear courses through us. Gillow warned us to be careful with the containment cubes. If it ruptures, it could explode.

We replace the fear with smug satisfaction. Yes. That's the idea.

We slash another blade of void across its surface, severing the circles and runes etched in its surface.

The following blast hits everything in the arena.

Chapter Forty-Six

Alive

Wrestling control from the predator isn't easy, but I do it. Its mind—like its body—is scattered, sent reeling from the explosion. Plus, a good portion of it getting sucked into the containment cube didn't hurt.

I mean, it *did* hurt the predator. That was the point. Anyway.

Now that I'm back in reality, back outside of the predator's influence, Echo's notifications are streaming through me. Fall damage, concussive damage, bludgeoning damage—yet somehow, through all that, I'm alive.

I'm alive.

The predator is, too. It's still there, lurking at the other end of our tether, though I'm keeping a tight hold on its leash. Enforcing as great a distance between us as I can manage. For now, it's not pushing back. The creature is confused, scattered, reeling. I might say humbled if I didn't know any better. Right now, I just do my best to box it away and focus on my surroundings.

The world quakes, sending the scattering of rubble and broken glass clattering over the stone floor. I roll onto my side, causing hundreds of microscopic fractures to send stabbing pains through me, and just as many new notifications from Echo. I brush them aside.

"Zyneth?" I call. At least my translator isn't broken. There's black ichor and broken stones everywhere—I can't see him.

Echo, help me find Zyneth.

[Affirmative,] Echo says. [The user will be notified when the Zyneth subject is identified.]

I try to stand, but one of my legs falls away. Dammit. I float the leg back up in place and go to activate a Sculpt, but—

[Mana: 0/111]

Shit. *Bonus Mana?*

[Bonus Mana: 0]

Between activating the portal to Earth and the predator sucking up every point of mana at my disposal, I'm bone dry. I guess the predator needed everything I had left to keep its claws latched onto reality. Pity it wasn't killed when the containment cube exploded—I guess I'll just have to take "weakened" for now. But I have other things to worry about.

"Zyneth!" I call again, trying to limp over a large chunk of stone. I slip, falling and shattering what remained of the broken leg. One leg, one arm. I can't be of any help like this. Unclasping my core from around my neck, I set myself down on the ground. My core is fractured, still damaged from Gillow's attack, but at least the harness and four legs I have secured around my vial aren't broken. Carefully picking my way through the debris, I reach into every shard of glass within my range, controlling every piece I can manage, and move them with me.

I activate Elemental Radar as I go, swirling the glass through the rubble.

The portal's spell circle is ruined. Lines in the stone are broken, runes blasted away, everything shattered by massive chunks of the coliseum's pillars that have fallen to the ground. Bits of void are scattered everywhere, too, though even now they're slowly, painfully starting to seep back in my direction like creeping black slugs. I ignore them, desperate to find Zyneth.

As I search, the world shakes again. There's a terrible roar somewhere in the distance. I levitate my head, as high as my range will allow, and turn it in a slow circle. Several white cracks run through my vision, but on the other side of the arena, nearest where the containment cube had been, I can make out where several of the pillars had collapsed and water is now gushing in through the side of our bubble.

The spell circles powering the air bubbles are damaged. Their magic is failing. We have to get out of here—soon.

I speed up. I need more eyes to find Zyneth, but the last time I tried turning on more than a few sources of sight, it was overwhelming. Too much to parse. And I'd only had a dozen pieces of glass, then.

The predator regularly uses several sources of sight—it wouldn't have a problem with this. But I'm not giving that monster even the smallest sliver of control—not now, when there's more of it than there is of me.

But it doesn't have to just be sight, does it? I'm already using a sense of touch in all of them.

"Zyneth!" I call again. Then I tell Echo, *Turn hearing on in all my pieces of glass.*

[Activated.]

The room becomes deafening. The same thundering sounds ripple through me, delayed a fraction of a second between my furthest pieces.

And somewhere amidst all that chaos, I hear a moan.

I push myself harder, trying to zero in on which glass had heard it. Not the ones to my left; I turn the sound off in all of those.

"Zyneth!"

I hear him again, a raspy breath. I turn off more glass. Push myself faster. One by one, I start whittling away at my glass, closing in on where I can now make out his consistent labored breaths. But he's still not answering my calls. I steel myself for the worst.

[Zyneth identified.]

I see the blood first, and I start shaking. Not with fear or regret, but rage. This is what the predator made me do. What the *predator* did. It hurt him, and I'm overcome with a violent urge to hurt the predator back. At this moment, if I had the opportunity, I would do unspeakable things.

But Zyneth comes first. He's on his back, several shards of glass protruding from his limbs, glass that had been outside my range when I'd first started looking for him. Apart from the stab wounds, a puddle of blood is forming beneath his head, and a large piece of stone is obscuring his left leg.

I Check him.

[HP: 45/150. Zyneth is suffering from a concussion, fractured leg, and multiple lacerations.]

Even as I watch, his HP ticks down one more point.

"Okay," I say. "I'm going to need you to wake up, buddy. I can't carry you out."

He's still breathing, but he doesn't stir. What can I do? I'm out of mana. A trickle of water streams past us, mixing with Zyneth's blood. *And* we're running out of time. I'm not strong enough to lift the rock off his leg, let alone pick him up after.

"Zyneth!" I shout, although the volume of my translator seems to be capped. I shake his arm with some of my glass. "Please, wake up, I need you to help me."

The void continues to creep back toward me, gathering its scattered bits from the battlefield. I try to ignore it, but its presence makes me think of something.

Echo, what's the state of my inventory? I ask.

[Inventory: 0/1]

My soul leaps. *There's one slot? I can use that?*

[Affirmative,] Echo says. [Although largely perforated by the attacks of the entity designated *predator*, a small fraction of the null pocket dimension is still functional as storage space.]

I don't even let her finish before I'm already racing to the rock on Zyneth's leg. I tap my core against it. *Add this to the inventory.*

The stone vanishes. At the same time Zyneth lets out a strangled cry, eyes snapping open as his body spasms.

His HP slips to 34.

"I'm here!" I rush back over toward his head. "It's okay. We're getting out of here."

Zyneth sucks in a tight breath, squinting through a grimace as he turns to look at me. His eyes pinch in a pained smile. "Little friend," he says between breaths. "Happy to see you looking like this."

Never thought I'd say the same, but me too. "Don't get too excited, I won't be much help to you in this form."

He closes his eyes. "That's fine. Give me a moment. Need to rest."

Not with his HP still slowly ticking down—and the water turning into a small stream beside us. "Uh, afraid not, buddy, we're about to get flooded. And then probably crushed by a million tons of water. Also, you need a healer. Like, five minutes ago."

"Alright." Zyneth lifts a clumsy hand to his head, wincing as it touches his temple. Then he screws his face tight, and pushes himself up. He immediately stifles a scream as his injured leg shifts.

"I'm not sure walking is an option," he says through a gasp.

The ground shakes, and with a sharp crack, another pillar collapses to the ground. Zyneth ducks his head and I tense as a cloud of dust and pebbles race past us.

"You have to," I say. "We're going to die here if you don't get up!"

"No, just me," Zyneth says, breathing heavily, as he takes in our surroundings. "You can make it back to the *Prismatic*."

"Fuck that!" I cry. "And then what? Twiddle my thumbs at the bottom of the ocean with no idea how to get back as I reflect on your death? Get up! You have to get up."

"Kanin," Zyneth says, pausing every other word to catch his breath. "I cannot stress enough how difficult it is to even be holding this conversation. I am very tired. I am in excruciating pain. Please understand, I make no suggestion lightly."

No. I won't accept it. He didn't give up on me when the predator had me, and I won't give up on him now. Options. Options!

The void is slowly pooling next to me, clustering around the shattered pile that was my clothes and body. It's keeping a respectful distance. Maybe it knows how pissed I am. Even at the thought, it shrinks in on itself, seeming to compress into a smaller pool.

Wait. Compress.

Echo what was that spell that the predator did before? With the null magic. When we teleported the Prismatic.

[Displace, Level 1,] Echo says. [Objects may be moved between two coordinates within an Attuned volume of void. Requirement: Attuned void. Mana: variable depending on size.]

How much to move Zyneth?

[Mana: 320]

Even if my mana wasn't totally extinguished, more than I can handle. But...

I Check Zyneth's mana as well.

[Mana: 335/640]

Holy shit. Just enough.

Just enough if the predator doesn't suck any of it away. Would it cooperate? It's only invested in keeping me alive, and it already tried to kill Zyneth once today. Can I force it to cooperate? Or would initiating that contact open a new can of worms?

A distant column collapses, then hits another. That one collapses, too. Water geysers into the arena, crashing into the ground and spreading out over the floor. By the time it reaches us it's no longer a wave, but a quickly moving stream. Zyneth plucks me from the ground just before I can be swept away. He holds me to his chest as the water races past.

"Kanin. You have to get out."

No time to waffle—this is our only shot. "I am—we are! Zyneth, I need your magic. All of it, as fast as you can."

"What are you—"

"No time!" I cry. "Do it now!"

Zyneth takes a steadying breath, then a comforting yellow light engulfs me.

[Bonus mana: 25,] Echo says. The counter starts to race up.

I turn to the predator next.

You're going to work with me here, I tell it. The predator's attention shifts to fall over me like an icy wind. *You were willing to work with me before. And after what you just pulled, you owe me.*

It doesn't reply, it only radiates frigid hate and resistance.

I frankly don't give a fuck, I say. *This is all your fault to begin with. If you hadn't attacked Zyneth—if you hadn't taken those souls—we might have been able to find middle ground. But you're only capable of thinking about yourself.* The words make me pause, even as I'm thinking them, but I press ahead. *Well now it's time to fall in line. Because if he doesn't get out of here, neither do I—and neither do you. If you take a single whiff of the magic we're getting right now, it's through. We're dead. So. Right now? You're working for me.*

The predator moves. Its mind presses forward, and I steel myself, ready to throw everything I have at it, ready to kill myself over this one final, desperate, most important act. But it doesn't attack. The gap along our bond closes, and for a moment I am seeing its thoughts as clearly as my own: Like looking in a mirror, it's focused on my resolve, my determination, my conviction. And I'd die for Zyneth right now. I really would.

This is one fight not worth having.

The predator lets me take the void. It lets Zyneth's stream of magic pass through its grasp. I can still feel its reluctance there, its unending hunger, but it's also radiating a new concept, one that a part of itself had only learned within the last few weeks: restraint.

I grasp the void, flinging half of it to the edge of my range. With the predator's mind this close, with it cooperating instead of fighting, it makes it all the way to the *Prismatic.* The rest I gather around Zyneth. I cluster all my remaining glass as close as I can manage as well, along with one of Zyneth's knives. The other, I can't find—either lost somewhere in the rubble, or destroyed during the containment cube's explosion. I know it's just a knife, but I still feel a sting of disappointment and guilt at its loss.

Another geyser of water burst through the bubble, this one closer, sharp lashes of water pelting against Zyneth's back. He hunches over me, eyes squeezed shut.

I Check Zyneth's HP: 22.

I Check my Bonus Mana: 310.

I swirl the void around us. "I'm going to need you to trust me on this."

[Bonus Mana: 315]

I can't see from my core anymore, Zyneth's hand obscuring my vision on one side and his shirt on the other, but my other glass has a front-row view as the nearest column collapses and the ocean thunders toward us.

Zyneth's hand, still gentle and careful as ever, squeezes tighter. "I always have."

[Bonus Mana: 320]

I activate the spell.

Chapter Forty-Seven

ADRIFT

Void wraps around us, and all light vanishes from the world. I pull the magic tighter, squeezing not us but space itself. The darkness collapses in. There's an inflection point—a tipping—and I feel the two separate points in the spell connect like magnets snapping together.

The roar of the wave vanishes. My soul lurches as I fall—Zyneth and I are both falling—but it only lasts for a fraction of a second. We hit the ground with a metal clang, a rush of water splashing around us, and all my glass crashes to the ground in a broken heap nearby.

[Spell complete.]

The void wilts around us, ebbing into the floor as light surrounds us once more.

We're in the *Prismatic*. I did it. We made it. We're alive.

Zyneth falls back with a heavy exhale, still weakly clutching me on top of his chest. The puddle of water on the floor beneath him is swirling with threads of pink and red.

"Zyneth?" I Check his HP: 18. "Zyneth, stay awake!"

"I'm awake," he mutters, eyes closed.

I wiggle myself out of his grasp, and he lets me go. "We can't rest now—we have to get you somewhere safe! Somewhere secure. The water—"

Even as I say it, an impact slams into the ship, and I'm suddenly airborne. I call my glass and void to me with a lurch of panic. The void gets there first (which is probably for the best, given the un-gentle nature of glass), catching me and staying my fall. A distant screech of metal on stone reverberates through the ship's hull as the water drags the *Prismatic* over the ground. I have the void set me down, but still hold on to keep me upright and grounded.

The impact rolled Zyneth onto his side, and he's making no attempts to roll back. From here I can see the half a dozen pieces of glass impaled in him—I can *feel* them in him—but I don't dare take them out. Not with his HP so low.

[HP: 15/150]

Every time I blink it's lower than before. This isn't good!

The ship rocks again, and Zyneth threatens to roll over onto his chest—onto the shards of glass. I lunge forward with my magic, catching him with a claw of void. It's massive, covering his whole chest in shadows, but it stops him from moving. Zyneth doesn't react.

"Zyneth? Zyneth!" No no no, not when we've made it back to safety. It can't end like this.

I can't kill someone else. Especially not him.

Echo, what can I do? I ask, desperate. *Are there any healing spells I can learn? Please, anything!*

[Negative,] Echo says. [Healing type magic is incompatible with your class.]

Why didn't I pick healer? Why'd I have to pick a stupid wizard?

[HP: 14/150]

No healing spells. No healer. What else can I do? What else do I have?

My soul lurches. I don't have anything—but Zyneth does. All those charms and tools he'd purchased in preparation for the trip—there was a healing potion in there, I'm certain of it.

I'm already racing for the door. I leave more of my void behind, keeping Zyneth pinned to the ground to try to keep him from moving while the ship continues to be buffeted by the rising sea-level. I hope it'll be enough.

As my glass and void sweep me out the door and through the ship, I realize I'm still able to keep a hold on the void I've left behind. Did I level up again? No, even that wouldn't account for such a huge increase in my range. It's the predator; it's helping me.

Summoning all my courage, I finally let myself Check its influence.

[Predator Influence: 50%]

The number chills me. Our minds are equally powerful now, which means it could take over without any warning. I'd be able to fight it off—eventually. But then, the same thing could be said for it.

Yet, it's not doing anything. It's lending me its power, and I'm not making it do that or fighting for it. Cautiously, even as I race for our quarters, I mentally turn my attention on the predator.

It's... *fighting* isn't the right word. It's in some sort of discourse with itself. Even looking at the predator, I feel like I'm seeing three versions of itself at once. Each slightly different copies of the same mind.

Something like this happened before, when the predator was able to pull some of itself from my inventory. It was like there were two versions: the version I had come to an uneasy truce with, and the newer version that had just come out of the inventory. They'd shared the same mind, the same goals, the same disposition up until they'd first become split: then the fraction of the predator that had lived with me—the one I agreed not to Attune, the one confined inside a bottle, the one that helped me break into the library—had changed, in the subtlest of ways. At the very least, it had gained new memories and experiences while the rest of it remained static inside my inventory. And when more of it had emerged, the two versions of itself found they were no longer entirely identical. The new piece had to learn from the old one. And what emerged was something slightly different from both.

The same thing is happening again now. This new piece of the predator is conversing with its other selves, absorbing the memories and experiences of its previous versions as it merges into one new identity.

Maybe it understands that helping me is better for both of us. Or maybe it's just too preoccupied with more important matters to pay me any mind. Whatever the case, I need its superior control of the void as long as possible if I want to keep Zyneth alive.

In our quarters, I find Zyneth's bag. I hastily slice it open with claws of glass and shadow, spilling its contents onto the floor. A faintly glowing bottle of blue-white light rolls across the deck. There! Confirming its contents with a Check, I snatch it up and rush back to the cargo bay, desperately hoping I'm not too late.

He's still lying where I left him.

[HP: 10/150]

"Zyneth!" I gently try to settle him on his back. "You're going to be okay. We have a health potion. You'll be okay."

I try to remove the potion's stopper and struggle with the cork for a horrific, laughable moment. A cork? A cork is what's going to thwart me? Then I dig the void in and rip the stopper away. A few drops of the potion spill and I freeze, carefully steadying the bottle.

"Can you drink?" I tip it up to his mouth. He's supposed to drink it, right? That's what they do in games and TV shows. A few drops drip between his parted lips, and I wait.

[HP: 10/150]

Nothing's happening. It's not going up or down. I pour a little more into his mouth. The glow vanishes down his throat—then Zyneth jerks, and starts coughing.

"Zyneth!" I pull the potion away so he can't knock it out of my grasp with his spasms. "Are you awake? Are you okay? Can you talk?"

[HP: 10/150]

His eyes open, tears pricking at the corners as he takes a shaky breath. He looks at the potion I'm holding and gestures it over. I move the bottle toward his mouth, but he shakes his head and grabs it before I can pour more in.

"Glass," he rasps to me, coughing again as he tries to speak. He taps at his arm, where one of my shards is protruding from his skin, coated in crimson blood.

"What?" I ask. "You want me to pull it out?"

He nods.

"But that'll cause more bleeding," I say. "And your health..."

"Remove it," Zyneth says, gritting his teeth. "Now."

I don't like it, but I know better than to argue. Cringing in anticipation, I yank the piece out of him as quickly as I can.

Zyneth growls between clenched teeth, splashing some of the potion over the wound. The liquid evaporates almost immediately as the magic sinks into his torn skin. And slowly, it knits itself back together.

[HP: 12/150]

Relief floods through me as Zyneth lets his head fall back to the ground and he pants heavily for a few moments. His health is going up. He's going to be okay.

Finally, after he composes himself, he tips his head in my direction. "All that trouble to avoid the ocean, and you try to drown me?"

I want to laugh and cry, but since I can do neither, I do my best to look ashamed. "I thought you had to drink it."

"Drink it?" he repeats. "I suppose you'd suggest I drink burn ointment as well." He smiles faintly. "It's almost as though you've never used a healing potion before."

"Would you believe it?" I say.

He chuckles, and it turns into a wince.

As Zyneth steels himself for me to remove the next piece, I sag to the ground, everything catching up to me all at once. Earth, my body, the predator, those souls. It's a lot for me to sort through, and I haven't had a second to process any of it. But Zyneth... At least Zyneth will be alright.

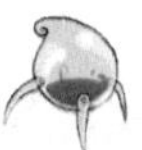

The *Prismatic* rocks as it's carried away by the ocean currents, aimlessly adrift. Most of the null arcana was removed from the surrounding waters when I activated the air bubble spells, and we'll just have to hope we're long gone by the time much more of the magic accumulates. The ship's designed to avoid the stuff, but without Gillow here, it's hard to say how much oversight the *Prismatic* needs to operate properly. There's not much we can do about it but hope luck is on our side.

Occasionally the jolt of some collision vibrates through the ship, but I don't leave Zyneth's side until his health creeps back up to a safe level. Even with his fractured foot healed and all the bleeding wounds closed, his HP still hovers around 75/150. I guess there's more under the surface that will just take time, but for now, I can live with it.

Once he's capable of walking again, we make our way back to the bridge. Zyneth sits heavily in the captain's chair, working through the controls as I dump all my worldly belongings (that is, tattered clothes and a giant pile of broken glass) nearby. And of course, all the void.

More void than I'd had before, but it's not as much void as when the predator had been in control. Not to mention, its mind then had been overwhelming.

Echo, what was the Predator Influence after we came out of the Between earlier?

[Although the Predator Influence stat fluctuated in that timeframe, the average value was 99.63%]

Shit. I really didn't stand a fighting chance. *What happened to it? Where did all that void go—and the predator's mind? Why is the influence less now?*

[Unknown,] Echo says.

Well that's not terribly useful. *Did the containment cube explosion kill it?* I ask.

[Negative.]

Is it back Between?

[Negative.]

Is it in my Inventory again?

[Negative. Inventory: 1/1. Contents: a rock.]

Then where? I ask, exasperated.

[Unknown,] Echo repeats. [This unit was unable to access the user for a duration of time while the nature of the entity designated *predator* interfered with the connection. After connection was reestablished, the quantity of void and Predator Influence was reduced.]

I inwardly grimace. I guess I should be glad that it's gone, but not knowing how or where it went is concerning. What if it comes back someday? Would I have any warning?

Then again, I've plenty of other more immediate problems to be concerned with at the moment.

The ship hums, streaks of light illuminating its magic circuits, as its list straightens out and the ship comes under Zyneth's control.

"That should do it for now," he says with a sigh. "I don't know how to get us back to Miasmere, but I can at least point us toward the west. We'll intersect land eventually."

"Will you have enough food and water?" I ask.

"And air," he adds. "Yes, I believe so. There was enough on board for Gillow and I when we first departed, and now that it's just me, it should be hopefully enough to cover however long it takes to reach shore."

Hopefully. I feel like he should be more worried about the fact that we're lost at sea and only have an inkling of an idea how to control the ship. Not to mention the monster infested waters we are drifting aimlessly through.

Maybe he just doesn't have enough energy to worry about all that right now.

As the *Prismatic* slowly turns, the shadows of Emrox floating by the window like phantoms, Zyneth pushes himself back and turns to me. He watches me for several moments in silence.

"Um," I say.

"Sorry," he says, rubbing his temple. "It's just with everything that happened—everything you just went through—I don't know where to start."

I don't either. I awkwardly shuffle my glass around, sifting through the pieces as if I could begin fixing the puzzle of my broken body. I

Check my mana: 0, of course. I guess this new version of the predator has decided our previous agreement is null and has gone right back to sucking up all my excess mana again. That's going to be a problem if I want to use any spells. Because I *will* need to use more spells eventually, won't I? I'm stuck here.

I'm never going home.

"My body is gone," I say. "Earth is gone." Voicing it out loud makes it more real than it had ever felt before this moment. Somehow, I'd felt it in my soul all this time. But seeing my own grave, knowing for certain, it fills me with a heavy grief. Yet, at the same time, relief. There's a finality now that wasn't there before. That queasy uncertainty has been washed away. I just feel... tired. Worn.

"I'm sorry," Zyneth says. "Maybe there's another way—"

"No," I say. I don't know if I can live through getting my hopes up again, just for them to be shattered a second time. "No. The spell circle is destroyed." I tap my way over to the window, looking down into the murk. Even as we begin to leave it in our wake, I can make out the ruins of the arena, the stone circle that had been inscribed there buried and broken.

I might be able to recreate it, in time. If the predator worked with me. If I grew powerful enough. "But you know," I say. "Even if I had another chance, I don't think I'd take it. Without my body, what would I be returning to? What I really want is to just move on."

I turn to look at Zyneth. "I'm sorry. I've been such a fool. This journey was cursed from the start and I dragged you into it. You were right. I *was* just using the predator as an excuse to try to rush into a solution for my body. And now the predator's stronger than before. I've been selfish and bullheaded and it nearly got you killed."

And that hurts me the most. Worse than the loss of my body.

He shakes his head. "I understand why you did what you did. And yes, you may have let your emotions drive you. But I think many would act the same in such circumstances. Besides, at the end of the day, we're alive, we're together, and that's what counts, isn't it?"

He smiles fondly, and I'm filled with affection. For the first time, I don't try to stomp those feelings out.

"I'm going to get both of us out of here," I promise. "I'm going to make sure we make it back to land in one piece."

He chuckles. "Glad I have you here to protect me."

He says it as a joke, but his words fill me with a fierce protectiveness. There's monsters before us, destruction behind us, and Zyneth will be counting on me to get us out of here alive. I'm the only one who can leave this ship and fight off whatever comes our way.

And I will. I'll protect him with my life.

"And when we get back to land?" he asks. When, not if.

"The souls." The memories make me shiver. I can't get the image out of my head of all those Earth souls that fell through the hole in reality while the predator held it open. They were the souls of the dead. People who'd died and were meant to pass through Between and into... whatever comes after that. But instead, I was there to stop them.

Just like what Trenevalt did to me.

"I have to find them," I say.

"Find who?" Zyneth asks.

"The souls," I repeat, guilt resurfacing once more. "It's my fault. If I'd never come here—if I'd never tried to get my body back or go home—they never would have fallen through. And I—the predator still managed to kill one of them. I couldn't save them. But I can help the rest."

Zyneth shakes his head. "Slow down. I'm not following. Those lights the predator had—those were souls? And you think they're somewhere in this world now? Assuming that is true, without any-thing to keep them anchored, they should have just blinked back into the Between and moved onto the afterlife on their own."

I suppose he's right. I'm only stuck here because Trenevalt's magic bound me to this bottle.

But I know that's not the end of it. Something *else* happened to these souls. When they passed through my spell, through my Attuned void, through the predator's ethereal body, I felt... *something*. And I still feel it, distantly.

Echo? I ask. *Can you shed any light? Do you know where those souls are now?*

[Negative,] Echo says. [The spatial displacements of the souls are unknown to this unit. However, the nature of the spell they interacted with—intending to seek out a body—coupled with the nature of the abundant null magic they passed through—the most powerful arcana that can be used for soul bonding—indicates they will have or are currently in the process of locating and binding to a new compatible vessel.]

I slump. I was right, then. I really did just pull a Trenevalt—only a hundred times over. Two hundred, maybe.

"They're out there," I tell Zyneth, my resolve crystalizing. Since I did this to them, it's my job to fix it. I won't be able to send them home, but maybe I can at least help them avoid going through what I experienced. They might be in a strange, new world, but they don't have to do it alone.

"I don't know where," I say, "and I don't know how, but I'll find them."

EPILOGUE

Thunder boomed through the temple as a god appeared in a flash of light. Brushing an errant lock of black hair away from the empty pits where his eyes should have been, he smiled.

"So. Who died?"

At the central dais, Lorata turned her head to cast a disparaging look over her shoulder. She moved only precisely as much as she needed to, as if the act of acknowledging the other god was beneath her. "No one's died, Shirasil."

"Oh?" Shirasil asked. "Then why the full house?" He swept an arm around the room, his silk sleeve whispering with the motion as he took in the few dozen other gods in attendance.

They were an odd sight to behold, every one of them almost passing as a different species of Lusio. *Almost*, as, though their likeness was based on the mortal species of their planet, their visages diverged in distinct and unsettlingly ways that were decisively otherworldly. Widengra, the orc god, had skin that swirled with living patterns of blood, barely an inch of green showing beneath his tattoos. Quimalad, an arachnoid, was ever shrouded by a white mist, their many limbs moving like shadows through a fog. Lorata herself might have appeared human, if not for the golden light which shone from her eyes and hair and clothes.

Ever the showboat, that one.

"That," Lorata said, turning her back on Shirasil, "is perhaps the first good question you've asked this century."

Shirasil cocked an amused brow as he strolled toward the center of the room. Some of the deities stood patiently nearby, hands clasped piously behind their backs, while others scattered toward the edge of the marble chamber, muttering and hissing amongst themselves. A few paced nervously near Lorata and the dais. Only one was reclined on a stone sofa, their silver hair spilling over the side of the marble and their silver face turned to the ceiling, which opened to the purple-blue nebula of the heavens. That one, Yua Tin, smiled pleasantly, as if the tense atmosphere of the room slid from their conscience as easily as water over a carp's scales.

Shirasil liked Yua Tin.

"What's this?" he asked, stopping before the dais. A shimmering, contorting sliver of nothingness floated in the air over the pedestal, like light reflecting through broken glass. A shattered fragment of living reality: a remnant. "You said no one died."

"No one has," Lorata repeated.

He reached a hand toward the remnant, stopping when his fingers buzzed against the edge of the containment spell. The broken space inside spiked and sizzled, as if trying to claw its way out. "Then where did this come from?"

"Step back," Lorata snapped, grabbing Shirasil's hand. Energy crackled between their skin, and defiance swelled within him like a thundering wave. Oh, how he'd love to meet this challenge with a show of force. How he desired to crush her smug, superior ego beneath his boots. It would be desperately cathartic.

Instead, he slipped his wrist from her grasp and stepped back with a respectful bow of his head. "Come, now, you treat me as though I've been tainted."

"Stop acting as though you are, and I will stop treating you as such," she said.

He shrugged helplessly. "What is a chaos god to do? It wouldn't be in my nature to leave well enough alone. The day I settle down—" He smiled, the expression as empty as his bottomless eyes. "—Now, that's the day you should really worry."

"Enough," Widengra grumbled, his voice deep and grating like a mortar and pestle. "We are all accounted for now. Lorata. Why did you summon us?"

Lorata stared at Shirasil for a moment longer, then flicked her hand to another god fidgeting nearby.

The halfling deity, god of fishing, moonlight, and the tides, stepped forward. "The remnant came from Emrox. Something happened there. Something big."

"What?" a nereid god stopped her pacing. "That's not possible. It was destroyed."

"It was," the halfling agreed. "It has been abandoned since the Frey. But something happened there recently, nevertheless. I felt it in the oceans. This remnant was collected at the same time."

"And we don't know what?" Shirasil asked. "Surely, Lorata, oh seer, our god of light, whose eyes pierce the darkest shadows—you saw this happen?"

Lorata scowled in exactly the way Shirasil had hoped, bringing him immense amusement. "I did not. However, I discovered something else." She made a sweeping gesture about the room, and a display appeared in Shirasil's vision.

"System users?" he asked as he mentally scrolled through the list. "I don't see what—"

Murmurs hushed through the room. There was a new name on the list.

"Who is this Kanin?" Widengra asked.

"Unknown," Lorata said. "Clearly, they didn't gain access to the remnant of anyone present. They must have found one another way. A new remnant."

"Impossible," Quimalad said. "Where would they even find one? This is without precedent."

"Is it?" Shirasil asked. "Not so in the early days. And we know many remnants fell dormant in the world before we could find and contain them. Others remained inaccessible. Perhaps they stumbled somewhere they ought not to be."

"That is my assumption as well," Lorata said, though her tone indicated she was none too pleased Shirasil had reached the same conclusion. "Something left behind in the ruins of Emrox, perhaps."

"Do we know how long this person has had access to the System?" another god asked.

Now Lorata looked uncomfortable. "That is... unclear. I typically run a status check on the System on a bi-decade basis."

Shirasil barked out a laugh. "They could have been walking around on this planet for twenty years without us noticing?"

"Absolutely not," Lorata snapped. "The last check was done seven years ago."

Shirasil laughed even harder.

"However," Lorata said, raising her voice, "I think it's more likely they received access today. Too many things have happened at once. This remnant collection might be an indicator of the event. Not to mention, there's an even bigger issue at hand."

"Oh, please." Shirasil grinned. "Do tell."

Lorata made another gesture, and their shared displays updated again. Instead of the user list ending with this new Kanin person, dozens—nearly two hundred—more spaces in the list appeared. They were all blank.

"Templates," Lorata says. "Auto created by the System. Potential new users that meet the requirements to be added."

"What does that mean?" Widengra asked. "Can they be removed?"

Lorata frowned, her lips drawing a thin line. "I do not have the authority."

Shirasil snickered. "Of course not. This is what happens when you dabble with magic older than the gods, Lorata. You pretend to have made it your own, but you're only fumbling your way along like a child playing soldier."

"This is no laughing matter," Lorata hissed. "Do you not understand the implications of this? If each of these new users imply the existence of new remnants which have been unearthed, we are potentially facing mass devastation."

There was a pause, then several gods started speaking at once.

"Surely, not all of these indicate acquisition of a remnant?"

"—an upset to the natural order—"

"You can't mean *war*—"

"Lovely," a voice said, tinkling like windchimes. It was not a voice Shirasil or any of the other gods often heard. The room quieted. "It's lovely, isn't it?"

Yua Tin flowed from their couch like liquid moonlight into the air, face still raised to the stars. "To be reminded we still live in our infancy in this vast space? That a thousand years is so brief. Look at us throwing a fit over the first small pebble we overturn. Here there are worms and fertile earth and cool ground. Look at how we witness an ecosystem and call it pests. It's beautiful to be reminded of our folly, isn't it?"

Shirasil marveled at them, wondering how anyone could think they might be tainted.

"You're suggesting we overreact," Lorata said. "Perhaps this is true. Though it is my belief that this would be preferable to brushing off this significant threat. It is our purpose to retain the order, is it not?" She turned to the rest of the gods. "Our duty. At minimum, we need to search out these new users. Learn what change has transpired—if there are new remnants waking in the mortal realm."

"I for one, agree," Shirasil said. Lorata raised a skeptical eyebrow. "Is this not why we raise Champions in the first place? To be our eyes and hands among the mortals—to settle matters regarding the remnants, should they arise?"

"Yes," Lorata said, eying Shirasil with clear suspicion. "Precisely. Now is the time to make use of our Champions." She stood straighter, shoulders back, managing to look down her nose at all the other gods—even the ones twice her height. "First we must settle the is-sue of finding a suitable vessel for this remnant—or *vessels*. It is so large, I think it will need to be split several ways; bring forward your submission when decided upon. Then, summon your most trusted champion. Send them looking for what has gone wrong in the world. To search for these templates and this Kanin individual."

"And if we find them?" Widengra asked.

"Evaluate the risk they pose," Lorata said. "Use your best judge-ment from there."

Widengra smiled at this, and Shirasil withheld a snort. Trusting Widengra to exercise good judgement was like trusting a nereid to live in a desert. The rest of the gods bowed or nodded respectfully and began to disperse, vanishing from the hall in wisps of light. Shirasil turned to leave as well, musing over each of the gods and which would require his closest attention.

"Shirasil," Lorata said, stopping him. "I wanted to thank you for the support. It is not often we see eye to eye, though in this regard, I suppose I should not have doubted."

"Is that your version of an apology?" he teased.

She smiled, tight lipped. "It's as close as you'll ever get. Though, after your initial comments, I am unsure why you changed stances."

"On the contrary," Shirasil said. "I enjoy mysteries. I enjoy the discovery of a tangle of things yet understood. This anomaly is the most exciting thing to have happened in centuries, and I crave to learn more. Suggesting we investigate is very much in line with my priorities."

She considered this with a slow nod. "I see. That is good to hear. Well then, I will hold you here no longer."

Shirasil inclined his head, turned on his heels, and let the hall of the gods fade into stardust behind him.

Oh, Lorata. Arrogant, naive Lorata.

He did intend to investigate, of course. His Champions would be eager for the action. But he didn't *only* intend to send them; some things required a more delicate touch—a more direct involvement.

He was the god of curiosity, after all. Maintaining the status quo was not in his nature. And this promise of mass disruption Lorata warned of—

Oh. It would be delicious.

ACKNOWLEDGEMENTS

First off, I want to thank my editor, Justine Manzano, for tolerating my adoration of em-dashes and polishing my story into something resembling a real book. I also appreciate the amazing cover art that MiblArt designed for me. It's perfect!

Huge thanks goes out to my critique partners and beta readers for reading the early drafts of this story and helping to brainstorm ways to course-correct when I went wrong. You guys had a huge influence on this story, along with all my books. Your insight is as valuable to me as your friendships.

And last but certainly not least, thank you, thank you, thank you to all of my readers from RoyalRoad and Patreon. I couldn't have done this without all of your support and motivation.

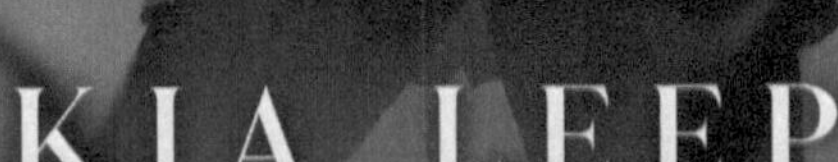

A LITTLE SALTY

NPSeeds SAGA

KIA LEEP

A LITTLE SALTY

SNEAK PEEK

The familiar orchestra of medical devices gradually fades into the distance as a comforting darkness envelops me. I relax into oblivion, knowing that this is the end. I'm dead.

Finally.

No more pain. No more tests. No more sobbing parents futilely trying to hide their tears from me out in the hallway. I've been ready to rest for a long time now.

Only... nothing really seems to be ending.

I peek one eye open. Then the other. An azure sky fills my vision as painfully white clouds drift overhead like cotton candy. Wind ruffles my hair, sending goosebumps racing across my skin. The air smells of grass and earth and fresh rain.

Well. That's not supposed to be in a hospital room.

I breathe in the sweet air, filling my lungs until they burn, fuller than I could ever manage before, and it feels like I'm taking a breath for the first time.

[New authority recognized,] a voice says. [Populating stats. Processing role.]

"Hello?"

Searching for the source of the voice, I sit up—and it's effortless. It's easy. Like it should be. I sweep my hand through the damp grass, reveling in the soft, cool sensation.

I'm alive. And not just alive, but healthy.

Laughter bubbles up out of me. How is this possible? Where even am I? I push myself to my feet, staggering as I stand too fast, and I laugh at myself again, giddy with excitement. I can't believe this. But it's real. It's really real.

I run my hands over my body: two legs, two arms, all the standard female parts. I'm wearing some simple clothes instead of a hospital gown, which pleases me almost as much as having a fully functioning body. My hair is long and black and blowing annoyingly into my mouth and eyes. Black is new: it was brown before. I comb it out of my face, tucking it behind my ears. My ears feel a little different, too. The shape's not quite right. And when I touch my face, the nose feels smaller, the cheekbones less pointy—even my teeth feel slightly off. My skin appears just as pale and sun-phobic as ever, but it's clear this body I've woken up in is not the body I died in.

Should that weird me out? Maybe. But I didn't particularly like that body, and it certainly hadn't liked me. Good riddance.

"I'm alive!" I shout at the top of my lungs, just because I can, just because I have the strength to. Whooping, I pump my fists in the air, spinning in a circle to take in my surroundings. The sun is toward one horizon, a forest opposite. Otherwise, I seem to be alone in this grassy, beautiful, amazing field.

[Designation complete,] the voice says.

I pause. Maybe not so alone after all. Though there's definitely no one around here but me. In fact, the voice doesn't seem to be coming from any direction in particular. Like it's all in my head.

"Hello?" I say again. My voice sounds a little different, too. Lower, and warmer, and louder. "Who are you?"

[This interface is a clone of the interface that has been designated Echo,] the faintly-feminine voice says.

"Uh, Echo, then," I say. "Why are you in my head?"

None of this should be making any sense. It certainly doesn't feel like the afterlife—but I also know it's not a dream. It's all too real and vivid—and my dreams are only full of pain and needles and shadows, anyway. An Echo in my head is exactly the sort of thing I should be questioning, but instead it feels as natural as the sunlight.

[This interface is designed to provide audiovisual guidance to users who fulfill the baseline requirements,] Echo says. [Activate stats?]

"Um. Sure?" I say.

A display of words and numbers appears in front of me.

[Name: Sally]

[Species: Human]

[Class: N/A]

[Level: 10]

[Attack: 20]

[HP: 90/90]

[Mana: 10/10]

[Role: Chef]

"Whoa!" I take a surprised step back, and the words float with me. I turn my head from side to side, and they stay within my field of vision. I mentally will them away, and they vanish. "Wait!" I say. "Bring them back!"

The words reappear. Excitement bubbles up my chest. No way. No way! It's just like a videogame! I really have a stats interface of my own? This is totally wild!

"Kind of short, though," I say. "Is this really it? You don't even have my last name."

[The current display is truncated as a result of a previous user's request,] Echo says.

Previous user, huh? That's interesting. "Well, can you give me more?" I ask.

[Affirmative.]

My vision explodes with words and numbers. [Gender: Female. Age: 18. Speed: 10. Weight Class: Medium.] I stumble back, hardly able to see any of my surroundings as text scrolls through my line of sight. No wonder someone else pared it down to the basics.

"Okay, okay, that's enough!" I say. "Set it back to the default for now. I can tailor it to my liking later."

[Affirmative,] Echo says, and most of the numbers vanish.

Just these few lines are already enough to chew on. I'm a human, which is no surprise. Level 10 sounds like some kind of default noob level, which is fair. Still need to get a class: that should be exciting. Mana indicates I should be able to do magic: the rest seem pretty basic.

Except that Role stat.

"Echo, what does it mean my role is Chef?" I ask.

[The Chef role requires the user to engage in cooking, baking, or elements of food preparation on a daily basis.]

Kind of obvious, I guess. "So, what, it's like my job? Do I get paid if I do my role?"

[Negative,] Echo says.

"Will it level me up?"

[Negative.]

"Do I get bonus items? Loot boxes? Unlock magic abilities?"

[Negative.]

I throw my hands in the air, exasperated. "Then what's the point?"

[The role requires that you meet the requirements of the role.]

"Created by the Department of Redundancy Department," I mutter. Well that seems pretty useless. "What happens if I don't meet the requirements of my role?" I ask.

[Failure to operate within expected parameters would result in strain on the system-user interface.]

Cool. Super helpful.

A grin spreads over my face. Honestly, though, who cares? If I have to slap some ham and cheddar on a slice of bread each day as payment for being reincarnated with magic and a videogame interface, count me in! This is real, and I'm not dead, and there's a world of possibilities ahead of me.

My eyes prickle with tears. I'm so glad I'm here, it hurts. An urge to do something wells up inside me. To jump, to climb a tree, to dive into a river. The excitement is building in me like an expanding balloon, until—*pop*! I take off running.

My boots pound against the ground, sending me racing across the field. Laughter bursts from my mouth as I run, exhilaration pumping through my veins, wind ripping tears from my eyes. When was the last time I was able to run? The last time I felt so free and strong and alive? All those days spent in my bed, dreaming of being whisked away to different lands, with a new body and a better life—and now it's real! I don't know how, but it's the best thing that has ever happened to me.

I was given a fresh start, and I'm not going to waste a second of it.

I skid to a halt, breathing hard, my lungs burning in the best way. The land slopes down into a valley before me. A lake shimmers like a sapphire at the bottom of the basin, birds speckling the air as they spiral down to the water. Forests nestle around the vista on every side but mine, and a stream lazily winds out from the woods to spill into the lake before snaking away again in the opposite direction.

"Hey Echo, have I got supplies or anything?" I ask. "An inventory?"

[The user has no items in their inventory,] Echo says.

My heart leaps. "I have an inventory then?" Awesome. Inventories are broken as fuck. "How do I access it?" Even as I ask, however, a display appears in my vision.

[Inventory: 0/1]

What. Are you kidding me? "It only has one slot?"

[Affirmative.]

"What the hell?" There's got to be an explanation. Maybe it's because I'm still a noob. "Can I upgrade it?"

[Negative,] Echo says.

"What?! Rip off!" I sigh. No, no, beggars can't be choosers. One inventory space is better than none—even if it seems pretty useless. But I have to look on the bright side. I'm sure I'll unlock a lot of sweet spells soon anyway that will make up for it.

"Well, guess I'll be needing supplies," I say aloud, just because I can, just because it feels great for every word spoken to feel effortless. "Water seems like a good place to start. And if you get lost, aren't you supposed to follow the river, because they're supposed to lead to civilization? I think I read that in a book somewhere. Right, Echo?"

[Query unrecognized.]

"I'm not really asking you a question, I'm just talking to you," I say, starting down the hill. "If it sounds like I'm rambling, you can just say 'Okay, Sal.'"

[Affirmative,] Echo says.

"Close enough."

I stroll down the hill, humming a happy nonsensical tune. Where should I even start once I get into town? I bet they have adventure guilds or something. That's what they had in the shows I watched. Since I'm starting out with what appear to be pretty basic stats, and no special abilities that I'm aware of, I'll probably have to do a lot of grinding. Do creatures here drop loot? Well, either way, I'll need to get some money and a weapon.

The birds I'd seen earlier caw in alarm and take flight as I approach the lake. I've never seen birds like them before: green feathers and bright yellow beaks, with long tails like a peacock. I watch them for a moment before crouching down at the bank to splash some water on my face and take a few tentative sips. Hopefully I won't get sick from this, but it's better than getting dehydrated.

The birds continue to caw angrily at me—I guess they don't like that I disrupted their little oasis—and then take off over the forest. Without their clamor it's suddenly quiet, and I feel very alone.

My heart stings as Mom and Dad flash through my mind. If I really died back there, then they're probably mourning me by now. I wish I could tell them I'm alright. I'm in a better place—literally. And now they can finally move on with their lives. They don't have to cater every minute of every day around me anymore. They can be happy again.

I slap my hands against my cheeks, trying to snap myself out of it. Come on, I can't get all sentimental now. Not when things are finally looking up. I stand back up and force a smile on my face. It's time for adventure! I plant my hands on my hips, surveying the two streams that branch out from the lake.

"Now, if I were a city, which direction would I be in?"

As I'm considering this, a distant rumble of thunder rolls over the hills. I squint toward the sky, but the few scant fluffy clouds don't look like rainstorms. And even more strange, the sound seems to be getting louder.

The lake ripples, and the ground beneath my feet starts to shake.

"Uh oh," I say, looking around. "Um, Echo? Any insights? I don't suppose this is, like, a small earthquake or something."

[Negative,] Echo says to my complete lack of surprise. The noise crescendos into thundering hoofbeats, and at the same time, a herd of creatures pours over the lip of the valley and begins racing right toward me. [The sound appears to belong to a stampede of pebblebacks.]

"Fantastic," I say, taking a step back toward the lake. I can't make out what the creatures look like at this distance, but they're big, there's a lot of them, and they're coming my way very fast. There's not enough time to run to the forest or climb a tree. And there's nothing out here to hide behind. I take another step back, and my boot splashes into the lake. When was the last time I took swimming lessons? When I was a little kid?

"You think they can swim?" I ask, ignoring the soul-sucking sensation of wet socks as I retreat into the lake.

[Affirmative,] Echo says.

Great.

"I bet they can't swim better than me, though," I say, hoping to will that truth into existence.

[The user's Swimming skill is level 1,] Echo says.

"Well," I say as the wall of creatures races toward me, threatening to put an end to my rather brief second shot at life. "Crap."

BOOKS BY KIA LEEP

Glass Kanin

A Little Salty

Friendly Fyre

Nyte in Shining Armor

About the Author

Kia is the author of their debut serialized series *Glass Kanin*, and specializes in writing comedic, quirky, queer fantasy. When not roller skating or sending people to the Moon, they can be found at home with a cup of tea working on any of their dozens of in-progress books.

You can find more about their projects on their website: www.KiaLeep.com